Altered States

Chapters

DEDICATION

I thank God for giving me the gift to write
about the people in the world I've dreamed about
for so many years.

My sister, Yolanda, was the person who encouraged me
and believed I could share my world with you all.
Thank you, Sis, from the bottom of my heart.

ACKNOWLEDGMENTS

To Keith, my oldest son, I asked you to create music for Lucas, and you did it. You made a piece of music that tells a story befitting of Lucas. Thank you, son; I listen to that track with my writing playlist. I love you and your brothers very much.

To my middle son Jay, you help me tremendously with everything, from listening to ideas to helping with CJ and more. I appreciate you, son. You are talented and so much more. You can do anything you set your mind to do.

To my youngest son, CJ, you have so much to learn, and you have to treat others the way you want to be treated. If you try your best and be patient, you can accomplish anything.

To my nephew TJ, you helped me with CJ and listening to my writing ideas when we lived together.

I love you all to my brother, James, my sisters Rachael, Kathrine, Zakiyyah, and my sister-in-law, Karima, brothers-in-law, David and Tyshawn, and my nieces and nephew. We need to have a family weekend!

To my granddaughters, K and J, as you grow up into beautiful young ladies, know that anything is possible! Go for your dreams!

Thank you to my chosen family, Enrique, and Tina: you know what you two do.

Thank you to my team, alpha and beta readers, my cartel, and my mentors. You all are amazing!

This series is for anyone who loves escaping into another world through reading.

Altered States

Book 1
Hidden Beasts

T. L. REIGNS

PROLOGUE

I'M Lucas, an elite tier demon, and I want to be with humans to discover what drives them. It's unfathomable that humans are born innocent, but by the time they're sent to Hell with me, their souls are blackened, like coal. I can teleport to topside (where humans live) and be there with them and return. Though I haven't done it yet, I want time to be there to observe them and experience everything I can as though I were one of them. My job is to design and monitor the punishment of the souls who get sent to Hell. It's a job that all demons want! Why was I chosen? I don't know, but I'm terrific at it. For one thing, it keeps me so busy that I'm away from other demons besides those who work for me. There are so many different levels of Hell for people who commit all types of sins, and they all aren't equal.

When a person kills someone and has been deemed self-defense by those angels up in heaven, they'll never see me here in Hell. When humans or supernatural beings die, the angels review everything they have done in their lives. If they committed vile acts, they come to me. After seeing what they've done, I decide which level of Hell they will experience.

I'm always wondering about the origin of my powers. Zyra, who is my creator, claims to be an elite-tier demon. Zyra has skills, but nothing like mine.

Tyrus and I are brothers; we are almost mirror images. I have all the powers, though. Since we were children, we were always isolated from everyone. We were never around demons, and we are the only beings who have been here since birth. We've grown up here.

Zyra's different from everyone else here, and she stays in her quarters. She doesn't interact with anyone besides Tyrus and me. She's an immortal and looks like us, but different from the other demons. I don't know what she is or where she's from, but it's not Hell, that's for damned sure!

She's very young, but the resemblance to both of us is incredible. She has taken care of us, but I don't believe she's my creator or mother. She is most definitely a relative, however. She won't disclose any information, and I'm not ready to try to use my powers on her again. It didn't work in the past.

I know for sure that the donor, as I call him, must be top tier since I am so powerful. Still, why hasn't he sought me out? No other elite demon has powers like I do; what if he's not even on the tier? What if my other creator is a Sempiternal? They have immeasurable strength and are indestructible. They are never around the lower demons.

Sempiternal is the result of two fallen archangels or angels who create a being together. They infiltrate human hosts for that purpose. Even in Hell, angels hate demons because they feel they are beneath them. Or what if it's something else entirely?

It would explain why Zyra always made sure I hid most of my powers as they developed. It makes sense, but finding this answer isn't part of my present mission. If I'm right, the opportunity will arise for me to investigate it in the future. I'm an immortal; unlike all Elite demons, I have time on my side. Elites live for centuries, and I've been here over a millennium!

Zyra constantly reiterated that humans were just worthless beings who are spoiled, greedy, and ungrateful. Unlike Zyra, I could always see the human side before the darkness invaded their souls—before they committed the vile acts that brought them to the torture of Hell. At one point, there were some beautiful souls inside all of them. So how does a soul change so drastically? That's the conundrum.

CHAPTER 1

PUNISHER/HEARTACHE

Lucas

IN my quarters, I pace around in my library, then grab one of the thousands of books on the mahogany bookshelves encircling the large room. I sit down at the desk and open the book. It's a new novel entitled "How Many Ways Can You Survive?" Speed reading, I flip through all 800 pages quickly to learn more about human behavior. Scraping the chair back against the hardwood floor, I get up, drop the book with a thud onto the desk, and stretch my arms, taking in this room that holds all my treasures—these books. I've been acquiring books since I was a teen. They have given so much to me. As I think about my bedroom, the room fades out with a flash of blue light, and I'm instantly there.

The massive, oval, levitating bed welcomes me, dipping so I can sit, but I'm not ready to rest. Porting to my closet, I open the door using telekinesis. The closet is full of my black work uniforms, numerous suits, jeans in various colors, pants, and shirts. I've been admiring the magazines I've seen when reading the souls, and I've discovered that I can think about clothes, and they appear.

Preparation is vital to my plan, and I need to be impressive. Many thoughts race through my mind, just thinking about how I will make this plan happen and not get caught.

If any demons topside ever tried to find me, I'd locate them first and kill them. I'd sense them way before they even connected to me. That's part of my powers; I can sneak up on anyone and not be detected until I allow it.

I have two names to choose from Lucas Enhells or Lucas Hellsin. I played with *sin* and *Hell* because you've got to deal with me for your sins. I like it, and I created identification cards. I'll figure it out. I've seen flashes from everyone who's been here showing identification. The wealthy ones carry black cards, so I've worked that out, too.

I enjoy books on Spain and Greece, so I'll pick one of those as my birthplace. I've read everything I could about humanity, adding more to my extensive knowledge base from what I've read through the billions of souls I've come across. I'm twenty-six years old and the Designer of Torture; I've also stopped aging.

Before I leave, I'll visit Zyra to ensure she won't search for me while I'm gone. I teleport from my quarters to check in on the second worse level of the torture pits. The crackling inferno engulfs Hell continuously, as eternal guests are always aflame. There is an endless view of vicious murderers, and witnessing their histories fills me with disgust and fury.

I'm the only one who can see the human side of these souls before tearing them apart. It's eternal damnation at its worse, but if you end up down here, then you were an evil motherfucker as a human! I hate them because every damned soul has complete darkness. They don't have the bright, beautiful, warm light that good souls have. These souls are dark, cold, and ugly. The darker the soul, the viler evil acts the person committed as a human.

The shrieks and screams from all the suffering the souls endure are deafening. They even beg and plead for it to stop, and some try to make deals! This is insane because there's nothing you can offer demons who are torturing you. I see the soul's human side burning in the pits of fire.

Dreadful, shrill shrieks echo in every direction from these murderers. The sound is deafening to human ears. They deserve all of the sufferings they endure. They wail and plead for their torturers to stop and to have mercy on them. They clench their teeth and cry until they are screaming uncontrollably, and their thoughts are all the same:

Please, please, no more! I can't take this anymore! What can I do to make it stop? I'm so sorry, God in Heaven, please forgive me!

Sorry, no, not sorry, God sent you here. This isn't purgatory to try to save your soul. This is Hell. It's either Heaven or Hell, no shades of damned grey. I shake my head and smirk, viewing the soul's human side burning in the pits of fire, and I cross my arms.

First, the demons wave their claws, and a waterfall appears over the soul. As it attacks the human side, it turns into shards of sharp ice that pierce small holes through them, revealing parts of their souls. And they clench their teeth at times while screaming from the immense pain. Next, the demons start twisting and pulling their claws in different directions.

Then, the black souls are fully revealed, moving in the same direction the claws are moving. Next comes the inhuman cries, bellowing through different layers of these ignominious killers. Their souls are stretched out to extensive lengths, blowing fire, burning them more, then slicing and shredding the souls until they are nothing more than fiery shards, quivering in agony!

With a clap, the souls come back together in human form, and the process begins again in different stages and for various lengths of time. Even though I personally don't care for demons, I'm so proud. They are doing such a great job! I've taught them everything about how to torture these souls, and there are countless ways of doing that.

I observe them, ensuring that they are giving their best effort. When my demons execute the techniques I've taught them, it gives me confidence that I can leave for a while.

I can shapeshift into anyone that a soul has ever thought about or seen. It's perfect because I can see every evil thing they've ever done to anyone. I use that to my advantage when torturing, as it makes it more psychological. Teleporting to another area and observing a new soul, a serial rapist-murderer, I shapeshift into one of his young female victims. Anthony's a murdering, filthy, despicable, rat bastard, son of a bitch. Anthony enjoys terrorizing his victims immensely.

Breathing heavily, itching to take control as my anger intensifies, my markings are glowing blue, increasing in color to a vivid azure. In the victims' voice, I taunt him. "You enjoyed raping, killing, and torturing me, right, Anthony? LET YOUR TORTURE BEGIN!"

With his eyes widening as his fear increases, he crouches to the ground, covering his head with his arms. I throw fireballs his way, making direct contact, and he screeches. I slowly balling my fists and raise them in midair, controlling and lifting him up. His body squeezes into a tight ball. Suddenly, my hands open, causing his soul to explode with a loud boom! His screams are among the loudest I've ever heard.

He wakes up on his queen size bed in his large bedroom. Breathing heavily, still feeling excruciating pain all over his body, he looks around, and relief washes over him. The comfort of his plants, his desk, and the sweet smell of his girlfriend's perfume lingering on his expensive sheets calms him down.

"Man, what the fuck was that dream about? No more babes, because that shit was crazy." He shakes his head.

Jumping up out of bed and shaking off the lousy karma he feels throughout his body, he smells bacon and walks over to gaze at the morning sun through his bay windows.

Exhaling deeply, he turns and walks into the kitchen to greet his beautiful, unsuspecting girlfriend. Singing in the kitchen, she has no idea who he really is at all. She's in his t-shirt at the refrigerator getting ingredients for his favorite Belgian waffles. Damn, life is good. Quietly coming behind her, he grabs her around the waist and breathes in her scent. He dips his head into the curve of her neck.

She shifts aside, putting the food on the counter, and hugs him back with a gorgeous smile. He leans in to kiss her as she holds her hands tightly to the sides of his face.

Her tongue greets his, but it expands massively, and he begins choking, trying to pull away. He can't! She has enormous strength, and he doesn't know where the Hell this is coming from. Her tongue turns into a sharp sword, impaling him through the back of his neck, through his skin, then wrapping around his neck! His eyes open wide in shock as his body collapses.

That beautiful girl turns into one of my female demons, Ursa, who is grinning diabolically at him. Her razor-sharp claws dig into his chest and arms, pulling chunks out as he trembles from the unbearable pain. He tries to scream, but there is no sound except for a gurgling noise from all the blood gushing from his wounds. Suddenly, the room begins to shake. The kitchen is crumbling apart, bringing him right back to my hell chamber!

I can transform how the area looks, so they think that maybe it was a bad dream. It's like you're waking up in your bed, and once you relax, I bring Hell right back to you! There are different levels of Hell with no way to escape, and my section is the worse. There are even creatures here that humans thought were just characters in fairytales.

I'M going to see another Demon, Jezebel. All in all, she has a thing for me! I need to find out how I can stay shifted as a human.

I transport up to her living quarters. "Hey, Bel."

Giving me the usual sly, sensual look, she replies, "Lucas, Lucas. Hmm, what can I do for you—or better yet, to you?" Licking her lips, she smiles.

As usual, she looks stunning. She has long, jet-black hair, her skin is tanned, and her eyes are smokey grey. She has deep dimples on each side of her cheeks as she smiles. Her teeth are perfect, while her full lips make me want to kiss her. Her body is just what I like: curvy, nice-sized boobs, small waist, and long, sexy legs.

She is wearing a little red skirt and a white cutoff shirt with red, puckered lips and says "Kiss me" in bold black letters. Her flat stomach is visible, and the gold chain around her waist accentuates it. Her red high heels add to her height, so the top of her head reaches up to my nose.

I know what I want her to show me and how I'm going to persuade her to give me what I want! I'm going to let her have what she's been wanting for so long: ME! No real mate bonding will occur with Bel.

I grin and let my bluish-green eyes slowly rake over her from head to toe.

"Bel, what do you want right now at this very moment?" I ask as I walk towards her deliberately.

She returns the exact look I give and slowly licks her lips. "You know what I want…you!"

Caressing her face, I touch her hair with my right hand, traveling lightly down the side of her temple, past her high cheekbone. I put my thumb on her lower lip, and she quivers from my touch. I lean my face to her, then stop at her lips.

"I can do what you want, but I need you to do something for me, Bel."

"What is it?" she asks, exhaling sharply.

"I need to learn how to stay shapeshifted for as long as I want. No questions asked, and it stays between you and me, okay?" I peer deeply into Bel's eyes.

Bel gazes at me, "Well, you stay with me and make it the best sex ever, and I'll show you how!"

"We're going to make this official," and I pull out Syre, an extremely sharp, long, black, squiggly, pointed sword. She's ancient, can grow massively, and only responds to me.

Gaping at Syre, then at me, Bel gasps, "What the Hell, Lucas?"

"Remember, I'm not your everyday demon, Bel. I'm full of surprises." I laugh at her expression.

Studying Syre, I trace the hieroglyphics on her handle, waking her up. She glows with the same azure coloring as my markings are at their peak.

"What do you need, Lucas?"

"Syre, I want to do a blood bond."

"Okay, I'm ready, Lucas."

I cut my right hand with the knife, and Bel gasps when she sees the color of my blood. Syre glows brighter, then Bel offers her hand, and I cut hers, too. We both hold our bleeding hands over my Syre, and our blood drips together onto the knife. My own blood is blue, while Bel's is black.

"This is an official blood bond that I, Jezebel, will help you, Lucas. I'll do whatever you want after we have our time together."

"Is that all, Bel?" I scrutinize the situation, deciding what may actually happen later. I keep a poker face, not allowing the disbelief to creep in because she didn't promise to keep it between us.

"Yes, I'm done."

"We have a deal," I say, and Syre glows red, then royal blue into flame blue, goes back to black. I pause for Syre's assessment of what just occurred.

Lucas, it is done; why didn't Bel promise not to tell anyone?

Excellent observation, Syre; that's why I asked her was that all. So, you need to be ready, Syre.

Bel gives me her bleeding hand. I wave my hand over hers, and it heals. Mine is already repaired. Automatically revitalizing is another power of mine, and I can also treat others. I tap Syre, and she disappears.

Bel smiles and wraps her arms around my neck, then says, "Finally!"

I kiss her, sucking teasingly on her bottom lip; she nibbles my lip before giving a slight pull. I pull her even closer and kiss her, and then she parts her lips to grant me access. Our tongues entwine, and she shivers with pleasure.

She moans, grabs my hair, then runs her hands through it down to the back of my neck. She rubs my shoulders down to my chest. My turn, breaking away from kissing her. I begin nibbling and sucking along her neck, moving to her shoulders and down to her breasts. I cup her breast; no matter what, I love a female body with a beautiful set of boobs and ass. I squeeze her and pinch her nipples gently at the same time, then with more pressure. Just a little pain to see how she reacts.

Her eyes change into a stormy dark gray—almost black. She shifts into her natural form, which is still as sexy as Hell. Her orange hair flows down her back. Her naked body is the color of steel, firm, and smooth.

She still has that chain around her small waist, and I look down further. I'm not disappointed. Her sex is glistening, and those long legs are sexy. I kiss her again while touching her breast, then bring my mouth down to her nipples, licking and sucking them, increasing the pressure one at a time.

Bel throws her head back and loses her balance, but I catch her and walk over to her bed and throw her on it.

She laughs and pulls herself up, leaning on her elbows, "What about letting me see all of you, Lucas? You got the full view of all of this!" She motions to herself with her hands.

Grinning at her wolfishly, I reply, "The question is, Bel, are you ready for all of this?!" Unzipping my uniform, I expose my broad, muscular, topaz chest, eight-pack abdominal muscles, and, of course, my massive biceps. I flex a muscle, just in case she doesn't realize just how big I am. I move my chest pecs up and down, and she laughs. My uniform is down to my hip; I glance at it and use my telekinetic power to remove it, throwing it to the other side of the room.

Her mouth drops wide open; of course, this power is something new to her. I know I'm the sexiest demon she has ever seen. Her eyes widen in surprise at the size of my shaft. Hell yes! I'm packing 13 inches of long thickness! Getting on the bed, I start kissing, sucking, and licking every part of her, except her core. I haven't touched any female's center with my mouth. I can smell her scent from a distance.

Touching her with my fingers, I play with her clit, flicking up and down and making circles, driving her crazy. She's trembling and breathing heavily and breathlessly saying my name. I slip two fingers inside of her, then a third. I reach her g-spot and go in and out, increasing my speed. She meets me with her thrusts.

She's moaning, moving her head from side to side while grabbing the sheets. "Bel, come for me now!" I growl. Her body begins to spasm as she screams my name. That's right; I do it to them every fucking time. She's ready. I lift her hips and put my shaft right at her entrance. Bel wraps her legs around my waist, and I slowly enter her, allowing time for her body to stretch to accommodate me. Squealing in pleasure, she pulls her hips up, gripping me tightly.

I ride her in deep, long strokes, and she's scratching me with her claws. Suddenly, she starts growling.

I feel her tightening up and throbbing inside; I know she's getting ready to have another orgasm. Her body went from steel-colored to a sparkling, dark gray! I feel her explosion coming, and I know I must get mine, too, before she is done! I pull out, and she screams, "LUCAS!" ravenously in a growling voice. I change my position, turning her around as she gets on her hands and knees. I'm on my knees, and I smack her ass. She squeals!

"You like getting your ass spanked, don't you?" She moans, so I do it again while repeating my question and emphasizing each word with a smack.

"You. Like. Getting. Your. Ass. SPANKED. Don't You?" After each word, a resonating smack of skin on skin echoes through the room.

"Yes, Lucas! I do like getting my ass spanked!" she yells. I see how aroused she is since she's dripping wet, her juices sliding down her inner thighs. I line my shaft up and plunge deep inside her from behind. My hands are gripping her hips as I grind her, stroke after stroke. Lifting her hips higher, I hold her legs, making hard strokes. I pull all the way out to my tip, then smash right back in, and go faster and faster.

She screams, "Oh, Shit!!!! LUCAS!!!!" I feel the gush of her orgasm on me, and my shaft grows even more prominent, that familiar tingling in my spine. I explode inside her at the perfect time. I look at her, and she turns her head, sighing, "wow," and then, she's unconscious.

Shaking my head with a chuckle, I disengage myself from her, then lie on the bed. Every female I've been with passes out after sex! Shit,

I could fuck every female I encounter if I wanted to. I could because they all want some Lucas! I'm just fucking phenomenal, in and out of bed! It damned sure doesn't hurt that I'm packing 13 inches, and I know exactly how to use it!

She came so much that the silver fluid is running down her leg. My sperm is clear, and it disintegrates since I'm not mating for creation. That fluid's blue. I guess I can sleep or relax for the next four hours. That's how long she's going to be knocked out. I'm going to enjoy rocking her world thoroughly.

We were like wild animals all over Bel's place, and it went on and on. Demons *can* sleep, but we don't *need* to sleep.

Finally, a very long time later, "This was well worth the wait, and I wish we had done this much sooner! We had the best fucking session ever! You did work, Lucas!"

"You were everything I imagined, and then some! You showed me some tricks!" I laugh.

"I'm satisfied, and I'm so ready to show this. You have EARNED this! Lucas, this is going to be easy for you. You know how you can see and read memories imprinted in their souls, right?"

"Yes, I know that part."

"Lucas, to stay in the skin indefinitely when you shift is to keep a crucial memory of that human. If it features many humans, you must always have those memories in the back of your mind. The longer you're in human form, the more human characteristics will tie their traits onto you. If you can shift back to yourself for short periods, you'll stop those traits from attaching to you. It's harder for me because I touch them, and I only keep my shifts for a short period for my deals. I can't go up there like myself to make deals with them. I need to look like them. But wait, why don't you use human skin and change your hair color? Shit, Lucas, you're a fucking gorgeous, sexy motherfucker! They'd be all over you up there!"

I raise my eyebrows in surprise because I had no idea it was this easy.

Should I leave Bel here? Maybe I'll have to kill her. Officially, she never said she wouldn't tell anyone about our shapeshifting lesson.

She may also figure out what I'm up to when I leave. I watch Bel calculatingly as she walks over and steps into the jacuzzi filled with hot, sudsy water. I watch her as she washes her body with the soapy sponge, trying to entice me into another round of play. My decision is made. She rinses off, licks her lips, stands up with the water dripping off her, and beckons me to come over.

I grab her towel, stride over, and dry her off. I lift her up, and she wraps her legs around my waist, lines up with my shaft, lowers herself, and takes me to her entrance. She moans as she kisses me. I give her everything she wants. With each stroke, while she's bouncing on my shaft, I'm giving her the most extreme orgasm she has ever had. She is in the middle of her orgasm. And she's unaware of anything else.

I think about Syre, and she appears behind Bel. Then, I think about her dying quickly, and Syre strikes! Bel's head is cut off with one swift swipe at her neck by the knife when I break the kiss! Her head and body collapse to the ground, and I stare down at Bel's body. Fire crosses my mind, and she's in flames. That's not enough for me, though; I need to make sure she won't be found, so my Syre slices her body in parts. I hide her body parts throughout Hell in super deep crevices. I did what I had to do.

CHAPTER 2

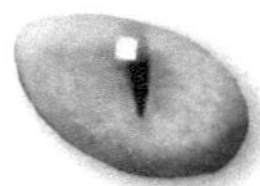 

THE COLDEST JULY

Lyssa

MY parents and identical twin sister were in a devastating car accident, hit by a drunk driver three weeks ago. My parents died ten days later, and this morning Lana was put in her own world. Leaving Lana's hospital room, I know I didn't just dream that she'd squeezed my hand lightly, but no one agrees with me. I hope she can hear us, especially Joaquin and me when we're talking to her.

Walking down the corridor, I wave goodbye to Lissette, Lana's nurse. Uncle Christoph says she must be put into an induced coma because this is her only chance. I hope she's going to come out of this, so we'll be back to ourselves, arguing about crazy stuff.

This is the only hospital I've ever been to that doesn't have the smell most have. Admiring the fantastic interior reminds me of an upscale residence. The walls are a beautiful lavender color, and lovely art, sculptures, a baby grand piano, marble floors, mahogany vaulted ceilings, and ten drum chandeliers that hang throughout the hospital. I walk over to sit by the piano guy and lean back to rest my eyes while waiting for Sasha to finish her shift in twenty minutes.

"I know she isn't sleeping; it's only 9:00 at night," Sasha says incredulously.

"She could be tired, Sasha; we're late," Marisol answers with a groan.

Opening my eyes, I smirk at Sasha's smart ass. "Do you seriously think I was sleeping? Hell no, I'm just waiting for your slow self to finally appear. I've been waiting for you for an hour and twenty minutes, Missy Pooh."

Getting up, my bones yell, cracking and popping, disagreeing with the notion of me moving anywhere. "We can pick up some Chinese food for all of us. Wait, Marisol, since you're sleeping over tonight, is that good for you, too?" I look at Marisol, waiting for her response.

"I love Chinese food, but I hate bean sprouts!"

I grimace at the words *bean sprouts*: I hate them, too. "Chinese food is our winner; let's order online for pick up." Walking out of the hospital together, I use the remote to unlock my Range. We all climb in, and I push the ignition button and pull off. After we get home, I'll eat, then illustrate the last couple of pages in my book before going to bed.

LANA has been in an induced coma for the past five months. After visiting Lana, I suddenly feel a searing pain in my head and chest as I drive home. I can't breathe! Immediately, I know. "Lana," I whisper with tears welling in my eyes. My cell rings. It's the nurse from the hospital calling me to come quickly. I speed to the hospital, praying that this can't be happening again.

I park my Range in the parking space that Uncle Joshua's fraternity brother, Mr. Micah, arranged for me. Running into the hospital lobby, I pass Jackson, the kind security guard who knows me. Well, they all do.

I step out of the elevator and glance at my family a few feet from the nurse's station. I see the same heartbroken expressions we all had just five months ago when we received the news that my parents were gone. Uncle Joshua sees me first, then everyone else notices as I turn quickly toward the corridor leading to Lana's room.

I run to my sister's room. *Oh, God! No, please.* I shake my head *no* as I get to the door. I observe the team of doctors and nurses working quickly on my sister. The doctor rushes, putting the defibrillator paddles on her chest and yelling, "Clear!" He is shocking her body, trying to get her heart beating again and bring her back to me. All I hear is that awful loud, long tone; then I look at the flat line on the monitor. It moves up once and goes flat again!

I slide to the floor, feeling waves of pain that are even worse than what I felt for my parents. All of a sudden, I'm enclosed in this warmth that touches my soul, and I hear Lana whisper, "I love you, baby sis, but I can't wake my body up. I tried." Then the warmth is gone!

A tremendous pain embraces me because a part of me has been ripped away! I feel and know that my Lana, my identical twin, is gone before they turn around. I hear a sound; then I realize it's my voice making this animalistic, gut-wrenching, horrifying, painful scream.

Everything is blurry; my eyes are full of tears that stream down my face. Someone's picking me up; then, I smell a familiar cologne. It's Josh carrying me. Shutting my eyes, I can't control the shuddering and sobbing that has overwhelmed my body. Josh walks into an empty room that a nurse is leading him into. He sits on the bed with me on his lap, then wraps his arms around me and cries with me. I feel a cold breeze, and our family comes into the room.

I lift my head and see my aunts hugging Joaquin; he has his head down, fighting his tears. Delia, Sasha, Naya, Ava, and Janae cry too; Uncle Danny and Jay lean on the wall with their heads down, in tears. Uncle Josh has his arms around Kyle's and Tony's shoulders, and they walk in crying. Uncle Christoph and Chris walk in and embracing the girls.

I WAKE up in my bed, breathing heavily, drenched in sweat. My sheets are damp, and I start to cry, screaming hysterically again. It's either my parents or Lana; I keep dreaming about their deaths three to five times a week! I keep going back to almost four months ago when my Lana left me. I dream about this too much! I cannot get to stage two of the five stages of grief. This hole has broken me. I'll never be the same, and I honestly don't think I can get help.

Janae, Naya, and Delia run into my room, and they get on my king-sized bed on either side of me. We lie there for a few minutes, then Janae and Naya start to sing one of my favorite songs, and Delia joins in, singing badly! There aren't any words they can say because the last nine months have been devastating for us all. Then, they hug me, saying, "We're here," but no matter what, this is not getting better; I feel lost.

We all just lie on my bed, and we have one good singer and another one who's trying! We hear Sasha come in downstairs; she calls, "I'm home!"

"We're in Lyssa's room," Delia stops singing to yell.

A few moments later, Sasha comes in and jumps on the bed. She looks at me knowingly. "Bad morning, Sis?" I nod my head. Then I remember I have to pick up my little brother.

"I have to pick up Joaquin and bring him to the airport. Remember, he's going to that baseball camp for eight weeks."

"Do you think he can handle this right now?" Delia frowns.

I look at her and take a deep breath, "Honestly, I don't know Dee, but he wants to go."

I check my cell and see that it's 9:05 am, so I have time to try to relax. Then, I'll jump in the shower so we can get to the airport at 12:15 pm.

Delia's cell phone rings with the old song "Sugar" by Maroon 5. We know it's her fiancée, Steve. I motion for her to answer, and she does. While she's speaking with him, she's smiling and observing me, so I turn and ask Sasha about her residency.

"You know they're working me to the bone as if the hospital is my life," she whines.

"Well, you want to take care of the people, and you picked medicine!" Janae replies, and we laugh.

Sasha rolls her eyes and laughs too.

"Ryan and Steve want to take a drive to Vegas in three weeks. Ryan has a great deal since his company has a block of suites for the next eight weeks." Delia looks at me cautiously as she shares this news.

All at once, it seems, they look at me! "What? Why are you all staring at me?"

Delia and Janae both give the famous *we need you there* expression. "You should get out, and we all can go together, plus have some fun. Not go overboard or anything. Ava said she could come too," Delia reveals.

Crap! Ava was close to Lana, not me! She's our cousin, but Uncle Austin found out about her a few years ago, when her mom died. Ava acts like a little Slut-Ho. Plus, she doesn't like me at all. I sigh and shake my head. "I don't see why we have to get any deal from Ryan. We have money; we can pay for our own damn rooms. I won't give that asshole any thought that he can say that he has done anything for me. I'll get our rooms."

It's not like Sasha is going to get six days off with this short notice! Sasha knows what I'm thinking and claims she can do some switching with other residents. I guess I don't feel like I'm ready to go out in the world just yet. I'm not comfortable hanging out with Ryan. Ryan has been acting more than a little weird. I felt like he has been subtly trying to make advances toward me! Ryan had just moved in with Lana two months before the accident. At first, I didn't want to be mean, telling him that he had to move.

Consequently, after almost two months of weirdness, I told him that he had to go! He flat out refused and told me, "Lana would've wanted me to stay and for you to take care of me!"

Then that bastard did the unthinkable: he damn kissed me! I pulled away and slapped the Hell out of him! When I told Josh, he came with his "brother from another father and mother," former Navy

SEAL Captain Christopher Castellanos. Our family has made Mr. and Mrs. Castellanos our honorary "aunts and uncles," and their children are our "cousins."

Chris is big, tough, brawny, sexy, and, to top it off, he was Incline Village's youngest police detective. They're in business together in Cyber Security, Software, and Game Development, meaning lots of money! By the way, he's just as big as Chris! Josh took Ryan's key, kicked his ass, and made him move out—and they brought a locksmith with them to change all the locks.

Josh said, "He's a fucking leech, and he probably has copies of the keys!"

Sasha was watching Chris from a distance, as usual. She has loved him since we were in 8th grade. Sasha is a year younger than I am; she skipped a class. This love materialized for Chris when he and Josh were in the 11th grade. Sasha's too chicken to give him a clue as to how she feels.

"First, Lyssa, you haven't been writing, so you are free. Just think about it, they have indoor swimming, a spa, a masseuse, and we can go to some shows. There are loads of other things we can do, too. Hell, it's just us! Ryan's a non-factor, and Steve will handle Ryan," Delia says.

I sit up and exhale, running my fingers through my hair, then my hand to the back of my neck, rubbing softly.

"Well, I could use a spa day! Plus, we can check out the shows to see who is there."

"There's that new club too; I've heard it's hot," Janae tells us.

I guess we're going to Vegas.

The girls leave my room, but I stay and pick out what I'm wearing. I look at Lake Tahoe from my bedroom patio windows, which I just opened with the remote. It's a beautiful day. I feel the crisp, fresh breeze wash over me and through my hair. I look at the gorgeous, calming, shimmering, blue waters, which have always relaxed me.

I miss Lana and my parents so much. I'm trying, but I think I need some help. I know I need to find a grief counselor or therapist. I'll talk to Aunt Alicia since she's been trying to get me to speak to a professional to help me. I turn on my music and walk over to my wardrobe closet to find what I'm wearing to bring Joaquin to the airport.

I pick my skinny white jeans, a sheer white blouse with royal blue designs, a royal blue tank, my lacy white bra and panty set, and my royal blue Jimmy Choo's. I go to my jewelry closet and get my sapphire earrings, necklace, and bracelet. I pick up my royal blue twist LV bag and put it on the bed.

I shower and get dressed, then go downstairs to eat a little something before I go. Sasha's curled up on the white chaise in the living room, reading a book with her Damien Escobar CD playing and the fireplace going. Sasha looks up at me. "Hey, sis, have you talked to Josh lately?"

I grin and hold in my laughter because I know who this will lead to, Chris! "I spoke with him yesterday, and you can call your cousin, you know!" I say.

She looks at me expectantly. "Why? Come on, Lyssa, tell me!"

"Chris just got back from seeing the clients in San Diego. Why don't you call him and ask if he's involved with anyone?"

"I don't want to seem like I'm chasing him."

"I don't think he knows how you feel. He has no clue at all! So why would you finding out mean you're chasing him?"

I stand up and walk into the kitchen and pull the refrigerator door open. I pick out a vanilla yogurt and open a container with peaches and pineapple chunks.

Sasha makes a groaning sound and shows she doesn't dare to let Chris know how she's feeling. I wash off my hands again, grab a spoon, then start eating. I don't have time to eat anything else, but I'm not that hungry, anyway.

My cell rings, and it's Joaquin. I answer, "Hey, bro, are you almost ready?"

He sighs, "I'm all packed up and just waiting for you, sis."

"I'm eating some breakfast."

Joaquin groans and says, "What are you eating? Wait, let me guess: yogurt and fruit, right?"

I laugh, "Yes, you get first place, bro!" he presses the camera view button, and I accept. So now he's shaking his head, telling me I need to eat some more.

"Lunch is my time. I'll have a nice one, okay?" he laughs.

I finish my breakfast and tell Joaquin I'll be there in about 15 minutes, and we hang up. I throw my garbage out and go over to Sasha, "do you want to ride with me to the airport?"

"Yes, can we stop by Chris and Josh's office on the way back?"

"Now that's what I'm talking about!" I beam my best smile. I'm so proud of her! We leave, and Sasha locks up.

We arrive at our family's home. Joaquin, Kyle, Tony, and Jay come out, and I'm guessing they will ask to come too. They come up to the window while Joaquin is putting his luggage in my trunk. They're looking at me with those pleading hazel and green eyes. Sasha says Joaquin can switch with her since he's so tall.

Joaquin gets in next to me and starts to ask, "Can they?"

I tell them, "Come on, it'll be tight, but we're family." Kyle, Jay, Tony, and Sasha are in the back with us in the front. Of course, Joaquin has his phone and wants to hook up the music to the car. So we get that straightened out, and we're listening to his music while we're riding to the airport, which is about 50 minutes away.

Joaquin's phone rings, and it's Mellissa, his girlfriend; well, any conversation I would have had is gone. We pull up to the airport, and he's still on the damned phone.

I tap his arm. "I need to talk to you. Tell Melissa you'll speak with her later."

He hangs up, turns to me, and asks, "What's up, sis?"

I look directly into his eyes. "Are you sure this is what you want to do right now, Joaquin?"

I see the same flash of pain that has been with me as a best friend since everything has happened. He inhales and exhales deeply. "When is it EVER going to be the right time? What, am I going to wake up, and they'll be back? I need to do something positive! It's the beginning of Spring, and it's only six weeks. It'll give me something else to do instead of being angry about that drunk driver that caused all of this! I love you, Kit Kat. Let me do what I need to do, okay?"

My eyes fill with tears; he sounds like my Dad, and that was my nickname. "You know we're both going through the same thing, right?

Even though we have extended family, you and I are what's left of our core. Our family was here one minute and gone the next. And it hurts like Hell; I'm awakened from the same nightmares or dreams where they are still with us, then I'm angry. And I wish that drunk-ass truck driver was dead, not them! I want you to know, Joaquin, you're not alone. I'm here for you."

I hug him. "Okay, do what you have to do, Lil Bro. I love you too. Make sure you call me every day."

My brother has tears rolling down his face; he wipes them away quickly and clears his throat. "I'm sorry, Kit Kat; since we aren't in the same house anymore, I didn't know how you were feeling. I'll let you in from now on, I promise. I want this, though; please understand."

It's noon, and we all walk him up to the point where we couldn't follow him, so all of us get our hugs and wave goodbye to my Lil Bro.

We get in the Range, and Sasha sits up front with me. Tony, Kyle, and Jay are in the back, wearing headphones listening to their music. I drive to where Josh and Chris's office building is. Just as I am parking, Sasha changes her mind and chickens out!

I shake my head, "Somebody else is going to get him if he doesn't know how you feel! You're beautiful, sexy, and brilliant! You have the whole package; don't waste it, Sasha."

Walking at the lake has always been a good thing for me. Watching the calmness of the water and the surrounding area always relaxes me. Being alone, just walking through the sand, and feeling the breeze used to revitalize me. Since my world has been blown apart, nothing brings me solace. My heart feels broken, and I don't understand how people say it gets better with time.

No one really knows how I feel, not even Joaquin. He definitely knows what I'm feeling about our parents, but Lana is—no, she *was*—part of me. I know I should think in the past tense, but I just can't do it. It feels so horrible to think of her like she's not here. I know physically that's true, but spiritually she's with me; I feel her all the time. I always pray for them. Lana and I are identical twins. We did everything together, even though we have different personalities.

Looking at the mountains, I can't help but think about everything she told me she wanted to do that no one else knew about. No matter what anyone says, you have a bond when you're identical twins, even when you have significant differences. She was like the wild night child, and I'm like the quiet, shy dawning of a new day. I feel such emptiness, and my heart feels like it'll never be the same.

There's no way in Hell that I'll ever be normal again or even get over this like everyone tells me to. Like they really understand when they don't.

Feeling a buzzing in my pocket, I get my phone, and right on time, it's Aunt Alicia, my mom's identical twin.

"Hi, Tia."

"Hola, Sweetie, come over. I need to see you. I miss you."

"Okay, I'm walking at the lake, and I'll be there shortly."

"See you in a few minutes."

"All right."

Hanging up the phone, I gaze at the water, let out a sigh, and turn to walk back to my Range. I see my mom's face whenever I see Aunt Alicia, so it's difficult to see her. Both of my aunts only want to help me, so I go back to our family home. Hearing my own heartbeat feels like a betrayal that I'm here and Lana's not. Shuddering suddenly, I freeze in motion as I'm attacked from within as flashbacks of the horrible night overwhelm me. I was supposed to be out with them celebrating, but my deadline was the following day.

I spoke to Mom, and we were going to go out with Lana and Joaquin the next day since Dad was flying out in the morning for a business trip. Collapsing on the sand on my knees, I'm overcome with pain. I scream, covering my face and rocking, as tears that are always ready slide from my eyes. I shouldn't be here either. I don't know how long I've been here, but the sun is setting now. Sometimes I just lose time when I have these…what should I call them? Episodes, maybe?

I get up and brush the sand off my pants—well, I try to because there's quite a bit left over. So, I just get it off of my hands, for the most part. I take a shaky breath and walk to the parking area where my

Range is; no one else is here, but I see a large truck; Josh is coming. Of course, Auntie sent him because I was late. Josh pulls up right by my Range and rolls his window down.

"What's up, Lys? Mom was worried about you. Wait, what the Hell?" He frowns, looking at my entire appearance, jumping out of the truck. He gently holds my arms while examining me.

"It's not what you think, Josh. I didn't get attacked or anything like that. I just was in the sand and got over-emotional."

He makes this weird-ass noise and shakes his head after rechecking me. "Let's get to the house; they all are worried now. Can you drive?"

"No reason why I cannot drive, Josh." Getting in, I start the Range and leave.

Oh, God, it looks like a full house; what the Hell? Why are so many cars out here? I park and go through the driveway since both of our families lived here. Well, it's more like a compound. My mom, Dad, her twin Aunt Alicia, and Uncle Joshua raised us together. They had every section built, and there's so much privacy, we had our separate family moments.

Walking inside, I hear my family's voices and smell the scrumptious aroma of spicy food. I go into the kitchen; everyone is in there while my aunts are still cooking. Aunt Alicia senses it when I'm close by. She looks up and rushes over to hug me.

"Oh, Lyssa, Chica, I was so worried; what took you so long?" She's feeling my arms—her way of checking for injuries. Both of my aunts are our godmothers, so we have an extra special relationship with them. "What happened? Are you all right?"

Returning her hug, I kiss her on her cheeks. "Yes, Tia, I'm fine. I just had a mishap in the sand."

"We are going to have dinner. First, you go freshen up." She sends me to the bathroom and claps her hands in excitement. "Janae, Sasha, Ava, and Naya, come, let's go set the tables."

Eating sounds much better than talking about my feelings—no need to worry anyone about my issues. I go into the bathroom and look in the mirror at my reflection, and I see why Josh and Tia were examining me. My eyes are red, my hair is a bit tousled, and let's not forget the sand stuck to my pants. The result is that it looks like I was in a bit of a fight. Rinsing my face and grabbing a brush for my hair, I get to work. Just because I feel miserable, it doesn't mean I have to look like it!

Satisfied with my appearance, I'm ready to face the 20 people in the dining room. They only want to help, but I just don't know how they can since we are all going through our own pain right now. I go into the oversized, formal dining room usually used for holidays or special occasions. It's not a holiday, so I don't know why we're using it today. This room is reserved for full formal holiday gathering time. We have a huge family, but it's not that, because all of the rooms here are spacious. I walk out of the bathroom and look around at everything, but it's the same; nothing has been moved or changed.

I see we have one person at the table who is a total surprise to me, and I think she's here just for me. It's Tia's best friend, Aunt Amy, a psychologist. I think Tony has a crush on her; he's always staring at her whenever she comes around, and tonight is no exception. Kyle is just sneaking glances at him and laughing. She's not what I envision when I think of a psychologist, and she's always been very kind to all of us. The girls bring out the food, and oh wow, this is a lot of food. Oh crap. I pull out my phone and notice the date. It's Uncle Josh's birthday.

It's nothing like we've had in the past. We always have celebrations with music, decorations, and way more people than this. How could I have forgotten his birthday? I hurry over to where I see him with my other uncles. "Happy Birthday, Uncle Josh!" I give him a hug and kiss his cheek.

Sorrow lingers in his eyes while he smiles and hugs me back. "Efcharistó, anipsiá mou, xérete óti eímai edó an thélete na milísete sostá?" (Thank you, my niece; you know you can talk to me, right?)

Nai, xéro óti boró, allá kai eseís ponáte óloi. Eínai tóso dýskolo kai lypámai pou den thymíthika ta genéthliá sou. Skéftomai egoistiká móno ton eaftó mou kai ton póno mou. Synchoréste me, theíe Tzósoua. (Yes, I know I can, but you are all in pain too. It is so hard, and I am sorry I did not remember your birthday. I'm selfish, thinking of only myself and my feelings. Please forgive me, Uncle Joshua.)

Putting his arm around my shoulder, "Come outside with me for a little chat. I like making sure you all remember our family languages."

We walk to the massive backyard, lit up with soft, colorful lights, exactly how my aunt and Mom liked it. The pool back here is its own oasis. There is a mountain of rocks with a waterfall trickling down into the pool, and it has slides and massage chairs poolside in the jacuzzi. We go sit at my favorite spot, the swings.

"You know, Amy is here for all of us because grief, mourning, it all hits us differently. It's all pain at the end of the day, and we will never, ever get over losing our family."

He squeezes my hand, and I feel the tears coming and see his. His voice cracks with emotion.

"I don't know how long it'll take for us to cope or make it through this. I want you to know that I've been talking to Amy's husband, and your aunts have been talking to her. Now, you young people need to talk to someone because I know we are going through Hell, and all of you are, too."

He hands me a clean handkerchief from his pocket. I wipe my eyes and blow my nose loudly. "I feel like I'm on a roller coaster, but it's only spiraling downward, not up; no highs, just the force of lows that I have no control over most of the time. I'm having nightmares, and I wake up hysterical, but I know if the girls hadn't moved in with me, I would probably be crazy right now." I exhale shakily. "I will see if I can talk with Aunt Amy. Maybe she can help, and it won't feel like I'm really seeing a psychologist because I've known her since I was a baby, right?"

Nodding his head, he gives me a long hug. "That's our girl. Remember, they are our angels and want all of us to get help." We compose ourselves and go inside to have dinner.

CHAPTER 3

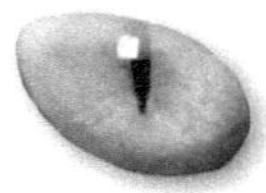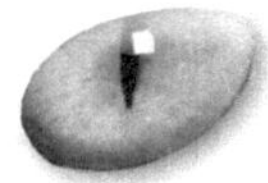

BREAKTHROUGH/NEW ARRIVAL

Lyssa

MONDAYS for the last four weeks, I have been talking to Amy, which has basically been like having regular conversations. She's confident, observant, encouraging, fearless, and trustworthy. Honestly, she is one of the most phenomenal people I know. How can I discuss what I'm feeling without crying like a baby? Maybe a stranger would be better than Amy; at least in that capacity, I would only see that person as my psychiatrist/counselor—whatever we want to call it.

Amy is part of our inner circle of people; I don't know if I can do this. The cell starts vibrating on the table; Joaquin's picture pops up, and I answer his call with, "Hey little bro, how are you, hon?"

"I'm okay, Kit. I know I haven't been gone that long. I really miss you all, and I'm not doing both sessions." He sighs with a cough.

My big sister's protective mode is activated, "What happened? Is someone freaking bothering you, Joaquin?"

"No, sis, I've gotten even more muscle and height in the last 4 weeks! The coaches are amazed, saying they've never seen a growth spurt like the one I'm having. To top it off, I've broken a couple of bats hitting home runs." Laughing, then groaning, he continues. "I've been feeling a little off, and I have a fever that won't break. The nurse called Aunt Alicia and Uncle Joshua, and they all think I should come home."

"I can book your flight for tomorrow."

"No need, sis; Uncle Josh said we are going on the annual Laskaris male coming of age retreat. Everyone is coming in on the jet tonight, except Tony and Kyle. Uncle Josh will be picking me up when they get here at about 7 p.m."

I stroll to the door, pausing to get my keys. "Well, I would like to see you, and you need a doctor's visit for this fever." Worrying is what I do now.

"Sis, remember Uncle Christophe and Uncle Stéphanos are both doctors; it's okay. Don't worry. They're some of the best physicians in the country."

"Okay, you're right. I guess I'm absolutely extra on worrying about you now. Accept this as our new normal, little bro. Call me when Uncle Joshua picks you up. You know how much I love you, right?" Opening the door to the Range, I step in, plugging the cell into its port.

"Yes, to the moon, stars, and throughout the infinite galaxies. I love you back more, sis. Yeah, I'll call you when Uncle Joshua gets here. Talk to you later, Kit."

"Later, little bro."

I start the ignition button, inhaling and exhaling and trying to stop my heartbeat from quickening because today is the day Amy wants to begin discussing my emotions. I take a quick detour by driving into the lake's parking area instead of going straight to her office. Tiny beads of sweat trickle down my skin in response to my anxiety about digging into my well of pain. I quickly go over to the lake, my safe place, and breathing in the sweet pineapple vanilla scents brings me some sense of calm.

The unique sapphire color of the lake in spring is just breathtaking. Mid-morning, there are only a few people around. Looking out at the lake, hugging myself as the birds' chirp, brings out a small smile. Sunshine infiltrates the sky, beaming warmth all along the lake. That's my cue to get to Amy's office.

I fidget and tap my fingers on the usually comfortable sofa in Amy's office, dreading the start of our session. I hear a quick knock, then the door opens, and Amy struts inside, examining me affectionately.

She smiles with a twinkle in her eyes. "Good morning, Lys. I need you to relax; it feels like you're ready to bolt out of here. I'm not the big, bad wolf." She comes over, hugs me, and rubs my back reassuringly. "We're going to peel off a little of what you have been feeling, and we will stop when you are ready. Okay? Remember, this is about you, and I'm here for you. And my top concern is you, Lys, because this is not just a quick fix. That's impossible. Like I told you before, this is a long process, and no matter what, you don't get over losing your family."

Amy turns on the recorder that's on her desk. Going to the other side of the sofa to give me my space, she leans back, takes off her shoes, and puts her feet up on the coffee table. "I'm all yours. Honorary Auntie Amy is in the building. Today, if all you can handle is answering one question, that's fine. I want you to tell me how it makes you feel that you didn't go to dinner that night when the accident happened. Wait, not just what you tell everyone else, either, Lys."

Gazing at the unicorn and dolphin paintings Lana and I painted for her as a birthday present when we were 11, a chill runs down my spine. That was a great day until the phone rang that night. Shaking my head, I say, "Amy, I don't think I can do this."

Looking pointedly at me, she replies, "Yes, you can, Sweetie. Say how you felt then and how you still feel right now. I'm right here; we can do this together."

In one part of my mind, protest builds up in contrast to that part struggling to be heard. Trying to breathe evenly and stop the tears, I force my voice to speak, stuttering, "I-I was so-supposed to be there with them! Maybe I could've seen that dri-driver and helped, or maybe if I'd have been driving, I could have taken a di-different route home!" Sobbing hysterically, I continue. "I shouldn't be here! They're gone; they left Joaquin and me!" Goosebumps prickle my skin as I inhale in shaky breaths. My heartbeat thumps in my chest. The room starts spinning, and Amy leaps off the couch and rushes to me. Then darkness envelops me.

Ammonia? Oh God, it's pungent. All my senses are being attacked by ammonia, ugh. My head feels like a drill is digging in it. Opening my eyes, my vision is blurry at first, then it starts to clear. Amy is staring at me worriedly.

"Lys! How are you feeling? You worked yourself up into a frenzy, had an anxiety attack, and fainted." Her nurse comes in, handing her a cloth, and Amy places it on my head. The coolness feels relieving on my head. I shut my eyes, hoping the conversation is over for now.

"Lys, I know you may not want to do this, but you have to. I need you to listen seriously to what I'm going to say to you. You are here for a reason, and you don't know what could have happened if you were there." She stands up, goes over to her desk, gets a bottle of water, and takes a slow sip.

"Sometimes, when people are in a traumatic, tragic accident—or even avoid one, like in your case, Lys, and some survive, and some die, the ones left here may suffer from survivor's syndrome, also known as survivor's guilt. You need to realize that you're not at fault for not being there; as a matter of fact, do you really think your mother, father, or twin sister would rather have you not living? Not being here to help with your brother? Not living your life? Since I grew up with your mother and was there when she met your father and was there when she was pregnant with both of her girls, you and Lana, I know the answer: Hell No!" Her voice is thick with emotion, and tears stream down her face. Lowering my head, I burst into tears uncontrollably.

Amy sits down next to me, wrapping her arms around me, crying with me, and rocking me like a baby. No one has actually explained how I feel the way she just did, but she is right because my family wouldn't want me dead, too.

Lucas

I'VE added a tanned human skin to my body, and with my flame markings against it, I look damn impressive! Like the song I've heard by Justin Timberlake, "I'm bringing sexy back!" I look like myself, and I've changed my hair color to black. I'll fit in, but I'm still a cut above the human males with all this. The only thing is my shaft is not happy in this human skin!

I'm on my way to see Zyra, and Tyrus is leaving her quarters. Now is the perfect opportunity to compel him to do what is necessary for my trip topside. I shift back into my natural skin and hair.

As he turns toward me, I snap my fingers, and the pouch with my essence appears over his head. My aura has my characteristics and a few physical traits.

"Greetings, Lucas." He reaches for my forearm, and I give him a quick hug. The pouch empties over us, and everything glows and goes blurry while he's morphing. Reaching exactly to my height now, he matches me perfectly. I give him my orders.

"You will be me, which means act just like I do in all aspects until I return and tell you to stop. You will only have my mannerisms and thoughts, none of your own. Your mind goes to sleep when I say. You will live in my old quarters. Do you understand?"

"Yes, I understand, Lucas."

"Your mind sleeps now. Go now."

I'm examining my results, and we're identical. Tyrus will do a great job! I believe that we can have the same mother but not the male donor. Why? Tyrus has none of the powers that I have.

Going over to Zyra's quarters, I knock on the door. When she opens it, her face lights up, and she claps her hands.

"My, Lucas, how are you, son? I haven't seen you for a very, very long time." She sighs and shakes her head. "I know you have this all-important job, but you could come to see me sometime. I miss you."

Giving her a great big bear hug and lifting her off her feet, "I miss you too, Madre. You know I'm extra busy. You are the one who always told me about how horrible humans are. You know there's a lot of them coming to Hell. Being in Hell seems to be a hot commodity."

Walking into her quarters, it's always been very feminine and pretty. We had our room in the back that she called "boys town." She has many pink colors throughout her space, so we never wondered what her favorite color was. There are many other things in her room that I've never recognized in anyone else's memories. So I don't know where she got the stuff for her room because I've never seen anything like it. It's very futuristic looking, though.

She has an oval, levitating bed, so what the Hell? Inside the bathroom, soap sprays from the shower. The soaps have some type of natural oil in them, so when you're done, you're feeling very nice. No, she's not going to give me any information if I ask her. I'm just going to let her talk.

"Of course, you have a very, very important job. You know that you and Tyrus are unique, unlike these demons here."

She touches my cheek, then rests her hand on my chest.

"You're going to be tested one day, son. Remember what I've told you; you have all these powers for a reason."

She grabs my hand, looking deeply into my eyes as if she's searching for my secrets.

"You are the Punisher, the one who punishes those who have committed the vilest of evil acts. You are not like them, demons, remember that." Raising her hand to give the stop signal, she says, "Don't ask me what I mean by that. I'm telling you this, and you make sure you remember it. Do you understand me?"

"I wish you would just tell me already about what's going on. Yes, I understand, and I'll remember everything."

"Tell me, how are you feeling, son? Just to make myself clear, if you ever need to talk, I'm here for you."

She's looking at me as if she knows, well, what I'm getting ready to do. That would be crazy as Hell if she could read my mind and just never said anything. Well, who the Hell does that shit? Wow, that would be absolutely insane because I really don't know what the Hell her power is.

I just assumed that my abilities were more significant than hers. What if Madre's even more high-level than I am because she's older; it just doesn't look like she is. She's probably just creeping around, not showing her power levels. I can mask mine, so she can possibly hide hers too.

"Well, I'm doing my job torturing all the souls that come to Hell. My team has mastered the many different ways to inflict the most agonizing pain to souls. I've only seen the worst of the worst souls. Not one with any good in them at all." I sit down with a flop. "At least, I can say that every soul I've encountered absolutely belongs where they are. Angels haven't made a mistake yet."

Tapping her fingers on the table when she thinks is a habit I've seen all my life. I lean back and clear my mind while she's studying me, just in case she can read me.

"Son, hypothetically speaking, say you wanted to live with people? Listen to me, living with humans or even getting involved in a relationship with one would bring unimaginable consequences that the world couldn't fathom. Remember what you learned about Pandora's Box? Do you want that level of ramifications to be on you?"

I stand up and give her a kiss on her cheek. "Madre, you worry way too much, and now I must go. I'll visit you more often." With tears in her eyes, she hugs me so tightly that I know that she knows what I'm going to do. Leaving her home, I just hope she doesn't try to stop me.

Where can I go and fit right in with these people? I've heard of many humans making deals with Crystal and Bel from Sin City, Las Vegas, and Hollywood, California. I decide on Las Vegas since it has the nickname "Sin City." I already have a suit in mind to wear from one of those costly designers I've been researching. You know, only the best for me. Everything I need to wear appears on my body. I'm wearing a black Brooks Brothers suit with a blue shirt and a tie with a mix of greens and blues.

I transport to Las Vegas right on the strip, where all the action is. I'm in front of a large pool of water, and I see the most beautiful sky! It's the only one I've seen in person, besides watching through the soul's thoughts or in books. It changes into a blazing violet with magnificent spots of angry pinks that make it appear like it's fighting to stay but losing the battle! I'm observing the sky still raging; it turns from deep violet into an all-consuming black…

Directly in front of me, there's a spectacular musical water fountain and light show going on. The water spouts up from the bottom of the pool. I tilt my head to the side, just admiring the show, in awe of how the water changes direction with the beat. I started counting the spouts of water, and I quit. The lights are changing colors, also moving to the rhythm of the music, giving the appearance of a choreographed dance! Shadows of a dragon appear; it's magnificent! Clapping and whistling people disperse when the show ends.

I see the tall buildings full of blazing bright, neon, colorful lights, which is a striking contrast from Hell! There are so many people, and the traffic is horrible; there are so many cars. Everything here is so congested. Even the air has a different smell. Well, I've never been in this city before, so maybe that's why I'm not sure.

The casinos and hotels look very interesting, too. There's one that has lights all over it. As I walk, I see the palm trees and people who probably work in the hotels. They're out on a break in their costumes, and each hotel has many screens outside showing what they have to offer. There are even screens selling marijuana. Oh yeah, it's legal here. That is part of the smell I mentioned.

Damn, I see bulletin boards for sexy, half-dressed women, boobs out, with nothing on but panties, waiting to have a sexual encounter. People can call the number and get the girl, and it's all good, okay. Wow, these hotels have some pretty good people here performing some video shows. There's one guy I like but don't see— Justin Timberlake. Now that's a show I would want to see. But I guess Justin's not here, because I don't see his picture or name on anything. Wow, there's even a guy with some animals, so I guess he's doing it. Whatever floats his boat right? Okay. There's another hotel, Lysine; it has a lovely fountain, but not like what I saw when I arrived. That was amazing to see.

Oh, there's a volcano show at one of these hotels. That's different; it seems cool; I'm going to check it out. They are beating tribal drums, and the fire is sprouting out. It's not at all like the water from the fountain that sprays with the beat of the music; it's just there. Then they have a massive volcano with sparks of fire shooting out of it. It reminds me of when a volcano actually erupts, and the lava comes out. I guess it was okay, but after seeing that fountain show, I don't think I'm going to see anything else here that's going to live up to that. One side looks busier than the other, and I'm on the more energetic side with all the people.

A mermaid show is happening down the street. Several beautiful women in gorgeous mermaid costumes are swimming and frolicking about near this man-made island at the center. There's music playing, and they are singing, "Come out to the sea, you'll soon be with me, and always be free, loving me in the sea."

They're rocking side to side to the music and using their hands, beckoning the men to come to them. At the end of the song, they dive back into the water and disappear. That was okay, I guess. I cross the street to explore the other side of the strip. Hmm, will this be interesting?

There are some women trying to get men to pay them to leave with them. They're wearing heavy makeup and not much clothing—prostitutes. There are some pretty women just walking, but not trying to get the men. Some of the men are approaching them. Don't they have to show what they can do for the women here? Show that they are a worthy mate for her? Damn, I remember some thoughts I've read from men and women upon entering Hell. No, many of them don't care about that.

I hear many people's thoughts, and it's mainly sex and money. Okay! Women even approach me, but I shake my head no. Some people are drunk or just high and unable to walk straight, just stumbling all over. I wander through the strip looking at everything, and with my powers, I can see through the buildings and decide where I'm going.

I see couples getting married and I see how they are with each other. What if I could have a mate? That would be the best way to see how it is to be with humans, right? My mate must be a match for me. How could that happen here when I couldn't find a mate in Hell in all this time? I have never felt the heat or fever for any demon, ever!

Once I find a mate, she's mine, and I'm hers. I know that I don't want any of the women I'm seeing that are just throwing themselves at the men. They don't seem clean to me. I'm not your ordinary demon, and I don't like filth.

I'm inside the Sweet Sensation Casino Club. There's a group of people who are having a good time in the restaurant, except for one young woman. First, she has a luminous aura all around her. It's drawing me to her, and I need to get closer, but her light is blocking me. Going over to the glass doors, I focus on getting through to see more of her. I feel electricity surge through me, and I know she's it! I'm determined to get this woman. SHE IS MINE! I can see that she has a beautiful soul; I want this woman for myself. I must talk to her, so I walk through the casino doors and go to the dining area.

She has long, dark, silky red hair, beautiful honey skin, and electric blue eyes that I could lose myself in. Her cheekbones are high, her lips are plump in a soft pout, and her peach lip gloss is perfect. She's wearing a short-sleeved, baby blue, satin blouse and a black skirt with a little slit. She is tall, very curvy, and has long legs. She's sitting with her people at the table.

I stop and inhale, smelling Jasmine, Vanilla, and something else; my head feels light, and I start breathing a little heavier. I feel a tremendous heat growing from deep in my chest and spreading throughout my body! I know this scent is from her. I quickly walk toward her, then a young woman rushes up, stopping me.

She smiles and breathlessly asks, "Sir, how many people are with you?"

I frown at her and look at her like she's crazy, "Don't you see it's just me?"

She apologizes and wants to show me to a table very far from the young woman.

I stare deeply into her eyes and use my powers of persuasion. "I want to sit next to that table where that young woman is." I point to the table.

Nodding her head in agreement, she says, "Of course you can," then leads me to the table. I flash a great smile, because I'm going to my future mate!

There's a little blond at the table who is staring at me, and smiling freakishly. I read her thoughts: Ava is her name, and she wants me and thinks I'm sexy! Not! Here I am sitting at a table for eight, and it's just me. I'm looking at the young woman who has her back to me and doesn't realize that I'm here. I read her thoughts and see terrible, heartbreaking events that have happened to her. A surge of protectiveness overwhelms me. "Alyssa." I whisper her name to myself.

I'm right, the scent's hers, and it's driving me a little crazy! My loins are more than erect, and I feel like I'm going to explode. I've never been this hot; smoke just rushed out of my nose! I have to control myself. I want to pick her up and carry her away! I want to make her mine right here! This feeling is more than strange, and I've never experienced any shit like this ever! The fever is beginning; in conclusion, Alyssa is my mate!

I order a stiff drink, and I'm pretending to look at the menu while listening to the other table.

"Alyssa, you have to stop being at home so much; your parents and Lana wouldn't want you to be so depressed and constantly missing them." The man, who is interested in her, is trying to rub her hand. I already read his mind, and I might kill him!

She moves her hand away, and another young woman glares at him.

"Ryan, don't be an idiot; you can't understand how she feels. Her parents and her twin sister died in a car accident!" Slamming her hand on the table, she scowls at him. "There's no schedule on grief; hell, we're still grieving for our aunt and uncle, too. Don't forget, they were also our Godparents, and Alana was our cousin and God sister! And keep your damn hands to yourself!"

"Delia, she has to snap out of it. It's been six months!"

Suddenly, Alyssa jumps up and yells at Ryan, "Who the hell are you telling me?" Everything gets quiet as the other customers stop their conversations. They all turn their attention to Alyssa's table.

She turns with tears running down her face and rushes away. "Why did I come here?"

I just want to break that idiot in half! I've never been this ANGRY! Bastard! I must do something! I haven't attached my essence to her, so I'll be able to tune in and find her once she leaves! I can't just run around trying to sense her.

I get up and see a couple leaving a table with a half bottle of wine still there. I look up at the chandelier; it's spaced above in the walkway. I use my telekinesis to loosen the bolts. There's a heavyset woman near the table walking toward Alyssa. I knock over the bottle with one look so the wine spills when the heavy woman is in Alyssa's path. She slips and is about to fall on Alyssa. At the same time, the chandelier falls!

With my ultra-speed, I reach Alyssa, pick her up in my arms, and spin away, and of course, I successfully save Alyssa from the chandelier! Consequently, the woman is hurt in the fall.

My head is spinning. Alyssa feels incredible! My shaft feels like it's going to rip through these damn pants! I want to take her with me.

Alyssa's cheeks are a bit flushed. "Oh my God!" she exclaims, and instinctively wraps her arms around my neck. I can't help it, and I smile at her.

Lyssa

I LOOK up to say thank you, and I'm shocked to see the most beautiful blue-green eyes I've ever seen! His eyes are two different hues of blue: cornflower turning into a baby blue, then streaks mixing into a light green. Everything stops while we're staring into each other's eyes. It's like we're having a conversation that no one else knows.

Damn, I can't breathe! I study the rest of his face; it turns out to be gorgeous! He has a fabulous tan, smooth skin, and has thick, black, super healthy-looking hair pulled into a ponytail. He has high cheekbones and full lips ideal for kissing! Wait! What's happening right now?

My heart is racing faster than when he picked me up and saved me! Feeling the muscles in his broad shoulders and arms is having a crazy effect on me. This iron-hard man has me hotter than I've ever felt in my entire life! Nope, adrenaline doesn't make you feel like this!

My skin is tingling all over, and even his smell is affecting me! His scent is like an aphrodisiac—woodsy, cinnamon, amber, with something else in it—a bold combination. I can't believe this; I feel my nipples harden! Oh, my God. I look up, and he's looking at me with this strange look in his eyes. I've never had a man look at me like this before, with pure hunger and something else, as if he possesses me. It just has me burning hot in a frenzy; then, I feel my panties get wet! My body is betraying me, because I don't do this!

He inhales, and I know it's impossible, but it's like he can smell my arousal! And the weirdest thing is that his eyes changed to all blue, and it's sexy as Hell. I'm losing my mind. Why are all these feelings coming on right now? I've never felt an attraction so powerful! I feel his muscular chest as he holds me against him, and his arms are incredible.

Lucas

I CARRY Alyssa a few paces away from the loud, crying woman while the restaurant staff is fast approaching to assist her. I can smell that I've stimulated her just from my scent and holding her close! I've awakened her as my mate; yes, this is very encouraging! I smile at her, and she responds with a smile and a breathless, "Thank you." I use my power to slow everyone down, so I can speak with her.

I act before she catches on. "You're as light as a feather. I'm Lucas. Whose life do I have the honor of saving?"

Alyssa blushes. "I'm Alyssa, and you're pretty strong, because I'm heavier than that."

We laugh. "Are you okay, Alyssa?"

She answers breathlessly, "I'm fine."

You're amazing! I'm thinking to myself. More heat is building, and I can't keep it together. She has inner beauty, as well as outer beauty. I carefully put her back on her feet, and she stumbles, so I hold her close to me to help steady her. Our bodies touch so closely, we're magnetite to each other. The sparks go off in our bodies, and she's confused, scared, and astonished by it. Reading her mind is intrusive, but that's what I do. All at once, we're interrupted by her family and the woman on the floor.

"Alyssa, are you okay?!" everyone asks. "Can someone call an ambulance!" the hefty woman on the floor cries out.

The women in the restaurant are all focused on me. Ryan, the bastard who was talking to Alyssa earlier, is staring at me with a deep frown on his face. Alyssa's friends surround us.

We make some significant eye contact, and a very young woman yells, "I'm Ava!" She grabs my hand and kind of eases very close to me. Hasn't she ever heard of personal space? I move away from her. Oh fuck, she's the one I read that wants me. I glance down, and she's a curvy, tall, attractive blond with a stylish short haircut, olive-toned skin, grey eyes, and super white teeth.

She starts shaking my hand vigorously, "You were right there; you probably saved Alyssa's life! You could save me anytime!" she exclaims with a broad smile and a sexy look in her eyes. It's the kind of look that says you're a piece of chocolate cake, and I'm a chocolate addict…

"I'm Lucas; I'm glad I was here for her," I say, looking right at Alyssa. I'm thinking, what in the Hell is wrong with her?

"Stop it, Ava, you act like you're going to have him for dinner!" another young woman says, shaking her head. "I'm Janae. Thank you for saving my cousin Alyssa".

She's beautiful: tall, with the same type of olive-toned skin, long auburn hair with reddish highlights, green eyes, and deep dimples in each cheek. She gives a genuine smile and shakes my hand much better than Ava did.

Another woman comes up shyly and says, "Hello, I'm Delia, Janae's big sister, and Alyssa's my little cousin. Thank you so much. My heart couldn't take it if something happened to her." She briefly puts her hand on my arm.

Delia is similar in skin tone to Janae, and she is stunning, because her eyes are an electric blue with green specks. Her skin is flawless, and she has shiny brown hair past her shoulders and a radiant smile. She's a little shorter than Janae with a fantastic body as well! Well, they are sisters.

"Hi, Lucas, I'm Naya; thanks for being here for my big cousin, Lyssa." Well, damn, she's very tall: at least six feet. She's another beauty too, with long, thick, curly brown hair with dark blond highlights and light caramel skin. She has hazel eyes and a lovely smile.

I think now's a good time to ask this: "Are you all visiting?" All of the ladies except Alyssa answered, "We live in Incline Village!"

"Are you from here or on vacation?" Janae asks. She looks over at Alyssa and moves slightly away, but she stands with Delia. I'm just watching and listening, within range.

"I'm new in the area, and I'm looking at different places and trying to decide where to settle."

"You have to see Incline Village, and then you'll love it! Not like Vegas at all, even though the strip is the only thing here. Hey Lucas, I'm Sasha. I'm her cousin too, and Naya's big sister."

She's an exotic beauty, like her sister, with long, thick, curly, dark brown hair, caramel skin, and hazel eyes. Her smile is amazing! She's very tall, too, the same height as Naya.

All the women in the group introduced themselves. All I can say is, what a beautiful family!

Another voice, this one male: "I'm Steve. Delia's my fiancé, so that makes Alyssa my fam too. Thanks a lot." He walks up and shakes my hand. What the Hell did I just see? Steve, no most of the family, has a huge secret.

Steve has to bend to get in the doorway, so he doesn't hit his head. He has curly brown hair, caramel colored eyes, a nice-looking face, and he's very muscular. Delia and Steve make a great couple.

Everyone except Ryan have introduced themselves, but he's away from the group sulking.

Ava called out, "Ryan, why are you over there? Come over and meet Alyssa's Knight in Sexy Armor!"

Ryan is also tall, though shorter than Steve, plus he's very handsome with his dark blond hair. He has dark blue eyes, tanned skin, dimples, and he's a personal fitness trainer, so his body is in damn good shape!

See, I can appreciate great looks, but with this guy, his physical features are the only thing good about him! If you're only paying attention to the surface, he could fool you.

He glares at Ava, Alyssa, then me with this crazy look of disgust on his face. For what? I don't know him and don't care to; I'm out!

He stomps off like a kid having a tantrum. Ryan was Alana's man, and since she's passed on, he was trying to get at Alyssa! I've been reading Ryan's thoughts, and I stop the frown that I feel appearing on my face. I'll fucking rip his ass apart with everything in my being if he tries anything else with my mate!

CHAPTER 4

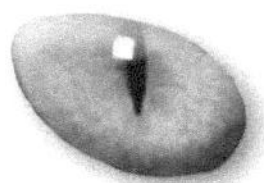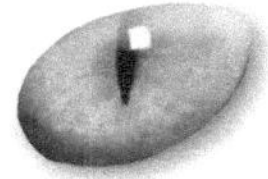

SEX PERSONIFIED

Lyssa

WHOA, what's going on with me? I could beat the Hell out of Ava throughout this entire building! Why was she all over Lucas? Well, he did maneuver her away from him. Why are these thoughts racing in my mind? I don't even know him. I feel such a powerful connection to him, and judging by the way he's watching me, he still feels it. My skin is just tingling everywhere since he picked me up.

Delia puts her arms around my shoulders and leans to my ear, whispering, "He's gorgeous, damn sexy as Hell! You better give him your number when he asks you for it. No hiding in that virginal closet." I glance over to the woman, who's screaming even louder, and I hear the ambulance sirens outside.

The paramedics and firemen enter the restaurant rushing to get to her. I look at Lucas, whose eyes are piercing right through me, then he smiles. I make contact with those eyes, and I melt. I feel myself getting hotter, and now my panties are soaked. What does he do? He takes a deep breath, and licks his lips and turns towards the group with an "Excuse me." He takes a few steps and is right in front of me.

I vaguely hear Delia's voice; well, I don't know; since Lucas is here, my focus is on him. "Alyssa, are you okay?" he asks while rubbing my arms.

I take a deep breath. "I think so." His scent is so alluring, and he's touching me. I sway toward him as my knees weaken, and he holds me up. I swear he's waking up something my body has never experienced before.

He leans into me and whispers, "Alyssa, you feel it too, don't you? You're mine. And I'm here to collect!"

What the Hell?! He kisses me on my cheek, looks right into my eyes, and I can't breathe evenly—my heart's beating erratically! He smiles, and I think I'm melting.

"See you soon, Alyssa." He walks away with so much swagger that every female in the restaurant watches him leave.

Damn, he's smoking hot, gorgeous, and just basically claimed that I'm his! I watch him go, and a pretty blond runs up to him at the exit. She's smiling, giving him the head to toe gaze, and she quickly puts her hand on his chest. He removes her hand and walks away; disappointment is etched all over her face! I can't help it. I laugh.

Delia taps my arm. I turn to look at her, and she has a smirk on her face and a sparkle in her eyes.

"Date or what?" I roll my eyes, "No."

Of course, she frowns, and here comes the dreaded question: "So what does he mean, 'See you soon', then?"

Heat creeps in all over my face, and I'm shaking my head.

"How am I supposed to know?"

The girls join in, and Ava is the first to speak. "Damn, he makes me want to rip both of our clothes off and jump on him like he's the last man on the planet!" They're all laughing; honestly, there's nothing funny, so I'm feeling more than a little pissed off! Janae tells the truth when she says, "We love you, Ava, but damn, why do you always have to be the group's slut-hoe?"

She has this surprised expression. "Why? Just because I say what damn near every woman is thinking, after seeing fucking male perfection-sexiness walking live in person!? I guess I'll be that, since being truthful is an anomaly!"

I clarify it, though. "No, that's not it, but what is slut-hoe behavior is when you damn near throw yourself at Lucas when he wasn't trying to catch your ass!"

Delia glanced at both of us and declares it's enough and time to have some damn fun. First, I have to run to our room to freshen up. Delia comes with me. We all walk out of the restaurant and go through the casino entrance. As we go to the elevator; my mind is still blown away in Lucas Land.

"So he is the sexiest man I've ever had the pleasure of seeing in person! Lyssa, what did he whisper in your ear? Come on, share! He has pure animal magnetism; every female in that restaurant felt it!" Delia exclaims.

We leave the elevator and I my head, "I've been attracted to men before but, nothing compares to this! I mean, this is crazy. I can't explain it, but oh my God!"

We get to my room, and I take a quick shower. I put on my sheer black blouse, black bra, and a rose and black print miniskirt with a little slit on the side. I walk out, and Delia gives the thumbs up.

"I'm so ready to go to the casino and win some cash!"

Gambling isn't on my mind at all! No time for that; my focus is on Lucas and how my body is still feeling after walking away! I guess I'll pretend at this point and go through the motions, since I did promise. I can't focus, so I go with Delia to the slot machines, because not much thinking is required.

Someone is watching me, the creepy weirdo type, and I look to my left. Ryan's staring at me angrily, while Steve is playing blackjack! If looks could kill, I'm convinced I'd be dead as a rotten piece of meat. I shake my head and roll my eyes, because he's really an ass! I will not be bothered with him, even though I have six more days here. I will most definitely steer clear of him!

"Oh, yeah, baby! I hit the jackpot, Lyssa!"

I see the light blinking, along with the loud sirens; yes, she won! I give her a high five. "Woohoo! That's great, Delia! The children's hospital has money coming! Yes!"

At the roulette table, she just won $100,000! We have a deal to send our winnings to our favorite charities. "Delia, you should cash out; you don't want to keep gambling."

"Come on, Lyssa, don't be the buzz kill."

"It's our first night; we have six nights to gamble. Save some for another night, okay?"

Delia pouts, "It seems like our roles have changed for this vacation. You've become the serious one; hopefully, Lucas changes that! Lady Luck is with me. I feel it in my bones."

Delia, this high roller, decides she needs twenty-five thousand dollars in chips because she has Lady Luck on her shoulder! I look at her, trying to change her mind. "How much did you spend to get that win?"

Delia looks at me like I've got 4 heads. "Lyssa come on, this is supposed to be a week of FUN! Don't be the joy killer police, damn!"

Seriously? "Whatever! Go. My lips are sealed. I'm done! Don't say ANYTHING to me, if and when this roll of yours turns."

We start walking, and she goes towards the blackjack tables where Steve and Asshole are, and I'm not going there. I stop and tell her I'm heading out to find Janae and the girls. I take out my cell, and I connect with Janae. Then, I call Josh to invite them down for Saturday and Sunday. He talks to Chris, and they're coming. Surprise for Sasha on Saturday night!

We meet at the restaurant across the street. We heard the food is delicious. There's a seafood festival going on, so we are here at the perfect time: there are shrimp, crab, and lobster dishes. YUMMY! I let the girls know about Ryan and what my plan is. We'll call for them right when we're done, so I won't be subjected to his asinine presence.

This is going to be a bad situation if I don't stay away from him! We're at the station, choosing our seafood and everything else. We can watch the chef prepare it on the viewing screen, then they'll bring it to our table. That hot, tingling, sensation throughout my body that I felt with Lucas is back. I look to my right, and there he is, waiting in line to come in here. He's looking in my direction, straight at me.

Damn, he's sexy as Hell! He has on a form-fitting, long-sleeved, electric blue shirt that outlines every single muscle. His eyes match, in my opinion, with blues and greens, and yes, it's working! He has on black jeans that fit so damn good! He smiles; it brings even more heat. Oh boy, my panties are soaked, again! I want to jump on him and have my way with him!

This is not how my mind works; I'm a virgin by choice. I want my first time to be with someone I love, not just a casual fling. Sasha, Janae, and I still have our V-Cards, since Sasha decided Chris is her destiny. Chris would know that if Sasha threw some clues out to him, but he has NO idea how she feels!

I smile back at Lucas. Now he's with the hostess, and he points at me and waves; of course, I wave back. She says something and nods to him, and he walks over to me, never breaking our eye contact. "Get ready, sis, your man is coming! Please give him your number; he has to be the one! Hell, he saved your life for God's sake!" says Sasha, giggling.

Lucas

SINCE I'm tuned into Alyssa, I'll always know everything about her—even when I'm back in Hell, and especially after I make her mine. She'll be a part of me, as I will be for her. I'll fix it so she won't have that full connection. Too much fucking evil shit going in Hell to expose her to!

This is a lovely, upscale restaurant; of course, this place screams money. It's the perfect place to demonstrate that I am Alyssa's match and also a provider. I observe these people who are waiting for their reservation, so I pass them. I stroll up, and I tell the hostess my party is where Alyssa is, so I can join them.

Damn! Look at my mate; she's gorgeous! That black and rose outfit is sexy. She's covered every curve, but I cannot watch patiently while these men ogle what's mine! I focus and command these fuckers to look at anything but her! Yes! Their eyes have averted to several other objects and people. A woman just jumped in my path, trying to introduce herself. I shake my head, not even breaking eye contact with my mate. I just step aside and continue toward my goal.

I'm walking to Alyssa, and all I can think about is how long it's going to take to make her mine? I want her to be with me on her own, using her free will. I'll never make her be with me because she's genuinely my mate, and she's made for me!

Yeah, I'm a demon, so how the fuck did this happen?! I don't know, but I'm going with it. I reach her, and we're both eyeing each other, although the ladies and some men are watching me. Alyssa licks her lips; you know, my eyes go straight to her lips, wishing to kiss and taste them.

"Alyssa, may I join you and the ladies for dinner, my treat?"

Before she can answer, Sasha, Janae, Naya, and Ava reply, "Yes! You can!"

She looks at me and laughs softly. "Okay, you should stand with me, so we can all order together."

I nod in agreement and move behind her, since the guy and his son who are also online didn't move back. I can't stand beside her, but I'm going to ease really close to her, so she'll feel my body and my heat, and it'll drive her a bit wild, since this is a long line! The only thing is that it'll have a worse effect on me; even more noticeable if these jeans were looser! When my body touches her from behind, she gasps, and her heartbeat quickens. Once again, I feel my aura flowing into her. I guess this is normal; I don't know.

I lean in and rest my hands on the railing, so she's encircled within my space. I whisper in her ear, "I've been thinking about you nonstop since I had you in my arms, Alyssa. Have you been thinking about me?"

She blushes and turns around. "What have you been thinking about concerning me? You don't even know me, Lucas."

I lift my hand and put it under her chin, so she has to look at me. I whisper in her ear, "We connect on a deeper level. I know you feel it too." I radiate more essence into her; I experience the heat rise higher in her body and mine.

My shaft has a full hard-on, and I just shift a small bit into her so she can feel it. She inhales sharply, and I already know she's turned on. I smell her sweet nectar; damn, I just want to devour her! Mine! Mine! Mine! She subconsciously leans into me, and right on my shaft! Her body is fucking marvelous. I can imagine being with her, and knowing I'm the first and last is…dammit, there's not a word to describe how fucking fantastic that is to me.

Shit! This is working; she feels it even more since she has a little more of my essence. Okay, I'm not going to force Alyssa, but giving her a little push makes her feel the mating pull stronger. It's not using my persuasive powers on her. It's our bodies naturally calling each other.

"Alyssa, are you going to answer my question with the truth or lie to my face?" I stare deeply in her eyes; she has to admit to me how she feels, even though I know it already.

She takes a shaky breath. "Yes, I feel it too," she says, so low that I barely hear her.

Yes! I have found my mate, and Alyssa admits to me that she's feeling it too, plus her body is calling me! I'm on a damn roll, but I don't want to overwhelm her, so I won't push anymore tonight. We start moving in the line, and we are basically walking together, since we're so close. Forget it. Fuck that; maybe I can get a kiss, at least?

We've all ordered our food from the different stations and are sitting at our table. I'm next to my mate, yeah, yeah, she's my future mate; whatever! She's mine; that's all I know.

I even pull the chairs out for the ladies: my woman first, of course. We're watching the chef prepare our food.

Ava sighs, "Lucas, you're too good to be true! On top of everything else, you're a gentleman! That's a rare breed for men, that's for sure."

The waiter asks about drinks, and I tell him to bring three bottles of their best champagne.

The waiter's eyes widen in surprise. "Right away, sir!" he replies, and rushes off to get bottles. He returns, and Ava is the first to see the brand: Krug Clos d'Ambonnay.

Ava nods her head at me with a smile. "Oh, oh, big baller, shot caller, I see you, Lucas."

The next thing I see, Ava jumps up a bit in her chair, with a pained expression across her face. I glance sideways at Alyssa, who was frowning at Ava, saying, "Why?"

Yeah, she just kicked the shit out of Ava under the table.

Janae intervenes. "Lucas, are you thinking about checking out Incline Village? It's lovely, and we live right at Lake Tahoe."

I gaze at Alyssa. "I've seen something so beautiful today that I don't know how anything could top it! But yes, I'm moving to Incline Village as soon as possible! And since I saved Alyssa's life, she should give me the grand tour of the city and end it with a date. I'll pay, but you know the area, so you can pick the place. The price doesn't matter. I need your number, and I'll give you mine."

Sasha quickly pulls out her phone and gives Alyssa's number to me. Alyssa looks at Sasha and shakes her head. "Wow, Sasha, I can't even give out my own number."

I pull out the latest phone that I brought from the shop next door. The young lady assured me it was the best, and I enter her number. Sasha just shrugs her shoulders with a grin on her face.

I call her, so now she has my number. "You can call me anytime, day or night, and I'll answer."

All three look at Alyssa then back at me, then they finally settle on Alyssa with knowing smiles. She just starts blushing, and our appetizers arrive.

Dinner is delicious, and the champagne is excellent. The waiter is thrilled with the two thousand dollar tip that'll help with college. The bill was over six grand because of those two bottles of champagne; they know I'm not cheap.

The ladies are all tipsy, and I offer to walk them back to their room. I don't tell them, but I'll be staying there as well. As we're leaving, Janae calls Delia about dinner. We walk across the street to the hotel and enter the lobby. The staff greets us. We go to the elevator, and while we're on, more people arrive. It's not that crowded; Alyssa moves back, then leans against my front. Damn she feels, well, you already know!

She drops her bag, and what does my little minx do?! She bends down to pick it up, moving her ass all over my shaft! She's going to kill me, an immortal! Well, let's face it, I've had a painful erection since the restaurant, and she's playing with me. I'm trying my best not to grab her ass up, throw her over my shoulder, transport her somewhere, and fuck her so brilliantly that she can't say her own name when I'm done! And she's trying me? This is what she wants, but right now, this isn't what she wants!

I'll forget she's an inexperienced virgin… When she straightens up, I spin her around so she's facing me, and she looks up at me with those stunning blue eyes. I have to stop time for this! Once again, she nervously licks those luscious lips, and I can't take it any longer!

I pull her even closer to me, and I crush my lips against hers—no gentleness or coaxing from my end. My tongue brushes along her bottom lip, and she opens her mouth for me; that's when I invade her like the destroyer that I am! She tastes like champagne, lobster, plus that chocolate cake we shared. Her sweet scent of vanilla and jasmine has me light-headed.

I'll devour any thought she has about slowing us down since she wants to tease me with that ass of hers! I suck on her bottom lip, then graze it just enough, then our tongues meet. I kiss her deeply. She moans as I let my hands roam, and damn, her breasts are just perfect! Her nipples are so hard from her desire for me, and I move lower, and I grab that weapon, you know the one, her ass that she wants to play with on my shaft. Damn, it's round, right, and plenty!

I stop the kiss, then move down to kiss her neck and suck on it to give her a mark. Yes, she needs to *see* I marked her, not just remember it. I should put her hand on my shaft, so she feels me, but that might scare her. It's hers, so one way or another, she's going to get to know it.

OH. My. God! Okay, I'm feeling super off the charts excited. My body is in overdrive! I have never felt aroused like this before. I drop my bag, thinking of what Delia said she did to Steven to get him to notice her. Well, he wasn't right behind her as Lucas is, and he has definitely seen me! Since the beginning, Lucas has caught me and carried me to safety, telling me that I'm his, very specifically. Damn, what the Hell did I just do? Stupid! Good Lord! I think his dick is a monster! It's huge!

I gaze into his eyes; they're filled with pure, hot passion for me. An unfamiliar tsunami of desire attacks me; whoa, my knees feel weak! His eyes have changed again! Sensational, sexy blue; oh, yes, this color won't ever be the same! It has me soaked, and God, that kiss has it running down between my thighs!

I'm burning up for him; oh, he grabs my hand and places it on his crotch to feel. Oh damn! I'm right; he's enormous, and the thickness is unreal.

"I'm yours, and you belong to me and this," his dick moves while I'm touching it, "is yours too," Lucas announces.

I feel even more heat emerging from deep within my core and spreading throughout my body. Goosebumps are raising up all over my skin. I'm light-headed, and I feel like I'm on fire!

"Don't worry, we'll get to know each other first, but you can't be teasing me with your sweet ass like you just did. My self-control isn't good enough to ignore that and not touch you."

He squeezes my ass, I gasp, and he kisses me again. He's gentler this time. My turn. I lightly bite his lip, then slide my tongue in, damn; he can kiss, but so can I. Over those jeans, my hands hesitantly brush his member; it feels incredible, but one day that is supposed to fit inside of me? I don't know about that... I can't believe this; it's my first feel of any man's dick! Now we have all been to strip clubs, so I've seen a few almost-naked men, but nothing like Lucas!

I move my hands up to feel the rest of him; he feels so hard and athletic. I touch his abdominal muscles by row one, two, three, whoa, four. That's an eight pack up to his chest. Damn, his nipples are hard too! I rub my thumbs on them and then give a little pinch for him to feel. My knees are feeling weak from just kissing and touching. Unreal! I bring my hands up to touch his face, then up to his hair just to run my fingers through it, and it feels fantastic.

We break from our kiss. We're both breathing heavily, and we hear the elevator arriving at the floor. I've totally forgotten where we are, then I hear a noise and I look to my right, and it's Ava. She's watching us with a sly grin on her face; at least my other cousins are pretending to look at the elevator buttons or their phones! Lucas turns me around, facing the people, so my back is against him, and he has both of his hands on my hips. He's now grinding my ass very subtly, and there's just a mess of my juices sliding further down my thighs. If I weren't so tall, it'd be past my knees!

We're the next stop; our group is left on the elevator. We move up, and it just passes our stop and goes up to the level before the penthouse. We press for our floor again, and more people get in on the way down. All the while, Lucas is steady grinding on me, and I'm joining him. We finally get to our floor. We're walking out, my knees buckle a bit, and I stumble, but Lucas has me and wraps one arm around my waist. I need the support, because my va-jay-jay and my body are throbbing so much. I swear it's the most intense feeling I've ever felt!

We walk down the long corridor to the rooms Sasha, Naya, and I share, and right next door are Janae and Ava. Of course, they all say thanks to Lucas and stroll into our room. Sasha closes the door and winks at us. I lean back on the door, and Lucas is eye-sexing me, his fingers caressing my cheek.

"Lyssa, are you going to call me tonight, or can I call you?" I inhale his alluring, intoxicating scent, unable to take my eyes off of him. Stroking his chest, I reply, "You can call me, Lucas."

He smiles, and he's just beautiful; damn, the most gorgeous man ever! He laughs like he knows the thought that just went through my mind, but that's impossible. I straighten up from leaning on the door, and now I'm so close that I feel the heat radiating from his body. What's that? I've been on dates before and never had anything like this happened!

"I guess I'm going in now. I'll talk to you if you call."

I start to turn to go inside; Lucas grabs me by my waist with both hands and lifts me up, so I'm at eye level. He picks me up like I weigh nothing at all! At 5ft 11, I'm curvy in all the right places, and my body is tight! I'm not skinny by any means, but I work out to stay in shape.

I put my hands on his shoulders.

"Alyssa, why do you say if I call? It's when I call you tonight, so we can talk and begin our process of getting to know each other, Sweetness." Lucas says it with so much sincerity that I know it's not a game to him.

His eyes are so extraordinary, I could just get lost in them. He leans his forehead in to touch mine. It's just what my Dad did and what my Uncles do with all of our family as a goodbye gesture since we were little. He's the first person outside of my family to do this. Lucas frowns and looks toward the elevator as it opens and who's stepping out? Asshole! You know, Ryan. He's looking down; hmm, maybe if he sees me with Lucas, he'll finally stay away from me on his own.

As if he heard me, Lucas leans down and starts kissing me; I wrap my arms around his neck and just grab the back of his silky, thick, curly hair. Oh! Sugar! Here we go. It's just so deliciously sexy that we have this blazing inferno!

He lowers one hand under my ass, and his other is there too. He guides me, so I wrap my legs around his waist, and we hear my skirt ripping. I keep my legs wrapped tightly around him. Oh, Lord! He lowers me just enough that I'm on his cock, and he grinds on my va-jay-jay, oh! This is so damn real, and for the third time today, I want this man; my entire everything wants him!

Lucas

HELL yeah! This bastard had better get my fucking message. She is—mine! My woman tastes scrumptious. I'm kissing her like she's all I have; well, that is the truth! She's damn soaked. Yup, I'm getting these panties to jerk off with tonight! Ryan's super pissed. I hear his thoughts as he watches us while walking to his suite, but he's still not giving up! She's so hot; her skin is really flushed. I slowly break off the kiss as I pull away; I lightly nibble that bottom lip of hers. I want to get deep inside her to the root!

"Sweetness, I'm going to put you down, and put my hand under your skirt, then take your panties. As I pull them down, just lift your legs and step out."

Her eyes open wide, and I grind against her; then she closes her eyes and quickly inhales. I slowly let her body slide against mine as I put her down and put my hand in to get her panties; she grabs my hand. She exhales, looks at me with so much hunger, and slowly shakes her head. I'm caught off guard and shit, I'm shocked! It must show on my face, because I know she wants me more than ANYTHING FUCKING EVER!

"We are not there yet, not by a long shot. We need to be further than this. I know; don't look at me like that. We need to have more than phenomenal chemistry, Lucas. Call me when you can," she whispers, then turns and goes inside.

Lyssa

I CLOSE the door and exhale, trying to calm down this raging fire of need that has erupted in my body. I touch my lips, which are swollen from kissing, and I can't believe I was just grinding on the damn hottest man ever! I use my hands to fan my face and neck as I lean back against the door. I shut my eyes for a minute, trying to get myself in control. Oh boy, it isn't working; why did I just have a flashback of grinding Lucas? Damn, what the Hell is this?

Oh God, here they come, all four of them, and in a moment they are about to become my own personal, nosey, pain in the ass squad! If our slut-ho Ava wasn't here, maybe we could talk, because I'm so confused by my reaction to this man. I'm not doing this right now. Sasha has her headphones around her neck, and she presses her Bluetooth speaker for all of us to hear. Sasha and Naya dance up to me, singing Bruno Mars, "That's What I Like!"

Sasha and Naya grab each of my hands, wink at me, and then get me to join in. They're trying to distract the girls, so I won't have to hear their questions. Ava dances up to us and yells, "So what's the verdict? Are you EVER going to give the sexiest man to walk in any of our paths a chance, so he can punch out your V-card?"

Oh, God, she's moving her hips like she's grinding. "Lucas is sex personified, gorgeous, and packing a body that's fucking amazing! He saved your life, Lyssa; you two were hot on the elevator, too. I swear you were like a different person. I was listening to you a little outside the door until Sasha pulled me away!"

She looks at Sasha, frowning and pointing at her. She's shorter than we are, especially Naya and Sasha, so, she only reaches Sasha's breasts. It looks funny as Hell!

"I have to get to know him," I say, as I dance with Sasha and Naya into our bedroom. Then I close the door on them.

"Seriously!" They both yell.

All I want to do is take cold shower number two, which will hopefully put a cap on this inferno I have in me! I have to think about the attraction I have for Lucas, and why in the Hell did he think I'd give him my damn panties? We just met. Okay, we kissed and felt each other up. I'm not happy that I didn't show more restraint; this isn't what I do, just let strangers kiss and feel me up! What the Hell is wrong with me?!

CHAPTER 5

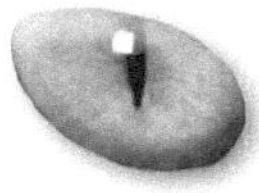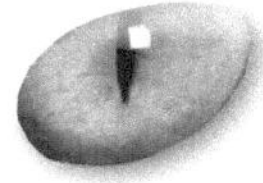

PROTECT AND WATCH

Lucas

OKAY, I guess I was somewhat presumptuous with the panty idea. No worries; this is still a successful night! I'm going to the lobby to get a room. Wait; no, I need the best place, like a penthouse. I need to do some more research on this dating thing, because of all the information I've read and seen in the soul's thoughts from Hell, there are different lengths of time before sex even happens.

Sometimes it happens on the first meeting, or days, weeks, or even months may go by. Months isn't going to work at all. I feel like I might have to help Sweetness along. I won't be using persuasion either; I'll just use her body against her.

Now that I know Ryan has a new approach, I need to make sure I'm as close as possible. That son of a bitch really thinks he can fucking drug my mate?! Have sex? No: *rape* her while she's passed out or knocked out; that's what it is. Then try to convince her that they had consensual, drunk sex when she wakes up? I really should just kill his ass tonight. I don't even want her on the same floor as he is. If she stays where he is, I'll exterminate him like the rodent that he is.

How can I ensure that Alyssa will be close to me during her stay, like on the same floor as I am, not just the same building? I arrive at the lobby, and there's a blond-haired woman with a young man at the check-in, giving him directions. She turns to me and gives me a head-to-toe appraisal. Here we go; she gives me the toothiest smile ever. Wow! She has a lot of teeth. I wince! I try to avert my eyes, so I'm not looking straight in her eyes.

I can't look at her; there's no way to avoid them. I search through her memories, trying to understand what's up with those teeth. It's a travesty to have to go through life with teeth like that. What if I have to come back down here again and be subjected to this? She can't afford the dental procedures. Oh boy; she's never even had a date! We have something in common, so you know what I'm going to do?

I'll fix her teeth so she can find somebody to rock her world.

At the rate these people mate; she'll probably end up in tears when she gets what she wants! At least she'll have a fighting chance, right? See what finding my mate has done? I stop time as I use my healing powers on her teeth. I open her mouth to get an excellent view; the teeth are very crooked in some areas and just too many. She has a few cavities I make disappear.

Focusing on her teeth, they began straightening, and the extra teeth dissolve. Also, I heal the holes in her gums left from those 12 extra teeth and whiten the rest. Okay, I didn't know she'd end up with turquoise on her face, but she doesn't have a mirror in front of her. It's okay, because her teeth look great now! I try to wipe her face with a cloth, but there's still a faint shadow of turquoise on her face.

"Good evening, sir. May I help you?" Her name tag says Alexandra, Assistant Manager.

"Good evening, Alexandra. I need two penthouses for one week."

Her eyes widen. "Okay, sir; how many bedrooms do you need in each one?"

"I need one to have at least three bedrooms. I'd really like the penthouses to be in very close proximity—next door, preferably. I want the best you have to offer."

Alexandra's on the computer. Meanwhile, the young man keeps looking at her, and he's freaking out about her face and how great her teeth look. I telepathically command him to ignore it and continue working. The frown is gone, and he walks through the side door.

"We have penthouses that have two and three bedrooms on the same wing, right next door. Both penthouses have king-size, extra-plush, pillow-top beds, 1800-thread-count sheets, super soft, like a baby's bottom. All the bedrooms have private bathrooms with amazing bathtubs, and I call them Jacuzzis, because they're marbled, huge, and you can have a few people inside." She laughs, and I smile at her. She's a cutie with her teeth done, and I can pat myself on the back.

"There's a game room upstairs, and both floors have butler pantries. The master bedroom is on the first floor, and the living room, and each floor has a powder room. By the way, the living room can seat 20 people. And guess what? These penthouse suites are $6,000 per night weekdays, and on Friday and Saturday, the price increases for the weekend to $8,000 per night. Since you want both penthouses for the week, the price is $96,000; with tax and fees, it comes to $105,600. Riding to the penthouse level is private and only accessible with VIP card keys."

Hell yeah! I get lucky; the penthouses are next to each other. I look around, ensuring no one is in the area, then I use my exceptional talent and make my briefcase appear in my hand with fresh bundles of cash in it. I put it on the counter, open it, and take out eleven ten-thousand dollar cash bundles.

Of course, when I hand her the money, she begins to explain, "Sir, we need a credit card, too, in case there are any damages." She scrunches her face to show her disapproval, but her eyes show that she's also surprised.

I show her my identification with a smile. "My name is Lucas Hellsin, and take this." I hand her two hundred thousand in cash as a security deposit in case anything occurs.

"Oh my; the incidentals are taken care of, Mr. Hellsin, and we'll have this in the safe." She enters all the information into the computer, humming a Justin Timberlake tune. I get the satisfaction of doing something for a fellow J.T. fan.

I explore the recesses of Alexandra's mind. "Listen, Alexandra, you will not tell Alyssa or anyone else that I paid for the penthouse. This is a complimentary upgrade for her family. You're going to call and give her that news. Do you understand?"

"Yes, I will call now. No one will ever know you paid, Mr. Hellsin." Alexandra gets Alyssa's phone number from the computer and calls.

What a surprise it'll be that I'm next door! She gives me my card key and explains that I have to swipe the panel in the elevator so it'll unlock, because only penthouse guests have access. Not only that, but there are also a lot of perks that are exclusively for VIP STARS.

Going to the elevator with the bellhop, I swipe the card key. Another number fifty-six appears, and I press it. I step out of the elevator and, in contrast, this floor is undeniably another world from the others. As we enter, I see gold marbled walls with twisted columns every couple of feet, costly artwork on the walls, and black marbled floors. Micah shows me the penthouse for Alyssa and her cousins. Walking in, I'm flabbergasted by what I see; this is truly exquisite. I approve.

I tip the bellhop two hundred dollars. He's thrilled, and he knows to keep quiet about my involvement. He's a young guy, 21 years old, and he's in college; he says his name is Micah, and if I need anything, he'll be happy to assist.

I call Alyssa; the phone rings four times before she picks up. "Hey, Lucas," she answers.

I reply, "Hey, Sweetness, what are you up to?"

"We got a call from the manager. She said there was an error made with billing, and to compensate for our inconvenience, we got an upgrade to the penthouse. We just took the suites that Steve picked from Ryan; you know, the jerk. We're waiting for someone to bring our access cards and escort us there."

Someone knocks on her door, "Lucas, can I call you back after I get settled?" she asks.

"Of course, you can, Sweetness," I tell her.

A few minutes later, since I'm specifically focused, I hear them coming out of the elevator. I hear Micah as he continues to explain the extras of being in VIP STARS, so I open my door to go out right as they're approaching. All the ladies are shocked to see me, and they can't hide the expressions on their faces!

"Lucas! Are you staying here too? Why didn't you say anything?" Alyssa asks me.

I look at her, shrug my shoulders, and respond, "You didn't ask me where I was staying, Alyssa."

Micah clears his throat and announces, "Your penthouse suite, ladies." He opens the door with the card key and begins the tour. Alyssa is standing by me while everyone else is walking inside; she looks at me and says, "well, I better go and see what's in there! I'll call you in a little while, okay?"

I grin and tell her, "I'll be waiting, Sweetness." She laughs and goes inside while I watch her sweet ass sashaying.

Instead of pretending that I was on my way to the STAR VIP Club, I go back inside. I know I shouldn't, but fuck it; first, I look right through the walls and watch Alyssa. I'm exploring her thoughts to see what she's thinking. Three of them are in the living room sitting around; Ava starts dancing and singing, "Lyssa and Lucas sitting in a swing, k-i-s-s-i-n-g! On what? A sex swing!"

Lyssa's rolls her eyes, "You are just a damn slut-ho!"

Janae rushes up to Ava, saying, "Shut the hell up, Squirt!" At the same time, Lyssa turns and walks into her room, slamming the door. Naya and Sasha appear from the kitchen with food. Observing the two ladies, they shake their heads and follow Lyssa.

Damn! She wasn't paying attention until Ava opened her big mouth; why? She was thinking about who? Oh, yeah, me! All right now! That's what the fuck I'm talking about! Her body temperature is up from how hot I made her, and it's even higher just from her thinking about it. She's perplexed and upset with herself that she's losing control, since she's never behaved this way. It's too late; the mating hunger is alive! I just know it, deep inside; and no, it's not a demon thing.

I can't even imagine how this is going to be with Alyssa; she's human. I have to use every ounce of self-control I have not to give in to these primal urges to mate her now. I'm trying to relax, lying back while drinking a shot of bourbon.

I also rearranged the furniture in this area just a little. I can look outside through the windows as I lay my feet on the chaise. The view of the skyline is astounding. The penthouse is fantastic, with first-class accommodations like stainless steel appliances and a wine bar fully stocked with top of the line liquor and plush furniture throughout every single room. The colors throughout are cream, tan, and rich chocolate, with blue accent colors.

She's getting ready to call me back; my cell rings. "Hey, Sweetness. How do you like the penthouse?" I ask her with a smile.

Lyssa

"I love it, Lucas. We have loads of space, and the view is beautiful, right?" I say to him.

"Not as beautiful as you are. Now that's a hell of a sight to behold! Nothing tops that. Oh, well, I guess when we come together, that will!" Lucas replies.

Damn, why must he sound dirty and so sexy? I should be totally offended, but I'm not. It's just making me hotter. With anyone else, I would just let them have a piece of mind, but there's something about him that is drawing me in like a bear to honey. We know he's big, and he can be terrible.

"Alyssa, tell me about yourself. What do you like? What do you do? What are your favorite things?" Lucas asks a load of questions. I reply, "Okay, hmm, after I answer, I have some questions for you. So be ready to answer them. Well, I love the outdoors, exploring new places, swimming, hiking, rafting, rock climbing, jet skiing, basketball, tennis, and biking. I love cooking, too. I work out regularly because I have to stay in shape, and even though it's rough, I love the feeling of accomplishment! I'm a children's author and illustrator. First, I was an illustrator because I'm an artist, then I started writing, and it came together perfectly. I have illustrated 30 books that aren't mine, and I'm the author and illustrator of 18 books.

"My absolute three top favorite things are cooking, traveling, and being an artist; that's my first love. Now answer those questions plus these: Where are you from? Tell me about your family. What do you do?"

He laughs. "You are amazing! Do you know that? Okay, here we go. I'm into intense exercise; I mean heavy. By the time I'm done, every muscle burns and feels shattered, then regroups. I emerge stronger, pushing my limits more and more. I enjoy playing ball, rock climbing, racquetball, swimming, soccer, and racing cars.

"You know I have to be doing something right to keep my body like this. I have my own business in investment trading, and I can retire anytime. More than anything, my favorite thing is getting to know you. You're my favorite subject from now to infinity. I have one younger brother. I'm a long way from home. This is my first visit here, and I got lucky to have found you. Did I answer the questions to your satisfaction, Sweetness?"

Wow, he's the impressive one to be able to retire now, as young as he is. "Wait, how old are you, Lucas?" I ask.

"I'm 26 years old," he calmly replies.

I have got to ask this. "How long have you had your business, and can you really retire?"

He's cracking up laughing at me! He says, "Since I was young, I've had a gift for investment picks, and I got super damn lucky! Yes, I have enough for a very, very long time! You know what that means, right? We're both great apart, but together we'll be fucking phenomenal!"

I know if he were right here, he'd see that I'm blushing at this very moment. "I am satisfied for now, Lucas," I tell him with some sass.

"Alyssa, by the way, I never got your age," he says. "I think you're about 24 or 25. Am I right? And would you like to have breakfast with me tomorrow, Sweetness?"

"You're right. I'm 24; my birthday is in two months. And yes, to breakfast. Where are we going?"

He comments, "STAR VIP preferred guest perks; we can have the private dining room. I'll schedule for 9 am, does that sound good to you? Or do you need more beauty sleep?"

I laugh; he doesn't know that I wake up at 6:00 am for my workout, so 9:00 am is perfect. "At 7 am, Sasha, and I are working out, so 9:00 am works out just fine."

I imagine watching Lucas work out with that magnificent, hot body of his, and whew, I'm hotter than I was! I hear a faint groan in the background on his end. Then he exhales, "You're killing me, baby-girl, damn. I'm going to call to make the arrangements for to-morrow morning. I wish I could tuck you in and make sure you have a great night. I can wish you a good night over the phone and have sexy dreams of all the things you want to do with me, Sweetness."

He enjoys doing this to me with that provocative voice. I put my hand on my head, "Good night Lucas. I'll see you in the morning."

He chuckles, and we hang up. All the while, I'm shaking my head, because he knows how to mess with my head talking like that. He wasn't vulgar or anything; he just speaks his mind.

Sasha comes in and sits on the bed. She looks at me, smiling, and asks, "Good talk?"

I laugh at her and nod my head.

"Well, this could be something, sis, especially since he's moving to our city!"

I look at her in doubt. "I'll believe that he's moving there when I see it. I mean, when he's got a place to live in his name, then it'll be real.

It's just incredible; too good to be true. I meet this sexy, gorgeous, mountain of a man who claims me as his and vice versa. We're coming straight out of…is this a movie or what?"

Sasha hugs me, "I think maybe it's just your time, sis. Maybe he can bring you some happiness. Just take your time to get to know him, and if it's genuine, he'll prove it to you. Because boy oh boy, I believe you'll have the time of your life with him. You need this, and you don't pass up someone like this!"

I look around our room with the gold, cream, and purple colors, and right then, I make the decision. What's good for me to do is also for Sasha to do. I verbalize my thoughts to her. "All right, Sasha, if I give this a chance with Lucas, then you should do the same by letting Chris know something about how you feel about him!"

Sasha's very surprised, and she shakes her head, but I nod yes. She frowns. "Come on, Lyssa, you can't be freaking serious! You can't compare our situations; I mean, Lucas has made his move for all of us to see he wants you. What the Hell has Chris done? Nada, nothing, zilch! Why should I make a move? He should chase me! I'm not desperate; he's the man!" she crosses her arms in frustration.

I close my eyes and take an intense breath, trying to explain this plan's logic. "You can force Chris to see you as a woman, instead of Josh's little cousin. You know, a teeny itsy bit of flirting with a sexy outfit on, so he has that epiphany that you're not that teenager anymore! Not asking him out our anything or confessing your feelings like spilled milk. By the way, I know your ass isn't desperate!"

Since Josh and Chris are coming here this weekend, we can knock out two birds with one stone! They can keep Ryan in line and have Chris see Sasha!

We have a full day tomorrow, but I need a cold shower since I'm burning up! I turn on the speakers in my bathroom. It's gorgeous; soft lavender with cream marble and gold trim and accents. There is a Jacuzzi and a full, walk-in shower with a built-in bench and a six-jet shower panel system. It's okay, but our showerheads at home are eight jets. Still, these should hit the spots just fine! There are double sinks, and we both have our makeup, skin, and hair products set up on each side.

The bidet toilet is a jazzy touch, and it's separate from the wash area. I blast my music, and I'm dancing around doing a striptease routine, and what happens? My mind visualizes that sexy ass man; yup, Lucas! My heart is racing, my breathing quickens, and my body responds as someone turns on the "and it's time to get horny" switch! I turn on the water, and damn, it's not helping; not one bit. What. The. Hell? It's like I've got a need that's so powerful that it turns into a strong, pulsing, physical ache throughout every part of me!

The shower sprayers are not calming my situation down at all; it's increasing! Enough of this. I wash and get the Hell out of the shower and take my sex-craved ass to sleep!

CHAPTER 6

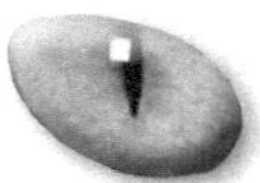

SEXY SUNRISE

Lucas

LISTENING to my Sweetness in the shower has me in a fucking, fuckery frenzy. Alyssa's feeling the pull as I am, but how can we speed this up? Walking to the shower and pulling my clothes off, I can't think of anything but mating her! Claiming her as mine is the only thing that'll get me back on track—experiencing life with a human and pretending to be one.

I turn on the cold water and step in, and my sheath is hard as a damn boulder. The chill from the water isn't helping the blazing in my member. I don't get like this; my control is beyond exceptional. But this is driving me crazy! I need her and like NOW. Like a human would, I soap up and rinse off, then brush my teeth and gargle. I don't bother with pajamas.

I lie down in the buff in the king-size bed, ignoring the continuous throbbing throughout my being, originating directly from my sheath.

I'm watching and listening to her dreams. Observing what shows are on the television may help with any information on dating an inexperienced virgin. No, I know what she wants. I've seen her thoughts, so treating her special is what I need for that dating thing. Can I wait for weeks or months without compelling her?

Yes. If I want Alyssa to use her own free will, I have to. So, I guess that means hundreds or thousands of cold showers. I know that I'll have to be extra careful when we finally do mate. This sheath of mine has never been in a human before, and definitely not a virgin.

Alyssa belongs to me, that's for damn sure! No man, especially that bastard Ryan, better put their hands on her. The way I'm feeling, he'd be a dead man, and that's not fitting in. Nope, that's me being a straight fucked up demon, all the way. Yep, I'd hate to be the man who touches what's mine.

What the hell am I going to do with that motherfucker Ryan? Just for thinking the sick shit he's planning for my Alyssa, he should be dead! He won't get the opportunity to make anything come true, but he needs to be put down. The question is, how and when? Accidental death or homicide?

Dawn's approaching, I'm looking at the skyline, and I see a bright, glowing object speed across the sky. Strangely, I get this shot of exuberance that passes through me as I observe it. Alyssa will be waking up soon to go to the gym and swim. Waiting is a bitch.

I'm on my way to the indoor pool for a swim. I get on the elevator and I'm whistling, "Dayum, Baby," by Florida Georgia Line and Sarah Buxton. I know Alyssa, Sasha, and Naya are leaving, so I can peek at her body in the swimsuit. The pool is empty except for two older women and us. I'm on the entrance in the front, and the exit's on the other side. I make that they don't see me at the swimming pool, but I see her.

She is divine, stepping out of the pool with water glistening and sliding off her body! I'm frozen in place, mesmerized by her, and my mouth drops open. The black and blue bikini I s perfect for her voluptuous curves in all the right places. Her plump breasts look ready for ravishing, her nipples are straining through the fabric, and her flat, toned stomach; damn! My eyes gaze downward, taking in every inch—from the tightness of her thighs to her calves.

Shit, I don't know how to keep from just immediately seducing or compelling Alyssa. I'll work all that out later. The three of them get towels, dry off, put on cover-ups, then walk to the exit. I'm sporting an erection that I can't hide in these trunks.

The old woman calls out loudly to her friend, "Oh damn, Christy! Look!" I leap into the pool with a splash, not welcoming the old ladies staring at my hard-on. Suddenly, Alyssa stops, turns around, and stares at me.

Lyssa

WE had a great workout. Swimming was terrific, and I have worked up an appetite. I worked much harder than usual, trying to get my mind and body off Lucas. We're on our way out, and as I'm walking, my body starts tingling and gets hot. The hair on my skin rises, and I feel a pull towards something. I turn around in the direction it's coming from, and it's Lucas. Everything stops. I mean, I can't breathe, and I only see him.

He's a magnet, and damn I'm drawn to him. He looks like the vision of the perfect man from his head down: that face, those eyes, the broad shoulders and chest. His entire left side—from his shoulder down, including both of those powerful, muscular arms, down his abs and his lower front leading to his, umm third member, to the sexy v that fit men have—is inked with black swirls of flames. Oh. My. God. I continue my viewing party, as my body is in the process of erupting like a volcano.

My eyes travel lower, but he's in the water. I slowly raising my eyes back up to his face after taking in all that magnificence, and my teeth bite down on my lip softly. He observes the motion and licks his lips. Grinning, he nods at me, then swims away. Sasha taps on my shoulder, clearing her throat.

She whistles, then she and Naya laugh. "You two are so damn hot for each other; you need to get together. Damn, Lucas is a smorgasbord of deliciousness. Get it!" she whispers.

Naya nods her head, singing the chorus to the song, "Butterflies." *"I just want to touch and kiss. And I wish that I could be with you tonight. You give me butterflies-"*

"Let's go!" I interrupt while walking out. He's going to give me a heart attack, because mine is beating like crazy! These two are laughing like there's something funny.

We get back to the penthouse and Naya bolts to her shower. Sasha keeps staring at me, so I ask her, "What?"

She gets up from the chaise, motioning for me to follow her to my room. Even though Janae and Ava are still sleeping in their bedrooms, I guess she wants to make sure we aren't interrupted. We sit on my bed, and then she takes this deep, dramatic breath.

"Okay, let's look at this thing you and Lucas have from all angles. First, don't be mad at me. I honestly think he attracts every female with hormones. Every woman in a room watches him, and some even get brave enough to approach him.

"What does he do? He turns them down in a hurry! He has tunnel vision focused entirely on you. Don't be afraid of your feelings; I figure there's a reason fate is bumping you two together. I'm not saying for you to have sex today, either! Just relax, okay?"

I frown at her. "Why wouldn't I be freaked out about how my body responds to this man I haven't known even one day! Dammit, every part of me wants him. That is scary as hell, Sasha! Since I've met him, I've been in a constant state of arousal, and it's not just that I want sex, it's him! And today was worse than last night!

"I'm going to shower and get ready; maybe it'll help me relax. And please take your own advice, since you've known Chris all of your life."

I get up, go into the bathroom, then turn on the shower. I look in the mirror, inhaling deeply and exhaling slowly. *I am going to get it together and show some kind of damn self-control.* Yes, I'm talking to myself, studying my reflection in the mirror while taking off my bikini. I have a little more than an hour to get ready, so I brush my teeth again and rinse with mouthwash, take my shower, and use my favorite scents. I wash, blow dry my hair, and style it. I apply some light makeup: just some eye shadow and lip gloss with a liner.

I go into the bedroom to get dressed. I put on my apple-green blouse, black jeans that show my curves very well, and my black pumps. I put on my diamond earrings, necklace, and the tennis bracelet my parents brought on my twenty-first birthday. Lana got the same set, too. I'm looking good; not overdressed or too sexy. I pick up my black Michael Kors bag and walk out. Both Sasha and Naya whistle, giving their thumbs up in approval. I laugh and head out since I have ten minutes.

I walk out as Lucas is coming out of his door. Damn! Damn! Damn! He is so freaking sexy.

"Good Morning, Beautiful. Are you leaving before I knock on your door to pick you up for our first official date? How does that work?" He looks at me expectantly, cocking an eyebrow and grinning. It takes me a moment to respond, since I'm still staring at this drop-dead gorgeous specimen of a man! The heat rushes through my body again; once our eyes meet, I clearly see desire in his.

"Good Morning, Sexy; oh, I mean Lucas! I thought we were meeting there, my mistake. I guess we were thinking alike today with our colors."

Lucas laughs, "So you think I'm sexy, huh? Right back at you, Sweetness! We look good as hell, don't we? I bet we're going to get some looks; as long as they don't look too long or touch."

I shake my head and laugh with him. His shirt is the exact shade of green that's in his eyes; boy, it hugs every big, delectable muscle, and I take it all in. He also has on black slacks that fit him like they were tailor-made.

"I hope you worked up an appetite; I did. Are you ready to go, Sweetness?" He puts his hand on my lower back.

"Yes, I could eat." My skin is tingling, and I think I need an ice bath. I'm burning up!

We walk down the corridor to the elevator while he guides me with his hand on my back. Then his hand moves across to hold my side, so his body is even closer to mine as we step onto the empty elevator. Then, my stomach embarrasses me and growls very loudly! Shaking my head, I feel the heat rushing to my face, and I put my hand on my forehead.

Lucas takes my hand and kisses it on the outside and inside. "It's okay; you worked out hard this morning, and you should be starving! I'd be worried if you weren't. I know I am!" He licks his lips, exhales, and says, "I have to do this."

He leans in and kisses me; oh, he tastes minty fresh. This kiss is so gentle; he nibbles on my bottom lip. I let his tongue in to meet mine, and I return the kiss. My heart is pounding loud, and fast; I think he can hear it too. I reach up to touch his chest, damn he is so hard and hot! I feel his pectorals, and I want to get my hands under the shirt to touch his skin.

The elevator bell rings, and we realize we didn't press a number; Lucas turns to do it. His eyes have changed to all blue, and for a second, his pupils look different. I blink my eyes to examine this weirdness, but I guess it's just my imagination. His pupils are normal.

He smiles and shows those perfect white teeth. "Now that's how you say good morning." He pulls me to him and finishes our kiss. He grinds on me a little, and the hardness and the length in that bulge is REAL. The elevator stops to let an old couple on, and we break apart. Lucas is gently turning me around, so I'm in front of him, and the lady smiles at us.

She looks at Lucas, then at me, and she says, "He's a keeper, Honey; make sure you hold on to him tight, and don't let him go!" She winks at me.

He smiles. "This young woman has me, and I'm all hers forever!" He hugs me from behind.

"You two make a beautiful couple. Get married and make some gorgeous babies," she advises us. I laugh nervously, because it's the first date, and she may ruin everything. I mean, what man is going on in the baby zone on the first date?

They get to their stop, and her husband apologizes for her and tries to lead her out. She playfully slaps his hand and looks back. "Make it happen, you two! You're perfect for one another!"

I look back at Lucas, who appears to be thinking about something. "Lucas, are you okay?"

He glances down at me. "Sure, Sweetness. I'm just considering what the lady said."

Chuckling, I shake my head. The elevator is at our floor. It opens, and we step out. I see to my right the charming dining room and the continental breakfast spread out for the guests. I start to walk that way, but Lucas picks me up by my waist, spins me around, puts me down, and leads us to the left.

"We are part of the STARS VIP; we're not eating there," he informs me with that sexy smile. I think my confusion shows on my face, and he laughs, leans in, and gives me a quick kiss. Okay, I don't need to get any hotter or wetter! We walk over to a set of bronze double doors. He swipes his STARS VIP card, and the doors open with a click. Holding my hand, he leads me inside, and the area changes from very charming to fantastic. The walls in the other dining room were tan with brown trim and crown molding, and I see lovely lights, dining tables, and chairs.

This dining area has dazzling gold walls with black accents and crown molding. The greeter is standing in front of the double doors. He introduces himself to us, and Lucas tells him his full name: "Lucas Hellsin."

Okay, that last name is very different. While we're being led to our table in the back, away from most of the guests here, I look up at him inquisitively, "Lucas Hellsin, that's some last name!"

He laughs, "I know, right?"

"Growing up, you probably were subjected to a lot of jokes using Hell as the punchline!" I giggle as we walk, gazing up at him. He nods his head, laughing.

Elegance is everywhere in this dining area. There are beautiful, round, black satin-covered tables ranging from an intimate setting for two up to eight people. The tables are set with gold tableware, and upon each one, there is a crystal centerpiece full of flowers. This setup is unique! I exhale and shake my head, thinking, Here we go again, as I observe the jaw-dropping, the gasps, and the ogling at my date! As usual, we've drawn the other guests' attention; no, Lucas has the attention of every female here.

We continue following Gavin, and he leads us into another section. He opens the door, holding it as we walk past. Whoa, a private room, only one table. The area is a replica of the dining area we just walked through. Lucas pulls my chair out while giving me the most devilishly sexy look ever! I've never had a man, no skip that, I've never *seen* a man anywhere who can pull that look off! I shiver from the inside, deep in my stomach, and I feel goosebumps prickling through my skin.

Of course, I'm already hot and wet from earlier, and now it's much worse. Since my panties are soaked, I pray that I don't leave a damp mark on the chair cushion. I feel the wetness sliding through between my thighs.

I sit and immediately notice the full effect of the table settings. It's beautiful; the white China with gold trim reminds me of the planet Saturn. There's a circle across the middle, then thin rings flow forward to the plate's edge, where's it's a little thicker, and the gold plate it's sitting on makes it pop. There are gold utensils and crystal champagne flutes with gold trim at the rim. To top it off, there's a tall gold vase with white orchids set in a lovely arrangement.

"So, Alyssa, what do you think?" Lucas is looking at me with this mischievous twinkle in his eyes. Oh, God, that voice; he says my name so damn sexy! More liquid trickles down my thighs; as if he knows, he inhales and licks his lips.

"This is lovely, just beautiful; my favorite flowers too." Gavin comes out pushing a cart with champagne chilled in ice, orange juice, and water.

Gavin asks, "Mr. Lucas and Ms. Alyssa, would you like straight champagne or a Mimosa?"

I smile, and we both order Mimosas. I order French toast, sausage, and a spicy cheese omelet. Lucas chooses sun-fried potatoes (from the description, they are home fries), eggs with cheese, and steak.

Gavin has our order on his tablet. "Very good." He grins and announces, "I'm a meat and potatoes kind of man, too!"

"I'm used to that; it's what my entire family is based on!" We both laugh at that, but it's the truth.

"Tell me about your family, Alyssa." I knew sooner or later this was coming. I began, "Six months ago, my parents and identical twin sister, Lana, were in a horrible car accident caused by a drunk driver. My parents died a few days later, and my sister—," my voice shakes. I try to tell him about the crash without totally breaking down, but I fail miserably. I look at Lucas, hoping the sadness that's infiltrating me doesn't show in my expression.

Lucas comes over to me and puts his hand out. I grab it. He pulls me up, puts his arms around my waist, and embraces me. I lay my forehead into his chest and wrap my arms around his back. He rubs my back in a circular motion for comfort, but it's like an electric current spreading throughout my body. I breathe in the scent of him, all woodsy and fresh. I feel a calmness enveloping me.

"Alyssa, I'm so sorry, Sweetness, you don't have to talk about it now, but when you're ready, I'm here for you, anytime. You hear me?" He lifts my chin and wipes the tears off my face with his other hand. Lucas is looking into my eyes. No, it feels like he's touching my soul.

I nod my head and softly agree. We just gaze into each other's eyes for a while.

"Ahem, Mr. Lucas, would you like to sit next to Ms. Alyssa?" Gavin sheepishly asks.

"That would be fantastic, Gavin," Lucas answers as he continues his visual assault of me with his mesmerizing eyes. Some staff come and quickly rearrange the tableware and move the chair, so it's next to me. I smell the aroma of the food as they set it up.

"Are you okay? Think you can put this food away with me?" Lucas asks, arching his eyebrow at me, like Dwayne "The Rock" Johnson, in those old movies.

I arch my eyebrows right back at him. "No problem! Show me what you got, big man," I laugh.

He kisses my forehead and leads me back to my seat, and we both sit down. Everything is delicious, and we actually share and demolish it all. I'm not one of those women who go out to dinner and don't eat because they're with a male on a date.

We talk more, and Lucas puts his hand under the table on my knee. I immediately feel his heat as he caresses me up to my thigh. I gasp; I'm already aroused. This is just increasing it immeasurably! My heart beats faster, my breathing quickens, and my body feels on fire. I turn to him, and he swoops in and captures my lips in his.

I can't help it, I part my lips for him, and our tongues intertwine. Blazing heat ignites my core, taking control of my body.

CHAPTER 7

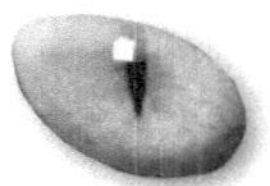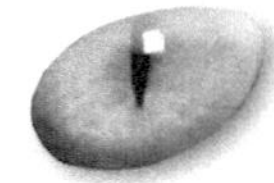

TABLE FOR TWO

Lucas

I KNOW I'm supposed to be on the slow train, and yes, I am. Hey, where I'm from, we don't even do this talking shit. I'm nothing like those other fucking demons. I could just tell you to have sex with me. I know Alyssa's favorite things, and I made sure to have some here, like her white orchids. I need to have some more contact.

She's so damn gorgeous and sweet, and I just want to erase the sadness she's living with. I feel her pain, my mate, so everything is enhanced. So is my need to protect her. I had to ask about her family. It would be fucked up if I didn't, leaving the impression that I don't care. She's mine, and it's my responsibility to assist her with her grief; it's not *if*, but *when* she's ready.

Feeding her some of my steak and potatoes, my shaft is more erect than it has ever been. If I had on loose-fitting slacks or shorts, I'd be in trouble. I have never given anyone anything before, but her opening her mouth and accepting my food was so damned alluring. She's not trying to be sexy, I know; she just *is*. She's telling me about her little brother, and I'm actually getting lightheaded from her scent. She's so aroused I have to kiss her.

The kiss is incredible. My hand touches the side of Alyssa's neck, moving down to her full, luscious breasts, and squeezing to let my fingers feel her hard nipples. I saw the imprint against her bra when we were on the elevator. My other hand is way up high, very close to that junction at her firm, tight thighs, and she's steaming hot and wet.

She moans into my mouth and shivers; we both know she's nowhere near cold. A small amount of my essence is flowing to her. I guess it's okay. I think my system is intensifying with my need for her. This has never happened before; it has to be a mate thing. I reluctantly break our kiss; opening our eyes, we both exhale.

Leaning toward her ear, I say, "I owe you that from this morning, Sweetness. You eyed me like a piece of meat you couldn't wait to sink your teeth into. You had me hard since then."

She blushes in disbelief, shaking her head and trying to break eye contact, but I stop her, gently lifting her chin with my hand. Her skin already flushed from our session, and now it's even more so, from what I just said. She's watching me with a desire that she's so plainly trying to hide from me. If she only knew there's nothing she can ever keep from me.

"What do you mean, Lucas? I was only admiring the same thing everyone else was, and by the way, I don't need you telling me the status of your member," she says sarcastically.

"Everyone else? You can't possibly be talking about those two grandma's who were in the pool, are you?" I ask incredulously with a smirk on my face. Is she crazy?

Alyssa crosses her arms over her breast. Rolling her eyes and making a face, she fires back with, "Lucas, everywhere you go, most women have to take in their fill of you! Some men, too. I mean, it's like they're starving, and someone just brought a gourmet meal for dinner! So, I was just taking my turn!"

She's jealous! This is fucking hilarious! I start to laugh, and I let it all out with a deep, bellyaching laugh! Seeing her biting her bottom lip with her eyes watering stops me cold. I take her face between my hands, and warm tears trickle down. I kiss them away and look deeply into her eyes. "Sweetness, you are the only female I see, the only one I want; the only one I will be with to protect and give orgasms to for the rest of your life.

"You don't understand it right now, but you will. For some reason, fate stepped in and created you as my mate, and that's forever. If I could, I would personally shake their hand and thank them for the gift of you. You are my everything." I pull closer and lean in and kiss her tenderly, trying to show her how precious she is to me.

What I really want to say is that I'll tear a motherfucker apart and rip his heart out of his chest if he even attempts to hurt you. Shit, I'll do it just for thinking it. Ryan, for instance, has to pay for what he thinks he's going to do.

She touches my face with her hand, and I stop kissing her for a moment. I hear the question already, but I'll wait for her to vocalize it.

"Lucas, why me?"

"Why not you, Sweetness? You're amazing, intelligent, gorgeous, sexy as fuck, and beautiful inside and out. That's why it's you."

I'm dead serious; she doesn't try. Alyssa's just everything I said and more. She has always been an introvert, while her sister was an extrovert. Alyssa is calm after the storm that was her sister. I read all of that, but unbeknownst to her, she has plenty of fire.

I'll be the first and last to ignite it! I growl and pull her closer to me. I should be tender and shit, but I need to convince her of what she does to me. I let the beast in me out a little as I kiss her fiercely; her body shivers, and she responds to me. I hear and feel the quickening of her heartbeat for me, and damn, it's fucking amazing. I pull her as close as I possibly can, with my hands on her sexy, round ass, and I grind into her, so she can tell just how hard she's making me.

She moans into my mouth and rubs back into me. Gavin's coughing and we break apart, both a little dazed—well, her more than me. She stumbles, and I quickly steady her. Wrapping my arm around her waist, I turn to face Gavin.

He smiles sheepishly. "I apologize for the interruption, but is there anything else you both would like?"

"We're good, thank you, Gavin."

We sit down to finish what's left of our delicious breakfast. We both have a hell of a lot more than food on our minds. She grabs a large strawberry from the fruit platter, slowly dips it in chocolate sauce, and whip cream. Damn, she brings it to her lips, and she licks the whipped cream while keeping those beautiful eyes on me. She takes a bite, dips it again, then offers the strawberry, teasing me with it by putting it near my lips. I take her hand and bite the rest of it.

She has some chocolate on her index finger. Grinning, I put it in my mouth and suck the chocolate right off and swirl my tongue around on it. She exhales sharply, and I know she's wetter than ever. She squirms in her chair a little. Her breathing is heavy with desire. She closes her eyes then covers her lips with her free hand to prevent herself from moaning. I slowly pull her finger out, then I kiss it. Holding her hand, I stand up, helping her up as well.

"Ready?" She nods, "Let's go."

We walk out hand in hand, and I caress the inside of her palm with my thumb. I'm also radiating more of my essence to her. Alyssa's pace is a little unsteady, but I know why, and I won't put her on the spot, even though it'd be fun.

Stepping on the elevator, it's packed with people. It rises slowly, stopping at almost every floor, and I'm patiently waiting. After the last group of people leaves, Alyssa swipes the card, and we're moving again.

Finally, we're alone. "Sweetness, are you okay?"

Nodding her head, she replies, "I'm okay; it's a little warm in here."

We arrive at our floor, strolling hand-in-hand to her door, and then we stop. Looking down at her, I move a strand of her hair that escaped the ponytail, brushing it behind her ear.

She's overwhelmed by her response to me, so I'll behave myself. She turns to me with her back at the door, and our eyes connect.

Fuck it. I lean in, kissing Sweetness softly. Lyssa wraps her arms around my neck, and all I feel is her searing heat. I want her; hell,

I need her more than anything. Her lips part, and I dive in, tasting whip cream and strawberries along with French toast. Her knees buckle, and I catch her by her waist. Then we both relax against the door, continuing our gameplay.

Suddenly, we're stumbling. Lyssa's falling backward, her eyes widening in fear, our kissing halted. I quickly pick her up and carry her in my arms. I can't have any type of injury happening to my woman.

The door is pulled open, and there are Ava and Janae.

"Oh, sorry, guys!" Janae quickly apologizes and turns to go back inside, but Ava stands there with a smirk.

"Well, it seems that you two are getting *very* acquainted with each other," she says, crossing her arms. "Hmm, only three days and Ms. Innocent is getting down and dirty? It's about damn time!"

I put Sweetness down carefully, now that I know she's not in any danger. I get so involved when I'm with her that my mind is focused only on her.

Lyssa

I LOOK at Lucas, and he has that mischievous glint in his eyes. He winks at me, and I turn around to face Ava.

"Ava, don't be so angry that Alyssa gets to touch *all of this!*" he responds, motioning to himself with his free hand.

She turns, tightening her hands into fists, cheeks flaming. She stomps out, passing us by and going toward the elevator.

"Umm, Lucas, I think she's pissed off with you right now," I say, laughing, and he shrugs.

"Hey, Sweetness, the truth is the truth. You saw Ava; she's mad." He nods his head toward her.

My body is driving me crazy! I'm not that person who gets into a situation like this. Well, honestly, I haven't been in any situation at all. I literally want to jump on him and get it all. I'm a blazing fire at this moment. My panties and pants are drenched from my honey. I've got to go take a cold shower.

"Thank you for the delicious breakfast, Lucas, and everything in between," I say, licking my lips as I gaze into those sexy eyes.

"Anytime, anywhere, anyplace, Sweetness. I've got you." It seems like he wants to just ravage me right here! The need and fire in his eyes are unmistakable.

"I've got a few business calls to make. I'll call you and see what you're up to when I'm done, okay?"

"Alright, I'll talk to you later." I go to walk inside, but he spins me around to face him.

"Not so fast, Sweetness." He cups my face and kisses me hard and thoroughly! Damn, I'm dizzy. He breaks the kiss; we're both breathing heavily.

"Now you can go in, Sweetness."

Stumbling inside once again, I lean on the door to regain my composure. I close my eyes, but my body is throbbing uncontrollably! Damn it! I have to try to get some relief! I open my eyes, and to my dismay, Sasha, Naya, Janae, and Delia are in the living room staring at me with goofy grins on their faces! I put my hand up to stop the questions before they start.

"I have to go to the bathroom. I'll be back in a few minutes," I blurt while rushing to my room.

I shake my head at Sasha as she's about to follow me. Oh, no. I need my time for real, seriously! I close the door, locking it with a click. I'm burning up; I walk into the bathroom, turning on my music from my cellphone. Looking in the mirror, I stop, shocked at my reflection. My skin is flushed, and my eyes look a totally different shade of blue. My lips are swollen from kissing Lucas. I gaze down, and oh, my God! My nipples are so hard that you can see them through my blouse! I can say one thing for sure, I'm a sexy kitty! I run the cold water in the basin and try to cool off, rinsing my face.

Nope! Shower it is! Turning the shower on, I hit the Bluetooth button on the wall. The music comes through the bathroom speakers, and "Bring Me Back To Life," by Evanescence, is playing. My mind and body keep going back to Lucas and how I feel when he is holding me, and my heartbeat quickens.

The heat that spread from my core to my body is rushing back! I undress and open the glass shower doors, and the water shoots out from the extra-large rectangular shower head hanging from the ceiling, plus the three sets of sprayers on the front, side, and behind me.

The water feels incredible against my body. Grabbing my fluffy shower puff, I slowly scrub my body. My mind goes to that spiraling-out-of-control feeling I only get with Lucas. I squeeze some feminine wash on my cloth, and as soon as it touches me, my va-jay-jay's throbbing increases. I start rubbing more as the soap rinses off, and the pressure from the water is right on my clit. Oh shoot, it's feeling so damn good!

My clit swells as I continue to touch myself, applying more pressure, rubbing in circles, going faster. As usual, I can't handle it anymore. This is when I give up and become very frustrated that I can't give myself an orgasm.

Lucas's voice urges me on. *"Keep going, Sweetness; sit down. Don't Stop!"* My legs are wobbly. I need to get this release, so I can think straight. Detaching a sprayer, I sit down on the shower bench. Spreading my legs, I let the water hit my clit while I increase the pressure a little.

My clit is super sensitive, but I continue to touch it with my other hand. I'm in unknown territory, and I'm climbing higher and higher to a pleasure center that's wild and woozy. I'm feeling lightheaded, and everything is tingling throughout my body. Trembling and jerking uncontrollably, I feel my climax bursting in waves, and I yell out Lucas's name. My heart's racing. Dazed, with my body twitching, I just sit there for a few minutes. The music covers my yell, so the girls don't hear, thank God! This is the first time I've had an orgasm. And fucking wow!

Lucas

I'M hard as fucking steel! I walk into my suite, rubbing my dick through my pants. I tune into Alyssa. Okay, okay, I'm fucked up, I know. Oh shit! She's in the bathroom, undressing for a shower. That body is amazing. My breathing is off; something's not right. I'm losing control and shivering, and everything is getting smaller, damn it. I'm changing back! I'm so into Alyssa, I forgot about what Bel told me.

I fight to get back into my borrowed human skin. I'm sweating profusely, but I get it back. Now I'm butt-ass naked with my sheath saluting the room. Whoa! What the fuck? I feel her, literally, her heat building, and damn I'm responding like I never have before. My essence is glowing bright blue on my flames. Walking into the bathroom, I step into the shower and turn it on.

I see her in the shower, looking like a sex goddess, so ready. She's touching herself while thinking of me. She needs relief; maybe I can help her. My hand goes to my sheath, which is dripping blue again—not the usual clear. I stroke my sheath, speaking out loud to my Sweetness and looking at her.

"I will make you mine in all ways possible, Alyssa, your heart, body, and soul. I'll learn and devour every single inch of you. Keep going, Sweetness, sit down. Don't stop!"

She follows my command, and I continue stroking my sheath faster, about to release. "CUM FOR ME NOW!" I roar! I erupt all over the shower wall, and she screams my name as she explodes at the same time.

Damn, that was unreal! I let the water hit me from various angles. I read that a cold shower is supposed to work. I guess it does for humans, but me? No! I see that even though she just had an orgasm, she's in need, too. It wasn't true satisfaction, but it will be when I show her everything she has been missing. I wash and rinse off quickly and come out of the shower, not feeling satisfied at all. I don't need a damn towel; I just air dry. I think better in the buff.

CHAPTER 8

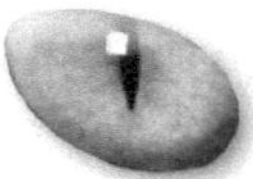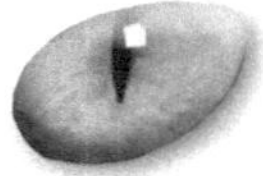

DUMB AND DUMBER AT FEVER

Lucas

I STROLL around just thinking of my next move and only see what my Sweetness is thinking about. Alyssa's talking to her cousin Josh because he's coming Friday with Chris to surprise the group at the nightclub, "FEVER!" I'm a damn genius, oh yeah. I go over to the laptop and get all the information, and I have a plan. I call the number listed for the nightclub. "Crap, uh, FEVER; how can I help you?" A grumpy-sounding male answers the phone.

"I'd like to speak to the manager, please."

"Please hold, and what is this about?" He huffs with irritation in every word, but I'll give him a pass.

"It's about the VIP area; I want to rent it Saturday night."

"Ahh, wait, you want a couple of tables, right? I can help you with that. We don't bother Mr. Rozowski or Mr. Martino for minimal requests like that. How many people? I'll reserve the tables." He's trying to speak in what I guess is in his *matter-of-fact. I am a professional* voice.

"What's your name? No, wait; never mind. I'll be there shortly!" I disconnect the call. I need the fucking manager, not a damn lackey. I'm back in my bedroom, thinking about a white undershirt and grey knit boxer briefs. I choose a navy blue Brooks Brothers suit and a black leather briefcase going into the walk-in closet. I'm all dressed in an instant and ready to go. I'll travel like humans do. I step out of my suite, walking down the corridor to the elevator. It's ridiculous; I can teleport anywhere, but here I am, pressing the damn elevator button.

I hear giggling as the doors slide open. It's a group of teenage girls. Of course, they stop eyeball me from head to toe. I give them a smile and a nod as I walk in. They just stare with goofy grins plastered on all four of their faces. I'm facing the doors with my back to them, and they're whispering to each other about me. The elevator makes another stop, and it's the elderly couple from breakfast.

The wife recognizes me, and she smiles. "Hello, young man. How are you, and where's your lovely young lady?"

"I'm excellent, thanks, and she's up in her suite with her family. How are you two?"

Behind me, the redhead whispers to her friends, "OMG, he's more than cute; he's damn gorgeous!"

The old lady chastises her. "Your behavior isn't ladylike," she says as she walks towards them. Looking back at me with a twinkle in her eyes, she gives me a wink.

"You get out of the elevator, *then* you talk about the super hot guy!" She laughs, then we do too.

A few more people get on the elevator. She taps my arm. I look down at her with a smile, and she returns one of her own. "What's your name, young man?"

"Lucas, ma'am."

She nods her head, "That's a real name, not one of those willy nilly names! I'm Pauline, and this is my husband, Nathan. So if you see us again, we know each other's names."

"Alright, Pauline and Nathan, that works! There's a meeting I've got to get to. Have a good day."

They both smile, "You too, Lucas,"

The elevator door opens, and I step aside so they can go out before me. The young ladies are smiling and laughing as they're passing me. The redhead has decided to get a long whiff of my scent. She walks by, and I catch her, stopping the fall she'd planned. She stares up at me, then her skin flushes with annoyance. I steady her at arm's length away from me.

"I can't believe that just happened! I'm so sorry," she whines in one of the most irritating voices I've ever heard.

"It's okay. I've got to go." I leave her standing there, looking confused as Hell.

This hotel/casino is a magnificent sight, from the beautiful color scheme to the grand architecture. I don't see why anyone would leave with all these stores and restaurants. Everything you need is here.

Once again, I'm noticed primarily by women. Two women, one with hot pink hair and the other black-haired with a broad neon green streak, are rushing towards me. I turn around and quickly reach the exit. It's not as busy as it is at night, but there are people out.

The club, well Vegas, never sleeps; it's 11:30 AM. As I pass by the Mirage, there's a lot of activity going on, so look inside. There's a double-decker Big Bus filled with tourists who pass me on the strip. I observe the area as I walk to the club; it's more of the same party area. There's a night club across the street, and it has a group of very young people there. I watch as they prepare to rehearse for a show this afternoon.

I'm glad this isn't the club they chose for Saturday. Two young ladies are coming out of the club with some young men, and they're wasted. I laugh and just shake my head because they won't even remember each other in the morning.

I walk to *FEVER*, and there are some bouncers at the door, trying to look tough. I'll show them what tough is! I walk up, and I emanate from my being, and they both start to shiver. The fear in their faces shows the terror I bring forth when I let a tiny bit of my demon out. They both move aside at the exact moment, and something drips onto the ground.

Glancing down, they've both pissed in their pants. Well, I literally scared the piss out of two grown-ass men with a bit of smidgen of me.

I stroll through the door, taking in the ambiance of the club. The lighting is soft red. There are chandeliers and spacious cages suspended from the ceilings on the floor. This guy gives instructions to the male and female dancers as they step inside. The women are wearing red and black lingerie, while the male dancers are wearing tight-fitting black jeans. They are strapped in, but there's a lot of wiggle room for them to dance around. I count twenty-five cages with two dancers in each, male and female.

There are different types of black, contemporary couches, sofas, low tables, and black partitions surrounding the huge rectangular dance floor in the center, straight to the massive stage. Above the stage, starting at the left is another level encircling the stage's right side. That's probably where the offices and the VIP area are. It has mirrored windows from the ceiling to where it ends at the bottom of the level. Shit, this place is impressive!

In the area by the bar, there are round, red tables with black chairs. The bar itself has tall, red and black stools with half-moon-style seats. The look is very chic. I nod my head at the young lady at the bar as she approaches me.

"May I help you, sir?" the petite redhead with violet eyes asks. I smile and check her name tag. "I really hope you can, Shareena. I need to speak to the manager."

She blushes a little. "Tyler is upstairs in his office. Can you give me some more information, please, so I know whether or not to disturb him?"

I turn towards the stage, point to the VIP area upstairs, and glance back at her. "I want to rent the VIP floor."

Her eyes widen. "Oh, okay, can I have your name, sir?"

"My name is Lucas Hellsen." I reach out and shake her hand. She hesitantly shakes my hand, swelling with delight at being treated like someone important.

"I'll be right back, Mr. Hellsen; I'm calling him." She quickly walks over to the bar, where she picks a cell up and uses it, I guess, to reach

Tyler. She glances in my direction and nods her head, then gives me the thumbs up. She rushes back to me. "He'll be down in five minutes, Mr. Hellsen. Would you like a drink while you wait? You know what they say; it's 5 PM somewhere." She laughs.

Laughing in return, I say, "Very accurate, but no thanks."

I turn instinctively and watch the door upstairs open. Tyler strolls out and my, my, yet another one with a secret. Damn, we all have something hidden around here. He's about my height and muscular. Well, with a secret like his, he should be. As he gets closer, I listen to his thoughts, and I'm surprised.

Tyler is thinking, *Is this a damn joke? Who rents the entire floor? I'm asking for payment in full before Saturday. I don't want to hear Nick's fucking mouth about us losing a dime.*

Humph, I rent the entire floor, that's who.

"Hello, Mr. Hellsin, I'm Tyler Martinez. You'd like to rent the VIP floor Saturday night?" He shakes my hand.

"Yes, Tyler, I would, and you can call me Lucas. I'd like to pay in advance, you know, to get it out of the way. I can pay in cash; how much is it?" I put my briefcase on the table.

Shock crosses his face. "Well, that would cover any concerns my partner will have about a no-show. Saturday is our busiest night, and the VIP section is a major moneymaker."

I withdraw $150k from my briefcase. "Do you think this will cover the costs? I have added extra; you can give the staff their tip from that."

"I must say this is the quickest deal I've ever made! We'll need the names of your party guests. I'll tip the servers for you from the extra money. I'll have Shareena bring back a contract for us to sign." He nods his head to her, and she goes up the elevator.

Shareena pops right over to our table with the contract. Tyler gives the paperwork to me after he adds my conditions. I read it carefully, we sign it, and I take my copy.

"Very nice doing business with you, Lucas," Tyler says. He gets up, shaking my hand.

"Same here, Tyler."

Tyler goes back to his office, and I give my number to Shareena. Listening to all the conversations that constantly swarm in my mind, I concentrate on one in particular.

In the back of the club, three men are headed out to the front. "That briefcase is probably loaded, man. The three of us can take him if—." Another voice interrupts with, "He may be in a suit, but he's built like a damn monster!"

The third male states, "I have a son and a wife, and there's no way in Hell that I'm fucking up my life, trying to rob some guy! Shut this crap down, now. This is stupid. You get caught, it's over, you're done and locked up. I'm going home to have lunch with my family." He walks away from the group, honestly thinking he talked some sense into the idiots. How very wrong he is about Dumb and Dumber.

They're dead men walking.

"Shareena, can you tell me where the restroom is?" I ask.

She turns from the register, using her hand as a guide. "Go straight down to the windows and make a right turn, and the restroom is on the left side."

"Thank you, Shareena; I gave you everything you needed for Saturday, right?"

"Let me make sure, Mr. Hellsin," she says while checking the tablet. "You're all set, and if you have any more people to add, call us."

"Thanks, Shareena. I'll see you Saturday. Have a good day." I smile, turning to go to the men's room. The music plays "Naughty Girl" by Beyoncé, and the dancers begin their sexy moves on cue. The floor vibrates from the bass in the song as I step. I turn right by the windows and bypass the men's room. I head out the back door to test my theory.

Two men, Dumb and Dumber, are outside, smoking cigarettes, plotting my demise. The area is narrow, and it stinks; there are three full garbage dumpsters back there. They both turn, and at the sight of me, one gives an expression of satisfaction and the other, fear.

"Well, well, well. Hello, gentlemen. Am I on time for your special surprise?" I look pointedly at Damon, who I've named "Dumb." Searching through his memories, I see that bastard, Ryan, orchestrated this. What the fuck? I was so deep in thought that I didn't realize he was following me. The thought of these two idiots trying to kill me is hilarious.

Looking at each other for confirmation, Dumb Damon reaches inside his pants pocket, pulling out a silver pocketknife. Grinning idiotically and flicking the blade open, his voice drenched with over-confidence. "Just because you're ripped up and got some height on you, don't think that you're fucking invincible. You can't take both of us on and weapons. Now!" Dumb Damon orders. Dumber Aaron clumsily drops his pocketknife, retrieves it, and opens it, and they both run up to me with blades in their hands, raised up in a stabbing motion.

Grabbing them both by their necks, their knives clatter to the ground, and I launch them high into the sky. I watch them shoot up to the clouds, and I leap high to catch Dumb and Dumber. They scream like babies. Their skin is sickly pale, tears spill down their faces, and the stench of urine attacks my nostrils. Using telekinesis, my hands guide them six feet away from me, alleviating the smell. Their bodies move frantically in the blue sky, arms and legs flailing in every direction.

Why did I fucking let Damon make me do this shit? Dammit, owing him one hundred dollars and him threatening to kick my ass isn't worth dying. This is my last day living on earth, and it's going to kill my family—mostly my parents. Meeting Damon was the worse day of my life.

Flying Dumb Ass Damon and even Dumber Aaron through the sky, I search for the highest building and locate it. Swiftly plummet-ing, their voices scream octaves higher as if they were bass singers pretending to be sopranos. The concrete is solid beneath my feet as I land. Dragging them to the edge of the roof, I force them to view the distance to the bottom. People and traffic are like ants from this distance. I throw them over; they squeal, plunging to the midway point, then I freeze time to bring them back up to me.

"Shut the Hell up! You want to kill me? For what?!" I growl. Before I know it, I'm beginning to shift into my pure form, my tanned human hand transforming into turquoise, my nails darkening into purple.

Their eyes widen, and they're openly crying and violently shaking in fear. I take a minute to focus on being human and gaining control of my emotions, and I shift back into the human skin.

What the Hell is this, dude? Ryan said to make it look as if it were robbery gone wrong. This is some bullshit! I'm not supposed to be the fucking dead one. Aaron just needed the right threat to bring him in; he's a punk ass, couldn't hurt a fly. Maybe I can trick this guy and have him think it was Aaron and that he threatened me.

"Please, we didn't know; we just were gonna rob you! You got to believe us. Please, I have to be straight, no bullshit or lies! Aaron was paid to rob and kill you, and I was forced to cooperate, or my family would be hurt."

He thinks he will fool me with this shit. Get the fuck out of here. I smack Dumb Damon in the face. "You're lying, motherfucker! I can see every thought you've ever had! You don't know shit about me! But guess what? You're gonna fucking learn, now!"

"Oh, God! No, please!" Dumber Aaron cries.

"Hmm, sorry, God isn't here, and he won't help you. If I can kill you, then you deserve it. Time to go!" I point at him using my finger, and blue lightning crackles from it instead of flames. He falls to the ground, unconscious but breathing. Dumb Damon screams bloody murder watching his partner in crime go down; he's the lucky one.

"Please, please, just let me go, and I'll never try anything like this again. Give me a chance to make this right." As if crying like this matters to me. Syre appears with her blue flames aimed at Damon. A glowing blue sphere of fire rapidly increasing in size emanates from my essence. I release Dumb Damon, and he runs to the roof door; next, my flames swiftly engulf him. He shrieks uncontrollably from my exquisite torture. "Oh, God! Ahhhhh!!!" Then it's quiet.

Trapped inside my fire sphere, there's no escaping, and this is only the beginning. Lifting my hand, Syre, her tip elongating so it's thin as a needle, zips through the air, piercing through my flames and stabbing Damon in every pressure point in his body. He convulses horribly, unable to use his voice anymore from the pain he's suffering.

I move closer to him to observe; it's crazy that his day ends like this for his human form. His physical body's near death, but his soul's torture is only beginning. His eyes are glossy as his life is sucked from his body, his critical moments flash before him, from his introduction to me to his meeting with Ryan, going back to the years that he brutally killed five young women and when he killed his mother and sister. His heart races: thump, thump, thump, then slows to a thump… thump…thump… Then Syre pierces it into silence.

Damon's body lies motionless; as his spirit rises, I grab it. Exhaling deeply, my essence and markings glow as I close my eyes, thinking about my natural appearance. The tanned human skin slides off painlessly, revealing my turquoise coloring. My body shudders. I grow to my full height, and my muscles enlarge, bulging out from everywhere on my being as everything evens out. My hair lengthens down to my mid-back, and dark orange replaces the black hair. Suddenly, the roof of the building begins shaking and cracking all around me. It's time to disappear.

Staring at his human form, my blue flames ignite, and his body burns blue as it disintegrates into ash. Waving my hand, ashes go flying in the hot breeze. He has been deleted. Teleporting back to Hell in my quarters in the library with Damon, I can begin his torture.

Loud snoring catches my attention, and I follow the source to my bedroom. Tyrus is knocked out asleep, but it's almost time to oversee the pits. Essence radiates from my blue flames, making a beeline for Tyrus's sleeping form. He's wheezing, but he's going into an even deeper level of sleep. It's now all clear for me.

"Lucas!" Halting my quick departure, I turn around, knowing that angry, high-pitched voice anywhere: Madre. "Why do you have a damn soul in your quarters? This is beyond—" she begins, until she's interrupted by the loud rattling sound coming from my bedroom. Dashing up to her while keeping hold of Damon in my other hand, I embrace her. "Madre, Tyrus stopped by, and he spent the night. And him," gesturing to Damon, "I'm on my way to the pits with this waste of life."

Scrutinizing everything, the fact that she's pondering what the Hell is going on here shows in her face. Skeptically cutting her eyes at me, she says, "Something's unusual about you, son. Your essence has changed, and it only does for one specific reason. So are you going to tell me, or do I have to say it?"

She knows something, "I have to go, Madre. I need to get him started." I gather up my essence to port the fastest I've ever done so I can get away from her questions.

Porting into the torture area, I drag Damon's soul along because he's the reason for my early return. The familiar sounds from the pain inflicted here embrace me, but I didn't miss it. Cracking my neck while waking his soul from its frozen state, I toss him into his pit. "Please!" He cries, and I mute his ass. None of that begging shit. I'm not trying to hear it. Slowly I begin ripping his outer layer.

Peeling him apart, bit by tiny bit, is giving me some satisfaction. I set forth a mini twister, and it's sucking his soul into a vortex. I snap my fingers, and he's back in one piece. I drill holes through him while his face contorts, screaming soundlessly. Flames begin internally, spreading throughout Damon's human side at a snail's pace. After a few hours of torturing this bastard's dark-ass soul, it's time to go.

I'll come back to visit, and I'll have Ryan here next; he's earned his spot. An uneasiness settles over me, but there's no reason for this. My markings are glowing. I can sense my Sweetness here, and a strange sense of fear and terror surround me. It has to be Sweetness. I haven't been here long, but it's time to depart.

CHAPTER 9

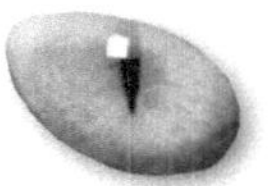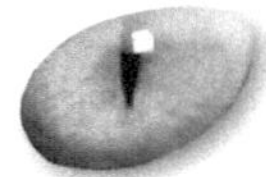

AVA'S DEMANDING GUEST

Lyssa

UNLOCKING the door and quickly checking for the girls in the background, I sprint over, tapping on Lucas's door. No answer. Doubt creeps in: all that talking he did about us, and I haven't seen or heard from him in two days. Well, this is the beginning of day two. "Let's go, ladies; the spa awaits."

"Lyssa!" Damn near jumping out of my skin, I spin around and face Ava. "Are you meeting up with the sexy one, and we're supposed to be having a spa day?" She pinches her face up, staring at me while the girls are coming out.

"Really, Ava? Why are you so concerned if I go with you or not? The only thing on your mind is finding your next old dude to get your swirl on with. Let's go." Rolling my eyes at her and shaking my head, I walk quickly to the elevator. No stressing about what's going on with Mr. Lucas; the spa is calling me.

Stepping off the elevator, scents of lavender, chamomile, and jasmine immediately knock me into a calm, relaxed feeling. I stop. Just experiencing these smells reminds me of Mom; these were some of her and Tia's favorite flowers. The house still has those scents when not being overwhelmed by the aroma from the delicious dishes cooking.

Entering the spa always brings relaxation; just viewing an oasis and the waterfalls effects in the background is so calming. There's something for everyone. There are soft lilac walls with white trim as we approach the receptionist to sign in. "Hello, ladies. Wait, don't tell me; you're the Laskaris Family, right?"

In unison, we respond, "Yes." Smiling, she says, "I knew it since we only schedule appointments, and your family is a group of 6."

Standing up, she waves her hand at us to follow her. "Follow me, and welcome to Paradise. This way to our dressing room. The robes, towels, and slippers are new and packaged separately in your changing area. They are also yours to keep, and they will be cleaned and brought to your penthouse later today."

There are pastel colors, cool blues, lilacs, and pinks throughout the area, with large, beautiful abstract art on the walls. It's all inviting us, and oh yes, we are accepting. I wait to go in, since there are only five rooms available. I rock and tap my feet to the light jazz playing while waiting for it to be my turn. As much as I want to call him, I refuse to, because this is some damn bull crap, even though ninety-nine percent of me feels he is the one. Everything ricochets back to Lucas.

Snap, snap. Oh damn, I open my eyes, and of course, it's Ava again. "I'm ready, Sleeping Beauty; you can have the room." Exhaling, holding my tongue and my fists, I go into the room and change.

Tossing and turning, it's evident that sleeping isn't happening for me. I guess Lucas must be working like a madman because we haven't seen him. Out of sight, out of mind, right? Hell no, he's in my thoughts all of the time. Going to the spa was relaxing, but, damn, it's exhausting.

Massaging the kinks and knots out hurts like Hell. Getting up to get a glass of water, I put on my robe because Ava went out and would try to bring a stray here. Hmm, no; she wouldn't seriously do that. Coming out of my room, I hear an unfamiliar male voice, along with Ava laughing. Unbelievable! This pain-in-the-ass girl has brought a damn man here! What the Hell is her problem? The thought of her doing this was a fleeting one. She does the craziest things out of all of us.

Who the Hell brings a random man to a place you're sharing with your family? Walking to the living room, I stop in the doorway. Shaking my head, crossing my arms, and tapping my feet, I say, "Janae, Sasha, Naya, come out. Guess what? We've got a man in here."

"What the hell? Why would there be a man here?" Sasha asks.

Naya and Janae look puzzled as they walk in. Naya frowns heavily. "Really, Ava, what is wrong with you, woman? So, you've decided to exhibit the one-night-stand Ho behavior now and bring him here with all of us? What the fuck is that? I could really knock the Hell out of you, and maybe you'll get some damn sense!"

Ava smirks at her, "Oh, please, just because I like to have a good time doesn't mean I'm stupid, okay?" Turning to the older man, she says, "This is Michael, and Michael, meet my cousins. Laskaris women in the building, oh yeah." She points to each one of us. She's an idiot! He looks like he's in his late twenties, and Ava just turned twenty-one.

A calculating look enters his eyes, and he clears his throat. "You mean as in Laskaris Corporation?"

I try to deflect, "Not—," but Ava interrupts, "Yes! That's our family."

A wicked grin crosses his face. "We've been watching your group, and I thought you were either part of a famous or wealthy family. We hit the jackpot!"

Dammit. I look around at my family. Everyone except for our idiot knows this is dangerous on so many levels. Immediately, the four of us, Janae, Sasha, Naya, and I, are on alert. As long as he doesn't have a weapon, we can take his ass.

Smiling and utterly oblivious to what's happening, Ava has no clue.

"Michael, you are so funny, there's no way we hit—," suddenly, a beep, a click, and then clanging noises arise from the hall. I ease over by the girls, so my back isn't to whoever the Hell is coming. Several quick, heavy footsteps are walking across the marble floor, approaching us. Finally, Ava looks worried and afraid; she's the gift that keeps on giving.

We're looking at the doorway with dread as the footsteps get closer. Silence engulfs the room, and two masked men, one husky and one muscular appear in the living room. He gets up to greet his partners while Naya creeps back to her room.

"Guys, we've hit the God damn motherload! These young beauties are part of the wealthy Laskaris family! How much do you think we can get for them?" Michael asks slyly. All three men nod at each other. "Shit; for the four of them, I'd say one hundred million." He cracks his knuckles and flexes his muscles.

Surprisingly (no, not really), Ava screams bloody murder and starts crying hysterically. Hmm, you bring trouble here, and you're breaking down? Only Ava.

Michael slaps her and roughly throws her onto the couch. Unexpectantly, there's a click, click, then Naya yells, "Popcorn!" We drop to the floor because that is the code word we learned from our bodyguards when we were younger.

Pop! Pop! Pop! Pop! Michael's knees buckle as he screams in pain, collapsing on the floor, hands reaching for his knees. The two accomplices fall backward to the floor, crying in agony as both of their shoulders are bleeding. Naya is standing in a triangle stance, holding a Fuschia 9 mm. She looks mighty damn comfortable shooting a freaking gun, too.

We get up off the floor. "Kick the guns away from them," Janae says.

"I got it, Sis. Call the police," Naya directs while striding to the criminals and kicking the guns away. Janae goes after her cell.

Instantaneously, several whirlwinds storm through the living room, and suddenly, Naya's next to me. There's movement from many different directions, sweeping through the room so rapidly. Identifying who or what is doing this is impossible. As quick as it started, it has stopped, like a complete standstill. What the Hell?! Our kidnappers are gone…there isn't a trace of them.

Lucas

"CHARLEE, take over for me and keep him muted." She's my best worker, right up there with Ursa.

"I will, boss," she eagerly begins.

Relocating to my quarters to take care of Tyrus, I communicate to his thoughts, *"Damon is with Charlee. He deserves her type of individual attention. Make sure he gets it. When you sense I'm gone, wake up and begin your day. Madre is pissed; avoid her, no matter what, Tyrus."* Shifting back into the human skin, I teleport back to the hotel.

Seeing the electronic calendar, my mind is blown by the revelation of the time difference. Damn, a couple of hours in Hell was actually two days here. I missed seeing my Sweetness. I peek in on her thoughts. What the fuck? Lyssa needs me! I port to their front door, ready to crash through it, but I'm too late, dammit; they're gone. Everything's clear, and all that is left behind is a scent. I'll find who helped and thank them. I let my mate down, and it doesn't feel right at all.

I knock on the door when it's taking every ounce of my control not to port into the living room. Opening the door, Naya's face is twisted in a mix of anger and annoyance; she lets me in without a word. I nod at her, "Hey, Naya," then hurry to the living room to my Sweetness. She's confused but smiles in relief. I breach the recesses of her mind: "Alyssa, sleep." She inhales with a shaky breath. Swaying, her eyes rolling, she passes out, and I catch her. Picking her up, I lay her on the couch.

"Lyssa!" They rush over to the sofa by her. "I think she's just overwhelmed by everything that's happened. Let her rest."

I need time to go through the ladies' memories to check if they may have seen something subconsciously.

"Lucas, it was crazy as Hell. Ava brought a damn criminal up in here, and he stole and made a copy of her card key. Then he passed it along to his friends. They were here talking about kidnapping us for fucking ransom!" Janae's getting more agitated. "You know why, Lucas?" She screams and points. "Ava's big ass mouth told him who we were!"

"Okay, Janae, what happened next? Where are they?"

"Lucas, Naya shot them, and all of a sudden, there was a presence that was as fast as Hell in here. And when we could see, the three of them were gone. There's no trace of them being here, not even blood. Crazy, right?"

"Yes, that's definitely in the crazy, mysterious zone for sure," I agree while searching through her memories. *What the fuck? A huge lion on the damn beach? He marked her when he licked her. Okay, she's got a mate who can't be far from her. He's here and most likely not alone.*

Wake up, Sweetness.

"Call down to the front desk, let them know that Ava lost her card key. Let the manager know that the cards have all been compromised. They're going to have to reissue new card keys for all of you. We're not taking any chances that nothing else might happen, and we don't know if he had partners other than the two who came in this room. You know what I mean?"

Naya answers, "I get that for damn sure; I'm calling right now." Grabbing her cell phone, she walks to the other side of the room. *Now I have to figure out what is going on. Is it the lion from her memories? And I see that Janae kind of realizes she has a mate. She's in a bit of denial, though.*

"We don't need to call the police; we can take care of everything. Whoever came in here did a pretty damn thorough job of getting rid of any evidence." Examining the room, I don't find anything. "So I'm going on a little mission to find out what I can since they came on this floor. These people have to be staying on this floor as well. Remember, we have to have this unique card key to get up here."

Janae nods her head. "Lucas, you know what? You are so right; I didn't even think of it like that. Well, I didn't have time to think of it."

Lyssa is groaning, waking up; I walk over to her and squat down, so when she opens her eyes, she'll see my face. Opening those beautiful eyes of hers, she gives me a sweet smile. "Lucas, I thought I was going crazy. I can't believe I freaking passed the Hell out. What is wrong with me? I crumbled under the damn pressure."

I shake my head with a frown. "No, Sweetness, a guy and his damn asshole fucking friends came in here with guns on you all, and that's a lot. Now, if you would have done something stupid and crazy like getting shot, then that's when you say, what the Hell is wrong with me? Not because you just passed out for five minutes after everything happened."

"Where the Hell is Ava?" she asks, looking around.

Looking towards Ava's room with Alyssa, it's not right. I want to say, "She's in her room feeling terrible about what happened. She's crying; remember, Ava's younger than you all are, and she has a different background than you do, so for that reason, she does the crazy things." I don't say anything, though, because how can I explain how I know what I know?

Alyssa sits up, sighing. "I hope she's going to learn something from this situation. Well, for one thing, I don't even know how to try to make her feel better. This was really taking being crazy, as you say, to a whole different type of level. There's a day that you wake up, and you have to grow up. You have to act like an adult. That day isn't coming anytime soon; that's obvious from what she did today. Ava isn't maturing at all.

"How can I keep something like this to myself, or how can any of us keep it a secret? Something can happen to her by her reckless, immature, stupid behavior. Yes, no other word plainly describes what she did today. What if we were kidnapped? What if Naya didn't have her friendly 9 MM that none of us knew she had with her? Let's be honest because that was scary as Hell."

Janae comes in and says, "Well, remember; we are older than she is, Sis, and she is the baby of the group. So, we have to remember that she's younger than we are. For whatever reason, she feels like she needs older guys or something. I don't know what to say about her. If we tell Uncle, it's going to be a big problem because she's going to be in trouble. You know that, and we all know that." Janae sighs, running her fingers through her hair. "What we should do, excluding you, Lucas, sorry, buddy. Is to go in there and make her talk to us. I know that, even though she's a pain in the ass, we do love her. Maybe that's it. Perhaps she doesn't think we love her or something. I don't damn know. Even though she came here when she was a teenager, she has always had a chip on her shoulder. I can't say that I never liked her or that I don't love her. So what we need to do is have a come to Jesus intervention so Ava can realize she is loved and so she doesn't have to do the dumb stuff she is doing."

Naya is frowning and looking like she's ready to explode. "What is it, Naya?"

Putting her hands on her hips, she yells, "I am 22 years old, and I'm not running around here doing what she's doing! So it is no excuse that she's young. I could deal with you saying that maybe because she's feeling unloved or whatever, but age? No, no, no, hell to the damn no! I'm not going for that one because right now, I want to punch her in her damn face, but I'm not because she's, my cousin." Naya's breathing heavily. Suddenly, there's a knock on the door, and Naya looks over.

"It's the front desk with the card keys. I'll go get the cards, and then we're going in to see our damn little Princess and find out what the fuck is wrong with her. And I'm not going to be nice about it because we ALL could've been killed today!"

Naya walks to the door, picks up the cards, and thanks, Micah. "Okay, Lucas, time for you to go; it's girl talk time, and you don't need to hear this. It's going to get loud, and it's going to get ugly."

The ladies are unanimously kicking me the Hell out of the penthouse.

"All right, Sweetness, I will see you later; I'll pass by to make sure you all are okay."

Caressing her cheek, I touch my forehead to hers. I need to show her I remember how much this gesture means to her. I get up and say, "Don't be too hard on Ava, ladies. Later." I walk through the hallway listening and tracking any voices having a conversation about the situation that just happened.

"Griffin, come on now; you can't be mad that he wants her to be his mate. Are you going to seriously just pace around being all pissed off? There's a reason why he chose her, and I bet once you get to know her, you'll know why he chose her, and you will choose her too." A persuasive male voice is speaking.

A furious, deeper voice yells back. "Sure, Grayson; it's not your mate who's out picking up a random guy and bringing him home. Well, I know it's a hotel, but you know what the Hell I'm saying!"

"Calm down, little bro; when have we seen an animal be wrong about his chosen mate? You never know who people really are deep down, and that's just what's going on with you and her. Trust your tiger, Griffin. I'm surprised that he found her so quickly. Hell, you weren't even thinking about a mate, and she's only 21. So you know that means you've got some years before you can go get her. Nothing is wrong with you befriending her, and you'll always be there to look out for her. To calm your tiger, you can mark her. What about your panther?"

Grayson intercedes. "Yes, I had to mark Janae because my lion would not stop trying to come out. Why? He needed to make sure she wasn't out there in any danger or dating anyone, and that was after one day of meeting her. What the Hell am I saying? I didn't meet her, I smelled her and saw her from a distance, and that was it."

I'm following the voices and bingo! On the other side of the penthouse floor, there is this PH-5608. Different men are groaning in pain in the background, which assures me that I'm at the right place. Hmmm, knock on the door or teleport inside? I will go with the surprise teleporting into the living room since we all are carrying some secrets.

Here goes nothing. Looking around to ensure that the rotating camera isn't facing my direction or other people, I teleport, vanishing into thin air and appearing into the room. There are four men. Two are identical twins. Well, no; reading them, they are triplets. The other brother, Garrison, is in the kitchen, and the youngest man has a twin.

So, a set of twins and triplets; okay. They are all brothers, with an undeniable family resemblance. Confusion crosses all of their faces. They look at me, and well, I guess I need to say something before we start fighting because they're ready to fight.

"Hey, guys, before the action upstairs starts, I know it freaked you all out that I just appeared here. There's a reason for that. We all have our own little secrets. For example, there are three lions, a panther, and a tiger in this room. The only reason I'm here is that you have three scumbags.

"They were trying to kidnap the young ladies, and I want to say thank you. My mate is in there, and before you ask, it's not Naya, Janae, or Ava. My mate is Lyssa." They visibly relax a little. "If you don't know what to do with those bastards, I know what to do with them. And they'll never come back again."

"Who the Hell are you? No, *what* are you, that you just appeared in the damn room with us, dude?" the younger brother, Galveston, asks with amazement all over his face. He walks around the penthouse, which is identical to ours. Maybe he's searching for a secret entrance; I don't know. The twins look at me thoughtfully, especially Grayson, and I can tell from his power levels that he is the strongest. Fucking wow.

Garrison is communicating with Grayson; I guess I need to let them know I can read their minds. I'm not in the mood for this shit right now. "Okay, guys, say something. I know what you think, and I know you're trying to think of a plan to take me down. Listen, guys, it's not going to happen. I'm here peacefully; I'm not going to do anything. I just really want to know what you are going to do with those bastards. They spied on and tried to fucking kidnap our mates!"

I turn to look at all of them and gesture to Griffin and Grayson. "That's it; if nothing else, I can go take them right now off of your hands. Believe me, what I will do to them is a million times worse than any-thing you could have ever planned. Okay, can we talk now?"

"I'm Grayson. Yes, Janae is my mate, and I'm here making sure she's safe. And my younger brother, Griffin, has just found his mate, her cousin Ava."

He shakes my hand with a very firm grip, and I return it with a secure grasp of my own. Looking into Grayson's eyes, they change from gray to chocolate brown. I figure that's his lion wanting to see me. Oh, okay, that's fine with me. Grayson walks over by his brother, and Garrison eases in next to Griffin.

"Now, we were getting some work done when I felt a surge of fear from Janae. Thank God for having speed and strength in my human form. I'm sure the girls, except Janae, would've been terrified if I went in there like a lion. Don't get it wrong; I damn sure would've; because I wasn't going to let anything happen to my woman."

The rest of us shake hands. "Let's go so we can see these bastards and figure out what we're going to do." Garrett leads the way. I'm finally going to find out what the Hell he means when he says what *we're* going to do when I already said what *I'm* going to do.

Garrett goes into the third bedroom, and I see the bastards. I guess they gave them a little first aid. Two of them have their shoulders wrapped, and the leader, Michael, has both knees wrapped up. Reading them is easy. I'm glad to know they're not part of any mob organization or anything like that. They're just a trio of assholes who are too lazy to go get jobs and are looking for the quickest way possible to make a dollar.

I'm wondering what we can do with them. It's not like I have my own personal jail cell to put criminals in up here. I don't want to take a chance of them going to prison and being there for a couple of years. This room is gold and purple, and it's immaculate. There's a beautiful king-size bed, the same as mine, and nothing looks out of place until you see these guys. They look comical and very out of place with their bandages and the rips in their clothing, which most likely happened when the brothers grabbed them and brought them here.

One of them has to know an alternative exit from the building, so they don't pass the front desk because my method is better. "So, how are you going to get the scumbags out of the building? Tell me how you're going to make that happen without being seen from the front desk? Do you have some hidden talents, which means you can coerce someone into not seeing you or forgetting that you were here?"

They all look at me like I have three heads. "We're really quick," they say. They start speeding through the room, so I can see just how fast they are. Okay, if I were human, I probably couldn't see them, but since I'm not, I can. I stop all of them in motion simultaneously. Yeah, that's how I roll using my speed; I stop Garrison and drop him on the bed, then grab Griffin and put him in the bathroom. Finally, catching Grayson, the fastest with the most power, I put him in the closet.

"What the Hell is that? Seriously, get the Hell out of here! What are you, once again, man?!" they ask incredulously.

"Let's not forget, I can transport out of here in a blink of an eye, never having to pass the front desk," I reply.

Grayson comes out of the closet. "You've got my vote, man; I don't give a damn about what you do to them as long as they never come back to hurt our mates again. Do whatever you need to do. By the way, do you have any hidden talents where you can make people do things or forget memories?" He watches me very closely; maybe he can tell if a person tells a lie. I don't know, but I really don't give a damn.

"Oh, I have a lot of hidden talents, and that's one of them. And since you brought it up, maybe I'll use it. They were coming for the money, not necessarily to kill them or hurt them, so I'll think about it. What are your votes Griffin, Galveston, and Garrett? Are you going to leave it to me so I can handle it?"

CHAPTER 10

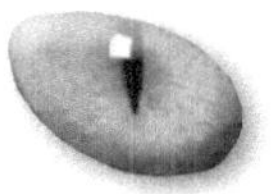

Taking out the Trash

Lucas

GRIFFIN cocks his head to the side, "Damn! You're terrific, Lucas. I would never want to get on your wrong side. I honestly believe you are going to fuck them up. If you can make them forget, they won't ever come back. First, let me do one thing. Wait, a couple of things." In a flash, he's standing over each one of the guys. He's beating the Hell out of them, using his speed to connect his fists to their faces and stomachs.

It looks funny as Hell because he punches them in the face so fast, giving some pretty damned good body shots, too. He's really taking out some aggression on them one by one. I grin; the enjoyable part of this is that if I let these guys live, they're going to be in a hell of a lot of pain. He stops, and they look like Hell, with their faces bleeding and their eyes swollen shut.

"I'm ready to go. I'll take these two first, and I am going to give them a gift from me. I'm going to erase their memories of each other and of this plan. I'll be porting them all to different parts of the world, so they will never get together again."

The four of them have shocked expressions because I can do what I do. I'm just that good; so, since they are mates of Ava and Janae, they're going to see me again. I think about the different awful places where I'm going to bring these douchebags. They won't remember anything about what they've done or who they are. They will know that this is a hard life and be forced to work like never before.

I walk over to the assholes with the shoulder injuries, grab them by the collars of their shirts, and teleport right out. We end up in the middle of the desert—the perfect place for me to do what I need to do. Watching my mate and following her around? Planning and scheming to take her away from me so they could hold her for ransom? Killers I can bring to Hell, but these jackasses? Who am I kidding? I'm going to try my hardest to have them suffer for what they've done. That's not who the Hell I am to let this go unpunished. I already gave a pass to Dumber. There is no way I can give three more passes. They have to die.

Teleporting to the savannah into a lion's den, I deliver a great meal to the hungry lions. I control their movements to place them just in the perfect spot inside the circle the lions are making. Nowhere to run and no damn place to hide, and I'm going to sit here and watch it all. They are shivering from terror and crying, "Please don't do this. We needed the money Mike offered, please!" As I sit them in their new home where they'll be a delicious feast, I say, "I bet you wish you could turn back the hands of time, right? You don't mess with my woman." I walk outside of the circle and wait in the grass to watch the show.

I yell, "Lights, camera, and action!" An excruciating pain shoots through my head to my chest, and I feel the grass my knees have landed on as Madre's voice bellows. "Lucas, you can't have them killed, because they aren't genuinely evil; you know this. They had no intention of killing Alyssa or any of the ladies."

Two lions leap at their prey but are immediately frozen in motion. Shrill screams are paused as time has stopped for the moment. What the fuck? She's been spying on me this whole time. Damn it, I really want to kill these idiots, but I've got to find something else, because I want these bastards to really be miserable after what they did.

I may not be able to kill them, but I will find something to my satisfaction that they will be wishing…no, I have to erase the memories. I just have to make sure that their lives are miserable. Do I want to see blood, guts and bones? Hell yeah, and they have to pay for attempting to kidnap my woman! I collect the two accomplices and then, unfreezing time, I watch the lions colliding into each other and teleport out.

Once again, I'm in the middle of nowhere, pondering what the Hell to do with these idiots. Studying their memories, I can see they weren't bad guys until they met up with Michael a few years ago. Okay, here we go; I carefully remove memories that have anything to do with Michael, Las Vegas, or each other and replace them with some intelligence, a lot of common sense, and independence so another Michael won't be able to come up and get these dummies. Well, they're not dumb anymore. I fixed it.

I teleport them both to different parts of the world, ensuring that they never meet up again. I'll check on them from time to time to see how they adjust to living close to the North and South Poles.

I teleport back to my new friends to pick up Mr. Michael, the little kidnapping group leader. He starts screaming immediately when I appear, and the guys are laughing and shaking their heads at him. I have some new friends; well, I don't have any friends. Let's start small; I'll call them comrades right now. We will do what we need to do to protect our mates. I drag Michael to somewhere unknown, so I can kick his ass, too.

Searching through his memories, I can see that he hates the heat and the rain. So what better place to bring him than the somewhere that he would hate the most—the rainforest—and I made sure that it stays in his memory that he hates it. I am porting to one of the poorest, least populated sections of the rainforest. Piercing through his memories, I change them completely. He believes that his life has been here, and no one knows him because he's been living in seclusion. I make sure that he now speaks his own language, not English, either, so communicating is a moot point.

There are beautiful animals and plants in the rainforest. A rainforest is indeed a dangerous place if you don't know what the Hell you're doing. So, if Mr. Michael survives in the rainforest, it will be because someone helped him. He knows nothing at all about the rainforest. It's raining heavily here, the animals are out, and the ground is saturated from all the rain.

Insects are all over the place, the kinds with diseases, which is especially bad if you don't have your vaccines up to date. Yes, I picked a pretty damn good spot, because he's not going to survive, and he will be in a lot of pain from the different illnesses he's going to catch here. I smile at him, knowing that everything is over for him. Life as he knows it will never be the same. I like that idea because, if it's not a crime punishable by death, suffering for the rest of his natural life sounds good to me.

Lyssa

WALKING into Ava's bedroom, we're trying to figure out how to approach this without her being defensive. "She doesn't have a choice in whether not she is going to hear what I'm going to say to her ass! The bottom line is she did some ratchet, slut-ho actions today. We all could have been kidnapped, raped, or killed because of her. So no, hell no." Naya is not going to let Ava get away with this crap at all. She's still pissed.

Opening the door, we see Ava's not in the room. We turn toward banging noises coming from the closet. We walk over, then Janae pulls the door open, and Ava's on the floor crying. I walk in behind her with everyone else. Thank God this is a big closet. Naya kneels down in front of her. "All right, I'm listening. What the Hell were you thinking when you bought that guy up here? Look at me; I am not playing with your ass!"

Grabbing both of Ava's arms, Naya shakes her. "I just shot three fucking people; yeah, three of them, because of your reckless behavior.

And you are going to explain to me what the Hell you were thinking!" Naya's yelling now, and Ava won't lift her head up. "You have them feeling sorry for you, even though we're pissed off. And it's not working with me, them saying because you're young is the damn reason. I am only one year older than you! Unless you want Uncle Austin to hear about this bullshit, you better open up your mouth and say something. This isn't a damn game, Ava."

I go up to them, with Sasha and Janae following close behind. Moving Ava's hair away from her face, I try to be comforting. "You know that we are family, and no matter what, we're here for each other, right? Now I really need you to explain why you did this. Bringing a stranger, male or female, in here with all of us is more than crazy. You went into dangerous territory, Ava. Now I'm waiting—we're all waiting—for your answer, and you need to realize that. We're not going to take I don't want to talk, or I'm not going to answer. Those options are not available, so we need you to get it together and talk to us now."

I'm not watching the time, but not getting any response is really ticking me off. Sighing, I say, "All right. Enough of this; what's up? It's time to get down to the nitty-gritty of it all. I'm just gonna ask: Why do you feel the need to be promiscuous, Ava? Did something happen to you before you came to live with us?"

Sasha's staring incredibly hard at Ava. At that question, Ava snaps her head up and backs away like a caged animal. She's visibly trembling, shaking her head. "What do you mean? Why would you say that? I was only 12 when my mom died. I didn't do anything. It wasn't my fault!" There's more fear than anger in her eyes. "At first, he was really kind. My mom told me he was a good guy, but then she started leaving to work, and he would be at the house with me. She wanted me to call him Daddy and all that stuff, but it didn't feel right because he wasn't my dad. Then my mom said he could be and basically made me call him Dad." Crossing her arms, she hugs herself tightly, trembling. "From there, he would bring little things home for me, small treats, and give me money. My mom said it was okay because he asked her to marry him, and one day he would be my dad. And that's what dads do for their daughters, you know? They take care of them. I never had my dad in my life. She wouldn't tell me anything about who my dad was."

She's breathing shakily. "And I relaxed because she told me that he just wanted me to be his little girl, even though I was 11. One day, I was getting something from the refrigerator, and he came up behind me and rubbed my back. My mom came in, and he said that he thought I might be cold. But I didn't tell him I was cold, and it felt very off, not right. Then another time, I was coming in from soccer practice, and he made a comment about how strong my legs were, and said my thighs would have an excellent grip." She pauses, putting her hands up to her forehead, massaging it.

"I didn't know what the Hell he was talking about. So, he said, let me show you, and he was feeling on my legs, moving up to my thighs, going up too close to my Va-jay-jay. It was creepy. I told my mom, and he told her he was just massaging my legs because I was at soccer practice. That he knew from when he was a kid playing volleyball that the leg muscles will quickly get cramped up after training. It was okay because he just was giving a massage to help the muscles relax. And then she smiled and said thank you for helping her.

"Every touch he had an excuse for, and she bought it because she wanted to believe everything he said. For my 12th birthday, he told my mom he had something special for me because he knew how much I love to draw. So he got a full art set, it was really great. But that really wasn't the gift. He paid a visit to my room that night when my mom went to work. He said it was my turn to learn what it was like to feel good. And that's when the real touching began, and I told my mom, he told her that was impossible. That I must've had a nightmare."

What the Hell? This is for Uncle Austin to handle for real. Ava's face is getting more flushed as she goes on. I don't think any of us are prepared for where this is going.

Ava continues with the story. "He said he wasn't even here, and that he shouldn't have left me by myself, but I must have had a bad dream. And you know my mom believed that crap? He waited a while, and he kept on doing the inappropriate touching, but then that night came. I guess he decided he was going to go all the way. He said it was time to take what he wanted. It was time for me to give. He was too strong. I tried to stop him, and I told her, and she didn't believe me! I didn't know my dad, so I couldn't contact him, and she still wouldn't tell me anything about him. Then the fifth time, she caught him."

She's getting louder, on the verge of hysterics, while pacing and hugging herself. Dammit, I didn't think anything like this had happened to her. Does Uncle Austin know?

"Oh God, I'm screaming and crying. He's going to hurt me again. My hands are tied to the head of the bed. Tied up with long straps to the footboard. He's covering my mouth with his hands, giving me that leering, evil grin. 'You are mine!' Busting through the door with a crash, my mom screamed at the scene before her. He leaped off me. She jumped on him, but he pushed her off and ran to the bathroom. She untied me, and I put my clothes on. Running to her bedroom and grabbing her gun, she ordered me to run, to get the Hell out of the house, and I did. And that was the last time I saw my mother alive! If I had just let him have his way and not fought and screamed, she wouldn't have found out. And she would still be alive!" Crying hysterically, Ava collapses on the floor.

We were stunned into silence. Everything was happening so fast. Anger like I've never felt before overcomes me, like a raging storm in full force just thinking about the bastard who hurt her. Walking over to her, we all get on the floor. I'm the closest, and I hug her first. We're all in a circle around her like a protective cocoon, holding her and crying. Protecting her is something we are going to do. Nobody else is ever going to hurt her again. We got to get some help for her as soon as possible—Auntie Amy, probably. After what seems like a long time, we slowly rise. Janae and I help Ava up.

"Ava, I think I'm speaking for all of us when I say that we didn't know anything about this. I know we all have questions. The first one is the man who hurt you—is he in prison, Ava? Does Uncle Austin know about what happened?"

She looks at me, panicked, shaking her head. "Dad would probably blame me; then where will I go? He only has me in his life because my mom died. What if he tells me to leave? I don't know; I'm terrified of what the outcome will be."

"Ava, your dad loves you so much; there is no way in Hell that he would ever kick you out. He won't blame you. He sure would want to know that this happened to you. We have a family that does what we have to do for each other, and this is something he needs to know right now. Just think about it; this son of a bitch who hurt you is walking around like nothing has happened, and that should not be allowed. They've got to get his ass because he could be doing this to someone else's daughter. You have to pay when you hurt someone. Come on, whether it be from some time in prison or getting killed yourself. I'm a firm believer in an eye for an eye Bible justice system. Yes, I am!"

Janae's livid. She's pacing with her fist balled up. "Hell yeah, that bastard needs to pay for what he did to you and your mom. There's no way that son of a bitch should still be walking around outside, no fucking way!" We all are giving each other the same shocked, angry expressions and agreeing with her.

When uncle Austin finds out, there's going to be Hell to pay. He is going to move mountains to find this guy. It's going to be like a category five hurricane and twister combined, but we can't say he doesn't deserve what he is going to get. Ava doesn't realize it; she is his baby, his only daughter. All my uncles are going to search for him. They will more than likely go in like they're the judge, jury, and executioner. He's so dead.

The long buzzer from the front door startles us, especially Ava, who damn near jumps out of her skin. Naya and Sasha go to check to see who it is. They come back into the bedroom with Delia, who's looking worried, and like she's about to explode. "What the fuck is going on, Ava? Naya told me what happened!"

Naya interrupts, scurrying behind. "Wait, Dee, you just became the damn Flash, dashing in here when I didn't finish explaining."

"Dee, we have a lot going on that you don't know about, crap, that we didn't know about. Calm down." She looks from Ava to me. "So, what the Hell don't I know that would make me say the bullshit that went down today is okay? Honestly, I can't think of anything that would excuse the crazy shit that Ava just did today. I'm all ears." Delia looks at everyone, then her focus is on Janae and me.

Going over to her and touching her arm, I say, "Come inside the bathroom with us so we can talk."

Bringing her with Janae into the bathroom as soon as we get in, I tell her everything Ava told us. Delia is the emotional one after Naya. She had the exact reaction that we all had. She needs help; we have to let Uncle Austin know no matter what because he's her dad. They need to find the monster who did this to her.

We go back into the bedroom, and Delia hugs Ava. "First, your father, who also happens to be our uncle, loves the Hell out of you. Ava, he needs to know what happened. You know they'll find him, and his ass will pay one way or another."

Ava nods her head and starts crying all over again. She's been dealing with this all on her own. "Okay, now, just because this happened to you, we don't want you thinking that being promiscuous is the way you should be. We're all in this together. You're not dealing with this alone anymore. When we get home, we can be with you to tell Uncle Austin."

This day has been full of revelations, more than I ever thought we'd learn. Now everything's changed. My opinion of her and most of the girls had been formed from actions that she'd taken. She'd been in so much pain and all alone that she'd just been throwing herself at guys. We can tell her that she doesn't have to exhibit this behavior, but she really needs help. We all thought she was just a spoiled brat, but we were so wrong about that.

My stomach growls loudly; an early dinner sounds good. "I think we should go out to get something to eat. I'm famished, and I know everyone could use some food. I think we can go to one of the local spots, instead of somewhere and the casino, you know? We can relax and just breathe because this was one Hell of a day. Do you think we can invite Lucas? Would it be a problem? If yes, just tell me, and I won't call him."

Ava calmed down quite a bit. Looking at all of us, she nods her head,

"He's really nice. I can't picture him ever trying to hurt any woman." Going into my room, picking up my phone, I call Lucas. "Sweetness, are you and your cousins okay?" he asks.

"Do you want to come out to an early dinner with us, Lucas?"

Closing my eyes, I can see his smile. "Hell yeah, I'm starving, woman. What time?"

Chuckling, I say, "Give us about an hour and a half to get ready."

"That's not an early dinner." He laughs at me.

"Whatever. See you in a while, Lucas." Shaking my head, I smile about this greedy man. Then, calling out from my door before closing it, I tell the others, "Be ready in ninety minutes, ladies."

Now I have to find something sexy, but not too sexy to wear, since I've invited this gorgeous man to dinner with us. This is a group dinner, so I don't want to appear like I'm trying to be sexy. On a date with Lucas, I want to look extra pretty, so afterward, he'll think about me. I'm going to wear my electric blue, wraparound shirt dress with a pair of black tights, and I have a cute pair of electric blue Gucci shoes that tie up over the top of my ankle. I want to look cute, but I don't want to look too extra.

After showering, I put my hair up in a ponytail and twist little curly ringlets to hang down each side of my face. I'm not putting on that much makeup. I like it natural, so I'm using a little eye shadow, bronze shimmer blush, and a bit of peach lip gloss. Putting on my favorite perfume, closing my eyes, and breathing it in is the last gift from Mami. Thinking about when he said I smelled good, that was me and not a perfume.

I pick up my matching Gucci bag and walk out into the living room. Surprise! Lucas is here. Sasha, Delia, Ava, and I are ready. We're just waiting for Naya and Janae.

"You're looking beautiful, Sweetness."

"Why, thank you, Mr. Hellsin. I have to look good; I mean, look at you. I can't be outside with you and not look good too." I'm grinning, joking with him. "Every female is going to look at you, that specimen of man-candy. For some reason, you attract women like bears to honey. No, let me say that right. Yes, Lucas is the honey, and all the women are the bears, because they just look at that man like he is the jar of honey, and they're coming after it."

Lucas is shaking his head, laughing. "Nah, I am not some damn honey. How about I'm a steak—a nice, big, juicy piece of steak. And they were on a deserted island. They couldn't eat any meat, just water and coconut juice, and some fruit, of course. That's what I am, not some honey, woman." He has us all laughing. I really couldn't picture him as a jar of honey that these women, well, no, bears, were hungry for. Right on cue, Janae and Naya walk in, and so, we're ready to go.

Leaving the elevator, we walk outside, and it is busy out here. There are so many people are out and about. As a courtesy, we can use the luxury van from the hotel during our stay here. Driving away from the hotel, we pass by several restaurants, and we're a little bit away from the strip. It's a fantastic Jamaican spot, and the food is delicious, from what Josh told me when he was here. We all adore spicy food. Crap, I hope Lucas likes hot food, too. Lucas gets out, and he holds the door for all of us to come out. He is such a gentleman.

I must say we all look fabulous. Janae has on white jeans and a black lace panel flare cuff blouse, and she has on her gold to make everything pop, as she would say. Naya has on her favorite color: pink. She has on a soft pink jumpsuit with a flared top that starts in the front and goes all the way around to the open back. There's chiffon on the side, and the back is cut out. Yes, that's our diva, yep.

Ava looks a little better than usual with a black and red mini dress, and she has her on her cute red Jimmy Choo shoes. Of course, they are heels. Delia, yeah, she's like the group's mother, and she is already with Steve. She dresses a little bit more conservatively than the rest of us. She's wearing a pretty, ice blue jumpsuit with bow ties at the bottom and waist and spaghetti straps on the arms, but she has a little sheer white jacket on.

Sasha has light blue skinny jeans and a white, belted, asymmetrical blouse that's tied in a pretty bow. Beautiful outfit indeed. Lucas has helped all of us out of the van, and I ended up being last, but it's all good. He's holding my hand as we're going into the restaurant, and I've got to say it's damn good.

CHAPTER 11

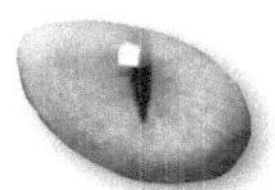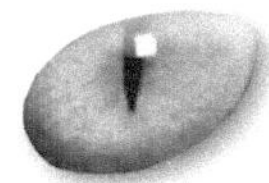

GUESS WHO'S COMING TO DINNER?

Lucas

I WAS pleasantly surprised with that phone call from my Sweetness, inviting me to dinner with them. Now the only thing is, I've got three of these ladies' mates who may not be too thrilled. I would say two, because Garrison and Griffin haven't marked Naya and Ava yet. *I concentrate, filtering out the other voices congregating in my mind, so the brothers can get my message to meet up at the restaurant.*

Okay, fellas, listen up. We're going out to dinner tonight. Get yourselves together so when we leave, you can already be outside. You can trail us from a safe distance, and then we all can end up in the restaurant. I'm telling you because your animals might go a little crazy when you realize that they're outside. Another thing; please figure out how you're going to mark your mates.

Griffin responds, "I still don't believe my tiger or panther picked this girl, well, young woman."

Griffin, you got to stop, okay? Ava is your mate. Now, you need to go and get to know her. This is why people do the crazy-ass things that they do. And you don't know; there could be some reasons. I'm saying that if you want to know what is going on with her, I suggest you find a way to get to know her. Tonight could be the start; that's all I'm saying.

We'll be there for damn sure.

You need to know what's going on with your mates, so you meet them as friends. When it's time to claim your mates, maybe it'll be more comfortable, because you'll be their friends. All right, so I'll see you at the restaurant. Perhaps we can say we're business associates, and you see me, and you pop over and say hello, and I'll introduce you. But you all know Janae and Naya, and so you actually could come over. Whatever you decide to do, I'll hear your thoughts.

Of course, I'm a gentleman, assisting the ladies out of the luxury van, making sure Alyssa would be last. Because when she walks into that restaurant, they're going to know that she's with me; no doubt, she's mine. Some damn good Caribbean music's playing here, and Alyssa's holding my arm, tapping her fingers on my arm to the beat.

My essence emanates from me to Alyssa, continuously increasing. It seems the more we're together, the more it binds us. Even though I may not know what the Hell I'm talking about, because it hasn't happened before.

Lucas, we're here.

All right, so how are we going to do this? Is it just reconnecting with Naya and Janae, and you know me from business dealings?

Grayson, yeah, we are going say we know you from our businesses, and we're catching up with them from when we were interviewed a couple of months ago. By the way, we're buying a large piece of land, close by where they live. Garrison and I needed to be close to Janae and Naya. Griffin, he's panther and tiger, so I don't know if it's going to be the same or worse.

See you when you make your appearance, guys.

Now I can focus on my Sweetness. "How was the talk with Ava? It feels like you ladies have made something happen, but there's a weird angry energy in the air. I'm here for you, you know that, right?" Even though I know what happened, I have to act like I don't know.

Inhaling and exhaling deeply, I gaze at Ava, walking ahead. "Yes, today there were some devastating revelations by Ava that no one knew about. So now we have real serious matters to share with my uncle. I know my uncle; he's going to go crazy, as well as my other uncles. We're much closer now than we were earlier today. Now we know that she has been going through her own personal Hell for years. She doesn't deserve to go through that."

Stopping, turning to face her, and lifting her chin with my fingers, I kiss her forehead.

"You are a brave, spirited group of women, even Ava. She's gone through whatever she has, and she's still here. I know your family will get her through this, and she's going to be all right. It's just going to take some time. So if you ladies need me, especially you, I'm here."

Giving that beautiful smile, she nods her head. "Thank you for that, Lucas. I needed to hear that."

"Hello, I'm Lydia, your hostess. Let me take a guess. Are you the Laskaris party?" The hostess, a pretty little redhead, smiles brightly at us.

"Yes, we are," the ladies answer in unison.

"Please follow me to our private waiting area. We need about five minutes to prepare your table." Leading us down the hall and making a right turn, she directs us to the waiting area.

"Lys, I thought you said this was a Jamaican spot?" Janae asks. Walking into the waiting area, I see she's right. It doesn't look like a Jamaican restaurant, maybe a multi-cultural restaurant with many different foods, which is fine.

She laughs, shrugging. "All right, it's my fault. I just remembered Josh said they had some great Jamaican food. I thought it was a Jamaican restaurant."

There are many different flags all around the restaurant. They must cook foods from all of the other countries whose flags they have up here, which should be interesting. The music is so good it makes you want to dance. So I guess nodding my head and tapping my foot to the beat will have to suffice. It would have been nice if I could have got a dance in, but after the day they had, that may not be appropriate.

There's a little stage in the back. At times, they have live bands here or something like that. The other host is a good-looking young guy. He's smiling a lot at Naya and Ava, and they're not paying him any attention. This is funny as Hell, because they're both mated, and they don't even fucking know it. On the other hand, it's a good thing they're not interested, because I really don't want to see the guys reacting to someone trying to take their mates.

The owners of this restaurant must have a thing for the color black. They have to, because everything is black, besides those flags on the walls. It's just really dark in here. The floor is a semi-gloss black tile, and there are black walls, ceilings, table covers, and chairs. Damn, everything is black: the plates, the candles, come on, those are also black. Even the staff are wearing all black. The restaurant's atmosphere is so dark. Hopefully, the food is good.

"Okay, Ladies and the lone, lucky Gent, your table is ready. By the way, my name is José."

Now, since all the ladies in our group are wearing dazzling colors, it's such a contrast that it's like they're bringing life into the place. The other people who are here are not dressed as vibrantly.

We get to the table, and I say, "Let me get the chairs out for all of you ladies. You know you have a gentleman here." Pulling each chair out, I assisting them, one by one to the table.

After the day they had, no one wants to be sober, because they're ordering drinks and asking for an extra splash of alcohol. Naya orders a Long Island iced tea. Sasha orders a hurricane, Ava and Janae both order strawberry daiquiris, Delia and Alyssa order pina coladas. My request is simply top-shelf Cognac.

"Jose, make sure the ladies' drinks are mixed with top-shelf, as well. If you're going to drink, you may as well get the best."

"Yes, sir."

"Lucas, thanks; I didn't even think about the top-shelf. Today has been a rough day. I don't think it would have been a great idea to just sit inside the penthouse."

We all agree with that. Even though I act like I don't know what's going on, I do. Looking at the menu, it does have an array of different foods from different countries. Great idea, because you never know what a person is in the mood for. They have food from about 30 different cuisines on here. Offering so many different dishes, tourist spots like this are moneymakers. Even though it's not on the strip, it's not very far from it. They do make a significant profit.

"May I take your order, ladies and gentleman?" Chuckling, the waitress says, "My name is Lylia."

Before we get to speak, Janae is on it. "We would like family size pans, and we can just serve ourselves."

Lylia's mouth drops open.

Janae orders. "We'd like two pans of jerk chicken, peas and rice, curry chicken, crab and callaloo, bammy, coucou and flying fish, beef and chicken patties, yams, and sweet plantains, and Creole bread."

"Wow! You really know what you want. I've never had anyone come in and be so confident in what the whole group wanted. I know you all ordered drinks from the bar, but do you want some water too, or soda, or juice?" Lylia's looking around at everyone, waiting. We decline. I think they might be on a mission to drink too much tonight; that's what I believe the ladies' goal is. So we have to make sure we get the guys in here as soon as possible before they start drinking too much.

Finally, the brothers are walking into the building. Immediately, Janae and Naya both have strange expressions, and both look in the direction of their mates. As they're strolling in with the hostess, Garrison and Grayson make a bullseye connection with Naya and Janae. Both of them inhale sharply, noticeably; now everyone else is looking at them with questioning expressions.

What a sight: Garrison and Grayson are relaxed and happy; on the other hand, Griffin looks like he's still pissed off about Ava being his animal's choice. The hostess is walking them to the smaller table right next to ours.

Grayson's smoldering gaze is fixed on his mate. "Hey, Janae and Naya. Who would have thought we'd be running into you ladies here. How are you two doing? You both remember Garrison and Griffin, right?"

Grayson eases next to Janae, holding his hand out to her. She puts her hand in his, and he lifts her up, hugging her. Janae blushes but hugs him back. Garrison walks over to Naya, who's sitting on the other side, and she jumps up, hugging him. I wasn't expecting that, but okay. She's confused, but she is drawn to him like a magnet.

Examining the empty table, Garrison looks back at Janae. "Are you all finishing up, Janae?"

Janae shakes her head. "I just ordered a mountain of food for us."

"Janae, since you just ordered, how about we join you? Not at this table; we can go right over there. We'll be right next to each other and catch up and talk." Janae looks around at everyone and at me.

"It's fine with me, and it's good to see you three again, Grayson and Garrison." Nodding at them, I say, "We've had several business deals."

"Sure, you gentlemen are welcome to join us. No, we'll join you at the other table." She smiles at him.

Grayson grins, "Great, let's get the hostess's attention. You all can move over to this table, and I've got you right with me, Janae." He picks up her bag and walks three tables over. He pulls out the seat for her, she sits down, and he sits next to her.

Alyssa has a puzzled expression on her face, because she doesn't know that these two have met before. Looking over at Naya, Garrison has her hand, and they're walking over to the table as well. Oh, look at Griffin. He did manage to find his way over to Ava. She's looking a little nervous. "Hi, I'm Griffin. Do you mind telling me your name?"

Ava shyly smiles up at him. "Ava is my name, Griffin."

"I'd like it if you'd sit next to me at the other table, Ava." He holds out his hand to her. She gives him her hand, and they go over too. I stand up and help my Sweetness out of her chair; we're going over as well. Steve and Delia follow, laughing about a joke he just told.

So who's left uncoupled? Sasha; yeah, we know that she has the biggest crush ever on Chris. For sure, she is not open to seeing anybody. I hope no one calls themselves talking about she's their mate.

The waitress comes back and reiterates the order that we gave. The guys ask for double of everything. Well, damn, I thought I could eat. I guess they're hungry for real.

Sasha looks at Garrison, "Where did you meet Naya and Janae?"

"Well, a few months ago, we did an interview with In-style Magazine where Janae works, and Naya was also there."

Sasha is in big sister mode, studying him, knowing that this guy is after her sister. "How old are you, Garrison?"

Garrison openly laughs, "I'm twenty-seven, Sasha. I'm not an old man."

Sasha, narrowing her eyes, crosses her arms. "Well, you are to Naya, because she's only twenty-two."

Naya interrupts, "Wait, I'll be twenty-three next month. Really, Sasha?" She smirks at her.

Shaking her head, Sasha, staring at Garrison, says, "You're still a baby."

Naya looks at her incredulously. "Really? How old are you? Not much older than me. So, Ms. twenty-three, going on twenty-four, don't act like I'm too young to date a twenty-seven-year-old."

"Whoa, little sis, calm down. Why are you getting all like this? I'm just asking how old he is because I've never seen him before. Of course, I'm going to look out for you. I'm your big sister. It's my job to take care of you. Even if I'm only one year older; what am I supposed to do, right, Janae? Janae!"

"Hmm, what?" Startled, Janae turns her attention to Sasha. She's been totally involved in whatever Grayson has been talking to her about and hasn't been paying attention at all to Sasha's little speech. They are hilarious. Chuckling a little, Alyssa kicks me. I stop before they notice that I'm laughing at them.

There she is in the pretty light blue dress and that red hair. Who the Hell is the guy with her? What the fuck?! That's my mate, why is she with someone?

Who the fuck is that?! I look up and around to tune in where this conversation is coming from. It's coming from outside. Leaping out of my seat, I say, "Be right back."

I rush out to the front to find out who it is and why the Hell he's calling my Sweetness his mate, because that's not the damn truth. She has never had another mate or even a serious boyfriend. I would have known it because I can read her damn mind. I want to know who the Hell is fucking delirious enough to think that she's his?

Opening the door and looking around, I search through thoughts from the people in the area but it's useless. I fucking lost him. What the Hell? Alyssa's fucking my head up. I could've stopped time and teleported to his ass, shit!

I turn around and walk back in, and Alyssa's looking at me questioningly. "I just had to go outside for a second. I'm good."

Lucas, what's going on? (The brothers are communicating their thoughts.)

I just heard something inexplicable from, I guess, another shifter, but he disappeared before I got outside. He described my Sweetness as his damn mate while thinking about her. But one thing is for sure: he won't be getting my woman. I'll annihilate his ass if his ass tries any shit.

All at once, Garrison, Grayson, and Griffin ask, How the Hell can he just think she's his mate, Lucas? You're going to have to mark her, ASAP. In case you don't know, that means as soon as possible, man.

It would be nice if I could do that, but I'm not sure how or what to do other than having sex with her.

How you don't know, Lucas? You've got to know how to mark your mate; come on now. You better go to your family and find out what you need to do, because if she's mated, he's not going to be able to come up to her. Your scent will repulse him. If you don't mark her, even if she doesn't want to talk to him, he will be able to approach her. If you can't, you know you're going to have to be around all the time.

How can you explain that, when it doesn't seem like any of them really know about their animal or anything? I hate that some families keep it from the females until they hit age 24 or 25. That's not even the half of it. Some parents give the children the elixir to quiet their beast, putting it to sleep indefinitely. Why? It's awful, man, damn.

Sweetness clears her throat. "Lucas?"

Turning to Alyssa, I say, "I'm sorry, Sweetness, I was thinking about something. What's up?"

Sweetness smiles at me and asks, "Are you sure you're okay? I was telling you that Saturday night we're going to this nightclub. It's called Fever. Would you like to come with us or meet us there? Whatever works for you. We haven't been there before, but we've heard it's a hot club."

You know, this is so damn perfect, since I'm going to be there anyway. "Guess what? I'm going to be there too. I have the VIP section for Saturday night. I met with one of the owners. I have some clients who love that club, so we'll meet and discuss our deal sign, then they can go do their partying."

She checks me out in amazement as the food is being brought to the next table. "Lucas, that's so damn crazy. How the Hell do we end up at the same place, on the same night, without knowing what's going on? So, we are joining you in the VIP area, Mr. Man, Big Baller, Shot Caller. Mmm hmmm. You just went and took over a whole area."

I laugh. "I always make sure my clients have a positive experience with me. My meeting is early. When you arrive, we all will have a place to relax and have a good time. If you're downstairs with everybody, you may not get a table, you know, and there's quite a few of you. Garrison, are you guys still going to be here on Saturday?"

Never breaking eye contact with Janae, he replies, "We were leaving Saturday evening, but now we'll definitely be here. So, my answer is yes. We'll be here, and we're coming to the club. I can see if Janae can work her body if she has some moves on the dance floor. Hmm, I know I got some."

Janae shakes her head, laughing. "I can dance; I can tell you that much. I minored in dance, and you better hope you can keep up with me, Mr., now there."

Grayson, shaking her hand, replies, "Challenge accepted. I hope you'll be ready, woman. It's going to be fun to see what Miss Janae has for me. You know that dancing is like foreplay, and if you can't dance, that's as bad as not having rhythm." He winks his eye at her, and she just laughs.

Right on cue, the servers arrive with our feast; damn. I take in all these beautiful, delectable dishes. Getting a whiff of the different aromas slamming through my senses is really making me want to eat: the sugary cinnamon in the yams, the brown sugar and vanilla from the plantains, then the savory and spicy smells from the jerk and curry chicken, along with the other dishes. This is going to be a delicious meal. For the second time ever in my life, I want to eat something. The first time was breakfast with my Sweetness.

"Thank you so much, Lylia. Everything looks scrumptious! Let's dig in." Janae's getting plenty of each selection on her plate. We wait for all the ladies to get their food, and there are no dainty servings here. Food is serious business.

CHAPTER 12

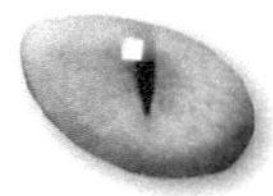

MOTHER HEN SASHA

Lyssa

ALL I can say is that these guys are pretty damn lucky, because I see that my cousins are totally into them. I'm trying to figure out when this happened. I thought that we talked, but I've never heard one iota about these guys. Sasha and Delia are the mother hens, and I understand not telling those two. We are like sisters, Sasha, Janae, Naya, and I, and I'm feeling very left out of the loop. We're very close.

I will get to the bottom of this; we're going to talk, to see what the Hell has happened, because I'm lost. Neither one of them has said anything about any of these guys. The way these men are acting, it's like they have something going on. There's more to this. There has to be, because of the way these two are into them. I'm even looking at the brother, who's looking at Ava.

Let's be for real: who gets lucky with three gorgeous hunks who are identical specimens of fine? It's unbelievable. This is just over the top, because no one has said anything. I know I have been in my own zone at times, but seriously, I would have remembered if one of them came up to me and said I met someone. Is it because I've been in my own place of grief that I couldn't pull myself out of that they didn't want to tell me? I want everyone to be with someone they could have a relationship with and build something loving. I'm trying to do what I have to do to get better. It's torture to my heart that it's never going to be the same again. I'm sad and depressed. Somehow, meeting Lucas has done something I can't explain or figure out.

I can't walk around, acting like nothing has happened. I lost my parents and my twin, and that's climbing a mountain with no gear. Aunt Amy is helping me, and the guilt isn't nowhere like before. As for Janae and Naya? We're most definitely going to have a come-to-Jesus, what the Hell is going on moment.

Once again, my stomach growls, and I gaze longingly at the food. Lucas touches my hand. I turn to him, nodding towards the food, and he says, "Eat, Sweetness; you're hungry." Getting up, I fill my plate with everything. Easing back into my seat, Lucas and the brothers get their food, making two plates of food. Women are tuned in to all of them, especially to you know who—Lucas. The waiter passes by, and he's not a small guy, but he doesn't even reach any of their shoulders.

The food is absolutely delicious! We knew it would be already, because Josh loves to eat, and he loves good food. If he gives us a recommendation, we know it's going to be delish.

Lucas keeps checking on me. I'm still trying to figure out what happened earlier. I don't know, but I really think something happened, but I don't know how to convince him to tell me. I just have a bad feeling because of how he jumped up. I can't shake this feeling that something is not right. I listen to my intuition when it tells me something is wrong.

"Excuse me, Griffin, how long ago was the interview where you all met?"

Oh, yes, I'm on a mission for information. Sasha and Delia are listening attentively. Ava and Naya aren't paying attention to anyone but Grayson and Garrison.

Taking a drink of his Coco Loco, Grayson answers, "We met officially at the interview. It was about, what, eight months ago, Janae?"

Janae blushes, "Yes, it was around that time, and just in case any of you ladies are wondering, this is my first time seeing him since the interview." She looks at each one of us.

"Grayson, you seem to be, um, very intrigued with our Janae. You haven't seen her in eight months, but you are very captivated by her. The same goes for your brothers and their attention to Naya and Ava."

"Sweetness, we've known each less time than they have, remember? We connect on a whole other level. Why can't they?" Lucas caresses my cheek with the back of his index finger. His eyes devour me, creating butterflies fluttering from deep within and spreading to the fine hairs on my skin.

I manage a shaky laugh. I'm feeling giddy because damn, he's telling the truth. "You do have a point, Lucas. I'm just curious, that's all. If they're happy, I'm good with that. I'm not a believer in whirlwind romances. That's why I'm so damn nervous about what's going on with us, Lucas. Wait; now isn't the time to discuss. I shouldn't have said anything here, sorry. Okay, I'm stuffed. As much as I would just like to sit here, we have to go soon, ladies. We have quite a bit to talk about, don't you all think so?"

"Oh, yeah, and we all want to know what's going on with Janae and Naya. Inquiring minds must know. We're going to be up all night tonight, just catching up with each other. We still have a couple more days here. Tonight is girl's night."

Sasha's beaming; she's going to be the chief detective, hunting for clues. We're all looking at Janae and Naya with smiles on our faces because we're going to keep them up tonight.

Okay, these three brothers are very interested in my cousins. And I'm not sure, especially with Ava. She has many issues that she has to deal with, so she definitely doesn't need to get into a relationship yet. She needs to get some counseling if she ever wants to be in a healthy relationship. Before she puts herself in any romance whatsoever, she needs to go talk to Auntie Amy.

"We had a fabulous dinner. I guess we will see each other at Fever Saturday night and have a good time. I'm getting ready to call the hotel so we can get picked up."

Garrison pulls his cell out of his pants pocket. "Oh, I also have to call. We got here in hotel transportation, too. No need to rent a car; they'll take us where we need to go, right?"

"Which hotel are you guys staying at, Garrison?" Sasha's finishing her third drink. She's on her way to being drunk.

"Sweet Sensation."

Janae interrupts, "What?! We're staying there, too. That's crazy, Garrison. How are we staying at the same hotel out of all the hotels on this damn strip? That's funny."

"Big hotel and lots of people. How long are you ladies here for, and when are you leaving?"

Jenae answers, "We're either leaving Sunday afternoon or Sunday night, so we can get back to work on Monday."

"How about we do something tomorrow? Something fun; we can go somewhere in the morning. Allow us to plan your day with us. We'll make sure you have a great time. Hey, Lucas, would you be interested in helping to plan the activities?" Garrison says, inviting us to a mystery outing.

Lucas laughs, "Sure, that would be fun."

"Wait, is this for everybody, or just for couples?" Delia, asks, grabbing a piece of Creole bread from the pan. "Because Steve can come too, and I can be there with my honey. I don't want to be sitting there stuck with the four of you talking to each other and all that great stuff, getting better acquainted with each other and all those little cute things people do when they're at the beginning of a relationship."

Drinking her strawberry daiquiri, she continues. "I've been there, and I've done that. I don't want to watch the blossoming of the flowers and all that. So, really, I would like to bring Steven, and we can come to have fun with you. I'm not going to be the third wheel."

Sasha rolls her eyes and shakes her head. "Yeah, make me the only odd one without a date, also known as the third damn wheel."

"Oh, damn, that sounds so messed up. I'm so sorry, Sash, but it's the truth, because we all see that Griffin likes Ava, Grayson likes Naya, and Garrison is all on Janae like white on rice. We all know Alyssa and Lucas. That's a whole different level, so that leaves you. Bringing Ryan is out of the picture, so you just will be the third wheel. We're all going to be kind of coupled up, but don't feel bad. It's okay. Your time is coming because you are brilliant, sexy, and gorgeous."

Sasha frowns, rolls her eyes, gets up, and walks out of the restaurant.

Did I really just hear that? I'm done. "What the fuck is wrong with you? That was so wrong. Okay, she's the only one here that is alone, but you don't know what's going on with her. You don't know why she chooses to be by herself! You don't get to make her feel bad about that." Taking a sip of my drink, I stand up. "She's your cousin. Why did you do that to her?"

I walk out to follow Sasha and to talk to her, and Lucas just nods his head at me while I leave. Walking quickly out to the front door, Sasha is tapping her feet with a hand on her hip, and I don't know why Delia would even bring that up.

"Sis, I don't know what the Hell is wrong with Delia. Why would she say that to you?"

She turns around, sniffling with watery eyes about to overflow. Shaking my head at her, I say, "You better not cry. She doesn't know anything, and so what that you are taking your time? I'm taking my time too. I just met Lucas. You know he may have got some kisses, but that's all. He's not getting anything else anytime soon. So that man will be waiting because nothing is happening. Anything else happens, it'll be in my damn dreams because I'm not that chick; we know that." A red Lamborghini stops in front of us, and the driver revs the engine. I wait until it speeds off, out of earshot. "And if Mr. Lucas doesn't know that he's going to find out that I am not the one to be out here being fast. You know that they know that, and I damn sure know that. Delia can't say anything. She's known Steven since they were what, like eight years old? For as long as she can remember, he has always been here, so she can't say anything about anyone they may meet as an adult. Delia's had Steve, the love of her life since she was a kid. She needs to cut her shit out. You can't be acting like you all that just because you got your man."

Hugging her tightly, "So don't you let her get you feeling any way; you hear me?"

Nodding her head, she wipes her eyes. "Can we just stay out here until the van comes, Sis? I really don't want to go back there. She really embarrassed the Hell out of me in front of people that we don't even know. Why would she do that? What's wrong with her? I mean, seriously, what the fuck?"

Standing out feeling the warm stuffy breeze, I would rather be inside with the fresh air. Looking down the street, some guys seem to be very intent on watching what we're doing, and it feels strange. Those little hairs on the back of my neck prick up, going down my arms, and raising goosebumps on my skin.

"Look, Sis, there's the vans—both of them, coming down the street." That was fast. I love service like that. I call Lucas to let him know that both vans are outside so they all can come out. Just watching the sites as we get on the strip again, it's pretty lively as usual. I love all the lights in Vegas.

Getting back to the hotel, we go to the elevators, and I just know that they're getting off before us, because we haven't seen them since we've been here on the penthouse floor the past two days.

"Can you ladies be ready by six a.m.? We can show you somewhere else other than the strip. What do you think?" Garrison smiles at Janae. Her eyes widen. "I hope where we're going is worth it, Garrison. That is very early, and I didn't have a workout planned, so I had every intention of sleeping in."

"We have to be ready by six? My God! That's early as heck!" Ava whines as she frowns at the thought. Cutting her eyes at Griffin, he grins goofily.

Lucas is smiling. This must be something they've discussed already. We're at the last stop before the penthouse floor, and they're still here. They're on the same level; how about that? We all get out of the elevator. We're going to the left, and they're going to the right. That's why we haven't seen them. They're on the other side. Now it all comes together and makes sense. While we are walking along, Lucas has his hand on my back, and that hand is so hot I; oh, yes, it is. We get to the penthouse, and we're left outside the door.

I look up at this gorgeous man who says he's mine. I still have a hard time believing this—yes, I do. In my mind, I'm just waiting for him to say, "You know I made a mistake, and goodbye, woman."

All of a sudden, his eyes twinkle, and he starts laughing like he just heard what I thought, but I know that's impossible.

He raises his hand to my cheek. "Guess what I did?"

Tapping my finger on the side of my temple, I reply, "I don't know what. Tell me."

"Well, you know I told you I want to see you, right? I mean really, really, see you. When I get to know you, we will be together, you know that, right? No, don't answer that. I'm going to show you that, so you know what's up with me. I bought a house not far from where you live." Those stormy blue-green eyes are piercing through mine, causing me to melt even more.

That announcement hits me like a splash of water, and I'm attentive, staring at him. I'm shocked, because he actually bought some property by where we live. Oh. My. God. "Are you serious? You really bought property by where we are? So, wait; you didn't rent. Buying is saying stability, permanence. I'm so surprised by that. I never would have imagined you would have done that right now." He lifts my chin up with his hand, so we're looking into each other's eyes.

"Didn't I tell you that I'm here? I'm not like any other man you've ever met. I'm here, woman. And I'm going to show you that I'm here, so you better get ready. Everything is about to change for you. That's what I do, and just to let you know, I've never done this before, ever. That is huge. As a matter of fact, you need to know that when I say I'm making this happen, it's for real, baby girl. I'm making this happen. I may go on trips from time to time, but you know I'm always returning to you. All we've got to do is come right down the street, and we see each other. Wish it was directly next door. You know I would have taken it. I did see some land next to you. I was thinking about purchasing it and building a home in a week or two. I told you you're mine, and I'm yours, and nothing is changing that."

Gazing into those gorgeous eyes of his, I swear I believe him. I don't feel like he's telling me some bullshit.

"I just want to let you know when you leave on Monday or Sunday, I'm moving too, and you'll be seeing me, and you owe me a date. So, I need you to think about where you will take me because I don't know a damn thing. You have the job of showing me all around your little town. Wherever you are, that's where I will be. If you go to Timbuktu, that's where I'll be; if you go to the hood somewhere, I'll be there too. Sweetness, I hope you're ready for me, woman. I'm ready to be wherever you are."

I am stunned, kind of dizzy, giddy, and my heart is racing right now. Leaning over, Lucas kisses me softly, tenderly showing me his gentle side, which is phenomenal. Just when I think he can't go higher, he takes me there. Lucas is my very own aphrodisiac.

I don't even need to drink around him. He quenches my thirst. How am I going to do this with him down the street from me? My mind is spinning, trying to comprehend how this all happened. It's only been a few days, and it feels like we've been together for some time when we're not even intimately together.

"Lucas, you know I feel like we have so much more to learn about each other because it's only been a few days. I hope you're ready for me because I will be taking my time to get to know you."

Reaching up, I kiss him softly. "I'll see you tomorrow Lucas. Have a good night." Turning to go inside, he turns me back to him, "You know, we've forgotten something." Leaning his forehead into mine, that telltale gesture just shows me how much he remembers how much that means to me. Wrapping my arms around his muscular waist to get closer brings a feeling of comfort and that heat that ignites every time he touches me. Reluctantly pulling away, I smile at him, then step inside.

CHAPTER 13

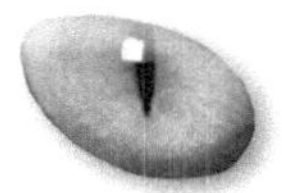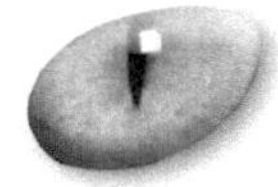

EXPLANATION TIME

Lucas

WATCHING my Sweetness safely into her penthouse, I remember those words, *"Why is my mate with him?"* Who in the hell was he? I shake my head at the absurdity of this fucking guy thinking he's my woman's mate! Fuck that shit. She's mine; I'll do whatever I need to keep her safe. Thinking of the brothers' penthouse, I teleport into their living room.

Appearing in the same spot I did when I introduced myself to them earlier today, the empty room's silence greets me, since the brothers are still with the ladies. Walking over to the chaise, the exact replica of the one in my living room, I sink into softness that's just right. Leaning back, I put my legs up, cross my ankles, close my eyes, and go over the weird situation I have going on now.

How is this even possible? The confusion in that guy's thoughts was sincere. So what is this? He's been, what? Stalking her? Or what, just popping up whenever? She has no idea that someone else thinks he's her fucking mate. Focusing on Sweetness and going through everything she's seen in the past, nothing is matching up. No one besides me has called his mate.

And I know for damn sure she's mine, so he'd better get the hell out of here with his bullshit. If I could've seen who he is, I could have found out the cause of his delirium. If I have to fight in a challenge to keep her, that's not a damn problem, even though she would be thoroughly pissed off, because she's not with the medieval times shit.

Listening to her thoughts is intrusive, I know. *Lucas actually bought a house right down the street. This is so unbelievable; dammit, this is really happening. I need to be in control. No matter how he makes me feel physically and emotionally, my mind needs to be straight. I've never felt like this before in my life, and if this is the real deal, it's fantastic! I can't understand how after a few days, if I'm honest with myself after the first night, everything in me is calling for him. Seriously what the hell is wrong with me? This is not normal.*

A familiar beeping and clicking alert me that the guys are back. Voices and steps are getting closer until they reach the thick, plush carpet in the foyer and they walk through the large sitting area before the living room.

Griffin sighs. "Man, Janae isn't that much younger, but Naya and Ava? One is twenty-two, and Ava's only twenty-one. Damn! And she's not ready for anything serious in the relationship department, judging from her actions with Mike the asshole." Entering the living room first, Griffin stops. Surprise and confusion spread across his face. "How the hell—oh, fuck, Lucas, whoa. You never knock on a door, huh?" He smirks at me while shaking his head.

Garrison and Grayson laugh. "You weren't paying attention at fucking all, bro. We caught his scent immediately. Is it that you're so worked up over Ava that you totally missed it?"

A loud thump from Grayson giving Griffin an extra hearty slap on the back for his error makes the other laugh. "You cannot be in Ava land, not paying attention. What if we weren't here with you and it was someone else here? Javier, for instance; you know that we have some special family members who don't want us alive; come on now, you've got to do better than this," Garrison tells him, walking to the loveseat across from me and sitting down.

Grayson goes over to the fridge over at the bar, pulling out a couple of beers and bringing one to each of us. Strolling over to the desk and turning on the computer, a frowning Griffin diligently presses on those keys like he's upset with them. In all reality, he's not too happy with Ava being his mate and the fact that he didn't realize I was here when he walked in with his brothers, and they did.

"So, Lucas, what brings you by? And Griffin does have a point; you really don't like to knock on doors." Grayson studies me, breaking eye contact to rub his hand on his eyebrows and through his hair.

Stretching out his leg and relaxing in the chair with his hands folded behind his head, he regards me with half-closed eyes.

"I had some questions about when you marked Janae, Garrison. I kind of saw from your memories what you did with your lion."

Garrison twists off the cap and quickly gulps down some beer while peering intently at me. "Seriously? Did you go through my damn memories? What the fuck, Lucas? You never heard of not your business, or it's not okay to intrude in other people's personal shit, Lucas?" Angrily pacing, he turns to face me. "Where are you from? You can't really think it's fine to do this, man."

I hole my hands up. "You don't understand; I don't just invade people's memories, Grayson. Do you know what it is like to hear everyone's thoughts? Let me share. It's like being in an overcrowded room, and everyone is scrambling to tell you information that you're not even asking for."

I sit up, uncrossing my ankles, folding my arms, and searching for the right way to explain what I do. "It's not a choice; I have to focus like hell to block out every single thought from anyone in the city. Earlier today, when we met, I saw all of your lives, everything you've ever done, and thought, I know, by the way. It is what it is, guys. I've been like this since I was a child, and there is only one person whose thoughts I can't hear."

Garrison is rubbing his chin, clearly deep in thought about me and what I am. *Lucas, are you an ancient shifter? Like a dragon? We do have those. They're not around anymore, but it is prophesized that they're coming back. You know, at this time, lions are the most powerful animal shifters. But if there are Dragons, they would be considered the mightiest of the shifters.*

"No, I'm not a shifter or an ancient shifter. No matter what, you're not going to figure out what I am exactly. And I'm not going to tell you, but we have mates in the same family, so that means we are good."

They're frowning, not happy at all, but they don't have any other choice in the matter. Griffin goes over to the large shelf, grabs a book, and strolls over to me. He glances at his brothers questioningly. They nod at him, then he looks back at me. "Lucas, can you tell me what this book is about? I just want to see it; you know the magic in action."

I'll show him magic, all right. Using my telekinesis, I lift the book up from his hands. Floating in midair, it comes to me, and each page turns as I read.

"Damn, Lucas." Griffin is checking the time on his watch. "You're reading that book like a speedster."

Closing the book, I laugh. "I'll tell you that the beautiful young woman and her brother are crazy, stone-cold killers. Robbing banks, stores, people; hell, they rob the jewelry from animals that belong to wealthy people, too. Then she fell in love with the undercover cop who ended up killing her brother. She kills him, buries him, then later finds out she's pregnant. Also—"

"Stop! I get it, Lucas. I know he asked, but he's not even reading the damn book. I am. Correction, I was." Garrison shook his head with a piercing gaze at Griffin.

"I really need some ideas on how I can mark my mate other than sex. Alyssa is my woman; as fate has planned it, she was made for me. Not that asswipe I missed outside of the restaurant. I'm not a shifter, but maybe there's a way."

"Well. You were all in my mind, and you saw what I did to calm my lion down. I had to mark Janae. Now, since you won't share whatever the hell you are, I don't know how we'll help you, Lucas. We can tell you about us, like shifters, on how to mark your mate. I can't begin to guess what else you have to do. Really, bro, I don't know; are you in contact with your family?" Grayson flops onto the other side of the couch I'm on.

Garrison picks up his beer. He's deep in thought, and I'm trying not to listen. Fuck it, I'll act surprised.

"Lucas, how about you try giving a light bite on her shoulder? If you can't get in touch with your family for information, you're going to have to improvise. Sex is sex; it's part of mating, but to claim someone, we have to bite each other on the shoulder, the area before the neck. When we mark, that will stop another shifter from approaching, as I told you during the mind conversation. I don't know what to call it."

"It's about keeping her safe and away from whoever the guy is, so, hell yeah, I'll do it. I'll see how this works out. I don't want to use this particular power on Lyssa, but in light of this new development, I have to do this."

The guys nod their heads in agreement. "Listen, Lucas, you need to do everything in your power to make sure Alyssa is safe. If you didn't, what kind of damn mate would you be? If I were in your shoes, she'd be getting a bite tonight," Grayson announces.

"I'm not sure about tonight; it's girl's night. Never mind, I'll make it happen; thanks a lot."

Griffin's back on the laptop, typing away, making plans for the outing tomorrow with the ladies. "You're really not going to let us know about what you are, Lucas? You are going to make me start wondering some really crazy shit, dude. Think about it: you pop up here and you have powers we've never seen before. You've already said you're not any type of shifter. I've got to say that's a hell of a lot to just take in and go with."

Grayson is not joking. I guess it would matter if I gave a damn. I laugh and shake my head. "All I can say is it's a good thing we're friendly, and we're getting to know each other. I'm getting to know you, and you guys are getting to know me, because you three already know each other. And since you all have mates that are part of my mate's family, we will be good unless you do something to hurt her."

The three of them have identical scowls appearing on their faces; I have to be honest to let them know my position in the scale of things.

"I've got some work to do. I have to figure out where I'm going to place this bite." Standing up, I say, "I'll see you guys in the morning; I'm out." Teleporting back to the living room in my penthouse, I scan the area while strolling to admire the view outside the ceiling-to-floor windows, wondering whether or not this will work.

Lyssa

WALKING into the penthouse and shutting the door with a soft click, I inhale and exhale slowly. After that crazy, unbelievable news that Lucas just told me, I need a moment to myself before everyone gets in here. Going into my room, I ease onto the chaise, so I can go over this conversation in my head. He is really going to be at Lake Tahoe with me.

Thinking of him has me in a damn frenzy of nerves, giddiness, excitement, and fear rolled into one me. This is a train speeding; I need it to decelerate it a bit. We will take this slow and get to know each other, even though every cell in my body is percolating for this damn man.

My inner conversation about Lucas is interrupted when I hear the loud tone from the card key being used, and I turn around. My cousins' loud voices are laughing and talking, along with the click clacking of all the heels.

I need to be there when Inquisitors Adelia and Sasha question Janae and Naya about Grayson and Garrison. They just popped up at the restaurant for these god sisters/cousins of mine. Closing the door behind me, I walk into the living room where everyone is sitting. I look pointedly at both Janae and Naya.

Sasha goes in. "Give it to me; I'm waiting to hear it. You know we all are waiting. We want to know how and when you met the brothers."

They both look at each other and start laughing. Janae says, "All right, I'll tell you all of it right now, okay? Remember when we went to Lahaina during my internship at InStyle? I'm going to start there, because that's where it began."

We're all in total shock. My mouth has dropped open.

"This is going to sound insane, but I want to know. When we went out to dinner at our favorite pizza spot and Lana asked if I okay, she said I looked a little flushed."

We nod our heads, and at the mention of Lana, all eyes dart at me. I guess those last few sessions before coming here with Auntie Amy have really helped. Tears well up and trickle down, but I wipe them away from my cheeks. "I'm okay. Go ahead, Janae."

"Well, I don't know how to explain this other than just saying it. While we were at dinner, I had this weird feeling like I was being watched. And let me clarify—not the creepy, stalker-like feeling. It was exciting and frightening at the same time. When we were leaving, do you remember, at some point, I was behind? I was speaking to our server, and I heard a growl, then a lion's roar." Janae pauses, and we all let out a medley of responses: "What the hell? Are you serious? This is freaking different, lions roaring. Wait, what?"

"When we had the interview with them at Live-n-Style, when he came into the room, it was like everything was frozen in time; it was the two of us. He captured me with his silver eyes. Even though Naya was standing right next to me, I forgot she was there. My senses were on fire; molten lava was erupting from my heart to my soul. I got scared, and Naya and I left near the end of the interview. Tonight was my first time seeing him since then. I believe he's been around me, though. You know, I think, checking on me." Janae looks at all of us, then leans back in the chair.

Our attention is now on Naya. "Well, I don't have that much to say; there were no roaring animals or anything like that when we went to Lahaina. The first time I saw him was at the interview, and I felt the same as Janae, but the only difference is I have avalanches going on with me.

We didn't get to talk or anything. Tonight was my first time seeing him and talking to him, and I think he's been around Lake Tahoe for months, because I've been having that feeling off and on since I first saw him."

"Well, damn, neither of you shared this with us; we're family. On top of that, we are friends; you've met two gorgeous, sexy ass men who have significant connections to you. Lava and avalanches, that's big." I say, watching both Naya and Janae.

Sasha, getting up going over to the window, says, "They're twenty-seven, and Naya, you're only twenty-two, and you need to be careful. I'm your sister, and I don't want to see you hurt. Furthermore, I'm not trying to rain on your parade, being a bitch or a control freak. You know I love you." She turns, walking to Naya. "You and Janae are both beautiful, intelligent women. Just don't rush into anything; take your time."

We all join in, "Here, here, I second that. I do too, let's talk to our youngest, Ava."

She dances over, sitting next to Ava on her right, and Delia is on her left. Giving her a hug, she says, "You need to just be friends, and no sex with Griffin. You need to work through what happened and heal. I think Auntie Amy can help; what do you think?"

She smirks and shakes her head. "Griffin isn't like the guys I usually date. He's on another level."

"We've had enough dating conversation; let's relax and go to the game room. We can shoot pool." Delia rises and walks towards the game room. We all agree and follow her.

Lucas

I PACE in the living room, as I watch my Sweetness, trying to figure out if now is the time to mark her. More importantly, will it even work for me, as it does for shifters? Since we're all going out tomorrow, she'll be with me; we shouldn't have any problems. I'll just listen to her at my favorite spot to relax, the chaise.

I grin at Alyssa's surprise and confusion when she finds out that Janae's and Naya's initial reactions to meeting their mates were even more powerful than hers. The only reason it was more powerful is that I choose to be subtle, not knowing what the outcome would be if I used more of my essence on her.

Leaving her thoughts, lowering my mental barriers, and expanding the levels of my distance to hear others, I have a slim chance of locating this guy. Skimming through all the voices infiltrating my mind, I'm right. This guy isn't in the area at the moment. Hell, he might even be sleeping for all I know.

Checking the time, it's not late at all; maybe his thoughts are silent, which I doubt. Sighing, I punch the pillow, creating a hole where down feathers escape in the air and fall on the couch. Waving my hand over the pillow, I repair it, and I continue listening to everyone in my damn head, including my Sweetness. She goes to sleep while I'm on the couch watching her dream.

Not long after the sun rises, it's time to get my Sweetness. Teleporting to Alyssa's door, I lift my hand, just as the brothers turn and walk down the corridor. I knock on the door, and they speed up to meet me before it's opened. "Good Morning, Lucas," they say together.

"Morning, guys."

"Did you have a successful night marking Alyssa?"

"No, I was watching them have their girl's night. Tonight I'll mark her. She'll be with us, so no worries about the delusional one. Ready to show our mates a good time?"

"You know it. Our mates are going to love it. And—"

Opening the door with her sweet self is my mate. "Good Morning, Sweetness." My eyes are caught by hers, those intense, sapphire eyes with electric blue, then down to her luscious lips, forming a smile that pings more electricity through my entire being. Examining further, she's wearing sapphire jewelry, including studs in her ears and a matching necklace and bracelet, a sheer black blouse with a black bra, sapphire jeans, and some kick-ass, low-heeled, lace-up black boots.

She moves back to let us in. "Good Morning, Lucas, Garrison, Grayson, and Griffin, come in, we're almost ready." She strolls in, allowing the guys to pass. "Good Morning, Alyssa," each of them says, grinning. They enter the penthouse and go into the living room. Shutting the door, she faces me, and I step closer to her, lifting her chin with my index finger. Leaning in, her lips part, and I gladly connect my lips to hers, hearing the quickening of her heartbeat and my essence. Lightly sucking her bottom lip, my tongue feels the edge before slipping in, meeting hers. It tastes minty fresh with a hint of cinnamon.

Her temperature is elevated, even though it's chilly in here. My essence has a mind of its own. As usual, it's flowing from me into her. The rush of want and need increasing with every passing minute has me on the verge of exploding. I need an ice bath. I pull away, kissing the tip of her nose, and both of us release shaky breaths. "Now, this is how we should say good morning every day."

Her sun-kissed skin is slightly flushed. Giving me a smile, she leads me into the living room. Grabbing her hand and interlocking our fingers, we enter the living room together. The guys are sitting having a conversation with Sasha. "They should be on their way out; let me go check on them." Sasha gets up, glancing at Alyssa, and goes upstairs, muttering about slowpokes. I'm chuckling, shaking my head, because if it were Christopher, she'd take her time as well.

"Would you like some water? There are some bottles in the refrigerator."

"We're fine, Alyssa, thanks." The bell from the elevator upstairs goes off and we hear the sound of footsteps walking down the stairs. Sasha enters, then the elevator lands, and everyone else comes in. We all are dressed casually in fitted jeans; the ladies have dressed their jeans up by wearing pretty blouses and boots. We have on button-down shirts, and Garrison is wearing a damn cowboy hat. Standing up, Grayson, Garrison, and Griffin walk over, each hugging their mate and speaking.

"Ahem, excuse me, can we walk out of the door so we can get going, instead of you all making googly eyes?" Sasha's impatiently tapping the floor with her boot while crossing her arms and shaking her head at everyone. She's feeling a little left out, but Christopher isn't here, and he's who she wants. He's never said anything to her, though, so he doesn't know how she feels because she never told him. I can understand where she's coming from, because she doesn't want to look like she's chasing a guy.

Lyssa

HONESTLY, the past few days since I've had Lucas in my life have been an inferno on my body. My emotions are syncing into his. It's so damn confusing and frustrating, because this isn't me at all. All he has to do is look at me with those eyes of his, showing the fire in them, and I'm melting inside. His reaction to my outfit gives me great satisfaction in my choice.

His black shirt and jeans fit him perfectly; the shirt hugs his muscular shoulders and arms—not to tight, but you see their outline. I purposely don't let my eyes stray down to his pants to get a closer look at his crotch. I know he'll catch me, then grin knowingly.

We are ready for this outing today. We all have casual clothes, jeans and cute colorful blouses, and boots. We know if we're going on an adventure, we have to wear something attractive and comfortable, because that means we will be walking.

Oh boy, those very cute, black and gold slingback stilettos Ava's sporting are to die for. She's definitely going to be limping by the end of today, if we are walking as much as I suspect.

Knowing Ava, she has a plan. It's going to be a challenge to get her on track, but we've accepted. Her black blouse with gold trim, unbuttoned, showing her shiny, gold camisole, says *I'm not dressing the way I used to.* Black skinny jeans and gold earrings, necklace, and tennis bracelet complete her outfit. Lifting her eyebrow, noticing me examining her, she gives me a grin and gives her full attention to Griffin. Winking my left eye at her with a smile of my own, I continue with my cousins' wardrobe assessments. Janae has on a white blouse with sheer sleeves, red skinny jeans, and black, knee-high, flat boots. She's wearing the pearl earrings and necklace set Tia and Tio gave her for her birthday.

Rubbing my back with familiarity, as if he's been doing it for years, Lucas ignites more fire that burns only for him. From deep within my core, it spreads throughout every cell in my body to my skin, where goosebumps are prickling.

Lucas is moving his hand away from my back. Grabbing my hand again, he clears his throat. "Ladies and gentlemen, come on, let's get out of here, so we can get to the vans before we're late." His attention is explicitly focused on the brothers; since we don't know our destination, it's all on them.

Garrison looks at his Rolex. "Yes, we've got to get moving. Time to head out. Let's go." Walking to the front door first, Lucas and I wait for them. We lean on the door for the slowest people, Garrison and Naya, to finally get out.

Turning to Lucas, my breath is caught in my chest; his eyes are filled with a storm of blazing passion. Pulling me toward him and wrapping his arms around my waist, he swoops in. I gasp, his soft lips capturing mine. My arms go around his neck, bringing him even closer. Our tongues are battling it out, with no winner in sight; I actually don't mind.

CHAPTER 14

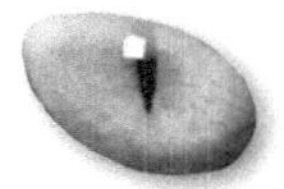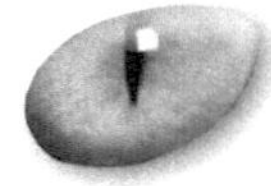

GROUP ADVENTURE

Lyssa

GARRISON laughs, "Okay, love birds, can we go now? We're waiting on you. We know you can get down to the lobby, but you don't know where we're going, right? Delia and Steve are waiting on their floor."

Lucas raises his left eyebrow at him. He glances from Lucas to me and chuckles at Lucas, putting his hand up. "Stop. I'm going; please hurry up."

Garrison quickly leaves. Sighing, I reach up, wrapping my arms around his neck, pulling him to me, and giving him a quick kiss that changes into a longer one. My heartbeat races like the propellers on a helicopter that increase speed to reach a destination in a rush. Dragging my greedy lips from his, I catch my breath, exhaling slowly. "Lucas, come on, let's go. They're all waiting for us." I give him a sultry smile. "You're the last one out. Please check the door and make sure it locks." We hear clicking and beeping from the door closing and locking, and Lucas catches up to me, taking my hand. As a couple, it's a good feeling. I'm not going to lie.

With my smaller hand in his, I feel his strength flowing into me, and it's crazy but true. We catch up to them. Everyone looks a wee bit impatient, but then the frowns on their faces change into smiles and smirks. The guys gesture for us to enter first; we do, and they follow.

You know I can't help but look around at all of us, and damn, we're a gorgeous group of freaking people. Yes, the hell we are, we look damn good. I mean, how often do you get on the elevator with eleven lovely people, seriously? Once get to our old floor and Steve and Delia get on, the doors open. Whoa, what the hell? Why is freaking Ryan coming on this fucking elevator?

Questioningly, I fix my gaze on Delia hard, because I don't understand why the hell Ryan is here. She just shrugs, mouthing to me that Steve told him. Lucas caresses my palm, automatically calming me down. What the hell is going on here?

"Listen, Ryan, you're not welcome. Man, I'm going to be straight up with you. I know what you did to Lyssa. We are not okay and never will be. So I guess you have to find some other place to go to entertain yourself." Lucas blocks the elevator door with his hand.

Why can I sense Lucas's anger? *MATE.* What the hell? I hear a voice in my head. Oh, my God. Squeezing his hand tighter, I feel a burst of, how can I describe this? It feels like strength, like I can do anything, and face it head on. My Lucas is here, and he won't let anything happen to me. Turning my attention to Lucas, his piercing eyes are on Ryan so hard he should be scared, because he looks like he can rip him apart. Wait, how does he know about what he did to me? I'm going to ask him about that, but not right now in front of everyone. Later, most definitely. I'm putting that in my file cabinet in my brain.

Ryan stares down at the elevator buttons, not backing down. "Last time I checked, this a free fucking elevator. I mean, really? Are you seriously going to act like I can't ride on the elevator? I don't have to go where the hell you go, but I'm riding on the elevator." He crosses his arms, shaking his head.

"If you don't want to get knocked the hell out, your eyes better not stray in Alyssa's direction. If you know what's good for you, you better keep on looking at those damn numbers, because those damn numbers are your friend. When you get to the lobby, you get out the elevator first and get the hell away from us. Listen very carefully, so you understand what I'm saying to you. This is a one-time warning. It's not going to be good for you, because I won't be telling you this shit again, dude."

The malice in his voice visibly affects Ryan. His skin's flushed, and his hands are trembling while his arms are crossed. His voice shakes slightly. "Yeah, yeah, I got it. I hear what you're saying. No need to act like you're the Godfather or something like that."

"Just shut the hell up, know your damn lane, just shut up."

The guys are observing the exchange. I guess they're assessing what the hell is going on. Even though we know Ryan is a bastard, how does Lucas see that he is? Retracing my conversations with him, I know I haven't said anything to him regarding Ryan.

Garrison, says, "When we get out, we'll give you some information about what we are getting ready to do. We have the whole day planned, so it's good that most of us are comfortable, so we can walk or run or whatever."

Griffin gives Ava the once over, with a slight chuckle. "Ava, maybe you should run back up and change into jeans and a pair of sneakers or boots without a high heel."

Eva smirks at him, rolling her eyes. "I'm just fine. What could we possibly be doing that I can't wear what I have on?"

"Okay then, suit yourself, and don't say I didn't warn you." Openly laughing at her now, Griffin just shakes his head.

"I hope you ladies, are ready for some adventure," Grayson adds, tipping that damn cowboy hat and wiggling his eyebrows up and down. We all bust out laughing, even though some of us are really wondering what the hell we're getting ready to do. I hope they're not talking about crazy adventure stuff, because I'm not so much into that. I like to have a good time, but I want to be safe. For instance, bungee jumping is not for me. I don't do that.

I look over at Lucas; he responds by giving my hand another squeeze, but he's still watching Ryan like a hawk. He's really going to make sure he keeps his eyes on those damn numbers. I believe if he looks at Lucas or me, he's going to punch the shit out of him, right in the damn face. That would be great. No, never mind; I don't want Lucas to get in trouble, so we're going to not call on that.

We arrive at the lobby. Ryan sprints off the elevator like a bat out of hell, going out of the hotel. Yes, he knew Lucas was going to fuck him up if he didn't. Lucas is holding onto my hand a little tighter and looking around. I look up at him and ask, "Is everything okay, Lucas?"

He looks down at me, chuckling. "Yep, all good. I'm just looking around. Always got to check to make sure everything is safe for you, my Sweetness, no matter what. You know what I'm saying?"

I nod my head. "Okay, okay, I get it."

Grayson points over to a different building across and down the street. "We're going over here. Let's go." We're looking questioningly, but they're all moving, so asking anything at this time is out. It's simply not an option. They know where we're going, so I guess we're going over to damn building number two. Going through all this traffic, you would think it wouldn't be so much at six-thirty in the morning, but it is. It's Friday, so what do we expect, right? Friday is the beginning of the weekend, so people are probably coming here right now for the weekend. Yeah, that's why it's so crowded.

Entering Swirls Casino/Hotel, we pass through the lobby filled with different assortments of swirls in an array of sizes on a black background with sprinkles of gold glitter. My eyes aren't adjusting well to the patterns. It has a dizzying effect, so I avert my eyes, because there are just too many swirls. Garrison goes over to the front desk and speaks to the receptionist. The young woman heads to the door marked "Manager" and returns, giving him a card key.

Even though there are several good looking guys here, the women are still zoning on my man. Damn, really? He releases my hand, wrapping his arm around my shoulders for all the ladies to see that he's with me. My turn. I lean into him, putting my arms around that muscular waist of his, and now they're gawking at us.

The couches and chairs match the colors in the swirl patterns. Uhm, this is color coordinating at its worst. Leading us to the elevator, Garrison swipes the card key and presses the very top button. R for the roof: it has to be. So we know we're going up to the roof; okay, what's on the roof? I guess we'll find out.

Ava turns to Griffin and says, "Let me tell you something and make one thing known because you didn't ask me. I'm not into bungee jumping or flying, just to go jumping out from the airplane. No, I don't do that. I don't do the parachuting thing or rock climbing, either, unless it's a fake rock and there are inflated cushions on the bottom for me to fall onto."

Using her hands, she counts off each one of the things she doesn't do. Janae and Delia begin groaning, "Oh, boy, here she goes," in the back.

"I don't eat weird foods or octopus or squid, but I eat regular food, okay? I love vegetables, chicken, seafood, some beef, a little pork. I don't do that delicacy stuff, no, no, no, I'm not into that. I am extraordinary, but I like regular things, you get me?"

Griffin cracks up, laughing hard. But I don't think he realizes Ava's staring at him like he's crazy, because he's laughing at her. She scowls at him, which has him and every one of us snickering and cackling until tears form.

"Eva, all the things you said, guess what? I don't do those things either, okay? So, we are on the same page. Let's just go and have a good time. We can get to know each other, because that's what I'm trying to do. And I have some news for you about what we were discussing last night. You all live at Lake Tahoe, right in Incline Village? Have you seen some work being done in the area not far from where you live?"

"Oh, yeah. A lot of acres were bought," Sasha answers.

As the elevator stops at another floor, Garrison says, "Well, that's the land we bought, and we're building a home there. Correction, we're building a couple of homes on that stretch of land we purchased."

Naya's cell rings. Her boss's face appears, and she quickly sends a message. Turning to Garrison, she asks, "What? Are you kidding? Are you serious? You guys are moving to Lake Tahoe?"

All three respond, "Yes."

"I'm moving there, too, as soon as possible, since I can't be without my Sweetness. Lyssa knows already, though."

Shaking her head, Janae laughs. "Lucas, that's no surprise. We had a bet on how soon you'd move to Lyssa, and I win, since I said you weren't going to wait. Booyah! Ladies, you know what you owe me."

They really made bets on him? What the hell? We arrive at the roof, the elevator springs open, and Griffin steps out first. Bowing and gesturing with his hands, he says, "Ladies, after you; our rides await." He grins as we walk out, I guess so we can see what the surprise is. Oh wow, luxury helicopters. Oh crap. I don't like heights, but okay. Everybody's like, "Oh yeah, let's go, we have helicopters!" I haven't opted to get on one, because I'm not a great fan of the chopper, and now I have to get on it.

Lucas squeezes my hand. I glance up at him, and he smiles. "It's going to be okay because I've got you, and we wouldn't go if I didn't think it was safe. I'm right here with you, so that's what I need you to focus on. I'm here with you, and you will be safe."

"How does it seem like you know what goes through my mind a lot of the time? I think something, and you respond; it's crazy. How the hell does that happen? You catch what I'm thinking like a snap of a finger."

"Sweetness, I looked at you, and I can see it written all over your face that you were nervous about the helicopter. I remember my first helicopter ride. As a matter of fact, I felt the same way you do. I never had the desire to ride a helicopter, that's why I'd never been on one, but then I had to for a meeting."

All right, let's get on this damn helicopter already. I've always visualized myself on one and having an adverse reaction. I hope that doesn't come true. My Lucas is with me.

Lucas

THIS will be interesting, because most of them are not into helicopters. But we'll see how they like it. They're going to be on this helicopter for a little while to the Grand Canyon and The Hoover Dam. I've got to keep my hands on my Sweetness, because she's very nervous about this ride. Walking over to the first helicopter are Naya, Garrison, Sasha, Sweetness, and me. In the other chopper are Grayson, Janae, Delia, Steven, Ava, and Griffin.

The pilot and another man and woman from the other side get out of the first helicopter. "Hello, ladies, I'm James, your pilot. This is Michael, my copilot, and Samantha, your hostess, will make sure you are comfortable during this flight." He goes over to Garrison and holds his hand out, and they shake hands. "Nice to meet you, James. We have five ladies who are virgins to flying in a chopper. So no extra tricks." Chuckling with the pilot, Garrison introduces everyone.

"I'll let Samantha show you around and get everyone seated and buckled up." Samantha smiles, "Please follow me, so I can get you all ready, and we can get your trip started." Glancing at Michael, she gives him a sweet smile that he returns. Obviously, they're together. Following Samantha to the point of no return, as my Sweetness just thought to herself. She begins to tremble even more as her nerves take over.

Onboard the chopper, my feet are sinking into the grey plush carpet, and I take one of the dark grey, soft leather seats that can clearly seat about eight people comfortably. Samantha gives us a tour, saying, "If you all look over here, this door to the right is the restroom. We would prefer you only get up after the green light is on over the door. James will also announce it's clear to walk around. Go select your seats, and I'll come over to check your seatbelts."

As I guide my Sweetness to a window seat, she's shaking. Emanating my essence into her, I check out everyone on both aircraft using my vision as we sit. Oh, great; her cousins have that edgy look, except for

Ava. I have to fix this, so slowing time down, I focus to telepathically communicate with the rest of the frightened women in our group.

Everything will be okay, of course. There's no reason for any of you to be afraid. Nothing catastrophic will happen. You are safe. There is no fear that you will have any kind of accident on these aircraft. Calm down now. Relax. Enjoy yourselves.

I watch them take a collective deep breath. The ladies visibly unwind. Grayson, Garrison, and Steven's animals feel that their mates are in a better state. That relaxes them as well. Everything is good, and I turn to my Sweetness and say, "Calm down and relax. Like I said, it'll be just fine." Helping her buckle her seatbelt, she's composed, and so are her cousins.

"I'm feeling calmer now. I don't know if it's just your presence, Lucas, that's making me feel like I can do anything. I know it sounds weird as hell, but that's all I can say."

We're all seated now. Sasha is across from us, sitting in a double seat. Naya and Garrison sit next to us on a three-seat couch with a mahogany table with drink holders separating the area. There's a double seat next to Sasha too. "Sweetness, you can do anything. Truly, all you have to do is believe that. I'm here, and no matter what, I'll always protect you; as I told you, we were made for each other. No one could ever say that's not the case, because I know that for a damn fact."

Samantha's coming over to each of us, checking, and moving the seatbelt and safety lock around, making sure it's secure. "Everyone's seat belt is stable, and we need you to stay in your seats during the flight, unless you have to use the restroom. Usually, we give the itinerary now, but this is a unique circumstance, since it's a surprise for the ladies. So we will tell you the destination when we arrive. I'll say this; you ladies have some men here who have really wanted to show you some beautiful spots around this area."

Giving a thumbs up and winking her eye at the ladies, she goes to the door leading to the cockpit. Pausing in her tracks, she turns to face us again. "If you look down at your seat belt, you will see a blue button. If you need me, click that, and I'll be alerted. I'll be in here before you know it. Does anyone have any questions?"

Sasha raises her hand. "Hi Samantha, I do have a question. Can you give us an ETA to where we're going?"

Laughing and shaking her head, Samantha watches Sasha pointedly as she begins to frown. "You could get an idea of the destination by putting the ETA on your phone. Be patient, Sasha."

"I should know the destination. For one thing, I'm not on a date like everyone else is." She huffs and crosses her legs. "Thanks for nothing, Samantha." She turns to stare aimlessly out of the window.

We nod and laugh at Sasha, and some of us do say, "Yes, got it." The best part is that no one had any questions, since she was very clear.

"Oh, I forgot to ask, would any of you like anything to drink? We have soda, bottled water, and red and white wine, too. I know it's early, but somewhere it's 5pm." She laughs at her own joke as we join in.

"I'd like some water, please," Sweetness asks, and Sasha sulks, "Me too, please."

"Okay, let me get those for you, ladies." Samantha goes to the other side, to the right of the entrance where the refrigerator is. I've helped Sweetness and most of her cousins calm down and relax because they wouldn't have enjoyed anything being so nervous. Racheal, the hostess in the other chopper, just asked about drinks, too. "We don't need liquor this early in the morning, but maybe a couple of cold waters would work," Grayson suggested. Steven agreed, but the ladies declined. Delia's not thirsty now, and Janae and Naya are thinking about their lip gloss coming off. Funny.

Lyssa

MY nerves have totally calmed down, given that there's a fantastic connection between the two of us. I've never felt so in sync with anyone like I do with Lucas. Who else could say it's going to be all right, and you just calm down? The effect that this man has on me is beyond strange. What is rubbing circles into your palm, and tranquility washes over you? How does this work? Mate.

Samantha hands me my cold water. I open it, take a gulp, close my eyes, lean back, and rest my head on the soft leather. Sasha will be singing a different song when Chris gets here with Josh. I can't wait to see how long it's going to take her to get ready if we all end up doing something together.

"Ladies and gentlemen, we will be lifting off in five minutes." Samantha goes into the cockpit and sits behind the pilots.

"Sash, did you bring that cute little black dress of yours with the red sequins? You can wear that to the Club if you have it." Moving my hands and shimmying in my seat, I look at Sash.

"Yes, Lyssa, I have it, especially since you know that's one of my favorite dresses. You all know that." Lifting her left eyebrow at me, I just smile. She's going to be so thrilled that she'll be drop-dead gorgeous when Chris lays his eyes on her.

That dress communicates; specifically, it states I'm a grown-ass woman! Using both of my hands, I give her the thumbs up, and she shakes her head, laughing at me.

Lifting off, it's not what I imagined it would be; most likely, I think, because it's a luxury helicopter. It's not a standard helicopter that's super noisy and shaky like you see on television. It's a very smooth ride. It's not loud. Surprisingly, we didn't have to wear those headphones for noise reduction. I can ride in a helicopter, like this one, I definitely can. Squeezing Lucas's hand just a little bit, he returns it.

He taps my hand. I look up at him, and he's giving me that sexy smile of his. "Sweetness, you're good?"

Searching his eyes, being drawn in, as usual, I reply, "Yes, Lucas, I'm good. This is nothing like I thought it would be. I'm pleasantly surprised."

"I told you, Sweetness. Now, let's relax and have an adventure. I know there's going to be at least one of us with sore feet by the end of today." Taking a glance over at Ava in those damn high heels of hers, he laughs. Griffin tried to warn her.

"Maybe he'll feel sorry for her and carry her when those feet get the best of her. If Ava says anything about it, she's stubborn."

Lucas

RIFFIN stifles a laugh, hiding it by coughing, to let me know he's heard every word. I know you heard me, Griffin, and you know her feet are going to be fucking killing her by the time we're done. So get ready to do your chivalry thing. Even if she doesn't say anything, just do it.

You know I'll carry my mate, even if she doesn't ask, because I know she will be too pigheaded to ask me to help her.

I can see why Sweetness and her cousins wouldn't like that feeling in a regular helicopter ride—the sinking feeling in the pit of your stomach, plus the loud noise. Instead, I can teleport—just pop around where I've got to go, but I can't do that now. Not with my Sweetness; so *not* going to happen. That would freak her the hell out. It'll have to come up one day, but no time soon. We have six hours between the helicopter ride and the stops we have to make.

"Lucas, can you give me an itsy-bitsy hint of where we're going, please, honey?" She's batting her eyelids and blowing a kiss at me; she's so damn funny.

"Sweetness, that'll ruin the surprise, so no, babe, I can't tell you. I'll let you know one thing, though; it's big—no, huge—that's a better word."

When they were small kids, I know they went to the place before, but that was a long time ago. Hopefully, they won't get there and say, "Oh, it's all coming back to me," which is not exciting. Twenty-five minutes have passed, and Samantha's coming back into our area. "Our first stop is a man-made wonder. If you look outside your windows, we're approaching it now." I move closer, so I can look out the window with my Sweetness. I can't act as if I can see and not be looking out that window.

"Oh, I know where we're going! I've seen this in my geology class videos. We're going to the Hoover Dam," Ava blurts out, giddy with excitement and almost bolting up out of her seat because she figured it out.

"Yay, Ava's right; there it is. Okay, it's humongous, but this is the great adventure we're going on? The Hoover Dam? Lucas, now I don't know the brothers. You? No, I would have never thought you would set something up like this. You are cool as hell, Lucas," Sasha states, shaking her head, clearly disappointed in our first stop.

"Enough, Sash, I can't believe you're acting this way. In fact, you've seriously got to be damn kidding me! Is all this necessary? You were the splash of cold water when all someone wanted was a nice, chilled glass of water to drink." Sweetness crosses her arms, scowling. "We're going to have a discussion when we get to the hotel. If you can't find a way to get yourself together and stop being so grumpy and miserable, I hate to say it. I don't know how long our day will be, and you're like Debbie Downer, and it's only the beginning of our day. Sasha, please, I know what is in your head, but you can still have fun and be solo. I'm here, even though Lucas is here too. You know I'd never ignore or forget about you. We all will have a good time together."

CHAPTER 15

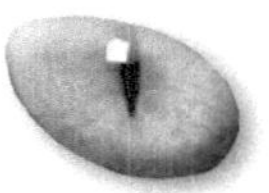

SUPAI VILLAGE

Lyssa

RIDING in this luxury helicopter has been a fantastic experience. Ava, for once, isn't exhibiting her usual awful behavior. We'll get to know each other on an entirely different level now that we know what she's been through.

"Ladies and Gentlemen, we are about to get to the main event. One of nature's seven wonders of the world extends very close to Utah and Nevada's borders. It's entirely in Arizona, though. Before I share, does anyone have any guesses?"

Samantha eyes Ava. "Since you did ask if I have any guesses, I'm going to say the Grand Canyon!" She's doing some weird dance with her shoulders and nodding her head to the beat of her own imaginary song in her excitement.

Samantha laughs. "Bingo! Give Ava a prize, because yes, she's the winner. Kudos to you, Miss Detective." Curtsying, as if Ava were royalty, she continues, "I hope all of you enjoy the majestic Grand

Canyon. First, we'll have an aerial tour, and if you didn't know, the view from up here is spectacular. Next, we'll land at the west rim for a light breakfast, and if you want, a ride down the Colorado River. There'll be cameras for you to take pictures, along with some other items some of you may need." Smiling, she focuses her gaze on Ava, with those heels on. Smirking, Sasha points at those damn boots, drawing everyone's attention to them.

Rolling her eyes, groaning. "Why are you all looking at me? I know how to walk in heels, and I don't think there'll be any type of problem. My boots are good, thank you very much."

Covering his laugh, Griffin coughs into the crook of his right arm. Swiftly giving him a sharp side-eye stare, Ava punches him hard on his other arm. He didn't even flinch. "Mr. Smart-Ass Griffin, what's so funny?"

"This isn't a good idea. We have more plans, and those stilettos aren't going to be a good combination for what we're going to be doing during the next few hours."

Sitting up, she leans forward, putting her hands on her hips. "You wanna make a bet, Mr. Mendasolas? I can guarantee that I'll be problem-free wearing my damn boots."

Shaking his head, Griffin grabs his water, swallowing it with a gulp. "Don't say I didn't warn you, Ava. I would like for you to take advantage of the items that await you when we land. You will need one of them desperately."

"Humph, don't hold your breath, buddy. I'll show you better than I can tell you. I've got this."

Sasha shakes her head, laughing. "I want in on this. I bet you, hmm, what?" She closes her eyes, clearly thinking, then her eyes pop open. "I've got it! A month of you doing my laundry and cleaning my bedroom. I'd add cooking, but all you do is burn food, so that idea's out." Smiling slyly, she knows Ava and how stubborn she is, and that she'll take this bet. And the funniest part is we all know she is going to lose.

Seeing both of their expressions, Griffin observes that they're not joking around and intervenes. "Listen, ladies, there needs to be a point of consensus. It's important to know that if I see that Ava's in pain, I'll pick her ass up."

Frowning, Ava turns back to Griffin, clearing her throat. "Let's get something straight. I'm not a damn baby! I don't want nor need you picking me up. I have two damn feet of my own that can make it wherever we're going."

Shrugging his shoulders, Griffin exasperated, sighs. "Young lady, you can say whatever you want to say, but guess what? It is what it is. Exactly what I just said is what will happen. So maybe you should back out of this bet right now."

Tapping her foot, she replies, "Whatever; you have not been assigned as the boss of me, buddy." Bringing her attention back to Sasha, she says, "We have a bet."

Giggling, Sasha agrees, "Bet." She smiles smugly, because she's getting a cleaner for a whole damn month.

Pulling out our cell phones, we take pictures as we're getting closer to the Grand Canyon and listen to Samantha's tour guide speech about the area. It's beautiful just seeing what nature has created, and man hasn't destroyed any of it. We're landing beneath the west rim, and I guess we really have something unique in store, because there are these big tents up. I don't know what's in them, but we're going to find out.

To the left, there's a boat dock with a wooden deck leading to three pontoon boats. Poor Ava; I don't know how she's going to be able to walk on the ground. There are so many loose rocks she could really get hurt in those stilettos. Griffin is right; he's going to be carrying her before our trip is over, and she's going to raise holy hell. Yep.

Getting up to go outside, Samantha, Ava, Sasha, and I leave first, and wow! We're at the bottom of the canyon. We see the Colorado River up close down here. It's seven in the morning, a beautiful spring day with a light mist, and it's not too hot. Stepping on this rocky terrain isn't comfortable at all, and I don't have a high heel on my boot like Ava does. I'm in awe of this landscape formation that the

Colorado River is responsible for. I slowly spin in a circle; this wild, unspoiled wonder of the world from nature is breathtaking.

"Beautiful." Lucas studies me as I'm enjoying the view.

"I know, right? This is amazing, nature at its best. We visited another part of the Grand Canyon when we were kids, but it wasn't anything like this!" I spread my arms out, admiring the vast, ferocious landscape we're in of over one million acres!

He grabs my hand in his. "Yes, you are, Sweetness; I'm not talking about these rocks. It's all about you."

Heat creeps up my cheeks, and I smile at Lucas; he's just something else. Checking on Ava, she's stumbling as she's walking on the rocks and pulling away from Griffin, nearly falling as he tries to help her. Sasha isn't far behind, laughing her ass off. This is going to be painful; she can't even walk straight. Her heels are very shaky on this rocky terrain.

Everyone else is coming off the other helicopter, and they look like they had an enjoyable trip, laughing and joking. We walk over to the tents to see what's in them. We see delicious croissants, muffins, and drinks. Champagne and orange juice are part of my favorite breakfast drink, which I'm preparing to make right now: a mimosa. Now that I think about it, what would champagne and pineapple juice taste like together?

Looking up, I notice there are several backpacks and cameras with straps lined up on two long tables and about two dozen hiking boots on the side table.

"Eleven backpacks and a bunch of hiking boots, Grayson. Surely I know we're not going hiking around here. That would be crazy." Janae frowns in confusion at Grayson.

Grayson is chewing on a croissant and taking a long swallow of his apple juice. He shakes his head. "Remember, this isn't our last stop, Janae. We're getting back on the helicopters. We're going to take those backpacks, and I really hope you find some boots over there for yourselves and put them on. Our boots are on the other side. These are all for you ladies to try on and see what fits, because we definitely need you all comfortable for what's next."

At that announcement, my cousins and I stop eating and look around at each other. What's next on the guys' agenda? I sneak a peek over at Lucas; damn it, he's looking at me with a big grin on his face. So I guess he thinks this is fun times too, this surprise event that requires us to have damn hiking boots. Quickly sticking my tongue out at him and shaking my head, I proceed over to the boots.

Now he's laughing at me. I take a size nine and try them on my feet, but they're a little tight, so I go a half size bigger, because comfort is a must.

"It's best if all of you wear those boots on the table because we're going to be hiking and walking for about fourteen miles," Garrison says, looking directly at Ava.

"What the hell!" Ava shrieks. Ava is the only one who hasn't changed into the hiking boots. Pointing to a pair of boots that are her size, I say, "Come on, Ava, put on the boots. We all have on hiking boots, because you know what Garrison just said; there will be plenty of walking."

Crossing her arms in irritation, Ava glares at Sasha. "That's not going to work, because you know I have a bet to win. I'm wearing my boots. I refuse to be Sasha's maid for a damn month."

She wobbles away, using her cell instead of the camera to take pictures. Griffin eases over to the boots and takes the pair I pointed out to Ava. Putting them in his backpack, he winks at us with a chuckle. This next wave of our group date is going to be a doozy. We walk around, taking pictures and then eating, then we go back and lift off in the choppers.

Samantha comes out of the cockpit, laughing and announcing, "If you look to the left, you'll see a parking area. This is called the Hill Top. People park here and use the trail that starts there, walking nine miles to the reservation. They can even pay for a helicopter ride to the reservation from the company that the tribe uses. The heat gets more intolerable the later it gets, and that's why most people start very early. We are seven to eight minutes away. Please enjoy the view, everyone." With a smile, she turns and goes into the cockpit.

Thinking back to what Garrison said, why do all this walking when we could just be on the damn helicopter and take pictures? Fourteen miles? Ava is going to have to change into those hiking boots. I close my eyes, counting to ten to myself, to calm down and just go with it like everyone else is. We're having a great time, and I won't ruin it. Hell, I'm mainly worried about Ava and her feet situation. How in the world is this going to work out?

Lucas

THIS has been funny as hell, since Ava is absolutely damn determined to wear those damn stiletto boots. She almost fell five times, and the real walking hasn't begun yet. I don't see how this is going to be good for her. Griffin has his hands full with Ava, and he doesn't even know about what she's going through.

We'll make it better when he finds out, because I know where the bastard is. Madre won't have any issues about saving his ass from the plans that I have for him. He has other crimes, even worse than they know about. Ava could be an entirely different young lady if he kept his fucking hands to his damn self.

"Lucas, if Alyssa gets tired during this fourteen-mile walk, Would you be a gentleman and just sweep her up off her feet and carry her the rest of the way?" Sasha asks with her goofy self, turning to Ava, because that's what this is all about.

"Most definitely, Sasha, I'd pick her up in a heartbeat," I say, wrapping my arms around Lyssa's shoulders. Laughing, Sweetness bats her eyelids up at me.

"Well, that is very kind of you, Sir Lucas. You are such a gentleman." Everyone laughs at her funny southern drawl, and she joins in. We watch the views of the Grand Canyon and take some great pictures as we enjoy this ride.

We land on the reservation's helipad, and as we're all unbuckling our seatbelts, Samantha comes out. "Grayson will be calling when you all are ready to be picked up. Have a great time, everyone."

"Thank you, Samantha," we reply, grabbing our backpacks and stepping out of the helicopter. In the area around us are one-level houses, two markets, and a café. It's a beautiful view, and there are trees and shrubbery, as well. The people who live here get to enjoy this magnificent geological display of layered rock.

Two Native Americans, a woman and a man, twenty-four and twenty-six, exit the store, dressed for hiking, and wearing backpacks. Walking up and smiling, the man greets us. "Hello, everyone, I'm Hania, and this is my younger sister, Aiyana. We're your guides through our reservation and to our breathtaking waterfalls. How was your trip?" He shakes all of our hands with a kind smile, with his sister following.

I reply, "The trip was good, and the view from above is unreal."

"First, let me explain that your group is fortunate to have gotten in for today. We usually book months in advance, but for some strange reason, there were exactly eleven cancelations. Plus, we usually have overnight bookings, four days and three nights, mandatory, not a day trip. I hope you all are ready for a mini adventure! We'll be walking and hiking six to seven miles each way. We're going to see four waterfalls and I really hope you enjoy their beauty." Examining our gear, Hania stops at Ava and frowns. "Most of you are wearing proper gear and footwear for hiking." Looking at Ava, she asks, "What's your name?"

Ava looks at him and replies, "My name is Ava, and it's nice to meet you, Hania."

Opening up his backpack, pulling out some maps, and unfolding one, Hania shows it to Ava. "I need you and everyone else to check out these maps. As you see, we are here," he says, pointing to the little square that's circled with a red marker.

"Now, we have to hike and walk through some rough terrain with plenty of rocks and gravel. For example, Mooney Falls is a 200-foot hike going down. It's very uneven, to top it off, so I need everyone to be careful, okay? Ava, you can't be serious about these boots, because you're going to get hurt. As your guide, I have to tell you it's a terrible idea." Frowning at her, he shakes his head and passes out the maps.

Rolling her eyes and crossing her arms, Ava looks him square in the eye. "I will be just fine, thank you very much. I have a point to prove, and furthermore, a damn bet to win."

Crossing his arms and glaring back at Ava, he says, "If that's the case, then I'm sorry to inform you that when we get to the hiking area, you won't be considered a member of this group, and you won't be given one of these wristbands. We always have our guests sign a waiver of non-responsibility in case they are injured or worse, but this is irresponsible. I suggest you change your mind, or you'll be waiting for us to return."

Ava yells, "Let's see how I do until we get there!" Huffing and puffing, she turns, stomping off unsteadily. Her right boot turns inward, and she falters again. At the moment, there's red dirt on the ground, not a bunch of rocks. Most of us are holding in our laughter, except for Sasha, and she's laughing so hard and holding her stomach, with tears rolling down her face.

"Everyone has bottles of water inside those backpacks, right?" Hania waits expectantly.

Grayson answers, "We do."

Hania, nodding his head in agreement, says, "Let's get this adventure going."

I grab my Sweetness's hand to ensure that she doesn't get hurt out here. We follow Hania and Aiyana along this dirt path that thousands have been through before us. Everyone else is listening to Hania and Aiyana describe the history of the Havasupai tribe being the guardians of the waterfalls and this part of the Canyon.

"Havasupai means 'people of the blue-green water.' We're the only Native American tribe that lives below the rim of the Grand Canyon. Before the Grand Canyon National Park was established in 1910, our tribe lived throughout the canyon."

Observing everything, we stroll by the one-level wooden homes, many of which have gardens. The group is listening intently to Hania except for Ava. She's rushing ahead, while Griffin's closer to us but keeping a close eye on her.

Hania continues, "Traditionally, we lived in two areas here, in Supai Village; this was our summer home. During the wintertime, we lived spread out on the South Rim in the area known as Grand Canyon Park. Our people planted crops during the spring and summer months here and brought the rest with us to the South Rim."

Passing by the tourist office and the Havasupai School, Hania points to it. There's a playground on the property, and the tall, wrought iron fence around the school is a damn good safety measure with all of the visitors that come. "This is the school our children attend from kindergarten thru eighth grade, and after our children graduate, they attend boarding schools for secondary education."

We're approaching a little brown church with a sign pointing in the lodge's direction, but we aren't headed that way.

Aiyana chimes in with a sigh, looking toward the other side of the canyon. "At first, our reservation here in Supai was only five miles by three miles. Our original reservation didn't even include our world-famous waterfalls. We still have a population of Havasupai living inside the National Park today. We have about six hundred fifty members right now. Many Native American tribes were from here in the Grand Canyon thousands of years ago. As our history says, many of the tribes separated and went their own ways. There's more, but I like to focus just on our tribe."

Walking past, we greet other people on the trail who are clearly visitors and wave to other members of their tribe. "Please don't take pictures of our people or homes. You may take shots of the waterfalls, the canyon scenery, or other visitors if they agree."

There she is, our pain in the ass, but she's a work in progress. We have to remember that. She can be so embarrassing, our Ava. Sweetness and the other ladies are all having similar thoughts about Ava.

Wobbling even more than she was at the west rim, she may break her heels in light of the rougher terrain here. Griffin shakes his head, takes long strides, and catches up with Ava, trying to have a conversation, but she's stubborn. She turns away from Griffin, speeding off, and it finally happens! The heel on her right boot is caught between two medium-sized rocks, and it snaps off. Losing her balance, her arms flail in every direction, and her body tries to stop the fall from happening. Despite all of her efforts, Ava tumbles, twists her ankle, and crashes on her ass, screaming.

CHAPTER 16

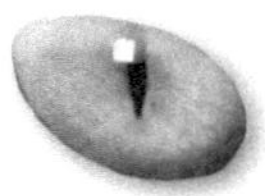 

HARDHEADED LITTLE HELLION

Lucas

I F I could, I'd laugh my ass off at Ava right now. That would up-set my Sweetness unnecessarily, though, so with this in mind, I laugh inwardly. Hania, rubbing his forehead, turns away from Ava, shoulders shaking, and tries his best to hold in his laughter. He wipes his eyes while letting out a dry cough, and Ayiana walks over to him, muttering, "She's truly ridiculous," irritated with the entire Ava situation.

Where did this young woman come from? Everyone else in the group seems to have sense but her. You see the family resemblance, so she's not a friend. I never judge a book by its cover, but she's spoiled rotten, in light of the actions that she's blatantly displayed. She may have ruined this trip for her family and their dates by being a nincompoop, using the term that my college roommate used for idiots in our dormitory.

Three small dogs scurry along the path with a teenage boy from the village chasing them. They race up to Ava. Sniffing her leg, they leap backward, showing their teeth while making low, rumbling sounds soaked with hostility. This causes Ava to get angrier. She roars back at them with a sound that's not entirely human. The dogs cower, tails between their legs, then turn, running in the direction they came from, speeding past the teenager.

The boy stares at Ava; he's confused by what's happened, and so is everyone else except for the brothers, and I know that the ladies have an alpha gene. Even I can't tell what beasts are sleeping within: after witnessing that shit with Ava, maybe it's a lioness, tigress, or some type of feline.

"What the Hell, Ava? This girl, I can't do this with her." Naya gives Ava a dirty ass look and walks away in the other direction, with Garrison close behind. *I know she's been through Hell, so we can give her a pass for some things. Ava not wanting to change into safe footwear is pure idiocracy. These men probably think she's freaking brainless, and why would we even have her come with us to Vegas in the first place? Thanks to Ava, my first date with Garrison has been annihilated. You can't choose who your family is, though, right?*

Garrison's following Naya with a smirk on his face. *Unreal. Ava is in a league of her own. I've never met anyone like her, and hopefully, she doesn't have a doppelganger that we'll ever meet. Ava's selfish, spoiled, and obstinate, or better yet, stubborn as a mule, as our Father would call her. She's the perfect match for Griffin's beasts. Damn, I'm glad I'm not him. I've never heard of a shifter's beast being wrong about a mate. Then again, there's a first time for everything. In the meantime, we shall see. Maybe there's much more to Ava than meets the eye.*

Janea and Delia's mouths drop wide open, and their shock shows on their faces. "Dammit, Ava." Adelia immediately breaks out, sprinting to Ava, with Steve and Janae not far behind.

Janae's taking slow steps; her thoughts are similar to Naya's. Why, why, dammit? Why, Ava? She never listens to anything that makes any sense. All she had to do was put on the damn hiking boots, and she wouldn't be on the ground right now, probably freaking hurt. Crap, the whole day is going to be ruined. Thank you, little cousin, thank you so much.

Griffin tried to help her, but she was, you know, being that pain in the ass. Even though I could have slowed time down to assist her, in my opinion, she deserves this one hundred, no, one thousand percent. People close by immediately surround Ava, wanting to help her.

"Miss, are you okay?" A young man rushes over and leans down to her. Seeing the broken heel of the boot, he picks it up off the ground, examining it and twirling it on his fingers, as he shakes his head. "Oh, wow, wearing these boots wasn't a good idea."

Ava's face and neck flush, and she wrinkles her nose, sneering at him. "I don't need you or anyone else telling me a damn thing! How about you mind your own business?" She waves her hand in a dismissive gesture at him.

"Then I guess I'll be on my way then. Suit yourself, girly." He gets up with a frown on his face at her rudeness. Dropping the heel next to her, he goes over to his friends, and they all glare at Ava.

"Boom! Yes, I knew it was going to happen! A hard head equals a soft butt. Well, in Ava's case, a hurt ankle and foot," Sasha gleefully shouts with her fist in the air. On the other hand, the rest are hoping that this fall of hers doesn't ruin our dates. Ava's damn irrational, foolish decision to wear her boots on a hike has landed her in this predicament.

Griffin, running to Ava and squatting down, gently pulls off her boot and sock. He examines her ankle and foot, touching it tenderly. She closes her eyes and clenches her teeth. Groaning, battling the waves of pain as her eyes threaten to fill with tears, she inhales sharply. Regret is plastered on Griffin's face because she's injured, and he knows that he could have stopped her. The rest of us sprint to check on Ava as Griffin lifts her up, putting her over his shoulder like a sack of damn potatoes.

Ava, hitting Griffin's back, angrily shouts, "Put me down, you big, muscled up—"

"Ava, are you okay?" Delia interrupts. She is the first to get to her, walking up behind Griffin.

"I'm fine. If Griffin stopped acting like a damn superhero, everything would be peachy. Listen, Griffin put me down! I'm okay; I can limp, I'm good," Ava yells, wriggling over his shoulder.

Exhaling, he curtly answers, "Ava, do you seriously want to do this crap with me right now?"

"I told you, I don't want or need your ass doing anything for me!"

"Fine!" He unceremoniously lifts her off of him, dumping her feet first on the ground.

"Ohhhh, owwww!! Griffin!" Ava cries out before falling, and Griffin catches her before she hits her ass again on the ground.

Once again, he picks her up. Now Ava is hanging over Griffin's shoulder like an overgrown sack of spoiled fucking onions. "Are you going to behave your damn self, young lady? Your attitude stinks, and honestly, it's unattractive and embarrassing. Next time, you're going to get something in return from me, and I guarantee you won't like it."

"Okay! I need your help, Griffin. Can you relax your macho man attitude?"

"Can you stop acting like a—crazy lady? Believe me, there's another word I'd say, but I won't."

Griffin shakes his head. Turning to Hania, he says, "The first waterfall is Navajo, right? Do you think I could bring Ava there for a while? I'll call for our helicopter if she gets too uncomfortable."

"Seriously? How about you ask me? Don't just assume that I want to go right there." Ava's back, being a damn little spitfire. She needs a mountain of cold ass water splashed on her.

Hania raises his eyebrows at Ava, then focuses on Griffin. "Yes, it is, but it's not going to be easy to get to with you carrying Ava. I recommend going to Havasu Falls, and we can meet you guys after we're done at Fifty Foot and Navajo falls for a while before going to the other two."

Actually, I could get there quickly, but then Ava would discover that I have some unique skills, letting the cat out of the bag about me being a shifter before I'm ready for her to know.

Pointing towards a group of people setting up camping equipment a short distance down the road, Hania continues, "To the right of the campsite, you'll see the first sign for Havasu Falls up there. After that sign, there are several more along the path leading you right there. By the way, just to give you fair warning, you have to go over a little bridge, but that's much safer than any of the other falls."

Lyssa

SASHA'S the only one taking her slow sweet time to check on Ava. She should have been the first one to Ava, as she's our doctor, the only one who is a resident.

"Griffin, let's walk up here to the campsite to sit Ava on a bench so I can examine her ankle. Ava, you know you lost the bet, right? Okay, you don't have to answer, given that we have all these witnesses to emphasize that you are a loser. After all, you fell on your ass. Yes, you did!" At this precise moment, Sasha is the smuggest young woman in the universe.

She must know that Ava's not severely hurt; I guess she has ESP, since she's dancing and making faces at Ava as she follows behind. We arrive at the campsite, observing several tents, equipment, and people heading out with their gear on.

I tug Lucas's hand, and he pauses. "Lucas, You know if Ava is seriously hurt, we may have to cut our trip short."

Shrugging, then rubbing the back of his neck, Lucas regards all of us. "No, Sweetness, she can relax with Griffin or even go get it checked out. Furthermore, no one else should have to miss the opportunity of viewing some of the most beautiful waterfalls in the country. This is Ava's fault, not to mention that it was absolutely stubborn and ridiculous wearing those damn stiletto boots here. Hell, no."

Lucas isn't joking, and he's very determined that Ava doesn't sabotage our plans, since she brought this on herself. He places a loose strand of hair behind my ear; that gesture reminds me of my mom. I have so many memories of her doing that since I was a young girl. I know Tia Amy has been telling me in our sessions that my family would want me to live my life, have fun, and definitely help with Joaquin. Even right now, sadness and guilt are creeping in. *This is not the time or place for this,* I think, as I take deep unsteady breaths while trying to calm my trembling.

"I need a few minutes with my Sweetness over here, so we'll be there with you all before you can miss us," Lucas tells the rest of our group. Grayson glances at Lucas then at me, saying, "We'll see how Ava is, but please don't wander off and get lost. Additionally, we have enough problems from little Ava; we don't need any more." Winking his eye at us with a chuckle, he strolls away with everyone.

Lucas and those mesmerizing eyes are gazing deeply into the depths of what may be my soul. Ripples of tranquility flow through me, halting the emotional turmoil that has been building inside of me.

"You know you can talk to me about anything, right, Sweetness? No matter what it is, I'm here for you, and we can discuss anything. No embarrassment or assuming that I can't help. Can you agree to that? If you don't want to burden your cousins or other family members, I'm here." He leans in for a quick kiss, then rests his forehead on mine.

"Yes, I can't explain it, but I know that we have an intense connection that I've never experienced before. There's something, maybe it's my intuition, that knows you would help with anything I need."

Lucas swiftly grabs me. He lifts me up by my waist, pulling me close as a group of people jog past, their boots digging in the path, creating dirt clouds. Every nerve is exploding in my body like we're magnetized, and he's the missing piece.

"Excuse us, sorry about that," two of the young men call out as they're passing by. What is it about Lucas that he has this effect on me?

"I need you to be able to invite me into every facet of your world. Nothing is off limits, and for the most part, I will share what I can with you."

"That sounds like two different meanings, but we can discuss it later, Lucas. I'm feeling better, so let's go see what the diagnosis is for Ava."

A warm breeze rustles the trees, and a small piece of shrubbery carried on the wind lands in Lucas's hair. As I remove it, I can't help but run my fingers through those silky, wavy curls. His gorgeous smile distracts me; subsequently, I forget what I was thinking about. *Oh my God, snap out of it, woman, get it together*, I chuckle at myself for once.

Watching Lucas, there's something extraordinary about him; just a few minutes ago, I was struggling to control my emotions, but when he touches or looks at me, somehow it soothes me. What the Hell is that about?

"Let's go check on Ava, even though we all know this is her fault. I really hope this is a minor injury."

Lucas

WALKING up to the campsite, Griffin delicately lowers the little Hellion, Ava, onto the bench. She grimaces, throwing daggers at him with her eyes. We all know she's miserable and in a considerable amount of pain. This is a perfect time for Griffin to get acquainted with Ava, because we're going exploring without her.

Damn it, now I'm stuck with cleaning Sasha's clothes and her freaking room for a whole month! Hell, if we were on a regular date instead of hiking, this crap wouldn't have happened. Our dates have gotten me in this predicament. This is Grayson, Garrison, Lucas, and mainly Griffin's fault that I'm hurt! Hopefully, I'm hurt enough to squirm my way out of this situation that Sasha is gloating about.

Freaking crap! How did I get hurt when I walked carefully on the uneven rocks and dirt? This is so unfair. Griffin; humph, who the Hell does he think he is? Telling what's going to happen the next time? He isn't the damn boss of me, and I'll show his ass as soon as I can walk on my damn own. I have to admit he is good looking, but he is kind of domineering with that next time sentence and what I get and his so-called guarantees.

This girl is truly a piece of work. How does she think this was our fault when she was told not to wear those high heels? Fuck, we even had boots for everyone, and she, being the adamant little Hellion, refused to wear them. This isn't due to her history; this is an attitude she exhibits frequently.

I don't know if there's any help for Griffin with this young lady, so, in other words, better him than me. She acts like an idiot, and she's way past headstrong. I honestly don't think I'd have the patience for her if she were my mate. I definitely would use my talents on her and damn the consequences, if any.

Ava's twenty-one years old, so that's four more years until she can officially become Griffin's mate if she chooses him. If he becomes her boyfriend shortly, I guess that would be acceptable to her father. I can guarantee that one of Griffin's animals will encourage him to decide how to subtly mark their mate. She's going to drive him to the mental ward if she doesn't get her act together.

Sasha walks over to a group setting up tents across from Ava. Their curiosity is sparked, so they're watching us. She approaches a young woman. "Hello, can I borrow your backpack chair, please? I'm a doctor, and I need to examine my whining cousin over here." She points to Ava while she pouts and cries louder, "Ow, ooh my ankle!"

"Oh, my goodness, sure you can. Dave, hand me the blue one." She turns to the burly man sitting next to her with the unoccupied chair behind him. "Thank you so much." Sasha beams at her.

Swiftly rising, his head hitting the tree branch, Dave scowls. He rubs his head, muttering to himself, "Fuck, how did I forget that was there that damn fast?" The rest of the group laughs and shakes their heads in disbelief. Why are they laughing? Dave's clumsy but the sweetest person in the group. Grabbing the chair, Dave smiles at Sasha, leading the way, and brings the chair to Griffin.

"Thank you, Dave," Sasha says.

"No problem. Glad to help. I hope she's not seriously hurt," Dave says to Sasha.

"My cousin over here is probably praying that she is severely hurt. Of course, I hope it's a minor injury. Let me get to work." She sits in the chair, lifting Ava's leg onto her lap. It's already beginning to swell.

Definitely in doctor mode, the joking around has stopped. Sasha's fingers softly apply pressure to Ava's ankle. Ava screams as if someone has committed bloody damn murder.

No longer pretending or exaggerating, tears stream down her cheeks. Ava sobs like a baby who fell out of its crib.

"Lucas, I think she's really injured, so we have to get her to a hospital to get an x-ray on her ankle or foot. Damn, I'm not comfortable just leaving her here, even though she's with Griffin."

"Wait a minute, Sweetness, it'll be like a date for them to get better acquainted. The only thing that's going to happen is that he will carry her directly down to the waterfall. We're all in the area, and we know him; correction, I know him. Oh, and I can guarantee that nothing will go wrong."

Glancing over at our little Hellion's foot, she does have a hairline fracture. I can't say anything, because then they'll ask me how the Hell I know this. Sweetness is shaking her head with a troubled frown on her face.

Sighing, I lift her chin with my two fingers to look into her eyes. "This is not Ava meeting some guy doing what she did the other day. So, let's go and have a good time. Seriously, what can you do? For example, if she has a sprain or even a little fracture, what are you going to do? Let Griffin cater to her right now."

She turns her attention back to Ava, watching Sasha tend to her as she still whines in pain. Griffin is watching with deep concern etched on his face, thinking, *I'm the unluckiest shifter fucking ever to have her as my mate. This has to be a fucking nightmare. Wake me up, please.*

Watching Sasha, she's thinking the same thing that I already discovered. *Crap, Ava needs an x-ray, and I'll be with her, so she won't be able to exaggerate her diagnosis. I could be wrong, but I believe she has a hairline fracture, requiring a boot or cast. Thank God she still lives at home and not with us.* Sasha shakes her head, opens her backpack, and brings out an ace bandage to wrap Ava's foot and ankle.

"Ava and Griffin, the adventure in Havasu Falls are over today for you two. We have a trip to the hospital to make. Call the pilot. No need for all of us to go and ruin a great time, so I'll go with them. I'll call once we know exactly what's going on with Ava."

Ava totally breaks down crying. She lowers her head, takes the tissues Griffin gives her, and noisily blows her nose. Griffin picks her up, and the three of them walk back toward the helipad. Grayson calls to get one of the pilots back here. My, my, my, maybe our little Hellion will listen to reason next time.

Chapter 17

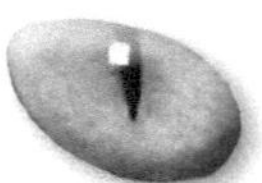

Exploring Havasu

Lucas

I REPEAT what I said to them before Sasha left. "Sasha reiterated what I told all of you a few minutes ago, and she was correct in saying we all didn't have to go. Now ladies, let's wipe those angry and worried expressions off of your faces so that we can explore more of the beauty in one of the Seven Wonders of the World."

Grayson sighs. "Lucas is telling the truth. First and foremost, if she were injured under a different set of circumstances, I'd consider leaving, but that's not the situation. It would be unfortunate for us not to take advantage of this opportunity. We couldn't do anything for Ava but sit and wait, anyway. Also, Sasha's with them, and she's a damn genius to be a resident at the young age of twenty-four. Ava's safe and in excellent hands between those two. What we can do is enjoy this time and continue with our date. What if we explore the closer waterfalls and skip seeing Beaver Falls since it's the furthest?"

Beads of sweat form on her forehead and pour in tiny rivulets down her face and the back of Naya's neck. She fixes her hair into a high ponytail and wraps it into a bun on top of her head. Getting a pink handkerchief from her pocket, Naya lightly wipes her face and neck.

"I want to see everything. I'm not leaving here for Ava, because as usual, it's her damn fault for being freaking ridiculous. We can show her all of the gorgeous pictures that we'll be taking from the waterfalls. Lead the way, Hania." With a silly expression on her face, she quickly spins and places her hands on her hips, facing Hania, with the group laughing at her. Naya has effectively broken the tension that her cousins were experiencing by talking about the little Hellion.

Hania, nodding his head in agreement, says, "If you want, we can skip the last waterfall; it's not a problem if you want to check on your cousin. Come on, so we can get moving before it gets scorching out here. Most people think they're prepared for our heat until they get a blast of it, especially during the summer months."

Grabbing a bottle of water from his backpack, Hania explains, "Secret number one is to stay hydrated and also check your backpacks for headgear, meaning the caps inside. In an hour or two, the sun will be bathing you all, and those caps are a necessity. Follow me to some of the most spectacular waterfalls you'll ever see and, you'll never forget. I call them our very own pieces of paradise."

Finally, we're leaving. I can't wait to see my Sweetness's reaction to these falls.

"Our land is sacred, and everyone who visits has different experiences for the most part, but there's one thing they all have in common. Please share with me your experience and what you got out of it at the end of the tour," Hania says as we walk. The sun beats down on us. Steven, Grayson, Garrison, and I are dry as cactuses, but our ladies are sweating quite a bit. Shifters have a much higher body temperature, and I'm not affected by hot or cold weather. Turning off from the main trail, Hania leads us down to a creek, and we cross over to the other side. Janae inhales and exhales deeply. Grinning and laughing giddily, she asks, "Is it me, or is anyone else overcome with relaxing, cheerful vibes? Delia, Lyssa, or Naya, or any of you guys?"

"I agree, yes, the peacefulness here is undeniable. I wish we could go swimming. You know, once we get to the falls, I'd love to cool off. If only we had bathing suits we could change into." My Sweetness is peering longingly towards the tree-shaded area where the water's streaming.

Naya strolls over to the edge of the creek, picks up a branch, and places it in, and it forms swirl patterns in the sparkling, wonderfully clear, and transparent water.

"We purchased some swimsuits overnight at a boutique, a couple in different styles for each of you; check your backpacks. We prepared ahead for all of you young ladies to go swimming," Grayson explains, turning and following Hania. With the little Hellion out of our way, this is a much better situation. Ava will eventually mature; of course, it will take some time.

Sweetness, stopping to examine a flowering cactus, says, "It's extraordinary how these flowers bloom in the day and close at night."

"It's a survival mechanism because if they don't close, they'll be susceptible to the intense sunlight and heat when it's at the highest point. From twelve midnight until four in the afternoon, the flowers stay in bloom." Naya joins in, touching the silky red petals.

Hania, with a surprised expression, nods, "That's correct, Naya, not many people are aware of this fact."

"I had a geology course as an elective, and I wrote a research paper about the five different ecosystems in the Grand Canyon. I learned quite a lot doing the research," Naya says.

"I know that was a lot to learn, especially about the differences in weather; for example, the North Rim's conditions." Aiyana and Hania both chuckle, giving a meaningful glance at each other.

Naya, sighing at the memories of her doing all of that work, replies, "Oh, yeah, over a million miles of the Grand Canyon, and the North Rim is the coldest due to the higher elevation, but I was surprised reading that it snows there."

Janae adds, "We all learned about the Grand Canyon, but we didn't get any information about the Supai or this area. You missed this, Naya."

"This area isn't what I was studying, Janae, remember? I studied Ecosystems of the Grand Canyon, not beautiful places to visit in the Canyon." Smirking at Janae, Naya shakes her head.

"Yeah, yeah, yeah, point taken into consideration. I retract my accusation. Are you satisfied, little cousin?" Janae says, grinning at Naya playfully.

"Yes, I'm ecstatic that you know that I thoroughly investigated the ecosystems here. By the way, I got an A-plus on that research paper. Boom!" She makes a silly face, sticking her tongue out and raising her manicured thumbs toward Janae and laughing. Unable to hold straight faces, we all join in with Naya, cracking up.

The closer we get to the falls, the more they relax; it has to be the aroma from the vegetation, along with the fresh water surrounding us. I restrain myself from using my gifts to look ahead and get a glimpse of our first destination. I'll wait with everyone else; then I'll get the total effect of the falls with my Sweetness and the group so that we can experience this together.

Lyssa

REVELING in the pure, untouched beauty, we have the privilege of this unique experience. This is an unusual first date. "So many different people are visiting. Honestly, I'd love to stay here, but in the lodge or one of the guest houses, not the campsites. I don't go camping anymore since a few years ago." Leaving the creek, we are brought into another world. The area is full of wild shrubbery in a host of different sizes, grass, and trees that hide sections of the pools of water.

I get my bottled water from my backpack. Drinking the cold water quenches my thirst, plus it has a cooling effect as it flows down. Unzipping the top of my bag, I take out the black cap with Havasupai written on it, and put it on my head.

"Oh, I need my hat on, too. Wait a second." Janae follows my lead, then Naya and Delia do the same.

"This is weird. We ladies are getting damp from perspiring, and it's a well-known fact that men sweat much more, but the only one who's sweating somewhat is Hania, and he is accustomed to this weather, so it's not surprising. The rest of you males, though, I don't understand." Naya stares suspiciously at Grayson, Garrison, Steven, and Lucas.

Laughing, they all shrug, looking at each other and then at us, and Lucas answers, "I can say we're some of the lucky men out of millions who don't have that problem." We all frown at that answer. What the Hell? "Ladies, don't hate; appreciate."

None of us want to hear that, so we continue strolling deeper into this wild, magnificent world of rock. In the azure blue sky, there are fluffy clouds that remind me of cotton balls. The bright sun shining on the tall limestone mountains reflects caramel, sienna, blue, and soft orange layers. It's incredible.

"What made you guys pick this for our date today, Grayson?" Janae asks. She plays with his cowboy hat, tilting it up and down.

"This was all Griffin's idea. Some employees came here about a year ago and talked about their trip and how beautiful it was to him. When we decided that we would have a group date, he was a beast man on the computer and phone, making inquiries about coming here."

"Griffin did all of that work and didn't get to enjoy anything, thanks to Ava. I'd never let her live this one down if I were him." Steve laughs, sharing his opinion on Ava's and Griffin's situation.

We hear clicking sounds in the distance, and as we're moving, it's also getting louder. A surge of curiosity causes me to focus my attention on the sound coming from high above us. Suddenly, several bats soar out of the humongous limestone. Their black wings are flapping, then spreading in unison, creating a row following the leader, whose clicks are the loudest.

"I think I'm crazy; this the first time I've ever seen bats flying outside in the daytime. I thought they only come out at night and fly back early in the morning, you know, during the sunrise." Delia is stumped at the bats being out in the daytime. I'm surprised as well, but I don't say anything.

Hania explains, "It's only a few bats; we do see this every now then, and there's no need to worry. Just remember one thing; never touch a bat. No matter where you are, in order to build cities, their habitat has been destroyed for the sake of progress. Bats are wild animals, and you don't approach them. They can't be domesticated, contrary to the opinions of many other people who have been here in the past."

Naya shakes her head. "Ava's not here Hania. None of us would go touching a damn bat. I'm just saying."

The bats fly in two circles, then up nearly to the top of another limestone, so it was a short outing for them. Garrison points out the other limestone that's their destination, so everyone can observe. The breeze is much warmer than earlier, with the sun lighting up the canyon.

My cell rings with Sasha's ringtone. "Hey Sash, how's Ava? I'm putting you on speaker." Tapping the speaker button on, everyone listens.

"She has a hairline fracture from her calcaneus; that's from her heel to her ankle. They're putting a cast on her now, and Griffin's in the examining room with the crybaby. They gave her some heavy pain medicine, but she probably won't need to use it all. She was ridiculous and embarrassed the Hell out of us."

"Only Ava. I have no sympathy for her butt, either."

"Griffin has the pilot on the roof waiting, so we'll probably be brought back to the hotel. She just took the pain medicine about fifteen minutes ago. I told her silly self that our bet is still on, and she'll pay up after she's all healed up in two to three months." Sasha is laughing again.

"Okay, we'll take plenty of pictures for you guys. I'll talk to you later, Sis."

"Bye, Sis, see you all later."

"We were just talking about Ava a little while ago, and then we get the call. I don't know how Ava's going to be out of commission for two to three months." Naya is frowning, and my cousins all know how Ava is. That girl can't sit still for long before she's up going somewhere.

"Griffin will find time to assist with keeping Ava at home." Grayson chuckles while sliding his fingers along the side of his cowboy hat.

Janae, shaking her head, says, "Oh, Grayson, I don't know about that; our Uncle Austin isn't too keen on male visitors. Ava hasn't had a boyfriend, you know; she, umm, has male friends that she, you know, how can I say this? She spends time with them. That's the best I can come up with as an explanation. Our uncle doesn't know about them, either, so it'll be interesting to see how he responds. Griffin is someone seriously interested in dating Ava."

Delia, watching a group of mules going towards another trail, comments. "Our Uncle Austin is more than overprotective, and soon it's going to be on a different level. He may have someone with her frequently. And then there's Griffin's age; she's twenty-one, and I can guarantee that's going to be an issue."

Naya interjects, "No, I don't think so; as long as Griffin show's he respects Ava, there shouldn't be a problem."

Garrison, chewing on a sugar cane stick, pulls it out to talk. "We all have respect for family, and our parents raised us the right way. Crap, our Madre would slap the taste out of our mouths if we disrespected any woman or her family."

Aiyana stretches her neck to the left then right. "Can we walk while you all discuss Ava and Griffin, please?"

Garrison continues, "Griffin will approach your uncle as an elder and talk to him about his intentions. Ava is a handful, and my brother has a magnitude of work on his hands, dealing with her. She's a special young lady, indeed, and it'd be a great disservice to her if any of you coddle her."

Naya makes an exasperated noise and replies, "I've never coddled Ava or anyone else in my life; she's only one year younger than I am. If anything, I'm the toughest on her out of my cousins. There's more than meets the eye when it comes to Ava." Taking an orange out of her bag, she holds it up. "An orange's skin is bitter if you try to eat it, but peeling it to the inside, it's delicious. Hopefully, Griffin has gained the patience he'll need to endure Ava, since it is one of the virtues."

Touching a boulder, Grayson laughs, "I've got to be honest with you all; as a matter of fact, I'm thrilled as Hell that I'm not Griffin. I wouldn't trade places with him for anything in the entire world."

"You've got that right, bro, neither would I. She's Hell to deal with." Steve gets an elbow in the side from Delia for his comment. "Hey, I'm not the only one who feels that way, babe. Don't get upset with me; you know how your cousin Ava is."

Kicking a rock clear across the path, Delia speeds up, walking past Steve, and catching up to Aiyana. Steve's in hot water with her, and he's so dense that he doesn't have a clue. The guys all know and simultaneously shake their heads. "What's up? Why are you all watching me?" Steve tilts his head in confusion; clearly, this man is lost and not at all in the loop.

"You're in the doghouse, man, and she's irritated; I'd say she's downright pissed off with you. That's your fiancé, and you don't know when you've upset her? We've just met, and it's obvious," Garrison explains, glancing at Delia then back to Steve.

"Rule number one: no matter what she says about her family, you're her support, her partner, and if you, for some reason, think she's going overboard in complaining, you can give positive comments. Never be the instigator or negatively talk about her family, Steve."

"Fuck, man, damn!" Steve breaks into a run, catching up to Delia. She shakes her head angrily and points her finger at him, probably telling him off. Aiyana watching them for about a minute then begins walking ahead, not desiring to listen to the argument that Steve is losing. If he just apologizes and convinces her that he won't speak that way again, she'll calm down.

"Hania, is there anyplace we can change into our swimsuits once we arrive at the falls?" Janae asks what we really should've asked once we found about the bathing suits.

"There aren't any bathrooms in those areas; actually, we only have some outhouses along some of the trails. You can find some shrubbery to hide behind and change. That's what most visitors do, unless they're wearing suits underneath their clothes."

We're basically out of the modern world; additionally, the thought of having to use the outhouse is unappealing, to say the least. I'd rather pee behind the damn bushes, then I won't be assaulted by other people's bathroom body waste using an outhouse.

Chapter 18

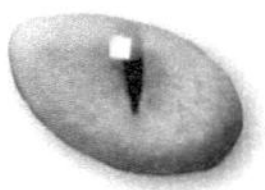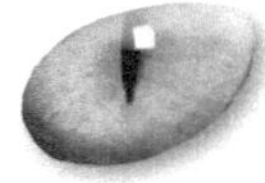

Cliff Jumping?

Lyssa

WE'RE almost at the waterfall; a distinct bubbling and burbling becomes louder. The freshness of the air, the water, the greenery, even the dirt is invigorating, but at the same time relaxing. I know that's weird, but it's what it is. It's precisely what was said earlier when we were at the creek: the area has its effect.

A cold mist hits my skin, bringing a refreshing chill. A few goosebumps rise on my skin. We come to a standstill, absorbing it all. The path shimmers with the heat from the sun. I pour a splash of my water on the ground, and some smokey steam is released. It's not that late, so it's going to be hot when we arrive at the other falls later.

"My God! This is, oh! This is freaking spectacular!" An enthusiastic Delia screams, "Hurry up and get up here, you guys!"

Speeding up from our slow stroll, we turn to the right, passing even more shrubbery and other greenery. I stop in my tracks at the view before me, gasping in astonishment at the layered pools of blue-green, glistening, bubbling water, whooshing down from one pool to the other. "I wasn't expecting anything like this!" Naya grabs the camera from her backpack and takes pictures, as a photographer would.

In awe, Grayson surveys it all, his voice filled with the excitement of a kid on his favorite carnival ride. "Wow! Just damn, wow! This is stunning. Griffin missed this. Damn, you know what? I'm videoing all of the waterfalls for him."

Forgetting to exhale, I have a coughing fit, and Lucas pats my back. Recovering, I say, "This is simply gorgeous! I mean, are all the waterfalls this color? First, I've never seen water similar to this color outside of the tropics. What causes this?" I'm speaking to Hania or Aiyana, never taking my eyes away from the water.

Grinning with a twinkle in her eyes, Aiyana laughs, saying, "It's the chemistry of the water, rocks, limestone, and minerals. The color has always been this way, and we want to keep it as it is, protecting the natural beauty of all our waterfalls."

"Damn, this is fucking incredible. There are four more waterfalls to see, and usually the best is never the first place you visit. Sweetness, I'm definitely glad that we stayed, and the expression on your face solidifies that. Who isn't enjoying this view?" Lucas winks at my cousins, grinning.

Janae and I both laugh first, and Delia and Naya join in. Janae gives Lucas a high five, saying, "I'm glad we didn't all go to the hospital, so, I admit that you and Sasha were right."

"Damn sure; we both were one hundred percent accurate; the only thing the guys and I are wondering is if you ladies have enough stamina to get through the rest of the activities we have planned." Lucas wiggles his eyebrows up and down after giving us this information.

"Lucas, Grayson, Garrison, and you, Mr. Soon-To-Be-My Husband, or maybe not." Delia pauses to scowl at Steve, then exhales and continues. "How about we enjoy the activities that we are partaking in at this moment? Sounds like a fantastic idea to me, and I can speak for all of the ladies." Delia's obviously still unhappy with Steve, even though she loves this scenery.

"Can we find somewhere to change so we can get into this beautiful spring?" Naya's bouncing on the balls of her feet, tapping on Garrison's arm. He takes her hand in his, turning to Hania to ask, "Hania, my date over here, is about to explode from the anticipation that's building. Where's the entrance to get in?"

Hania points from where we standing on this cliff overlooking the area and explains. "We're seeing lower Navajo Falls; you'll see Upper Navaho Falls as we walk up ahead. It'll be easier to start from Upper Navaho Falls and travel down. Once we're at Upper Navajo Falls, you can swim or do whatever you'd like to. There are plenty of areas to take phenomenal pictures in each of the falls. Now, I can turn a blind eye if someone wants to cliff jump into the falls here. With the other falls, cliff jumping isn't gonna happen. Upper Navajo is fifty feet high, and lower Navajo is thirty feet high, and they connect. Many years ago, it was one fall, then we had a flood. We won't try the shorter way of tumbling straight down through the rocks, shrubs, and dirt; as tempting as it may look, it's dangerous. Are you all ready?"

We all signal that we are ready. Naya gives a thumbs-up, and Hania and Aiyana wave at some teenagers, calling out to them from the trail behind us. I appreciate the landscape and the serenity it brings me. I peek at my phone; time passes quickly. Will we even be able to see all of the falls?

A group of sizeable thick shrubbery and large boulders look like an inconspicuous place for our wardrobe change. I tape Lucas's hand, and his eyes meet mine. Pointing to that area, I say, "That appears to be a private area where we can change into our swimsuits. Ladies first, and then the men can go." Raising my voice, so everyone hears, they all glance over. "That seems to be a spot we can go to. I'm praying we won't need to use any of those outhouses; instead, I'd rather go in the grass." Janae shares my sentiments right on the nose.

"The guys got perfect styles and sizes for all of our swimsuits. To be honest, I was worried that there'd be slutty suits; you know how some men are." Naya, checking out our suits, says, "I mean, they thought of everything: coverups, suntan lotion, towels, hair care items, and swim shoes." I don't know how, but we all have our favorite colors and bathing suit styles. I'm wearing an adorable two-piece, royal blue, lattice-front tankini top with a black and royal blue printed pant skirt. And I have an extra bathing suit in my bag, so I'm guessing that Lucas liked both and decided to get two for me. I'm not complaining or saying anything to my cousins.

As we come out from the changing area, the guys greet us by whistling; Clearly, they appreciate their swimsuit choices immensely. "Wow, we have great taste, because we picked out those suits on our own and only had a saleswoman assist us with determining the correct sizes. Oh, Lucas didn't require anyone to help with Alyssa's size." Grayson admires Janae with a smile, putting a flower on the right side of her hair.

"Wait a minute, Steve, you needed help finding my size, too?" Delia meets Steve's eyes with a scrutinizing gaze.

"No, I told her your size, and the suit looks great, Babe." He gives her a sloppy, wet kiss, then goes to the hidden place to change.

"Lovely, Sweetness. Damn, you'd make a paper bag look good." Lucas, licking his lips, winks as he joins the guys to change. Laughing at his sexiness is the only way I can stop myself from kissing him.

"I cannot wait to see Garrison in some trunks, but I don't think he's a Speedo guy. If I were taking bets, I'd put my money on swimming trunks for all of the guys." Naya's confident in her assessment.

"We don't need to bet, because I think they'll be wearing shorts. I don't believe any of them will have on the tiny weeny briefs. What if they get, you know, excited? That would be embarrassing as Hell if that happened. Imagine." I added, laughing at that scenario.

"Oh, I can't take it, you know the visual of that is freaking hilarious!" Janae, clapping her hands, giggles at first, then breaks out into a gut-aching roar with tears sliding down her cheeks.

Lucas

ALKING to the changing area, the guys start speed changing. I snap my fingers, and my clothes disappear, then swimming trunks appear on my body, and I'm ready. Leaning on the boulder, waiting patiently, Steve yells, "What the fuck? Shit!" Grayson and Garrison are ready, and they turn their attention to him. He's standing there, holding up some Speedos that aren't the trunks Steve brought from the store when we were out last night.

"Where did those come from, Steve?" I tilt my head with a confused expression on my face, rapidly going through Steve's memories, seeing him at the boutique. He's paying for his and Delia's swimwear, and the saleswoman has several bags on the counter. Moving away to answer the store phone, Steve gets impatient and grabs two bags, one with her items and another one, which he didn't bother looking inside. Well, it didn't contain his trunks.

Steve's distraught, breathing heavily. "Lucas, man, I don't have a damn clue. I got the bag last night and just put the bag in the backpack. I was concerned about Delia's swimwear more than mine, since so many women's items were lying on the counter. Maybe they'll fit better than I'm envisioning."

We're laughing at that because they're not going to. Steve's irritated that we're laughing at his expense; well, this is on him.

Lucas, Steve is a nice guy, but wow, he's not attentive, and he hasn't marked Delia yet. He's a prime target for another shifter to come and sweep Delia off of her feet. If they were having issues, he could lose her, and he's so dense it could be someone right under his nose.

Steve is a nice guy, but sometimes nice guys finish last, and that would be fucked up. I hope he gets his shit together, so he can keep his woman and be attentive to her. Ultimately, she chooses who she wants to be with in the end.

Remember, Lucas, some shifters won't take no for an answer. In fact, they'll kidnap, mark, and mate them, and bringing an alpha woman to their family is a great accomplishment. Once mated, the only way to break the bond is through death, so it's asinine for a family to keep this quiet from the young women. I don't have a fucking problem killing anyone to get Lyssa back.

Steve looks ridiculous. It's official: Steve is the funniest fucking guy in this group. Seriously, how do you buy swim trunks and not open the bag until you are here? He has some other dude's Speedos, who's average height and scrawny, not six foot six and built like a linebacker who's all muscle. Like Naya said about the little Hellion, I just can't with this guy.

Lyssa

"OH, damn, how in the Hell didn't you check your bag, Man? I don't know, it's not like you're not in great shape; it's obviously for someone much smaller." This worried voice may be Grayson or Garrison.

A muffled voice answers incoherently, then we hear a booming laugh that's immediately recognizable as belonging to Lucas.

"It's up to you, that's all I'm saying, and I'd keep them on until I was ready to get in the water. Let's get out there, come on."

Oh, no, a familiar voice is groaning, "Damn." That's Steve; what the Hell is wrong?

The guys come out from our private changing area, and our mouths drop in unison, staring at Steve. I blink my eyes several times, since my eyes have to be deceiving me. Walking over to Delia, he leans down to her ear, speaking to her, and her body begins shaking and putting her hand over her forehead. She inspects Steve from his feet to his waist.

Steve's wearing a neon yellow Speedo that is two sizes too small. Oh, my, this is bad. Even though he's awesomely physically fit, the material's cutting into his waist. I can't look lower, but from what I gathered when he arrived, his manhood is profoundly outlined in that itsy bitsy swimwear. If I were Delia, I'd be laughing my ass off too; as a matter of fact, Naya and Janae are doing that now.

Inhaling Lucas' tantalizing scent, I turn towards the path we used waiting for him. Garrison and Grayson come out, and even though they have a pleasant scent, theirs are nothing compared to my Lucas. Yes, they're also handsome men, and I know my cousins are thoroughly enjoying them. Citrus and sandalwood tease my senses as he emerges. Damn! That Adonis—no, he's better than that. Every bulging muscle and that eight pack is coming at me with purpose.

The mischievousness gleaming a promise in Lucas's gorgeous eyes is just for me. Our swimwear matches; he's wearing royal blue and black swim trunks. Those black tribal tattoos, I assume, only have a trace of blue on the outline. Hmmm, that's strange; it was more when we were at the pool.

"Lucas, I've got to say this, you'd make a paper bag look good, too. Whew." I pat my chest lightly to get my breathing together. *Lust is something else; no, no, no, it's not in control here.*

Lucas openly laughs, as if my thought were verbalized.

"We're fifteen minutes away from the falls, so let's pick up the pace and get moving," Hania advises, even though we know we're close.

"Wooooo!" A group of female and male voices screams ahead of us, an ecstatic, exciting sound. We laugh and speed up our pace, because we know we're almost there. Walking along the path, we arrive; not only are we here, but we're also at the top of Upper Navajo Falls! The Canyon is on the left side of us, and people are climbing on the edges to get up here where we are. Maybe they didn't want to take the long route that we did.

The sun reflects brightly on the limestone, giving the appearance of entirely different colors, such as subtle blues, reds, and greens mixing in the ridges. Burbling streams cascade into other segments of stones, creating an unbelievable sight, angrily thundering down into pools, like several water spouts, foaming at the bottom for us to cool off in if we want to.

The limestone is smooth and very slick, and if I weren't stepping carefully, I'd slip for sure. About twenty feet beneath us to the right is

Lower Navajo Falls; this place is extraordinary: the beauty of nature, untouched by man. It's a blessing that this place is protected. People are playing and swimming in the turquoise water, and there are many stones in various shapes and sizes throughout. Taking pictures on some of those rocks is going to be fantastic. Poor Ava; she's the selfie queen out of all of us, and she's missing this.

Clapping his hands and all pumped up, Garrison attempts to get our attention. Conversations from the others cease as we all turn to him.

"Oh, yeah, baby, who's cliff jumping with me? Nah, let me rephrase that; who's not afraid to go cliff jumping with me right now?" Garrison, staring each of us down, is waiting for an answer.

Lucas watches and raises his eyebrow at me, silently questioning, and I nod in response, giddy with enthusiasm and just a little fear. "I'm in! One jump, and that's it for me, and Hania did say this one was the only one he'd not say anything about. I'm nervous, but I'm going for it. Ladies, how about it; are we going to do this together?" Peering down at the long way down, I close my eyes, because this is something I've never thought of doing.

Janae nervously strokes the handle of her backpack. "Well, I don't know; we have these—"

"It's okay. We'll take your bags down with us and meet you when you come out. Listen closely, everyone: make sure you take a deep breath and hold it right before you jump. Keep your legs straight, and keep your arms up by your head." Hania demonstrates what he just said and takes the guy's packs. Ayiana takes ours, and they both leave, going down the side.

"I'm so ready to cliff jump! How are we doing this? A group jump?" Naya's doing this side to side dance, voguing with her hands.

"Yeah!" "Yes!" "Hell yeah!" Everyone is answering, and adrenaline is surging through us. Opening my hand up, I say, "Let's count to umm, how about five?" Glancing at Lucas, he grins, nodding his head, and we all line up at the edge. The brisk water swirls over my feet, and the chill of it reminds me to at least try bracing myself for what's coming.

Checking us all out, I put on my goggles and take deep breaths to calm my nerves. Shutting my eyes, I promise myself that I'll open them before hitting the basin. Grayson walks to the front of the line, and he's doing the count. "Ready? We will jump at five. Naya, use that camera and don't let go of the selfie stick. One, two, three, four, five!"

Closing my hands, I take another deep breath and hold it, slightly bending my knees, lifting off on my toes, and springing off the falls! Hearing the loud, nonstop crashing of water into more water, I open my eyes quickly, and exhilaration overcomes my fear. I plummet toward the water, keeping my legs together, smashing into the swimming hole, and looking around as my feet touch the ground. Lucas's muscular arms wrap around me, pulling me to the surface.

Exhaling, I catch my breath, and Naya comes over with the selfie stick. "Video is recording everything! Jumping the waterfall was amazing! How did it feel for you, Lyssa and Lucas?"

"It was exhilarating, and I can cross waterfall jumping off my things-to-do list."

Laughing at my answer, Naya focuses the phone on Lucas. "Your turn, Mr. Lucas."

"Oh, I've cliff jumped before; it's electrifying. The view here is astounding." Lucas goes underwater, grabs my legs, and puts me on his shoulders. He stands up, and I hold onto him, so I don't fall. I start giggling uncontrollably, as Lucas has found the ticklish spot on my thighs and is taking advantage of it.

Chapter 19

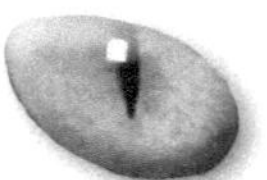

Blue Blaze

Lyssa

THE other two waterfalls, Fifty Foot and Beaver Falls, were captivating. The best is yet to come, though, according to Hania and Aiyana. This whole hike would have been pure Hell for the little Hellion, Ava. When we meet up with the three of them, I'll have to read how the hospital visit went, since she embarrassed them. The people I'm with have positive, bright, spiritual energy, even Ava; she's sickening, that's all.

"Sweetness, I'll rub some of this sunscreen on your back for you. We can't have that silky skin of yours getting burnt." Beckoning her to me, she comes over and turns so I can get to work.

I squeeze the sunscreen out onto my palm and rub the creamy lotion onto her shoulders and back. She takes a sharp breath. Goosebumps appear on her body, and her heartbeat increases. The shifters hear it; glancing at me, they give knowing smiles.

Hey, guys, focus on your own mates and igniting their passion so their own hearts start racing.

Well, Naya isn't going for that; see, Janae is applying the sunscreen on her, and vice versa. We can't attempt that kind of move on our first dates. We're not you, Lucas the Almighty; you know you have something unique, and we all wish we had it.

Wait a minute, Grayson, you've already marked Janae, so she's yours, right? No other shifter or male will even approach her, so it's not about my, uh, so-called uniqueness. By the way, Alyssa is mine, but I'm getting to know her as a person, because she's made it clear that I can't have my way. Sure, I could use my gifts to help her along, but I need her to want to be with me.

We don't want to be with our mates just because our beasts chose them; we have to fall in love with these ladies for who they are to us. To do that, we need to build a relationship, and Grayson and I have two wonderful women we're getting deeply acquainted with.

Lyssa

AS soon as Lucas applies the sunscreen on my back, I'm in trouble. I start breathing extra heavily, and my heartbeat thunders in my ear. Lucas's hands are fire, igniting the torch that is my damn body. Ferocious heat spreads from my skin throughout my body to my core, to the tips of my toes. My va-jay-jay is throbbing and pulsating, and my own personal flood streams into my swim panties from this overwhelming need that I've only experienced since meeting Lucas. My breasts are aching for his attention, and my nipples are hardening from desire. This man drives me into a frenzy every time he touches or even watches me, so how about I tease him a bit—just enough to get him aroused?

Lucas

I'M done with making sure my Sweetness has sunscreen on. I lean over, kissing the back of her neck lightly and letting my tongue swirl on her skin, tasting her. Moaning softly, she faces me and reaches for the bottle, and I hand it to her. She gives me a sultry look, and there's a sparkle in her eyes as she twirls her hand in a circle. "Your turn, Lucas." I'm not going to invade her privacy by reading her mind at the moment. I'll be surprised. Grinning at her and turning around, I don't have to find somewhere to sit, since Sweetness doesn't have a problem reaching my shoulders.

I cross my arms and wait for her. The warm lotion is poured across my shoulders and slides down my back. Sweetness rubs her hands together briskly, then lays both of her warmed up hands on my lower back. Damn! I've never been affected by temperature before until this woman touches me. What the fuck? It must be a mate thing. Her hands are like molten lava, stroking upwards and creating slow circles that move up, then slide down, spreading throughout my entire being.

She reaches my shoulders, and I inhale and exhale, let out a long whistle, and ignore my instinct to do what I want with her. Every cell I have is sizzling. Fuck; my markings are glowing. Shit; this is a problem. I open my channel to those around me. *No matter what, you don't see anything out of the ordinary when you look at me, and you're not going to remember this. It'll just be there, a subtle reminder.*

Yeah, I'm using my powers on every single person in this fucking area; it is what it is. My essence flows into her uncontrollably, strengthening our bond, and blue smoke rises from my fingertips. What the fuck is this? I wish I had someone to explain this mating situation to me. This woman has me so damn ready. My dick is waking up, and I know for a fact that she's not going to help him out.

At least I'm not wearing the neon yellow men's bikini, like Steve, or I'd be fucked. She switches from putting on sunscreen to an all-out assault caressing my back. Fuck this; I can't. Freezing time, I turn to her and say, "You love trying me, don't you, Sweetness?"

Licking her lips and playing Ms. Innocent, she replies, "What do you mean, Lucas? I was making sure you had sunscreen on."

"Sure, you were, Sweetness. It's time for me to give you a little special gift." I pick her up by the waist and let her body slide against mine, and she wraps her arms around my neck. Holding her still against me, her full breast lines up against my chest. My Sweetness's breasts are luscious, and her nipples are like pebbles, protruding through her top. Her eyes are darkening with desire, but there are also golden specks that I've never seen before. Her heart is racing and her lips part; her breathing's heavy, aching for me. Our mouths meet, and I suck on her lower lip then gently nibble it, sliding my tongue in to play with hers, and she shivers. Her fingers stroke my neck then touch my hair, pulling me closer.

I'm in charge of this moment, not Sweetness. She had a great time with my back. Her honey is flowing and her heat's radiating to me and intensifying my need for her. Teasing her is punishing the fucking Hell out of me, because I know nothing is happening but me jerking off, either in the bed or shower. We could have another session like the first time she was able to give herself an orgasm. That was all me, and she was thrilled, thinking her imagination got the best of her.

She's going to need me so fucking much she's going to be touching that va-jay-jay of hers this very night. I guarantee that, and I'll help her with every touch.

Relaxing Sweetness's mind so she's unaware of what I'm doing, we teleport rapidly to our private changing area. *Keep your eyes closed, Sweetness.* Focusing on the slab of limestone, thick patches of greenery and shrubbery appear. I'm still holding her up, and I walk over to it. Leaning into her against the stone, I kiss her hungrily. Her body flushes, and she wraps her legs around my waist. Hell yeah, baby, that's what I'm talking about.

Unlike Ava with the dogs, a low growl or moan escapes from her throat. What the Hell was that? What the fuck is sleeping inside of my woman?

Grinding against her, she gasps, arching her body into mine, our passion building feverishly. Leaving those delightful lips of hers, I trail hot kisses along the length of her beautiful neck. Stopping at the base of her shoulder, sucking her neck, a primitive notion overcomes me. Mine!

Lyssa

FOR some reason, my eyes will not open, it's like they're glued shut, and I'm not even worried about that. As usual, kissing Lucas brings an eruption like a volcano with hot, steaming lava oozing out. No matter what, I'm always responding to Lucas, and everything else is on mute.

Madre would say, "No, Bueno, I can't get involved so deeply with this man so quickly." I have a one-track frequency wave to Lucas's channel, and I'm the number one subscriber. I may be one of many women who melt from just the sight of him, but I know for damn sure that Lucas ignites from my actions, too.

Returning his kisses, my body intensifies like the strings on an instrument ready to be played. I need to feel closer to him as he presses his body into mine. I hold on to his neck and wrap my legs around his hips. Oh. My. God. His cock is at my va-jay-jay, and under those swim trunks, it emits red-hot heat. Gasping at the heat, hardness, length, and thickness of him as he grinds into my swimming panty-covered lady bits, my clit swells like it did in the shower.

A memory flashes through my mind. It's not one of my own, yet it's familiar: a storm of fire, rain, ice, and electricity wreaking havoc in a village, somewhere, a very long time ago, I guess, in another country. It fades out quickly, and I'm back in the present. As fast as it appeared, it's gone. What in the heck was that about?

Lucas

I MMEDIATELY, my birthmark begins to pulsate, and I ease off of Sweetness to examine what the Hell is happening to me. A strange tingling is beginning internally and spreading to my skin, and an incredible amount of my essence flows into my Sweetness.

I'm as utterly damned confused as a fish out of water, because my birthmark is metamorphosing. It's turning away from solid black with azure edges, lightening until it's fully glimmering azure.

Fuck, this is crazy! An identical copy of my birthmark in glowing azure shadow is transferring from my skin and floating over my Sweetness's body! Each mark is separating until there are enough pieces to cover her entire body.

Lyssa

M Y breathing falters. From my center, an inferno explodes, rushing through me. I can't move; a deafening humming increases until it overcomes all of my senses. A magnificent blue fire blazes in my mind, and a sleepy voice says, "Our mate." I'm losing my damn mind, and is this really what lust does? I'm hallucinating and hearing voices. They're going to throw my tail into an asylum.

Lucas

"SHE'S your mate, and you must claim her now."

Who the fuck—

All at once, my birthmark pieces penetrate Sweetness's skin, from her head down to her toes, becoming a fiery blue and engulfing her! An inhuman, animalistic purring or soft growl from Sweetness resonates throughout the immediate area. Her legs buckle, and she's sliding down, "No, no, no! Stop!" Instantly, I catch her. I'm ablaze as well; our bodies and spirits are intertwining, becoming one azure flame, and it has a soothing effect.

Lyssa

WHAT the Hell is going on? There's a tremendous amount of pressure on my skin as if something is trying to get through. I can't open my eyes or speak. What the fuck?! Suddenly, the intruder succeeds, and every single area of my body is riddled with mild, stinging pains, digging through my skin and into my bloodstream. Racing through my vessels, bones, organs, and lastly, my heart, it's giving me a significant dose of strength. My brain is lighting up like a blue Christmas tree!

Sparkling blue electricity crashes through me, bringing light shocks within me, even in my soul. Internally quivering, my heart stutters, and there's an echo of another heartbeat! Oh. My. God. What is going on here?

Lucas

"ALYSSA is ours, and you needed to mark her. It's done. Now maybe our third head will calm the fuck down."

I'm shocked and frowning at the fact that my essence has spoken to me for the first time ever. My powers have existed since I was born,

and now that I have a mate, out of the damn blue, my motherfucking
powers decide now is the time to fucking communicate?!

*Sweetness, everything is fine. You know I wouldn't let anything wrong
happen to you. Stay relaxed. You're not in any pain, Sweetness. Keep
your eyes closed, and you won't remember I was in your mind.*

Lyssa

FEAR overcomes me. My breathing quickens, then my body relaxes, and calmness enters me, I know I'm all right; my intuition
knows a great deal that I don't.

I see a larger-than-life Lucas disguised in turquoise. His hair is
long and dark orange, and his pupils are shaped differently, like di-
amonds. He's someplace I've never seen before. He may be in one of
those deep caves, but it could be anywhere in the world. If this were
for real, I wouldn't ever ask for a trip there; why would I? The cave is
somewhere excruciatingly hot and except for the shadows thrown by
flames, it's in darkness. I sense pure fear and despair; why do I imagine Lucas here and in that form?

Lucas

TAKING her hand in mine, the fire recedes without any pain
at all. I don't know why the Hell my birthmarks are scattered
all over my woman's body like this. Can anyone else see them?
Keeping my arms wrapped around her, I teleport with her back to
the group, where they are all as we left them. Sweetness's eyes are
still closed, and her appearance is freaky as Hell. Here it comes, the

moment of truth, and what am I going to do, if, in fact, they can see this all over her?

I adjust the time and ease everyone back into what they were doing so it will be an easy reconnection. Janae's rubbing suntan lotion on Naya while Grayson and Garrison have their own conversation. Steve's outright ridiculous in those Speedos; I'll help him out in a few minutes. I can't have him ruining the scenery anymore. Delia's putting lotion on, while Steve's covered up with a towel. You know those Speedos can't be out in the open long before people start staring and making Steve uncomfortable.

"Sweetness, open your eyes," I say, touching her arm and tracing the outline of one of my markings. Her pupils are azure for a second; then, blinking her eyes, the original sapphire coloring returns.

Lyssa

OPENING my eyes, it's like I was sleeping, but I'm still standing, so how does that work? "Ours!" Who the Hell is that, and why is she saying that? I know it's inside of my head, and it's scaring the Hell out of me. I'm adjusting my eyes, since I see shiny blue markings, and I blink several times, because something's definitely wrong. Finally, my vision is back to normal; it must have something to do with our location and all the spirits around in this area. I have to remember that this land is sacred. I must be extra sensitive to the energies here. That's the only explanation I can come up with, and if that's the case, why haven't I seen my family? That's crazy; no, I do not see ghosts, so it's not that.

I know one thing that has happened today, Lucas has me in some type of predicament with all this sexual tension. There may be a hot shower in store for me today, like the one after our breakfast date. Now he's turned the tables on me; first, he succeeds in his mission of getting me all hot and bothered with that sexy massage of his. Returning the favor, I was accomplishing my goal, until he kissed me. I wonder if he went through any of the weirdness like I did?

Lucas

S WEETNESS is freaking out about something, but I can't read what happened. It must be the marking, but how is that? She would be talking to me about it, so it has to be something else that transpired, but why am I blocked from it? No one is looking at her screaming or anything, so let's test this out.

Hania, it's time to go; tell everyone, so we can pack up and go over to the trail. You came up with this on your own. Also, my voice isn't in your head.

Hania stands up and brushes off his shorts, announcing, "Time to get moving, people, break time's over. We'll use the trail over here." He walks to the trail and waits, with Aiyana close behind.

"Here we go. Sweetness, are you ready for Mooney Falls?" Smiling at her, I hold my hand out for hers.

"Yes, I'm ready as I'll ever be." Sliding her hand into mine, I can see every mark on her.

Janae and Naya pass us. They don't seem to notice anything strange. That's great, oh yeah.

Lucas! What in the Hell did you do to Lyssa?! Jesus, you both have glimmering blue marks all over your bodies, man!

All three shifters are staring at my Sweetness with expressions of shock and disbelief. They clearly see the same thing I do.

Your tattoos are not black anymore; they're the same color as whatever those marks are on Lyssa. I don't think those were tattoos. They're something much more than that, right? Unique, because tattoos don't just change. I have plenty, and none of mine have ever done anything like this. This is part of whatever you are.

I don't know either; remember, we discussed this before, Grayson.

I turn my attention to Steve. *Steve, don't say anything about Lyssa's appearance to anyone, do you understand?*

Steve damn near jumps out of his skin, confusion replacing the shocked expression on his face. Oh, damn, his towel slips off, and he rushes to cover up those yellow Speedos.

Yes, Lucas, I got it. I'm really wondering just what kind of shifter you are. I've never in my life heard of anything at all like I'm witnessing with Lyssa. My family has told us so many stories about marking a mate, but this is bizarre.

Steve, don't worry. I've got Lyssa. She's just fine, and some things are just unexplainable.

"Steve, bro, I just realized I have an extra pair of trunks in my pack. You can have them. I just bought them last night. Be right back, Sweetness." I'm thinking about some black and navy blue swim trunks in my size, since we're similar in stature. Unzipping my backpack and pulling out the swim shorts, I hand them to Steve. His eyes light up, and he hugs me tightly. "Thank you, Lucas, you just don't know how fucking happy I am right now. Hang on, let me run and find a quick spot to change."

Jogging through some shrubbery, Steve yells out, "Yes!" Laughing at his enthusiasm, Delia says, "Thanks, Lucas, I'm glad you remembered before he had to take that damn towel off again."

"Delia, I'm glad I remembered it too, because I couldn't take one more view of those fucking yellow Speedos on him." Laughing, we hear Steve returning and we welcome him back into the world of wearing shit that fits by clapping for him.

CHAPTER 20

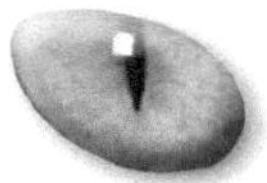

DEATH TOWER

Lyssa

THIS has been a hell of an adventure, and I, for one, will never forget this beautiful, spiritual, serene section of the world we live in. We walk through what I call mini limestone mountains. Yes, I called the majestic Grand Canyon that, even though I have gone mountain climbing and this feels nothing like it. That's why I said limestone mountains.

Climbing the makeshift ladders, I keep a close eye on my footing, because I know I'm not trying to slip and fall. "Hania, I've noticed that the flat-lying ladders on the water and the ones against the limestone are old. How often are they redone?"

Hania bursts out laughing. Why is he laughing at me? The guys join in, so my cousins and I are out of the loop and left wondering what's so funny. Eyeing Lucas with some irritation, he stops chuckling. "Hania, please explain what's so funny."

"Ladies, the reason we're all laughing is that we had this discussion already, while you were all changing into your swimsuits. Even though some of the ladders are a little worn, they are perfectly safe. We check everything and provide maintenance every few months and construct new ladders if needed." As he's talking, he strolls over to the foggy, blue-green creek where some of those flat ladders are, and steps on and off, testing them.

Laughing at myself for thinking crazy thoughts, I say, "That means none will break while we're climbing up those ladders; that's good to know. Now let's get over to Mooney Falls." I gesture to Aiyana to lead the way. Shaking his head at me, Lucas grins. We need to get to those falls quickly, because the drinks are losing their chill factor. Warm water in the damn heat isn't good at all.

Another scorching breeze punches through us while the sun continues its glaring attack on everyone here, especially the ladies in our group. We've been to three of the waterfalls; one was Beavers Falls, which is the farthest away. I'm thankful for the swimsuits; honestly, I know my cousins would've joined me in all those waterfalls, even if we went in with our regular clothes on. At least our clothes would keep us cooler after getting wet; our swimsuits dry too fast.

Naya abruptly stops, causing Garrison to grab her by the waist to prevent her from falling as Delia bumps into her from behind.

"Oops, sorry, Naya." Moving over and shaking her head, she says, "You stopped without any warning, and I didn't realize how close I was to you."

Naya laughs and begins coughing. Clearing her throat, she says, "It's okay. That was my fault, not yours, Sis. Now I've got a question, and any of our dates can answer this. Since you all have the entire day planned for us, are we going back to our hotel after our adventure here to umm, freshen up?" She eyes each of the guys before settling on Garrison.

Garrison, nodding his head at Naya, responds, "We're going to bring you ladies back to the hotel so we all can get ready for part two of our date. We'll have about sixty minutes."

"Thank God we have five bathrooms. Maybe, just maybe, one hour will be enough," Naya replies, making a worried face. "You're asking a lot from five fashionistas. One hour? I don't know."

Laughing at her, the guys really are acting like she's joking. They're sadly mistaken. The guys notice the shocked expressions on our faces and stop goofing around. "We have to shower, wash, and dry our hair, plus get clothes to wear and dress, plus apply some make-up. We need at least two hours, guys. Call whoever you need to fix your scheduling, because we need that time to get ready." I give each of them an intense stare, so they know that I'm serious.

"Yes, I do know that you ladies do take your time getting dolled up," Lucas says, wrapping his arms around me and nuzzling my neck. "You know, each of you ladies are such natural beauties that make-up is unnecessary. I just wanted to share that."

I reply, "Oh, Lucas, we know we're lovely and intelligent young women; our family always made sure we knew that from a very young age. When you don't know your self worth, it leaves you open for assholes to take advantage of you," Janae states matter-of-factly. "The main one who makes awful choices is Ava, and we have to get that handled soon as we arrive home."

"That's right, and we don't even go heavy on make-up. That's not even an issue," Janae adds, pointing her finger at her face.

"We'll rearrange our plans to give you ladies two hours of preparation time. No more, no less; we have two more places to go. Dress casually, but no skirts or stilettos," Grayson announces.

"Casual to me means a pair of pants, shirt or blouse, and comfortable footwear, Grayson. Except for Ava, the rest of us are appropriately dressed today, as you guys requested last night." I had to say that because it's the truth. My stomach growls loudly, reminding me and everyone else that we ate breakfast quite a while ago.

All this activity has built up my appetite. Slowing my pace to a complete stop, I gaze at Lucas. "Can you take out one of those boxes of raisins or trail mix from the side pocket of the pack for me, please, Lucas?"

He hands both to me; the trail mix has more, so I put the raisins in my pocket. "Thanks."

"Anytime, Sweetness; you know I've got you." Pulling out a sugar cane stick, he bites a piece off, then chews on it. His eyes widen in surprise, a slow smile appearing on his face.

"Lucas, is this the first time you've ever had a sugar cane stick?"

"Yep. What made you ask that, Sweetness?"

"When you first chewed that stick, your smile showed it was a new experience, and you were enjoying it. It was that first taste of discovering yummy goodness."

Laughing, he nods, "Oh, yeah, I agree with that."

As we're hiking this steep ass hill, I'm hoping that the last waterfall, Havasu, isn't far. Sweat is rolling down my chest and back. If I had my blouse on, I'd definitely be uncomfortable. Thank God I have this swim top on. I'm in good shape, but damn, I don't think all these waterfalls were meant to be explored in a couple of hours.

The bottom of my feet are throbbing; after three and a half hours, these boots aren't comfortable anymore. There are rocks in various sizes and shapes everywhere. Janae slips and nearly loses her balance, and she tries to prevent her fall by holding onto a large rock. Grayson quickly pulls her close to him, so he was her savior, but she had it under control.

Another misty breeze hits us, and the sprinkle of that cool mist is aiding in my quest to cool down. Finally, we reach the top, and oh, my God, it's the top of Mooney Falls. We're on the right side.

Naya excitedly yells. "Hania, you could've told us we were coming right here; I mean at this very moment. I needed to be prepared to take video and pictures of the view and, most importantly, everybody's reactions." Taking out the Fujifilm X-14, the badass camera that the guys had for everyone on the table in the tent, she begins snapping pictures of everything.

This is wonderful! We are much higher than we were at the previous falls. This is why Hania said no to cliff-jumping at any of the other falls. This particular waterfall is very different than the other three, like different melting, angry expressions imprinted throughout the limestones. It has loads of personality. Janae is pointing out to Grayson a way to get to the bottom. Please don't say we're going down there this way.

"Wait, Hania or Aiyana, how tall is Mooney Falls?" Naya stops taking pictures, looking at them for an answer.

Clapping his hands, Hania answers, "Mooney Falls is the tallest waterfall here, about one hundred and ninety feet high. Guess what? We're all going down to the base. Get excited!" He points to the area Janae was showing Grayson. "Let's get over there."

"Wait a minute. Who said we are going down that?" Delia voices what I'm thinking.

"Yeah, this is a serious drop, and it looks rough," Janae adds, frowning.

"Janae, don't worry, we will be fine. Just don't slip!" Steve suggests, laughing. He's punched on each arm by both Janae and Delia. The only one of us who doesn't appear to be nervous is Naya. I guess she's in her photography zone. She's always loved taking pictures, and that camera has her in her second element; food is the first.

"Ladies, we'll keep you safe. Each of us can get in front of our dates and be your personal bodyguards." Garrison, flexing and making a silly face and wiggling his eyebrows, gives a good suggestion.

Easing over close to the edge of the cliff, I decide I should look down. Swaying at the dizziness that comes over me, Lucas pulls me back to him, holding my waist. I guess that since it's almost two hundred feet, it may be too high for me. The other three falls didn't affect me like this one does. I look at all the greenery sitting in patches throughout the base and the water plummeting and streaming into the basin. It's still unbelievable that this turquoise paradise is here.

"Sweetness, you know you don't like heights, so don't go too close to the edge to see how far it is to the bottom." Lucas shakes his head, leans down to my ear, and speaks softly.

They're all following Hania and Aiyana; I pause, turning to Lucas. "I was curious, but I didn't know it would hit me like that. Lucas, please just stay close to me; I'm nervous", I say, as we start down this incredibly steep, almost two hundred foot monster. Taking deep breaths, I rub the goosebumps that have prickled up on my arms.

Turning me to face him, Lucas does that magical thing that he does: calm me down. "I've got you, Sweetness. Never think that I'll let anything happen to you. You are safe with me." He kisses me on my forehand, then tenderly on my lips.

"Ready?" He squeezes my hand, and his heat radiates through me. Standing on my tippy toes, I kiss him in return, feeling like I can do anything. Grinning and nodding my head, I reply, "Yes, let's do this."

Speeding up, we come to a sign that reads, "Mooney Falls—CAUTION: No Lifeguard on Duty. No Diving or Jumping into Pools, No Rock Climbing."

"That's why no diving is allowed. Can you imagine if it were? This isn't a joke. People have died trying to cliff jump from this waterfall," Aiyana explains. I doubt that any of us are trying cliff jumping over here. They have nothing at all to worry about on that issue. I slow my pace, so Lucas and I are at the end of the line in our group.

I tread carefully, since the terrain here is the worst of the three, in my opinion. I slide a little on this narrow, bulky, rocky, rugged, curvy, colossal limestone cliff with Lucas close behind, and he immediately grabs me. "Careful, Sweetness. I'll stay up here, so I'm closer." The slope is getting worse as we go down, and my stomach is getting that sinking feeling.

Heavy steel chains in low steel rods are placed along the cliff's edge, leading us to where we need to go. Noticing how our group is significantly ahead of us, I say, "Lucas, I guess we're too slow for them, since they're all rushing." Wow, what if something happened to us?

"It's fine, Sweetness. The guys know that I can take care of you."

I'm unable to walk fast at all, because I may fall before Lucas can catch me. Yes, I do trust him, but what if my body cannot control itself? Moving in sync with each other, we come to another sign, and we stop to investigate. The sign is attached to a steel post in the ground by the edge; it says, "DESCEND AT OWN RISK."

My mouth drops; I wasn't expecting this. What the Hell?! Oh, man, am I ready for this? With this gorgeous waterfall and canyon in the background, if I were someone else, the beauty of it might distract me from the danger that's screaming at me.

"Sweetness, don't worry, I told you already that I won't let anything happen to you. Please just trust me."

Exhaling, I answer, "Okay, I'll relax and trust you, Lucas."

"You won't regret it, Sweetness." The single chain line changes to a double one; watching where it may lead, I see there's a small cave. It doesn't make sense that this cliff has a small cave. My family and their dates are almost there. How in the Hell are all of us going to fit into that?

Lucas

SWEETNESS needs a little help in the fear department. *Sweetness, stop walking; close your eyes, and listen to me. These thoughts are yours. They are not coming from me. On second thought, the height of this cliff isn't as bad as you thought. Now you can enjoy this experience, and you know that I won't let anything happen to you. You're perfectly safe.*

"Lucas, you know I trust that you won't let me fall off of this cliff," she says. Then, turning around, she kisses me with those sweet lips. Those marks on her shouldn't excite me, but damn, they do—every single one of them, because she is mine. I didn't think it would be possible to be more attracted to Sweetness, but I am. Who would've thought it was possible? I was more attracted to this woman from day one than any other female I've ever been with.

What the fuck is it with the low placed chains? Why aren't they higher? I mean, what is their purpose? They won't stop anyone from falling. It's perplexing that these chains are this way. Sweetness slips on the rocky surface, and I reach out, swiftly catching her. "Whoa, that was close, Lucas." Leaning back against my chest, her heart skips a beat, and she inhales. The sweet jasmine and honey scent from her hair plays with my senses. Warmth spreads through me; what the fuck? What is she doing to me? I close my eyes for a moment, breathing it all in.

"Lucas, you know the only reason I'm doing this is that you're with me, right? I would have seen this towering scary-ass cliff and told everyone, Hell no, I don't like heights.'" She places her small hand over mine as I run my hand across the bumpy, rough rock wall. The golden sunlight streams down over the cliff. The chains on the ground are attached to steel pegs every few spaces and continue to the cave entrance.

We're catching up with everyone else checking it out, because we have to climb through it down to the basin.

What the Hell? Lucas, bro, do you see this? It's a tight ass squeeze for someone of average height. How the fuck are we going to get through these damn caves? Yes, Hania said there are two of them; as we exit this one, there's another one a couple steps ahead.

Grayson, we'll be all right; I'll make sure of that. Let me enter first, with Lyssa behind me.

Cool, Lucas, do your thing, bro.

"Hania, I'll go in after you and Aiyana. Sweetness, let me get in front of you. You know we're going into the cave, and I'm going in first to make sure it's safe."

Laughing, Sweetness stops. Walking in front of her, I grab her hand and she smacks my ass with her free one. "You're feeling mighty spicy, Sweetness. You know I'm more than willing to return the favor. Later on, I've got something for you."

Smack! She does it again. I laugh and shake my head at her, because I will keep count. This damn cave is narrow as fuck; Hania and Aiyana go in first. Hania says, "Everyone, these chains are for your safety, so please hold on to them."

Letting go of Sweetness's hand for the moment I place my hands on each side of the entrance and concentrate, freezing time. Rapidly observing the others, I see that everyone's like statues. Focusing on the cave, then stepping inside, I can't fit my upper body properly. I'm the tallest here, so once I can get in, the other guys can, too. I press my hands at the top, where my head is, as I'm scrunched up.

There's a rumbling and shaking throughout the cave as I push to temporarily expand the area. Falling rocks and dust cover poor Hania and Aiyana. I move debris telepathically, so they aren't injured, and within about two minutes, it's complete. I summon the wind to blow the debris from them, so they're back to normal.

Straightening out my body, this feels damn fantastic. Snapping my fingers, time is back in motion, and Sweetness enters the cave, holding onto those damn chains. The others are following, with Grayson and Janae next. "Lucas, hold on to those chains. I can't lose you, man." Her hot hand rubs against my back.

"Sweetness, I'm fine, but I'll hold on for you." I smile at her concern for me; that's my woman. I grab the chains on each side of the cave, using only a little of my strength, and the chains and pegs shake. I release my grip and just cover the chains with my hands to give the appearance that I'm holding on. I adjust my eyes so I can see in the darkness, and I count the links between the pegs. There are eighteen.

The path grows steeper with every move I make, and I can hear Delia's and Janae's heartbeats racing with fear.

Delia and Janae, calm down. You're safe. Garrison and Grayson are here with you, ladies, and they won't let anything happen to you. So please take a couple of deep breaths and enjoy yourselves. Step very carefully. This idea was all yours.

Both Delia and Janae inhale and exhale a few times, their fast fluttering heartbeats calming down to an average pace. "Ouch, dammit." Smelling iron, I know immediately that my Sweetness scratched her hand. "Are you okay, Sweetness?"

"Yes, I'm fine. I just scratched my hand on the rock."

"I know you may think this is a crazy-ass question, Lucas, but I'm going to ask it anyway. You tell me to make sure I'm holding on to the chain, yet you forget to do it?"

Daylight shines through the cave opening, as we step out onto two large flat rocks, very close to the cliff's edge. The waterfall is there, but there's still a lot more treacherous cliff to get down. There are more chains hooked through the steel poles curving into the other cave that I already expanded when I did the first one. Sweetness is right behind me, trying to put a Band-Aid on her palm. I put it on for her, lifting her hand, and kissing it. She'll be healed and as good as new.

There are about five to six steps before climbing through the second cave, but this one is shorter. Sweetness is damn near on my back. This is hilarious. At the end of this cave, Sweetness is not going to be too happy with this shit at all. Hania and Aiyana are carefully going down the cliff that Sweetness may have a breakdown about.

Lyssa

WE come out of the second cave behind Lucas. What the Hell is this crap?! Lucas is waiting, and he says, "You can do this, Sweetness; I'm right here with you. Just keep your eyes on the chains and where you're walking."

"Dammit, Lucas, I don't like this at all, but I'm very calm. It's strange as Hell." Overlooking the long way down this cliff, a part of me screams *No!* Something is keeping me together, and I can only come to one conclusion: it's Lucas. I know it shouldn't be possible, but we live in a world where many things can happen without an explanation.

Grabbing onto the chains, I slowly step down the array of uneven, wet, slippery rocks leading down this deathtrap, and once again, I think I'm crazy to be doing this! Oh, damn, my hands, slipping from the wet chains, are soaked like the cliff stairs from the water spraying off the falls. Water is everywhere; heck, it's even getting on me. Suddenly, I'm sliding down uncontrollably, grabbing those chains with all my strength, and Lucas is there in a flash. How? Janae screams in fear, "Lyssa!"

"I'm fine, Janae. Be extra careful coming down; it's slippery like a damn seal!"

"Sweetness, how about we turn around facing the cliff? We'll go down slowly, and I'll watch you."

"I'm willing to try it that way." Letting go of the left chain and stepping down to the next rock with my left foot, I slide my right hand down. Still holding on to the chain, I slowly turn around, bringing my right foot down and grabbing the chain with my left hand. Cool drizzles of water hit my body, and I can't help but giggle a little. Lumpy, uneven rock causes some pain to my feet. I'm still wearing the boots.

Lucas taps the side of my thigh. "Come on, Sweetness, you've got this, and I've got you."

"I'm coming, Lucas." Strange stairs melded in different areas in the limestone make this descent tricky as Hell. Slowly stepping down, I focus on this damn cliff, so I don't slip again. Then I arrive at an area where there aren't any steps. "Sweetness, take two jumps down, and there are ladders here, too."

Pushing away with my legs and counting to three, I take a giant leap. Landing a reasonable distance below, I repeat it again,; it's a success. At the beginning of the first ladder, the chains continue down on each side. I breathe an enormous sigh of relief; the rest of this descent was easy as eating a slice of my favorite banana cream pie.

Climbing down the last ladder and turning around, I bump into Lucas's scrumptious body. "Oh, Lucas, you know I could crash into you all day long, right?"

Wrapping his arms around my waist, he says, "Sweetness, you know I'd love that, and I'm ready, willing, and able." He gives me that sexy smile with a glint of promise in his eyes. Everyone else is coming down, and we can admire the waterfall. First, we are the only people here, and I know why. They didn't want to come down on the death tower.

This is the tallest waterfall here, and no doubt the wettest. There's no mist here and we're getting splattered from the water. I don't regret climbing down the death tower for this.

Vibrations from the ground beneath my feet make me ask Hania a question. Walking over to him with Lucas, I ask, "Hania, is the vibrating we're experiencing from the force from the water?"

Nodding his head, smiling, "Yes, it is Lyssa. Since it's coming from almost two hundred feet, that is what happens: a great deal of water plummets into the pool."

"Well, I'm ready to explore another beautiful turquoise beauty of nature. Come on, Lucas, they'll meet us in the water." I untie my boots and take them off, then retrieve my water shoes. I run into the water, splashing, and playing with Lucas and the rest of our group as they join in.

CHAPTER 21

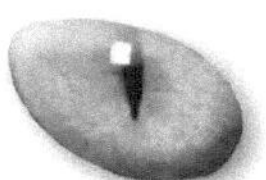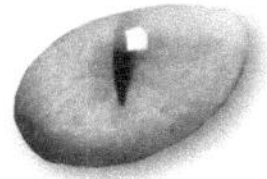

IN CONTROL

Lucas

MOONEY Falls was fucking fantastic. Climbing up Mooney was as bad as going down was for the ladies. We're almost at Havasu Falls now, and Janae notices a young man and woman we'd seen at Beaver Falls. "Hey guys, how was that climb down and back up Mooney Falls?"

Shaking their heads and laughing, the young woman answers, "Oh no, we took the short cut we found out about online, so we only had to climb up Mooney Falls."

Each and every one of the ladies expresses shock on their faces. Janae's and Sweetness's, mouths drop open. We all look at Hania and Aiyana, and Hania laughs. "No, we don't take anyone that route, because it's not the safest way to go. Yes, it may be faster, but it's not the best way. Our number one priority is to make sure our visitors are safe."

Janae cuts her eye at Hania. "Well, that cliff isn't the safest way; in my opinion, it is a towering monster. And I'd prefer climbing up, instead of going up and down that thing. I know it's a gorgeous sight, but I'd go the way they went any day."

Aiyana shrugs, "Well, I guess next time you can try it their way. Let's get going to our last and final stop down here." We're following them, and I'm laughing my ass off, and *smack*, Sweetness does it again. Three times; oh yeah, I'm going to pay her ass back for sure, that's a promise. "Lucas, that's for laughing at Janae; behave yourself," she says, pointing her finger at me.

Nodding, I just stare at her, licking my lips, and she puts her head down. "Don't worry, Sweetness, I'll have plenty of attention to spare for you later tonight." Two can play this game, and I may not get what I need tonight, but I'll turn her on like a six-alarm fire.

Damn; this fall is the best one—about one hundred feet high, the water cascading into the shimmering blue-green water. I forgot to breathe. I clear my throat while taking this astonishing waterfall in. This area is packed with people, and there are picnic tables and benches out here, too. Water shoots down this waterfall more powerfully than the others, and there must be more minerals, since the blue-green watercolor is more pronounced here.

"Okay, this is our last waterfall, and Hania and Aiyana saved the best one for last! We need pictures and videos, so break out those cameras in your backpacks, people!" Naya yells enthusiastically. She's not kidding either; she's motioning with her hands to all of us. Laughing at her together, we follow her orders as we prepare for our last swim of the day.

Lyssa

I CAN'T even say anything to Janae about being pissed off about climbing twice on that damn deathtrap cliff, Mooney Falls. Don't get me wrong, it's beautiful, and all, but the drop is horribly steep. Hania could've warned us before arriving there, and I still think Lucas has something incredible; if it could be sold in a bottle, it'd be a best seller.

Naya is crazy, and she's funny as Hell. Honestly, I've never seen her this excited before, and we've been on countless family trips together. Either the waterfalls in this area have hypnotized her, or she will rub this in Ava's face. I think it's the latter.

Havasu Falls is magnificent! I'd be thrilled to come to this one waterfall; it's truly an oasis all by itself. The water is more blue-green here. Those other falls were just the tease, as appetizers are before the main course. It's also louder here—even louder than it was at Mooney Falls.

Going over by Aiyana and Hania at the lower pools, I ask, "Hania, how high is this waterfall?"

"Havasu Falls is ninety-eight feet, and the water comes down this waterfall faster than it does at the other ones."

"I thought that was the reason; the rumbling in the ground was more intense. And I can tell you what I've gotten out of this adventure. Even though my feet are hurting and I'm tired, it's beautiful and serene here. I'll never forget this experience, and thank you both for guiding us, I could've done without the two climbs on Mooney." Laughing, I give Lucas a moment to give his opinion.

Grabbing the camera from the backpack and motioning for Lucas to come over, I say, "Let's take shots of the different pools leading to the waterfall and everything over there."

"Sure, Sweetness, that sounds great to me. How about we get pictures under the fall?" Lucas answers.

"Let's get this area first, then move inward, taking shots, until we're under the waterfall. We can take some great photos. It's gorgeous here; I'm glad Hania saved the best for last." Lucas follows me as we take pictures of the trees, shrubbery, pools, and the canyon.

"Come over, Sweetness, it's your turn. Time for your photoshoot, with me as your photographer. Now, strike a pose, woman."

Lucas waits expectantly, and I put my hands on my hips. I give him a sexy, come-hither expression and blow kisses. Then, I show him vogue moves from the old Madonna video. "Oh, yeah, sexy lady, bring it. Keep it coming. These are just for us, so give some poses for the family."

Moving into the water, it's my turn to be the photographer. I move towards the vivid but ethereal waterfall. Lucas is my model. He's yummily delicious, and I snap shots of those eight pack abs of his. Damn. He goes underwater, swimming around in a circle, then coming up and splashing me.

Water is dripping off him, and those tattoos of his, as usual, are the center of attention from the females. He smiles, never taking his focus off me, and I return my attention to him. Next thing I know, we're under the crashing water of Havasu Falls.

I inhale and hold my breath, and Lucas moves us to the wall behind the falls, so we're hidden and not getting hit by the water. Leaning into me, he places his hands on my waist, his leg between my thighs, and his warm, minty breath welcoming me. We stare into each other's eyes, and my hands move to his face, sliding across his warm, smooth skin to his wet, silky curls. Grabbing his hair, I pull his face down to mine. Wolfishly grinning, he lowers his hands to my butt and lifts me. I wrap my legs around him, and our mouths meet.

I close my eyes and graze his lower lip, but he breaks our kiss. I frown at him; what the Hell? I open my mouth to speak, but he places his index finger on my lips. I bite his finger in frustration; this man has to be in charge all the time, and yes, he has sexual control issues. I don't know exactly what it is, but it would be nice to lead for a change.

"Humph, really, woman?" Taking my hand from around his neck, he places it on his umm, member, and it's rock hard. "You drive me into another fucking zone, the same as I do to you. Yeah, I owe some playtime from you smacking my ass in front of everybody. And believe me, you will enjoy every moment of what I have in store for you." He unwraps my legs from his waist and puts me down. Dammit, Lucas. Gasping in confusion and irritation, I quickly grab his hand, which is on my waist.

I pull his hand up to my chest and place it over my heart. My heartbeat quickens. "Do you feel that, Lucas?" I yell over the roar and intensity of the plummeting water.

"Yes, Sweetness, I feel your heartbeat. Why do you ask?"

"This is what you do to me, and I'd like to be in control sometimes so I can do that to you."

Chuckling, he concedes. "All right, you can do whatever you want to me. I thought you already knew what you do to me, Sweetness." He moves closer to me, and oh, my God, he is sex personified, as Ava called him. Our bodies touch. "I'm all yours, madam; do whatever you want. I won't stop you." He bows down toward me.

Now I'm the aggressor, so where do I start? Wherever I want. I smile at that realization, licking my lips, and Lucas laughs, shaking his head. "Decisions, decisions, decisions. What are you going to do, Sweetness?"

I move away from the wall of the falls, as Lucas intently watches me. My hand trails the length of his arm to his chest, then over each one of those eight hulking abdominal muscles. I play with the edge of the waistband of his trunks, and he looks at me, raising his eyebrow. I tug on his swim shorts and walk in a circle with him following, stopping when he's against the wall.

Oh, God, here we go. Goosebumps are prickling on my skin, and I get as close as I can to him, so we're touching. Waves of heat are emitting from both of us. Standing on tiptoes, I lift my hands to his face and gently pull him to mine. My lips meet his, and I gently squeeze his lips with my teeth and slowly pull back as his lip slides slowly through my teeth. Caressing his chest shakily, my hands get familiar with his naked upper body. When I reach his hard pecs, I squeeze them both.

Lucas inhales quickly, his fists by his sides. I reach up for another kiss and gradually, with deliberation, I suck his lower lip, and he growls, losing control. He swiftly picks me up, turning faster than I've ever seen anyone turn, and pushes my back against the wall. He slides his tongue next to mine. Yes! I've made him break down. I taste caramel on his tongue, and inside I'm burning like a forest fire.

He drags his lips from mine, and I open my eyes. Suddenly, I exhale sharply, seeing that his eyes have changed to emerald green with shiny blue speckles. He covers my neck with kisses. Then his tongue sneaks out, and fireworks go off inside of me. He's making a mark on my neck, and I plan on returning the favor. He's sucking on my neck like a damn lollipop, and it feels so freaking good. A need is crawling through me, and I'm craving so much more from Lucas.

Lucas

THIS woman is going to drive me fucking crazy! She wants to be in control? Why doesn't she realize by now what she does to me? Dammit, I've changed how I operate for her. Hell, I'm waiting for whenever she will be ready because of her morals. I've never gone through getting to know any female, ever. She's my mate, so I'll do whatever she wants, but she has to figure out that she has the power.

Sweetness knows she's not giving in to me today, but she wants me all fucked up and not able to think damn straight. I've been extra careful, being easy on her and holding off on touching areas because she's a virgin. I'm patiently waiting, because she's made it abundantly clear that she's not about just acting on her desires. Her words were, "We have to get to know each other, Lucas." Well, if it's good for her to have me tied up in sexual frustration, then it's an ideal situation for her ass, too.

It's official. I'm getting Sweetness to the point of no return, or very damn close. My mission is to teach this woman a lesson. It's hard as Hell to fall asleep when you're in need. It may be cruel, but she has to know what it feels like to be on fire and get nothing to douse it. I'll be putting both of us through this. If we get back too late tonight, then, tomorrow night after we get back, it's on.

I admire my handiwork on Sweetness's neck, I'm satisfied with that red mark on her skin.

Lyssa

GETTING back to the helicopter is more than a welcoming sight. That means soon I'll be in a hot shower, and I'll probably flop on the bed before finding something to wear. This was incredible, and the only thing I wouldn't try again is climbing Mooney Falls. My cousins and the guys look like they had a great time, and we'll get into more detail if they want later. If Ava were here, even in the proper footwear, she'd be the drama queen out of all of us women.

It's one in the afternoon, and my stomach's growling once again. I take out the box of raisins, which will only tease my appetite. "Sweetness, I have something for you." Turning to look, I see he has my favorite candy bar; smiling in pure joy at him, he gives it to me. "Thank you, Lucas." I blow him a kiss and, leaning to my ear, he says, "I didn't forget; tonight is payback."

Heat rushes to my cheeks as my heartbeat quickens; he's as serious as a heart attack. I still feel what our kissing did to me earlier. "Hmm, we have so much to do with our group date; we'll need a raincheck on that, Lucas." God, please let this group date end late, because my body can't take another session with Lucas like the earlier ones.

He arches an eyebrow at me and grins, as if he knows something. Ugh, he's driving me out of my damn mind, because there's no way this man knows what I'm thinking. Taking my hand in his and lifting it to his lips, he kisses my palm. Electricity speeds from my palm, up to my arm, and throughout my body, bubbling in my core. Here we go.

"Hey, now cut it out, you two. No smoochie—smoochie in front of us; we don't want to see that," Delia says, shaking her head at us.

"What? All I did was give a quick kiss on her hand—nothing out there. Relax, big cousin Delia. I'm not all over her or anything like that. I'm just showing a little affection to my Sweetness." Putting his arm around my shoulder, he pulls me close as we get to the two choppers. Sash comes out in the doorway waving to us, and we wave back, speeding up our pace toward her.

"Sis, I thought you were going back to the hotel. Where's Ava and Griffin?" Naya gets to her right before I do.

"Princess Ava is inside with her King Griffin; yes, it's official, that man knows how to handle our girl. I couldn't picture having to sit in the hotel with her, even though Griffin got her to behave her damn self." Sash turns to walk inside, then Lucas and I follow her. The rest of our group reluctantly go into the other chopper. They want to know what happened. Oh well, we're going in the helicopter we came in.

Stepping in with Lucas, Samantha closes the door behind us. Surprisingly, Ava is asleep, with her legs propped up in Griffin's lap. "Hey Lyssa, hey Lucas, how was everything?" He greets us in a low voice, obviously trying not to wake Ava.

Ava's knocked out. Her cast, up to her knee, is painted half pink and half purple—her favorite colors, of course, and in bold neat letters on the pink side, Griffin has written, "Compórtate Bien, Mi Lo Loba Princesa," in purple marker. *Behave Yourself, My She-Wolf Princess.*

"Uhm, Griffin, why did you call Ava a she-wolf?"

Sasha laughs. "Really, sis, you have to ask that question?"

Griffin brought his attention directly to Ava. "Well, she scared the Hell out of those dogs earlier and acted crazy in the hospital. I figured it's a perfect name for her."

Putting my hand over my forehead and going to my seat, I glare at Sash, and she shakes her head and raises her hands defensively. "Oh, no, I was on the phone with you when he did that. I know what your thinking: Uncle S is going to flip out when he sees it."

I fasten my seatbelt, knowing somehow we have to explain that this is a joke, because it's too early for Ava to be Griffin's anything. Our uncle is old school, and he's not going to be thrilled about this; not one bit. That's a promise.

Lucas

AWW, Sweetness is worried about what her uncle will say when he reads that cast. Since he's a shifter, he and Griffin will work it out, even though he hasn't had the opportunity and blessing of meeting his mate yet. Ava's father does know what happens if they're forced to be apart.

Sitting in the same seats we were in previously, I buckle my seatbelt.

Chapter 22

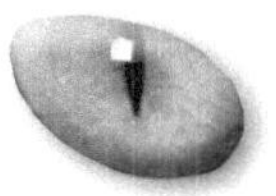

Taking a Bite

Lucas

WHILE Sweetness discusses Ava's situation with Sasha, it's time to see what the Hell happened at the hospital with the little Hellion. I'll explore Sasha's memories first; hers should be the funniest.

Sasha's experience includes Ava's whining as the helicopter lands on the helipad on the hospital's roof. Griffin picks her up, walking out and into the hospital elevator. "Ava, can you calm down, please? You've gotten louder, and you aren't even walking on it, young lady."

Following them, Sasha scrunches her face and shakes her head, pressing the emergency room button. *This damn girl is acting like an idiot, blaming the guys for her stupidity. All Ava had to do was change into the freaking hiking boots. If I were Griffin, I'd let her ass hop on one leg, not carrying her with her talking crap. It was funny when she fell—I can't deny it, and I have a maid for thirty days as soon as she's able.*

The elevator slows down on the fifth floor and people get on. "Ava, please act like you have some sense. We have people coming on the elevator, and we don't need you embarrassing us here." She gives her the side-eye while she wrinkles her nose.

The elevator doors slide open, and three doctors, two male and one female, enter, followed by a male attendant.

"My foot is really hurt, and I'm in a lot of pain! If you guys would've chosen a common place for a date, this wouldn't have happened, so this isn't my fault! You had me in a weird position."

Just great; now they're looking at us curiously like we were in a three-some. "Excuse me, are you on your way to the ER?" The female speaks to Ava. Her ID badge states, "Dr. Claire Willis, Intern."

"Yes, we're going to the ER. My date over here caused me to hurt my foot and my ankle. Some positions are not meant to be tried."

Ava gazes slyly at Griffin, and he shakes his head. "This is Ava, and she's lying; she's stubborn as Hell and acts like a wild child who's been away from civilization for a long time."

Their attention goes from Ava to Griffin, trying to figure out who's telling the truth. I clear my throat with a loud cough, and they turn to me. "I'm Dr. Sasha Laskaris. This young lady is my little cousin, Ava, and right now, she's acting like an idiot." I shake my head, wanting to slap Ava so bad my hand is itching.

"Really? I'm a damn idiot? Well, you made a bet with this idiot. So, what does that make you? I know, an even dumber, dateless idiot!" Ava is seriously going to make me punch her ass in the damn face.

Thank God the elevator is at the ER now. The doors open, the staff move aside, and we walk out, searching for the triage nurse I was referred to. Oh, crap, several arrows are pointing to different areas. The black marble walls care overed with red, green, yellow, orange, and lavender arrows. We need to focus on the red one for the Emergency Room. Looking over at Griffin, we both point in the right direction and speed up our pace before she starts again.

Passing by the gift shop, Ava pouts, "Griffin, I'm hungry. We have to hurry so I can eat something, because I'm going to start getting kind of cranky if I don't eat."

Griffin stops at that statement, eyeing Ava incredulously. "What? You mean the way you've been acting is, uh, nice?"

"I'm not being mean or anything; I'm hurt! This is so damn unfair that I'm stuck having to be in the ER." Ava whines like she's the only freaking one here at this hospital. She is sickening, and dammit, I can't wait to get home.

"I can't stand being at the hospital with the antiseptic smell and the fact the people die here all the time. I don't want to be here, Griffin." She gives Griffin her pleading, puppy dog eyes.

Sighing, Griffin glances at me and I shrug, shaking my head. "Ava, you have to get an X-ray to see what's going on with your foot. Your foot and ankle are significantly swelled up, so something is happening. We need you to cooperate and act like—how can I say this without you taking it the wrong way—"

"What he's saying is to act like you have some damn sense, Ava; the crap you pulled in the elevator wasn't cool at all."

Rolling her damn eyes, as usual, she grins. "I was only joking around. Geez, can't I have some fun with you two?"

Finally, we're at the emergency room entrance. Walking over, I press the button to open the double doors. There are only four patients in the waiting area. At the registration area, there's an older woman there who's not very friendly; she crosses her arms and clenches her jaw as we approach her. Whatever. I look at her nametag, and say, "Hello, Raquel, I'm Dr. Laskaris, I'm looking for Valarie in Triage. Can you please call her for me and tell her we're here?"

Her funky attitude changes into a better one, and she picks up the phone and asks for Valarie. "She's on her way, Dr. Laskaris, and can you give your cousin's insurance information, please?" She smiles, even though a few minutes ago, she was rude as Hell, before knowing I was a physician. I hand Ava's insurance card and identification to Raquel, who collect the information and returns the cards to me.

The double doors open. An attractive young woman comes out, and her attention is immediately on Ava. Smiling, she offers me her hand. As I shake it, she introduces herself. "Hi, Dr. Laskaris, nice to meet you in person."

"Hi, Valarie, nice meeting you in person, as well." Releasing my hand quickly, she focuses her attention on Griffin. She's transfixed, I might add.

"Hello, there, fine sir. I'm Valarie, and you are?" she says, with a beautiful smile that, in my opinion, would cause any red-blooded, unattached male to light up.

At first, there is confusion in Griffin's eyes. Then, after a quick glance at Ava, who gives him a dismissive wave, he offers Valarie a sexy-ass grin. "Hey, Valarie, I'm Griffin, and this here is our patient, little Ava."

Don't get me wrong; Griffin and his brothers are gorgeous, but I don't see any of them the way Valarie obviously does.

"We can go into triage to get her vitals and head straight to orthopedics; she'll need an x-ray for sure. Let's get Ava a wheelchair and free those arms of yours, Griffin." Winking her eye at him, she turns, strutting her stuff, as we follow her to triage. Griffin chuckles. Peeking over at him, it seems that he's watching Valarie giving him a show. Ava frowns. She lifts herself up and bites the Hell out of Griffin's shoulder, and he actually growls! What the fuck? Since when in the Hell has Ava started biting people?

Get the Hell out of here! I've got to get into Griffin's mind right fucking now. I know Griffin was upset about invading his memories before, but what the Hell? He'll never know I was here unless I tell him.

Griffin's experience—*Why am I being punished? This girl has been whining since we've been on this damn helicopter. After Samantha told us we were five minutes away, Ava got even louder.*

Panther—*Ava is our mate. It's NOT a punishment that she is ours. She'll take some time to tame, that's all. A mate is our gift; be grateful that we are part of the lucky ones who find their mates.*

Tiger—*Yes, you'll have to be patient with her. Remember, she's very young. We'll be there to assist with her maturing into the woman we'll all love and provide for. I'll rip apart anyone who messes with our Ava.*

Griffin—*Relax, you two. I really can't believe she is our mate. She's spoiled rotten, immature, a pain in the ass, and a bitch. Please let her get better as she gets older. Come the Hell on, a threesome? This damn girl—no, she's not a grown-ass woman—this girl is being fucking ridiculous, giving the impression that we're having a damn threesome to these doctors.*

I swear, I'm going to put her over my knee and spank her ass. Hmm, knowing my luck, it'll turn us both on. This all began over her refusing to wear the damn hiking boots. Fucking unbelievable. She's beautiful on the outside, and from what I've witnessed, this is only on the surface. I'm praying I'm wrong.

Tiger—*We're aren't wrong about her, and there's much more to her than on the surface.*

She's made some bad decisions lately, and no one's perfect. She is our mate, and when her animal wakes up, we will be right there for her, just like we're here for her now. No one else will touch what's ours!

Griffin—*Calm the Hell down, please. I know she's ours, and I'm the only one out of our trio who isn't thrilled. I'm trying to get to know her, and both of you should be paying attention.*

Panther—*Grif, she's hungry, we have to get her something to eat. We have to provide for Ava.*

Griffin—*Ava's definitely not starving, and her injury is more important than getting her something to eat. You two know what we have? A pain in the ass named Ava. After we get her checked out, we can feed her, so does that satisfy you both?*

What in the Hell does she mean, if she doesn't eat, she'll get cranky? What does she call the crazy-ass way she's been acting? If there were a way I could reject her ass as my mate without losing the two of you, I'd say those words the moment she began to shift.

Panther and Tiger—*Hell no!*

Griffin—*I said if 'I would never do anything to risk losing either one of you. Get a grip. I can't, and both of you and her in my damn head and ear. Just watch, and relax, dammit.*

Valarie's definitely flirting, and Ava's acting like she doesn't care. Well, all right, we'll test the water and see how she reacts to me answering Nurse Valarie in a flirtatious manner. Little wild princess, Ava.

Griffin—*After my answer, Ava needs a little lesson, since I'm pretending that I'm watching her ass as she walks ahead of us.*

Tiger—*Grif, I don't think that's a great idea—ROAR!*

Panther—*PURRRR!*

Griffin—*Suddenly, I feel a searing pain in my neck and shoulder. I look down, and what the fuck!? This girl just bit the shit out of my shoulder! Fiery tingling races through my body, paralyzing me, and an unfamiliar roaring is ringing through my brain. A kaleidoscope of colors is invading my vision. What the Hell?*

Panther and Tiger—*FUCK YES!*

Tiger—*She bit through your skin at the curve of your neck and shoulder. Her animal's DNA is surging through you right now, and our DNA is doing the same to her. Mates!*

Griffin—*This is impossible! Ava's never shifted before; this couldn't have just happened. How can this shit be for real? I've been marked by a shifter whose animal is fucking sleeping? I've never in my damn life heard of this before. With this crazy-ass young woman, anything is possible.*

Panther- *It's fate, Griffin, that Ava got jealous of us with another woman, and, somehow, her intuition guided her to mark you. Marked mates: we're hers, and she and her animal are ours.*

Griffin—*So what the Hell does this exactly mean? I had four years to get to know her and watch her ass hopefully grow into maturity. What the Hell? How do I explain this to her father?*

Tiger—*It'll be great once he calms down from the shock of you taking his only baby girl away from him. He can't kill you. Ava will be devastated if she loses you, and best of all, she did this to you. To be honest, she's a prime example of why families shouldn't keep being shifters a secret.*

Panther—*It's the truth, Grif; you didn't mark her. We didn't see this coming, and it's unprecedented. Ava's unique, and to top it off, she's a little wildcat. We'll have to move closer to Ava, since she doesn't live with her cousins. We need to be with her, and living down the road isn't close enough.*

I'm finally able to move, and my vision slowly clears. I immediately see Ava, and she's stunned into a trance as well.

"Hey, Griffin." Sasha's snapping her fingers in my face.

Keeping my eyes on Ava, I answer, "Yes, Sasha?"

"Griffin, you're bleeding! I can't believe you, Ava!" Sasha is a bit upset with her cousin.

"I'm fine, Sasha. It's just blood, and I've lost more than this at one time. Yeah, I was the accident-prone one in the family during my younger years."

"Ava! What the Hell? Since when have you started acting like a wild animal?" Sasha's talking to an unresponsive Ava.

Sasha claps her hands in Ava's face, and she finally snaps out of it. Staring at me in fear and confusion, she exhales shakily. "I need to talk to you, privately, now."

"Excuse me, you two, this is a hospital, and I have a job to do. We probably need to get you a rabies shot, Griffin, since you were bitten." Nurse Valarie speaks with some irritation, pointing to the room she was leading us into.

"I'm great; no need, Valarie. Would it be all right if Ava and I go into triage alone for maybe five minutes?"

She shakes her head and frowns, but Sasha goes over to her. "Please, Valarie, just five minutes, because obviously, they need to have a quick conversation."

"You have exactly five minutes, and, no you-know-what in my triage."

"Uh, I said talk; besides, I'd take a helluva lot longer than five minutes." Laughing, he strolls over to triage with Ava in his arms.

Ava, you little Hellion, here I come to find out what's going in that whacky-ass mind of yours.

Ava's experience—*First, I'm disappointed that my cousins went on their dates, and I'm hurt. I never would have done that to any of them. No, I'm more than that; I'm hurt, too. I'm physically and emotionally injured, and that's a hell of a lot to deal with. Griffin didn't know, but I watched him when those doctors came in, and those women were checking him out, so yeah, I said the threesome comment.*

GROWL. My stomach rumbled loudly, and neither one of them act like they heard it. What the Hell? Feed the injured woman over here. I'll even take a candy bar. I'm not requesting a meal at this very moment, damn it. If I don't get some kind of food in my stomach soon, I'm going to be a very cranky young woman, and he'll think I'm bitchy.

Finally, we're in the emergency room, and I can get an x-ray of my foot and ankle. Then I can get something to damn eat. Sasha has everything under control, and I've never felt so comfortable with any man besides the men in my family before. Leaning my head on Griffin's chest and listening to his heartbeat causes me to smile. He could be someone important in the future. Something about Griffin connects me to him, and it's confusing as Hell.

I've never felt this way about any guy; it's always just been about me getting them excited then leaving them hanging. Everyone thinks they know so much about me being promiscuous when they don't know a damn thing in reality. I don't know, but since I've met Griffin, it's like something's slowly waking up inside of me. What the Hell could that be? I'll find out whenever the time's right, I suppose, as Mami used to say when I had questions when I was younger.

I've never been attracted to any of the guys I've gone out with. Griffin is the first man I've felt this strong urge to jump on and have my way with. Why am I possessive over a man I met not even twenty-four hours ago? Here's the nurse Sasha was speaking to on the phone. What the Hell? Why is she checking out my Griffin? Wait a minute. I must be imagining the sexy undertones in her voice, and she's talking to my damn man! I can't show how this is upsetting me, so waving my hand and rolling my eyes at Griffin seems to be a good idea.

What the fuck does he think he's doing, talking to her like he's interested in her and watching her switch her ass down the corridor? Hell NO! Rage like I've never experienced before overwhelms me, and every cell inside of me is rapidly burning, increasing, until I can't see anything, but an inflamed animal roaring the words He's mine and yours! Ours! Claim him NOW! I'm not in control of my body right now, and it's listening to the animal's voice.

This definitely is an out-of-body experience, looking at Griffin and listening to his heartbeat between hearing the word mine after every beat. Quicker than I ever thought I could move, my head's by his neck, and I'm biting down hard as I can into his shoulder by the crook of his neck. What's happening? I'm frozen in place with my teeth sunken into Griffin! There's some type of liquid flowing from my teeth into him. Oh, my God, what is this?

After what seems like forever, I release Griffin from my, um, what? Animal instincts? Oh, God, why am I licking where I bit him? What. The. Hell? A flash blinding white light and blazing fire surges through my being from my hair follicles down to my toenails. I lose my breath momentarily as I hear the roaring and purring of animals in my mind. You are ours! I see Griffin, with a tiger on his right and a panther on his left. Why do I see animals with Griffin, who are stating I'm theirs? What the Hell is going on here?

Hell, maybe we all should've gone to the damn hospital with them. Damn; Ava's animal doesn't seem like she's going to wait four years to introduce herself!

CHAPTER 23

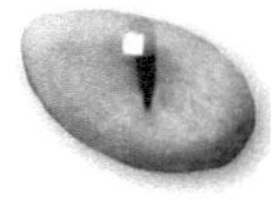

SOMETHING'S INSIDE

Lucas

SWEETNESS'S voice snaps me back to the present. "Lucas, honey, are you all right?" Damn! I turn to her with a smile, but she appears troubled. Oh, yeah, she knows what Ava did.

"Yes, Sweetness, I'm okay; just deep in thought, that's all." Checking outside, we're back in Vegas, about to land on the hotel's roof. Glancing over at Griffin, he's watching his little sleeping hellion.

"Lucas, while you were extremely deep in thought, Sasha caught me up on the events at the hospital. You're not going to believe this, because I damn sure didn't. Sasha thinks Ava was jealous of the pretty nurse. Valarie was flirting with Griffin, and when he returned a little attention to the lady, her crazy ass bit Griffin on the neck. Look at his neck; it's as if he were a delicious, thick piece of chocolate cake—her favorite damn dessert." Sweetness is staring at Ava and then back at Griffin, trying to figure out what the Hell is going on.

Griffin shrugs and shakes his head. "Like I told Sasha, I don't know what's going on."

"Damn, Ava really did that? Well, Griffin, you better make sure you never, ever do that shit again." I point to Griffin's little sleeping Hellion. "That young woman with her legs on your lap takes you better not look or speak to another woman to another level. Good luck."

I'll get him talking to me, so all he has to do is get the Hell out of this chopper with Ava when we land. "Griffin, are you going to stay with Ava, or are you going to see if she's up to going out?"

"I'll wait to see how she's feeling, then I'll decide." Griffin's very suspicious.

Lucas, were you running around in my damn mind? What happened to boundaries, man? And I thought we discussed this shit. Come on. And you know I know you did, want to know how? You asked about Ava in the sense of her being mine. You would've gone to Sasha with that question, as her older cousin.

I'm just asking because Ava's your damn mate, and I know how your animals are about leaving her. And look at your fucking neck.

No way in Hell I'm going to let him know I was in his head to see that shit, especially when she marked him, but it'll come up one way or another when his brothers see his neck. Or maybe he plans on wearing fucking turtlenecks from now on, even though he's watching me as if he knows that I saw something in his fucking head; not to mention the fact the bite is out in the open. I'll never admit it, though.

Lyssa

I CAN'T believe Ava bit Griffin! Seriously, what the Hell is wrong with her? She's been asleep the entire ride, then Griffin's picking her up from the couch and she sighs, wrapping her arms around his neck. This girl is knocked the Hell out; what kind of medicine did they give her? Sasha sped out of here soon as we landed, probably ready to tell everyone what Ava did.

Smack! Ouch, Lucas slaps my ass and looks back at him as he's grinning and nodding his head. I won't lie; that slap gave off some spark, and it was hot, too.

"That's just a taste of the payback from earlier Sweetness. I have plenty of surprises for you, Lovely. You know you enjoy what I do to you." I shake my head, but I have to laugh at him. Stepping out of the chopper, Sasha paces impatiently and holds Ava's purple and pink crutches while the others are exiting from the other helicopter. Griffin's expression is one of pure irritation, and he's whispering into Ava's ears as she sleeps. That's not the way to wake Ava up. That girl sleeps like a log, and that's without the assistance of medication.

"Ladies and Gentlemen, I have news to share with each of you. While we were at the hospital, Ava had some type of weird-ass type of mental break, and she bit the Hell out of Griffin's damn neck!"

"Wait, what did you just say?" Grayson and Garrison ask in unison. They're frozen in place and their eyes and mouths are open from shock, I presume.

"I know you heard me, but Ava got highly upset when Griffin had an attractive woman flirting with him. Then Ava went psycho when he flirted back just a tiny bit and watched her strutting down the corridor." She lifts up one of the crutches towards Griffin, who is by the elevator with our Sleeping Princess.

"Damn, I never thought Ava could shock the Hell out of me, but dammit, she has done it! Who the Hell does that? Honestly?" Naya throws her hands up, putting her hand on her forehead. "Let's get to the hotel and get ready for the second half of our dates." Saying goodbye and thank you to the crew, we set off to the hotel.

Getting back to the hotel, Griffin looks apprehensive about leaving Ava here with us. This man is kind of cute, but we have been around Ava since she came here after her mom died. What the Hell would we do to her? She's our family, and even though she's our personal pain in the ass at times, we love that girl.

I want to ask Griffin so bad about that damn bite, but I think Ava's the one we need to ask. "Wake up your she-wolf Griffin. Ava needs to wake the Hell up, so we can know if she's going out." Janae has a point, because we do need to know how Ava's feeling.

These inquiring minds have to know what the Hell happened in the damn hospital. Sitting on the couch and still carrying Ava, Griffin shakes her gently, and calls her name softly. Oh, I can't take this; why is he acting like this girl is all damn fragile and delicate? A bit frustrated, I walk into the bathroom, pick out a clean washcloth from the linen closet, turn on the faucet, and wet the cloth with cold water. Squeezing the excess water from the washcloth, I go back into the living with Sleeping Beauty and Prince Charming, shaking my head at the fact that she's still sleeping and he's doing the same thing he was when I left.

Walking over to the couch, I lay the cold rag on Ava's head and shout, "Ava, wake the Hell up, girl! In a minute, I'm throwing ice water on you."

Naya runs into the kitchen, and, of course, she returns with a large glass of ice water. "Please don't wake up, Ava, so I can splash you with this damn water." Shaking the glass excitedly, she may get to pour a little ice water on Ava.

Watching us as if we'd suddenly grown two heads, Griffin pulls Ava up and sits her on his lap. "Come on, Ava, time to wake up; I have to leave now. Come on, Princess."

"Come on, Pixie, wake up, now!" I'm laughing at our childhood nickname for her. Griffin looks at me strangely. "Ava was so tiny and had light hair; when she moved, she reminded us of a magical Pixie. So, we called her Pixie for a long time."

Oh, no! A splash of icy cold water hits my arm, and ice falls onto the carpet. At the same time, wait to see if Ava is waking up, but Griffin moves out of the way so fast that I know my eyes have to be playing tricks on me. There's no damn way that I didn't see him move, so maybe I haven't been paying attention like I thought I was? That has to be it. Also, we walked about 18 miles today. I'm a little tired, but the day isn't over yet.

"Ahhhh, oh, man, I'm awake!" Ava stretches her arms over her head and arches her back in Griffin's arms. "You carried me all the way here, Tiger?" She smiles goofily at Griffin. He nods, and a slow, satisfied smile lights up Griffin's face. I guess he likes being called a tiger! Speaking in her ear, Ava nods to whatever Griffin's saying to her, then shakes her head.

Clapping my hands and clearing my throat, I say, "Griffin, I'm sorry to interrupt you two. As you know, we are on a schedule for the day you guys have planned for us, and we have to start getting ready."

"Okay, I'll go and get ready myself, and Ava can go on the second part of our date, but we'll have to sit out the last part. I'll carry her to her bedroom, because today she should be taking it easy."

"Griffin, we have an elevator and five strong, young women to help Ava. She's as light as, well, not as light as a feather, but we have it under control. No matter what she says, we've got the situation under control." I cross my arms and arch my eyebrow at both of them.

Griffin laughs, and Ava frowns at him. "Lyssa, I'm going to take you at your word and take care of her; she's special to me."

He lowers her onto the chaise and fixes the pillows under her feet. Giving her hand a light squeeze, he looks at her for a good while longer than any goodbye I've ever seen. Griffin gets up and checks his phone. "Ladies, Adios; we'll see you all in about one hour and forty minutes." The five of us give him an "Adios" as well, and Janae follows him. We hear the beep from the door and the clicking of the lock, and we wait for Janae to return.

Janae runs across the foyer, then she enters; we look at Ava, then all scream, "What the hell happened at the hospital?!"

Ava, still confused, looks at us with her face flushed and tears building in her eyes. Breathing shakily, she speaks. "I can't tell you all everything, but one thing is for sure, I'm bat shit crazy! I have something else inside of me, and I couldn't control myself!"

"Uh, what do you mean you have something else inside of you, Ava?" Janae speaks as we all were about to say the thing.

We walk over and sit on the sectional, looking at each other, then back at Ava, waiting for clarification. Naya taps her foot, watching

Ava keenly. Rubbing her hand on her forehead, Ava sighs and leans her head back on the chaise, shutting her eyes. "I don't know how to say this, but I'll just let it out. I was fine until I saw women being attentive to my Griffin."

"Uh, huh; I agree with you this is crazy. Since when did Griffin become yours, Ava?" Naya's words are laced with sarcasm, plus she's wrinkling up her face and crossing her arms.

"How in the Hell am I supposed to damn know? I can tell you that I felt so comfortable with Griffin, and we have a connection. When that heifer, Nurse Valarie, started flirting with my Griffin, yes, I was angry, but when he acted like he was interested in her, we were both enraged."

"Oh, God," Janae, Naya, and I all said in unison. Delia shakes her head and asks, "Who the Hell is we, Ava?"

"I told you already! There's an animal of some kind inside of me, and she was enraged and took over!" Tears trickle down her face, and she angrily wipes them off.

"Calm down, Ava. So take us through what was happening when you bit him." Sasha is calmly and carefully listening to Ava's responses.

"I was there, but it was some type of animal, and she controlled me. It was made clear to me that Griffin is ours, not just mine. Griffin damn sure doesn't belong to anyone else. I was a spectator, and I didn't have any control of my body when that bite happened. If I say anything more, I'll have a one-way ride to the nuthouse, and Griffin will have to come and rescue me."

Janae jumps up, pacing. "So, how does Griffin feel about the fact that you bit him? I mean, if you did that shit to any other man, you could've been charged with assault, or another guy would've even knocked the Hell out of you."

Ava immediately shuts down, visibly. "Griffin understands, and that's all I can say about that."

Naya and Sasha both say, "What the Hell?" Naya adds, "What do you mean I can't talk about that? We're your damn family, and something freaky as Hell is happening to you. How can we help you, dammit?"

"You all know I love you, right?"

We nod our heads. "We love you, too, dummy." Well, the dummy part came from Naya, of course, smart ass number one.

Rolling her eyes at Naya, Ava continues, "There are some things you won't be able to help me with. Just like there'll be times when I have to let you deal with your special issues when they happen." She glances at the clock on the wall. "Believe me, we'll all have our moment. Don't we have to start getting ready? We don't have much time."

Rooted in my seat, I point at Ava. "Guess what, Pixie? You're more important than going on dates, and this is a serious situation. What happens if or when this animal decides to appear again?"

"Yeah, something is going on, and we can't just act like nothing's happening. You're younger than we are, so the question is, why you and not us?" Sasha asks thoughtfully.

"I don't know what else to tell you, and if you need more information, ask Griffin or my Dad. The older people in our family may know. I can't tell you anything else." Ava's stomach growls loudly, "I'm starving! Can we please get ready to go eat lunch?"

We look at each other, because it's evident that we won't be getting any other answers from Ava. Delia walks over to Ava, whispers in her ear, then kisses her on the cheek. Facing the rest of us, she sighs and says, "I've got to go down to our suite and get ready myself. Y'all got so damn fortunate, getting this penthouse."

Motioning around the room and spinning, Janae sings, "There's room for you, but you wanted to be with the yellow bikini man, your fiancée, Steve."

Silence falls over the room, then laughter erupts from everyone except Ava. "What's so damn funny, and why are you singing with your non singing self about Steve wearing a bikini?"

I stop laughing to try to explain. "At the—"

Suddenly, Janae intervenes. "Nope, you had to see it to believe it. This was a moment you could only get if you saw it."

"Oh, God, you are so crazy, Janae. I'll see you all in a little while." Delia leaves, going to her bikini man.

Naya and Sasha go over and help Ava up off of the chaise. Naya says, "Listen, Ava, today we'll help you with crutches, but starting tomorrow, you will have to use them. You'll need help in the shower, and I understand that, but that's it." They help Ava to the elevator while she hops on her uninjured leg. Disbursing from the living room, we all go to get ready for our afternoon date.

Lucas

I CAN'T pass up the opportunity to join the brothers to hear Griffin's explanation of being marked.

"Lucas, is something going on with Ava that we don't know about? She had to know what she was doing, right?" Garrison is pacing, and he's freaking the Hell out. He's going to have a damn heart attack.

"No, Ava's scared to death about what happened. I can you one thing, though; her animal will not wait four years to emerge. After what happened today, it's going to be much sooner. Calm down, both of you. Griffin's on his way here." I'm relaxing on the chaise; it seems to be my favorite piece of furniture, other than the bed.

We're waiting here with these guys in their penthouse while they have all these questions bombarding their minds, and I want them to ask them all. Will Griffin be sincere with us, or will he act like this isn't fucking his head up? I hear the beeping tone from the card key, and the door swings open. The lock clicks closed again, and the questions begin.

"How in the fuck are you marked? What the Hell is going on?" Grayson and Garrison are both yelling at the same time. Here we go…

Griffin enters the living room. "I don't know why, how, or what the Hell happened! Fuck, I was busy making Ava's ass jealous since she was acting all nonchalant, and the next thing I knew, she was biting the shit out of me!" Griffin stomps off to the kitchen and his brothers look more confused than they did before he walked in the door. Coming back with an eight-pack of beer, he hands a cold one to each of us. "I need a damn drink, but nothing too strong, since we're taking our ladies out soon."

We open up the beer and raise the bottles. "To our mates. Let's hope that my Ava will be able to convince her cousins not to worry about her biting me."

Drinking a swig of beer and sitting it in the cupholder, I voice my thoughts. "If you think that Ava will be able to get those women to stop worrying about what happened today, you must still be suffering from the side effects of being bitten. Seriously, they have no idea about the shifter world, and now they're going to ask a Hell of a lot of questions. This has been caused by their family keeping secrets, and nothing else."

"What the fuck is going to happen when I meet her father? Is he going to understand why I was out on a date with her and didn't introduce myself to him first?" Griffin opens up his second beer, guzzles it down, and lets out a long burp. This guy is worried about Ava's father's reaction to all of this. He starts pacing, then he goes over to the window, stares outside, and rubs his free hand over his forehead.

Garrison strolls up to Griffin. "Bro, listen; how in the Hell can he be upset with you when he has kept this from his daughter? And there's also the fact that she bit you!"

"Remember, we have Alpha blood surging through us, as well, and we don't have to ask anything of our mates' family when it's a Raveinah, and Ava is most definitely, without a doubt, in that category." Grayson nurses his beer.

Not wanting to be rude by going through their thoughts to find out information, I wait for a second for clarification. Since no one has said anything, it's my turn. "Guys, what the Hell is a Raveinah?"

"Oh, shit. Sorry, Lucas; it's when mates are fated—in other words, true mates. We can be with other women who don't affect our beasts." Taking a gulp of his beer, Grayson continues. "You have people who fall in love and have families together, but they're not true mates. Their beasts haven't connected spiritually, even though their hearts have. When our beasts connect, they're each others' Raveinah. Once we meet our fated mate, we can't be with another after we're marked. Honestly, once you see your Raveinah, you don't have any desire for another."

Bringing my attention back to Griffin, "Since Ava's your Raveinah, her father shouldn't have a problem, in my opinion. If he didn't want her to meet a shifter, then he should've kept her in the fucking house."

"You know I've been thinking that today is some weird-ass nightmare that I'll be waking up from at any time. Hell, I even pinched myself, but I didn't wake up." Griffin's shaking his head, frowning, and crossing his arms.

"Bro, I'd think after that bite Ava gave you, it would've been clear that the pain was definitely happening," Grayson said, shaking his head in disbelief. Yes, Griffin, this is reality; you're not dreaming, that's for damn sure.

"We need to start getting ready, because we've got about thirty minutes before we have to pick our mates up. Let's go. And Lucas, just transport back in when you're ready." Griffin is anxious to see his Reveinah. We all have super speed, and we can be showered and dressed within five minutes.

CHAPTER 24

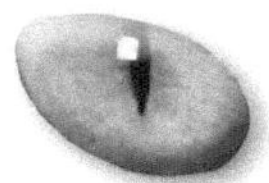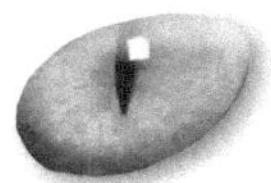

MYSTERY MANOR

Lyssa

WE'RE back in the helicopters. I'm leaning on Lucas's shoulder and, opening my eyes, I realize I fell asleep. Approaching an airport, there are two luxury vehicles parked by the runway. Of course, this is another surprise, so I won't even waste my time asking the typical question, "Where are we going?" Tilting my head, I look over at Sasha, and she raises her eyebrow at me. Yes, we're both wondering if this will be lunch and maybe something crazy like bungee jumping.

Samantha comes out from the cockpit. "Ladies and gentlemen, we're going to land in three to five minutes. Please fasten your seatbelts if you're unbuckled."

"Sweetness, you did enjoy the waterfalls, right?"

"Yes, you know I did, Lucas. Those were incredible waterfalls, and the company was the best."

"So why are you so worried about where we're taking you all out to eat? We've proven that we have fantastic taste."

"Speak for yourself, Lucas, and I do remember that Griffin planned this entire trip!" I giggle a little, shake my head, and point at him.

Lucas smirks. "I already proved to you that I have excellent date planning skills. Did you forget our first date, Sweetness?"

How could I not remember that sexy first date we had? "Yes, I take that statement back, and Lucas, you are a magnificent planner."

"Oh, God, really? You both are too funny. If you want to keep our destination a secret, just say that, please. I'm not really that interested in hearing about how sexy Lucas and Lyssa's first date was," Sasha announces, goofily rolling her eyes.

Griffin gets up, carefully laying Ava's leg on the couch. He goes to the refrigerator, opens it, and takes out a bottle of black cherry soda. Twisting the cap open, he brings it over, handing it to Ava.

"I hope we'll be there soon after we land, because I'm damn starving!" Ava says, looking at everyone like it's our fault she's hungry.

Sasha takes her shades off. "How do you act as if you're the only hungry person here? We walked and climbed for about 20 miles. We built up appetites too, Pixie, and it's not all about you. All of us are probably starving at this very moment."

"Okay, I'll include everybody. How about this? We're starving! I hope we will get to eat soon." At least she's thinking about the group and not just herself.

"Pixie, that's much better, and yes, I'm starving too, and I can't wait to eat." With that being said, my stomach growls, then Lucas and Sasha start laughing.

"We can tell you ladies that our destination is about 30 minutes away from this airport. And yes, there will be delicious food for us all to chow down on," Griffin says while helping Ava up off the couch.

The chopper descends onto the runway, close to luxury vehicles like those at the hotel. "Have a great time at lunch, everyone, and we'll be here when you all are done." The pilot sends us off into the world of more surprises.

The driver greets us. "Hello, Ladies and Gentlemen, I'm Luis, your driver, and I hope you all enjoy yourselves today."

Opening the passenger doors, he motions for the ladies to enter first. Of course, Griffin carries Ava in while Sasha holds her crutches. I go in after Sasha. I go over to sit in the oversized, cream-colored leather seats. I lean back, relaxing and listening to the jazz music playing. The seats against the wall are arranged in a half-moon shape. There's a large screen television and a small refrigerator, which Griffin opens. It's loaded with soda, water, beer, and, yes, candy bars.

"Griffin, oh, yes, please bring me a candy bar!" Ava yells after spotting what's in the refrigerator. Ava's bouncing in her seat, like a child about to get a treat. Taking a few candy bars out, Griffin brings enough for all of us to get a snack. Peeling the paper off, I take a bite, close my eyes, and savor the yummy, creamy, melting chocolate on my tongue. I exhale, lick my lips, then devour the rest of the candy bar.

Everybody's quiet, and we are all listening to the music playing when the vehicle slows down to a complete stop. "Ladies and Gents, we have arrived." Luis hops out of the driver's seat, but Lucas opens the door before he gets around the vehicle. "It's okay, Luis, I've got it. Also, we are gentlemen who open doors for our dates." Helping me out of the vehicle, Lucas moves me over to the side. "I need you to face me, and when Griffin and I give the word, then you turn and see where we are. Okay?"

I nod, wondering what's with all of the cloak and dagger stuff. The others must be inside already, since I don't hear Naya's loud voice. Sasha walks next to me, saying, "These guys take a date to another level. If I had a date, I don't know if I'd be irritated or intrigued."

"Think about it, Sash. It's cute that they want us to experience something new with them. If you knew who did this for you, you'd love that he took the time to plan this."

"Yeah, Sasha, come on, if you had that someone you care about here, I agree with Lyssa—you'd enjoy it one hundred percent."

Lucas chimes in, "Hell, yeah, she would love it." Griffin agrees, and Ava punches him on the arm.

"All right, ladies; turn around on three: one, two, and three!"

We spin around and, damn, this is definitely unexpected. Oh, my God, a creepy all-black, three-level mansion. Ugh, who wants to have fun here? I know I don't… What the Hell? There are black frosted panel windows with weird-ass eye designs on some of the glass. "What is this place, Lucas and Griffin?"

"Sweetness, it's a restaurant, and we're going to have lunch here."

My eyes narrow as I try to figure out what the Hell is going on here. I have no desire to eat somewhere that reminds me of a damn horror movie that I'm too scared to even go watch.

"Dammit, if my foot and ankle weren't hurt, this would be so awesome! How many times have I imagined going into a building like this!? Thousands!" Ava lets us know that this is her dream coming true at the worse possible time. Hopefully, running isn't involved, because she's very slow with those crutches.

Sasha puts her hands on her hips and turns to both men. "I'm just wondering who in the Hell picked this place? This looks like a mansion of horrors, and I'm stuck here because our ride has left."

I hug Sasha tightly, inhaling and exhaling and calming myself down, first, before speaking. "Listen up, my Scary, Sparkly Spice Sasha, we are all in this together, and we will not get hurt here until each and every male is either dead or unconscious. So, get it together, and above all, we are Laskaris women and can handle anything." I laugh, because I know damn well that Lucas won't let anything happen to any of us.

"This isn't what any of us were expecting as a lunch date, Grayson. We're going into a house of terrors; if the outside looks like this, how is the damn inside?" I turn to the left, hearing Janae's voice. They're walking from the back of the house.

"I'm excited to go inside. Just think: it'll be fun going into a possibly haunted mansion! Why did we get dropped in two different areas?" Rushing up to us, Naya's eyes glisten with eagerness and excitement. "We were in the spooky ass backyard, and if you think this is scary, you haven't seen the half of it. The back of this mansion leaves you speechless."

"We wanted to make sure that you all would be surprised and didn't give anything away. For example, if we all arrived at the same time, and someone, not mentioning anyone in particular, couldn't wait for the countdown and was to turn around before everyone else." Everyone in Janae's group is staring at Naya and nodding. Yes, she's the second impatient one, after Ava.

Even the long stairway, nestled in the middle of two massive black marble statues of hideous gargoyles spreading their wings, is black. Touching the smooth surface of the gargoyle's head, a chill goes down my spine, as if something sinister is in my presence, observing me. Grabbing Lucas's hand, he intertwines his fingers with mine, squeezing lightly, reassuring me that we're safe. At the top of the stairs, two more gargoyles sit on each side, as if on watch duty.

In the middle of each of the double black doors there is a lion's head knocker. Everyone is at the front door, except for Ava and Naya, and the rest of the women look at the guys like this is crazy! Why? Do they believe that this mysterious, scary place will be fun? I don't joke around or play with the paranormal, because I'm not trying to get any spirits pissed off at me.

I cross my arms and tap my foot, and Lucas steps up behind me, rubbing my shoulders. Naya runs in front of all of us and lifts the heavy lion's head and releases it with an ear-splitting *bang*! I damn near jump out of my skin. Lucas wraps his arms around my waist, and his body heat comforts me. Janae, Sasha, and Delia visibly do a tiny backward leap.

"That scared me, damn, why is it so freaking loud?" Sasha asks. I shake my head and bring my hand to my forehead. Sasha adds, "It's giving haunted house vibes all the way."

"Ladies, it's not a haunted house, okay? We're looking at off-the-charts creepy, I agree with you, but it's not a haunted house," Garrison finally says, after seeing our reactions. Lucas turns me around to face him and leans down, putting his forehead on mine. "Sweetness, do you honestly think I'd bring you somewhere that I know you wouldn't like? I remember everything we've talked about. I know you never said I love haunted houses, so I figured you didn't like them if you never said it."

The door opens, and an old man in a butler's suit answers, "Good afternoon, Ladies and Gentlemen, can I please have the last name the reservation is in?" Standing there, he seems almost as creepy as this mansion, but not quite.

"Good Afternoon, sir, the reservation is under Hellsin."

Nodding at Lucas, he gazes at us and introduces himself. "Excellent, Mr. Hellsin. I'm Dudley, and welcome to the Manor. Please follow me."

We follow Mr. Dudley into this creepy damn house, with its blood-red walls with different black and white types of art, some in abstract and prints. Walking on the black-and-red-checkered marble floor, with this dim lighting, increases the sinister factor. Walking up a flight of stairs, I raise my eyes to the ceiling, and—what's that!?

A statue of a man is suspended from the ceiling with a chain wrapped around his waist. Maybe it's a dance reference; his legs and arm are posed like a dancer's. I don't know what the Hell that's all about. This is way past the creepy stage.

"What the Hell is this? Oh, this is some craziness happening in here." Janae is freaking out. I slow down as we walk upstairs. I'm not excited about this place at all. Reaching the top, the only light is on the stairs; the rest of this floor is in complete darkness. Weird.

Suddenly, soft lights come on upstairs in the stairway. A man walks down the stairs in a hurry, carrying a pack of papers, and approaches us with a kind smile. "Hello everyone, my name's Tristan. Dudley, I'll take it from here."

Dudley, turning to us, says, "I bid you farewell, ladies and gentlemen," abruptly walking away while we're saying goodbye to him.

"Well. I must say that was weird as Hell," Ava remarks.

Tristan looks at Ava. "Oh, don't mind him. He's trying to get back because he's clocking out now."

With skepticism written on her face, Ava appears unconvinced, but she let her stare speak for her.

Tristan hands some of the papers from his packet to each of us. "Ladies and Gentlemen, please don't look at your documents just yet. Let me explain what you will experience in the next three hours of your day. This is called Masterpiece Mystery Dining, and while you and the other guests who will be here are all having lunch today, there will be a murder."

In the background, Janae, Delia, Sasha, and I are all saying, "What the hell?" Naya and Ava are high-fiving each other, saying, "Woohoo, oh yeah, we're going to solve a murder!" Those two are in extra excitement mode doing little dances, and Ava slips from under her crutches, with Griffin catching her.

Tristan continues, "Yes, there will be a murderer, and you will either be investigators who will find the killer or killers, or you will end up being a victim yourself. If you get too close, and no one else can protect you, you may die trying to discover who's the murderer. Let me clarify, you will not really die; you will just get hit with a paintball, and then you'll know you're dead. You'll no longer be in the competition to find out who did it."

"Oh God, oh God, who said that I'm not into this? Okay. Wait a minute. Why are we getting hit with damn paint-balls? I'm not trying to ruin my clothes." Janae realizes what I already have. Tristian's looking around at the ladies with a bit of fear. Right now, we're all giving him the evil eye. None of us are going to be okay with getting our freaking clothes ruined!

"Thank you, Lucas, and the rest of you guys. You mean to tell me we came here and are about to be acting like we are the investigators? Let's go! I'm ready, and I hope you're all ready because guess what? I'm going to find out who the killer is, and I'm not going to die. I'm damn ready to solve the case," Naya announces.

"No, sis; I'm going to find the killer, since I want to get the Hell out of here because, no matter what, this place is creepy as Hell. I better have fun, do you hear me, Mr. Grayson? And this sounds fun as long as I'm not the victim." Turning to Grayson, Janae kisses him on the cheek. "I'm sorry if I sound a little cranky, but I'm famished, and I know this won't be a regular meal, because we will be trying to find out who killed the victim. At least we're going to have lunch first before the murder happens."

Tristan clears his throat and says, "It's going to happen during lunch, so that means it could happen at any time. Maybe as soon as somebody sits down or in the middle or at the end: boom, someone's on the floor dead. Follow me into the dining area, please."

Ava, Janae, Delia, Naya, Sasha, and I look at each other then turn to the guys with different expressions all equaling pissed off women. Janae and I cross our arms, Naya and Sasha put their hands on their hips, and Ava is ready to explode. "We better get to eat before they start this damn murder crap!"

All I want to do is eat some good food. Now, I've got to focus on the other people around me, because someone's going to damn die. When I get some real food in my system, I know I'll feel better.

"Can I just eat my food and not play this game, please?" Ava whines. "As you see, I'm injured and on crutches and medicine. So I can't think about being an investigator right now. What if I get hurt while walking on the crutches checking out the crime scene?" Ava is using her injury to the fullest and, well, I can't blame her. If she gets hurt trying to play this game, that would be a horrible situation.

"How about I make it easier for you? You don't have to walk around, and you can investigate from your seat, but that still means you can be killed." Tristan comes up with a decent solution that won't get Ava injured even more.

The lights slowly brighten to a soft red glow that's weird against the blood-red walls. I don't understand why someone would want that, but being that it's a murder mystery house, I guess it adds more scariness. Oh wow, there are several gaudy-looking, life-sized, red and black statues from the Roman and Greek eras scattered around. There are bats and crows suspended in the air, too. Oh my God, this is just crazy. I'm trying, but this is creeping me out.

Ava's struggling with the crutches. Breathing heavily, she says, "I just don't know what to do with this, but I'm going to see about solving the murder mystery. I'm just hoping that when this person dies it's not bloody and he or she just falls down, you know? I mean, because if we're supposed to be eating, it's not going to be cute for us to see some type of bloody person while we're putting food in our mouths. I'm just keeping it real, because that's not cute at all, not cute." Tiny beads of perspiration appear on her forehead, and Griffin helps her.

"Well, I've got to say Ava has made some valid points." Naya is the first to point it out, and we all agree. We're walking into the dining area, and it's almost full of customers. I guess a lot of people like to solve murder mysteries. Our group has just turned this into a heck of a lot of people; eleven people added to any group is a significant difference. Altogether, there are forty-two people. Hmm, one of us should be able to solve this.

There are many round tables in different sizes, and of course, we have the largest one. The guys are always gentlemen, pulling out our seats and holding out the chairs for us. Aww, Lucas has even helped Sasha into her chair, since she's not with a date. That's my boo. Oh yeah; even though I've never said it out loud, he's my honey, but I've got to take my time. Here they come with the menus; let's see what they have to offer, because we're all starving.

This has to be a damn joke. We all frown at what we're reading. It's not cute at all: everything on the menu has red sauce all over it. I guess this is about a murder, and so the menu reflects it: blood bath shrimp, bloody fries, bloody chicken parmigiana, and death by gooey pasta. I can honestly say I don't have any idea what I want to eat. On that note, my stomach growls angrily. I guess this is death eats. I look at Lucas, and I think it's showing on my face, because he's not smiling anymore. This menu is awful. This isn't even like spaghetti; it's weird combinations with red sauce.

I can't believe this. Next time, guys, please, please go and check the place for yourself before bringing people. Everyone is looking at the menus in pure distaste, even the guys, who set this up. It doesn't look appetizing at all. I'm getting irritated. I'm just going to eat some bread, because nothing on this menu is appetizing. The staff messed everything up, trying to make it murder mystery food.

"You know, this is ridiculous. Why don't they have regular food names? These damn names have made me lose my appetite, but I can bet it'll be better when we leave. I can literally cry right now because I'm so angry." Sasha's not happy at all, and there are tears in her eyes as she tries blinking them away. How can we focus on the murder when we are hungry as Hell?

"If there aren't better choices, we're going to have to leave, and you demand a damn refund." Lucas motions to the waiter, and he comes over. "We need a menu without all these crazy names for your dishes. Tell your manager if we can't have regular menus, we'll be leaving and demanding a full refund, including the generous tip." Annoyance drips from every word as Lucas drums his fingers on the table. Shaken, the waiter almost drops his tray. He responds, "Yes, sir, I'll tell him now." He speeds off to give Lucas's message.

Returning with another set of menus, the waiter goes over to Lucas. "We do have regular menus, and my manager sincerely apologizes. Let me take those and give you these. The majority of our customers enjoy the death references for the dishes, but we have regular menus as well."

"Yes, food that I can relate to! Chicken parmigiana, steak, and now I'm ready to order." An excited Ava claps her hands with a smile that could light up a Christmas tree.

I laugh and check out my menu. Yes, I can order something. "Damn, I've got to say that if we had to leave with six hungry women, there would have been Hell to pay. We never would've lived this down. Lucas, you are the man!" Steve's praising Lucas, and oh yeah, he should, because we'll never let him forget the yellow Speedo.

CHAPTER 25

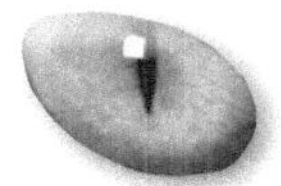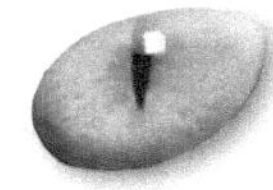

THE HUNGER GAMES

Lucas

HOW in the fuck do they give these dumbass menus to their customers? I had to fix this shit. My woman wasn't happy, and I'm not having that at all. I open up my mind to hear what the damn food is like from either the customers or the employees.

How's the food here? After you answer me, you won't remember anything. The food is average, and I only come for the murder mystery; it's fun.

This food sucks if you get dishes that require more work. Stick to the simple meals, like spaghetti, steak, French fries.

The food isn't what I'd write to anyone about. It's the fun; you have to figure out who the killer is and not get killed yourself.

The food's not tasty, so I'll order something simple and make sure the rest of the group does the same.

Since you're starving, Ladies and Gents, make sure you order something quick and easy to make. All your idea, ladies, and you won't remember I was here in your heads.

Most of us ordered steaks and fries, and Sweetness and Sasha ordered spaghetti.

"Let's take a look at the instructions that Tristan gave us." Sweetness is right; we do need to know the rules.

Flipping over the title page, reading as slowly as possible, I got the rules down.

Hey Lucas, bro, I just thought about something.

What's up, Grayson?

For the game, you can't use your mind thing to find out who the killer is. We all have a chance to win, but not against the mind-reading thing.

I won't use my mind reading power on anyone during the game to find out who the killer is.

Cool, and thanks for the heads up on the food.

Anytime.

Looking at my Sweetness, I smile, because she's going to get it tonight. It's only fair that I pay her back for earlier. She's going to love every minute of what's in store for her.

The waiter's bringing the food already, and that was kind of fast. This may be one of the really terrible food days.

Placing the food on the table, the waiter is nervously shaking in his shoes. "If there's anything else you need, please let me know." I nod at him, and he rushes back to his break area.

I examine my lackluster steak with its dark, crusty sides and edges. It's lovely that food isn't a necessity for me.

I guess I'll eat the fries, because this steak is crap, and I'll eat something else when we leave.

Fuck, what the Hell? I'm still going to starve with this nasty ass steak and the overcooked, dry fries.

Well, I'm not the only one unhappy with this.

"This is the worst meal I've ever had in my damn life! This burnt ass steak and overcooked French fries! What the Hell? How can we think about who the killer can be when we have this slop that we can't even eat? You all walked and hiked damn near twenty miles, and this is your first meal since then. I don't know how you can function with this as your meal. I know damn well that I can't!" Ava throws her napkin onto her plate, out of breath.

"Ava's right, guys, this is horrible," Sweetness chimes in.

Ladies, I know these meals are awful, please don't think about food until we leave.

Drew, you will fire every incompetent chef or cook, whatever you call them. Then you will hire people who can actually create delicious food for your customers. Call your staff and tell them the murder mystery will be solved in one hour. After the game is over, you will give a full refund to every customer here. You will not re-open until you have people who can cook, and you will pay them fairly for their talents.

Who the Hell is this?

If you wish to keep your establishment and not end up with nothing, you'll do what the fuck I'm telling you.

And start giving a sizable donation to charity and homeless people in your area. Do you UNDERSTAND WHAT I TOLD YOU, DREW?

Yes, sir, I understand. Thank you for telling me how to be better!

Get to it.

Lyssa

POP! POP! POP! Knowing that this is a murder mystery theater didn't stop me from going to hit the damn deck. As I'm going to the floor, my waist is grabbed, and I'm pulled back into my chair. "Sweetness, murder mystery; you're safe, and nothing's happening for real."

"You know, it was so loud that I forgot." Looking around, I can see all of my cousins must have forgotten too. Sasha's on the floor under the table, and the guys caught my other cousins. Sasha didn't have a date here to stop her. Across from me, there's a lady on the floor, lying face-up, with three red paint-ball circles on her chest. Ominous music plays while three men and one woman enter, all in tan trench coats with sheriff's badges.

"I guess this death happens right at the beginning of the meal because no one wants to eat this crappy damn food." Ava's throwing insults about the food.

The waitress brings some rolls, which is my chance to eat some bread. Oh no, they didn't. They grabbed all of the rolls, and I didn't get one; damn, my stomach's growling, too; how embarrassing.

"Here, Sweetness." Lucas slides a saucer to me with a warm roll on it. Lucas deserves a kiss for this treat.

I lean over to him, press my lips to his, and pucker up for a quick kiss. "Thank you, honey, you are the best." I pick up my roll and smell it; the buttery bread with a hint of cinnamon is music to my senses. Wait, did Lucas have one? "Did you have one, Lucas?"

"No, I got that for you, Sweetness. Go ahead and eat it."

Breaking the roll in half, I feed half to him and eat the other half. The explosion of flavor in my mouth from the cinnamon and the butter is yummy. What's so ridiculous is they know all of us are here at this table, so why would they only bring out one bowl of rolls? What is wrong with these damn people?

The first "detective" with the Sheriff's badge steps into the middle of the room. "Someone here is a killer. The person followed our victim into this restaurant and committed a cold-blooded killing here while eating their lunch. And everyone needs to be questioned to find out what they were doing when the shot was fired."

They split up and go over to people's tables. Finally, he gets to our table. "Hello, I'd like to know what you all were doing when the shot rang out." I looked at him and replied, "I was inspecting the unappetizing spaghetti I was given."

Lucas shakes his head. "I was examining my steak that was burnt and dry."

Ava, smirking, added, "Well, I was telling everyone that I'm starving, because your food is horrible here."

The cop answers, "I have nothing to do with the cooking; that's not my job. I'm a police detective." He looks around and focuses on Janae. "Miss, what were you doing when the shots rang out?"

"I was putting a buttered roll in my mouth because I'm starving too, because your food sucks."

Then he looks at Garrison. "What were you doing, sir?"

"I was sitting here just thinking about what I'm going to do when I leave here, because everyone was unhappy with your menu. So that means that I failed at showing my people and, most importantly, our dates, a good time here. Basically, I'm trying to figure out how I will make it up to them when we leave this place. And I was eating bread, too."

Benny looks over at Naya, our other smart ass. She says, "Wait, wait, I'm ready. You want to know what I was doing, right? I was just sitting thinking about how somebody could come here for this show when the food is horrible. And you know why I say that? Because I'm a chef. It's ludicrous that the menu is this bad, and I don't want to hear that's not my problem. I'm a police officer in the show, and I have nothing to do with how good or bad the food is in this establishment, ma'am."

Then he looks over at Sasha, another one of the smartasses. "Hey, do you think you can remember what you were doing when you heard the shot, Miss?" She tilts her head back, observing him like he's crazy.

"What are you trying to say? What do you mean if I can remember what I was doing when I heard the shot? I'm not stupid, and Hell yeah, I remember what the Hell I was doing in this whack-ass establishment. Only eight rolls were brought out for eleven people. I wished for a piece of one of those rolls they brought out here, and that's what I was doing, yeah."

He shakes his head at Naya and notices Grayson. "Sir, what were you doing when the shot happened?"

Sighing, Grayson replies, "Oh, well, I just was sitting here looking at the roll, thinking about how I really wanted real food. I took a bite of the roll, and while I was chewing, the shots started."

"Sir, what were you doing when the shots rang out?"

Steve just starts laughing. "I was just thinking about how hungry I am, and all I have is this damn roll. I couldn't even get a piece of butter, since they only sent out four packets of butter, and there are eleven of us."

"Okay, thanks for that," the fake Sheriff responds to Steve. Going to Delia, he asks, "Ms., What were you doing during the shooting?"

Delia stares at him and just cracks up laughing. I mean, she's laughing so hard that she's crying. She pulls herself together enough to say, "I was eating the other half of Steve's roll right here."

"Thank you so much. Well, it seems that you all have alibis. We're going to need you to join the team of people looking for the killer, but be careful; you don't want to get killed yourself. Take these shields to show that you are investigators." They're little gold stick-on shields to put on your clothes. Oh, my God, this is hilarious.

"The quicker we find this killer, the faster we can get the Hell out of here to get some real damn food. Do we have an agreement? If we can't find the killer, use whatever you can to get him or her, so we can leave." Grayson announces, and I believe he's ready to get out of here.

"Yes!" We all answer together. We ask the people to find out what they were doing or if they knew the victim. This is stupid as Hell; there are too many people here, and we're not getting anything to find the killer. Everyone's giving the same damn answers, and they were doing the same thing. Someone's lying, and we all stay in groups, so we don't get killed.

Lucas, Sasha, and I look at the black, satin-covered tables and the red plates with black trim and red satin napkins. There are red satin-covered tables and black plates with red outlining the edge, black satin napkins, and both have black goblets for drinking. Lucas goes over to one guy and grabs him, and says he's the killer.

"Wait a minute, how do you know?" One of the sheriffs asks. Lucas goes into the guy's vest pocket and takes out the little cardboard gun.

"We're done, yes!" Lucas says, "Let's get the fuck out of here." He grabs my hand, and we exit the spooky house that I'll never go to again. Our cars drive us back to the airport, where both helicopters are waiting. We ride back to Vegas, and wow, they're looking to see where we're going to go eat, because we all know we have to eat before we do anything else.

Grayson hangs up his phone. "I found a place with an excellent buffet. There aren't many high-quality buffets anymore, and there are only a few of them where you know you can tell they care about the food and the people eating the food."

Garrison interrupts. "Wait, we've got to do this thing I planned first before we eat because we can't it if we eat right now."

"Oh, no, come on, Garrison, I'm speaking for all of us. Are you for real?" I have to say something because I'm so hungry my stomach is hurting.

"I promise you; it'll be quick and you're all going to say this is freaking cool. Then we will go right to eat, and everything will be freshly-prepared, Grayson can call to have the tables on hold."

Naya groans. "Oh my God; we better be quick, and if I don't eat soon, I'm going to freak the Hell out."

We're all hungry, but I guess we're going to do this activity really quick. "Are you sure we won't have to wait for this activity, Garrison?"

Garrison says, "No, we don't have to wait. I reserved the time just for us, so, no waiting in line or anything."

We're doing another fun activity, and I hope it is fun, because the second one was a bust. When we were kids, we went to the Grand Canyon, but just the regular part. Lana and the girls loved looking over into the vast Canyon, unlike me. I'm so surprised that I handled the waterfalls like I did. In all of the places I've been to I didn't participate in activities that involved heights.

I've been running away from the grief and sadness of my loss. It was suffocating me every day except for the past couple of days, and I guess that's because Lucas has been around. It comes in waves, and it just hasn't been coming as much. I think it's because I've been out doing stuff with Lucas. I'm still trying to figure out what it is about Lucas that calms me down.

Lucas

*L*UCAS, *can you give me a little assistance, bro?*

What's up, Garrison?

We have about forty-five minutes until we get back to Vegas, and I'd love to get to Naya better. Any ideas on how I can do this and not be obvious?

I'll think of something, and I need you to just be ready for it when it comes.

Thanks, Lucas.

I could ease something into Janae's and Sweetness's minds, and it could benefit all of them.

Janae and Sweetness suggest the group plays a little "get to know each other while passing the time" game. You can make up the rules. Again this was your idea.

Sweetness picks up the phone to the cockpit. "Hey guys, how long do we have until we get back to Vegas?" Smiling and nodding, Sweetness hangs up. "We have about forty-five minutes before land in Vegas. How about we play a getting to know you game? How we play is whoever starts first can pick a subject and then ask a question, and after the answer comes in, that person becomes the questioner, and you have to answer. I think it'll be a great way to get to know each other."

I don't mind volunteering to go first. Naya's thoughtfully watching Garrison and says, "Sports."

Smiling, Garrison answers, "What do you mean? What do I play or what do I like to watch, or both?"

"Hmm, both would be great," Naya answers, giving him thumbs up.

Garrison says, "I play basketball, football, volleyball, racquetball, lacrosse, and I used to run track. I also love to swim. I watch basketball, football, volleyball, beach volleyball, swimming, bowling, I ski and snowboard, and I like to watch skiing and snowboarding. That's about it. If I think of anything, I'll let you know."

Naya's eyes widen in surprise. "Wow, you're a sportsman, for real.

I love swimming, playing beach and regular volleyball, skiing, ice skating, roller skating, bowling, snowboarding, and watching all of them. I also watch basketball and football."

"That is awesome! Now you two know what sports you both like and know which ones you can actually play together. Garrison, so far, you and Lucas are the avid sportsmen of our group. You know we have to have the others play our game too."

I glance over at Lucas, and he's sporting a sour expression. Oh boy.

I trace my finger up his sexy, muscular, beautifully tattooed bicep, and sincerely express how I feel. "I know, Lucas, that you do all those things too. You're also the man; I would never forget you, and you know that. Stop looking like that."

"Garrison, it's your turn to give her a subject."

"What foods do you like to cook, and what do you like to eat? I know you're a chef, and I've been told that most of the time, chefs don't like to cook when they come home, because they cook at work. Is that true?"

Naya is about to go in, and we all know she doesn't like cooking at home.

"You know what, Garrison? That is kind of true, sometimes. Since I cook all day and damn near all night at work, I don't cook much at home. I work twelve to fifteen hours a day. I would say my favorite foods are lasagna, baked macaroni and cheese, steak, shrimp, chicken, or beef and broccoli, and fried chicken. I can cook all of those dishes. How about you? What are your favorite foods, Garrison?"

"That's easy for me: all meat."

"So, you are telling me that meat is your favorite food? What the Hell is that? Why would you tell me that is your favorite food? What type of dish? Please be more specific, okay? Thank you." Naya laughs, but she's not kidding.

"Okay, woman. I like steak, chicken, ribs, pot roast, pork and all kinds of meat, and sides."

There's a moment of silence before Naya speaks. "I don't know what to say. I've never had anyone who said that all their favorite foods are just pure meat. I mean, you don't like baked macaroni and cheese or lasagna?"

"Well, maybe it's because I don't have anyone who knows how to make it right. You know what I mean?"

"So, if I said I'd cook one of my favorite meals for you, would you try it?"

"Hell yeah, woman. All you have to do is tell me when and where; I'll be there because I appreciate delicious food. If you can't cook, I damn sure won't eat it. And to be warned, I can eat, and I don't do those tiny servings of food. Be prepared to feed me, Naya, because there's no small appetite here." Garrison points to his body, lingering at his eight-pack abdomen.

"I can tell you have an appetite, Garrison. I mean, look at you. Damn, if anyone sees you and feels that you're a lightweight in the food department, they must be high on something." Naya shakes her head, laughing.

"Now that you guys know about each other's favorite foods, let's think of another subject. Garrison, can you go next, and I'll take the next two, please? I'm trying to think of some good subjects."

Garrison nods. He is focused on Naya, thoughtfully rubbing his chin. "Your favorite type of movies; give me your top five."

"My favorite kinds of movies are thrillers, horror, comedy, and action. Every now and then, I'll watch a drama. I'm working hard being a chef. I wasn't kidding when I said I work damn near fifteen hours a day. I don't work like that because I have to, but because I love what I do. I could take the easy way out and let my family take care of me and help. The way I was raised, I would never do that. My goal is to have my own restaurant, but I have a lot to learn right now. Why are you looking at me like that? Garrison? Just because I have money, it doesn't mean that I'm ready to run my own restaurant."

Garrison, shaking his head, says, "I wasn't negatively looking at you, Naya. Missy, you must have some issues about what your goals are. As for the movie question, I don't get to the movies when they are out in theaters. I see them later on. I work a hell of a lot, keeping a billion-dollar empire running. My favorite types of movies are action, comedy, thrillers, and I'll watch a drama every now and then. There is this new actor, Zack, I forget his last name, and he's pretty good. I've watched all of his movies. He is outstanding as an action actor."

Naya, Sasha, and I look at each other knowingly. Naya turns back to Griffin and bursts out laughing. "Guess what, Garrison?"

Already arching his eyebrows at her, he answers, "What, Naya?"

"Zack is one of my best friends. I have a story about him that is so funny. When you and your brothers came to Crush Buzz for the interview, Zack had an interview there earlier that morning. I thought Zack was tall from all the movies he's in, but Zack's short. The camera can make anyone look taller than they really are. I used to have a crush on Zack, but it was over after meeting him that day. Zack was shocked that I didn't respond to his mack. He tried to take me out on a friendly lunch date after I declined the romantic dinner invite from him. On the way to lunch, we got stuck in an elevator at the magazine office building. I wasn't interested in him, but I did introduce him to the young lady who is now his fiancé."

Garrison is stunned, then shakes his head, laughing. "Well, damn, who would have thought that you are besties with Zack? It is a small world."

Samantha comes out of the cockpit. "Ladies and gentlemen, in about fifteen minutes, we will be at our destination."

Garrison watches Naya. "It's your turn, and I hope it's good."

"I'm ready with the next two questions. Number one is when was the last serious relationship you had, and why didn't it work out?"

Garrison chuckles. "I see what you've done, and that's cheating. I haven't had a serious relationship. I've been all about either the family business or now, mostly our business. The majority of women can't relate to what I deal with on a day-to-day basis."

Naya frowning, says, "If that's the case, why are you interested in me if you don't have the time required to put into a relationship?"

Griffin raises his finger, shaking it. "I'll answer that after you answer the previous one."

Naya playfully rolls her eyes. "I was so involved with your answer that it skipped my mind. I haven't been in any meaningful relationships either, due to my insane work schedule. I tried once, and he just tried to move in with us and tried to convince me that it was the only way for us to make it work. No thanks, buddy."

Griffin coughs from laughing so hard. "That guy really tried to move in with you? What the Hell? People like us who are extremely busy with work or businesses can't be involved with people who work regular schedules. While they're off of work, they have more time on their hands; hence, they get angry with us, because they have nothing else to do with their time. I can adjust my schedule for you, Naya."

Naya smirks, "You better, man, if you want to see where this goes."

Griffin gives her a smile that's so hot, it's probably melting her insides. I have to ask her.

CHAPTER 26

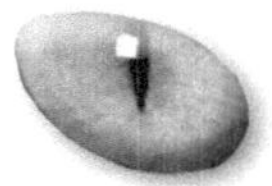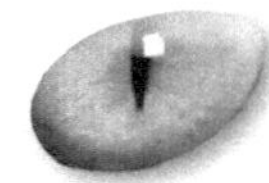

SPEEDING THROUGH THE STRIP

Lucas

WE'RE close to the surprise Garrison has planned. We'll find out if this activity is one that our ladies will want to do. We still have to go and eat this late lunch. On top of that, we have to get them back in time to get ready for the concert tonight.

Garrison hangs up the phone. "Are you ready, ladies? Our transportation is waiting, and this is an activity you all will all en—"

Janae interrupts, "Oh, my God! Can you just tell us, please? You're very confident that we'll love this, I must say."

Garrison rubs his forehead. "What, you don't like the surprise factor?" he asks with disappointment written on his face and voice.

Janae exasperatedly shakes her head. "We're a group of starving women, man! None of us want to be surprised right now.'"

As we step into the stretch SUV limousine, Garrison makes his announcement. "Ladies, we're going ziplining down the strip."

Every female stops and stares at Garrison as if he has grown two heads. Ava screams, "Come on, Why??!!?? How do you think I'm going to zip line with a broken damn foot?"

Griffin responds, "Ava, remember when I told you earlier that there was one part of the date that you were not going to participate in? This is it."

Janae sighs. "Do you really think this was necessary? I am tired. Now you want me to zip line across the damn strip."

Garrison, taking her hand, pleadingly says, "Please, Janae, I'm trying to make up for this afternoon. You can do this. We have to do it today because tomorrow, we have two meetings, then we're going to the club, and then Sunday, we're all leaving."

Sasha interrupts. "Actually, the club is late tomorrow night. We could have gone zip lining tomorrow morning or, better, tomorrow evening, since you say zip lining will be so fast. We all know you guys like getting up early as Hell."

Janae looks at Sasha. "It's okay, Sash. Let's just do it and get it over with. The faster we do this, the quicker we'll get to the restaurant. We're all starving."

The limousine comes to a stop. Ava whines, "Oh no, we are here! I'll be waiting right here in this damn seat, and so will Griffin."

We all step out of the limousine. Sasha says, "You know what? I've never had the desire to go zip lining in my damn life, but I guess there's a first time for everything."

A young guy walks over in zip line gear. He smiles at everyone and introduces himself. "Hi, guys. My name is Cage, and I'm one of your guides. My team and I are going to show you how to safely zip line. Who's excited?" None of the ladies answer. The guys only nod, and the tension is so thick out here from the women, it could be cut with a knife. Don't screw with these ladies and their damn food.

Cage motions for us to follow him. "Come on, let's go, guys." This guy has a hell of a lot of energy. We go with him into a building and get onto an elevator. Cage presses the button to go to the roof.

These ladies are really pissed off, and I hope that the concert tonight makes them feel better. Actually, getting some good food should do the trick.

Stepping out of the elevator, there is a whole team up here. Cage checks us out. "Who are the couples? We have three separate zip lines, and I need to have groups of two." Sasha is all alone.

Lyssa thinks to herself, *another height activity. Damn it!*

"Sasha, come over with us." I know she and my Sweetness are really close, so she should be with us.

Lyssa

LUCAS takes my hand. "Sweetness, you know I've got you. Nothing will happen, and you know, you're safe with me."

How in the Hell does he have me, when I'll be ziplining alone? I still don't want to zip line, but my feet walk over to the first zip line as Lucas pulls my hand.

A young lady with gorgeous long red hair is waiting for us with harness gears in her hands.

She smiles, "Hello, I'm Mya. Can you tell me your names, please?"

"I'm Lyssa, he's Lucas, and she's Sasha." They both say hello.

"Can you all please put these on so I can make sure that you're secure before we hook you up to the line?"

I put on my helmet, then put my arms in the gear and fasten the straps. Mya comes over and makes sure that everything is attached correctly and secure. She explains, "This is what is going to happen." She lifts up the clip and shows me. "We're going to hook this clip into the trolley. I need you to grip the handles and take a deep breath, then leap off the platform." I check on Lucas and Sasha; they're also in their gear. Sasha smiles shakily, and Lucas smiles confidently. Maya hooks the clip onto the trolley, smiles, and says, "You've got this, Lyssa. Remember: grip, deep breath, and leap."

I'm supposed to leap off of this damn building! Why?!!? Just tell me why? Looking over at Lucas, he is grinning like this is the best thing ever. What is wrong with these damn men here?

I raise my hands and grip that damn bar like my life depends on it, which it does. Stepping to the edge of the building, counting to three, and taking a deep breath, I close my eyes and leap. ZZZZZZ HHHHHHHH! The trolley whistles as it glides on the zip line.

I know I should be excited that I'm flying over some buildings, but I'm not, because all I can do is think about my growling stomach. As I speed past, I open my eyes. If it were later in the evening, the colorful lights would be on, and it would be a better view. The brakes kick in, and I slow down until I come to a complete stop. The guys pull me to safety on the rooftop at the end of the zip line. I open my eyes and see an unhappy Janae and Delia shaking their heads.

Lucas

EVERYONE is full, fat, and satisfied with the delicious food from our lunch at the restaurant's buffet. We can say that these ladies do not believe in tiny portions like salad. We arrive at the hotel in the limousine at a quarter to five.

Guys, I'll tell the ladies now about the concert, but we will let who's performing be a surprise.

"Ladies, our last event will be tonight at 8 p.m., but we need you all to be ready by 7:30 p.m. We need you all to start getting prepared when you get upstairs."

Grayson announces, "Ladies, we are taking you to a concert this evening. Please be ready in two hours."

All of the women are giving Grayson the evil eye. Janae says, "How do you tell six women to be ready in two hours when they only have three bathrooms? Delia and Steve have their own bathroom, but the rest of us have to share. You really don't understand the female process of getting ready to go out."

Lucas says, "Oh, hell! Let me see if I can help. I have an idea. You know I am right next door, and I'm alone. I have the same number of rooms as you. So that means that I have two bedrooms with private bathrooms. How about two of you use my bathrooms? If you are uncomfortable, I can get ready first and let you have the penthouse to get prepared. That will help you with your time."

Sasha and Naya both yell, "Thank you, Lucas."

I guess that they will be using my bathrooms.

Lyssa

WE'RE ready to go to the concert, and I wonder who is performing. I just finished putting my hair up in a high ponytail with twirly curls on each side of my face. I am wearing my gold cocktail dress, and it is adorable. The dress has slinky shoulder straps, and I added my wide black belt. I'm also wearing black pumps and accessories. I look at my reflection, shaking my head, because I don't like the belt on this dress. I take it off.

Naya, as usual, is the lady in pink, and she can't help herself. She has on a lovely soft pink cocktail dress. The cocktail dress has ruching that accentuates her curvy waist. Naya's make-up is heavier than usual, and it's beautiful. She is a tall glass of caramel latte.

Janae is wearing a jumpsuit with sheer chiffon material at the bottom that flows behind her as she walks. It is beautiful, and the color is a lovely baby blue. She has on white accessories and white pumps.

Sasha is looking fierce in her red mini dress. It is snug-fitting, and it shows her curves. She has on gold Gucci pumps and gold accessories.

Last but not least is our little Ava. She has on an ice blue cocktail dress that matches her eyes perfectly. That dress is a knockout. How is she going to walk with one heel and that cast? Will Griffin like her dress? Ava has reverted back to showing too much skin.

We're heading out to meet the guys at the elevator, and when they see us, BAM! They're looking absolutely gorgeous in those damn suits. Grayson, waiting in the doorway, checks us out and says, "I'm not trying to be cocky or anything," as we get on the elevator, "but damn, we all look good."

Griffon and Ava look amazing together, even though we know she has some issues. Is she even ready to be in a relationship right now? If Griffon really cares about her, he will be willing to wait for her. Hell, she bit him, and he's still here. Who am I kidding?

The elevator slows and stops on the fourth floor, and who walks in? The cute little old couple, and the lady comes up to Lucas. "Hello, young man. Look at you looking so dapper. You all just look lovely. I love seeing young people dressed well. You're going to be the talk of wherever you go. Back in our day, we didn't have all the activities that you have now. It's a lovely thing to see. Hello, missy, how are you?"

I smile at her. "Hello, I am fine, and how are you doing?"

The little old lady replies, "I'm doing just fine, but you are doing way better than I am. Remember what I told you," she says with a smile. She winks her eye at me. Oh, God! "As long as you have each other, you will always do great. Never let anyone come between what is yours. Also, when it comes to relationships, no matter what, communication is critical. Trust is the foundation for anything worth having. Never rush into relationships, and take your time to get to know one another and become each other's friends. You do not have to be best friends, but you do need friendship. Do you understand what I am saying?" Her husband takes her hand, looks at us, and mouths, "*I am so sorry.*" You never know when you are going to get some wisdom.

The little old couple gets off the elevator. Ava says, "Boy, she talked a lot," and we all just look at her.

We get off the elevator and head toward the limousine to leave the hotel. Is Lucas the person I am meant to be with? Could I grow old and have a family with him? What I want is our relationship to grow and to become more than a mind-blowing crazy attraction. I am not looking for a *wham-bam, thank you, ma'am*, and *I'll see you when I see you.* That's why I told Lucas he will have to wait to show me that he is worth it and not just because he likes me.

There is no need to rush into anything. So if Lucas wants to be with me, he will take his sweet, slow time. I'm not saying that I have to wait until I get married. What I want is something real and someone I care about.

Stepping out of the limousine, there's a line of people outside of the Mystique Casino. Grayson leads us over to the front of the line, and the people in line get upset and yell at us. The bodyguard looks at his clipboard and motions for us to come in.

Grayson shakes the bodyguard's hand. "Come on, guys, we're going to see someone you all lo—" Ava interrupts, "Oh, my God! We are going to see Caprici and Justin Timberlake!"

Janae yells, "Oh my God! Yes! Let's go!" Janae grabs Grayson's hand pulling him along, and he laughs and follows. I can't help the big grin on my face as I look at Lucas, and he is smiling at me.

They actually did great. I give him a quick kiss and tell him, "You did awesome—two out of three. You made up for the horrible lunch and the spooky mansion." Lucas laughs. "Oh yeah, I remembered she is your favorite singer."

We all caught up with Janae. Sasha puts her two cents in, saying, "Caprici is amazing, and she can sing her butt off. She is not about stupid songs like a lot of artists. Her songs are meaningful and powerful. They get down into your soul. You don't get that from everybody."

Lyssa said, "Oh, no! Delia wants to give a concert trying to sing one of Caprici's songs with her no-singing self." Walking through the crowd is very annoying when they don't step aside when you say *excuse me*. Griffin's behind me, and a man's falling into him, but he quickly swings Ava to his other side. So, the man hits Griffin's back instead of Ava's head.

"Oh, sorry, man, I tripped a little, but I thought I was good. Sorry to you, too, young lady." The older gentleman regains his balance and goes into his row.

Lucas goes into the third row in the center. Damn, we have the entire row. "Lucas, did you and the guys buy the entire row?"

Lucas nods. "Yes, we did, Sweetness. We're big guys, and we need our space. Even though we're out on dates together, we don't have to be crowding each other."

We all get comfortably seated about five seats apart per couple, and Sasha's with Lucas and me. The lights dim, and the curtain rises. There are multi-colored flashing lights around the stage leading into the center, then down the steps. We clap and cheer with everyone, and Sasha and I get caught up with the people jumping up and down. Overhead, there's a massive, flaming circle encased in some type of glass. Booming music starts with thundering bass that I feel everywhere. The floor is vibrating to the beat of the bass.

The band, the background singers, and the dancers run up the steps to the front, wave to us, and go to their spots. Whoa! The flaming circle is slowly lowering, and when it lands, wow, it's another stage with a flaming oval on top. The oval rises, and the eight dancers go to the stage, surround it, and throw shimmering gold, red, black, and silver long materials onto it. The music stops suddenly, and the dancers run away. The light goes out, and it's pitch black. Melodic humming starts, and I'd know that voice anywhere. The spotlight hits the stage, the material lifts up and slides off, revealing Caprici, wearing a gold sequined bodysuit. She is about to give us one Hell of a show!

The crowd wildly screams her name, "Caprici, Caprici," the excitement around us builds, and we all join in. Lucas steps behind and wraps his arms around my waist. The drummer starts to play, and we all start moving to beat. With Lucas behind me, our bodies are swaying together, and his body heat is welcoming me as I lean into him. The electric guitars blast in, and the saxophones blow like the roof is on fire! "You ready to have a great show tonight?" Caprici yells into the headset microphone. "Then say, hell yeah!"

"Hell yeah!" we scream, and then the diva extraordinaire began to sing one of my favorite songs. We clap our hands and sing along with Caprici as she is genuinely impressed that we all are singing the words and even when she motions the band and dancers to stop, we are still singing in beat not missing a lyric when they join back in. "You guys are one of my best audiences! If you can keep up with me on this next song, I'll have a surprise for you at the end of the show!"

We rock the next song, "*If you were my man.*" She even has the right, left and center, where we are in the audience, battling it out singing the song. One of the stage guys come down and comes over to Ava, she smiles at him and the next thing I see is Griffin carrying her up to the stage! My cousins and me are in shock looking at Ava.

Caprici smiles, "Hey gorgeous, what's your name?" Of course, Ava beams and answers, "Ava," and Caprici asks, "Do you know this song, Ava?"

Ava nods, and says, "I know it, yes."

Caprici smiles up at Griffin, she holds the microphone towards him and asks, "Sexy man with Ava, what's your name?"

Griffin arches his eyebrow, and glances down at Ava, then back at Caprici. He gives a smile and says, "I'm Gr—" Ava inhales and quickly covers Griffin's mouth with her hand!

Ava turns her head, first to Griffin and if a look could slap the hell out of someone, it'd be him. Then back to Caprici with a sweet smile, but irritation clearly in her eyes. "Caprici, there's no need to know his name because he's mine. Now if you really want to hear your song I'm more then ready to blow your mind."

Caprice laughs, and says, "You got some talent, Ava? Show me and this audience what you've got." She hands the microphone to Ava. Our girl doesn't wait for the music she starts singing the intro of the song, and Caprici widens her eyes in shock, and Griffin does the same. "Sweetness the little Hellion can sing her ass off." Lucas bends his head to tell me in my ear. I smile and look at my cousin. Ava hits high notes that are beautifully done and her rendition of Caprici's song does blow everyone's mind, except my cousins and me. We all can sing in my family. Ava finishes, and the audience claps and hollers her name. She smiles and bows her head smiling. "Now you owe the audience the surprise you promised." Ava says to Caprici.

Griffin brings her back to our row, and Caprici announces that the entire show is being videoed for her upcoming documentary. After a couple more songs it's Justin Timberlake's time and Lucas is excited. I can feel it, and I don't know how it's possible, it just is. Lucas knows every song that JT is singing. He has even more dancers, background singers, and musicians then Caprici. He is still in shape, dancing around and singing not getting out of breath.

The concert was marvelous. Both Caprici and Justin Timberlake were stupendous! We could tell that Lucas likes Justin Timberlake. Oh, hell yeah. The slogan, *Vegas never sleeps* is so true. You see more characters out here than anywhere else. Some are hilarious in their costumes, but when the hookers try to approach your dates while you are standing there, it really makes you want to punch the Hell out of them.

We opted to walk back to the hotel instead of taking the limousine. Poor Griffin. We didn't think about him having to carry Ava around and listen to her complain along the way. Since she's giving encore performance number three of Caprice's song "Why?" My other cousins walk ahead with me.

"Sis, look," Janae calls to me. I stop and turn around to see what's going on. Some people have stopped to take pictures, and not of the volcanoes or the buildings. They're taking pictures of Lucas.

What is wrong with them? Four other gorgeous guys are walking with us, and as usual, every female is drawn to mine. I feel like I'm being punked right now. Honestly, we can't go anywhere without some woman trying to jump his bones or something. In no way, shape, or form does he show any interest in them.

Some of these women are something else, and they don't know how to control themselves. I lose control of myself, but you know it's because he does things to me. He's not doing anything to these heifers, and they are all over him.

A chill goes down my spine and, in my bones, and I freeze. Goosebumps prickle on my skin, and I shiver. Something's not right; the hairs on my neck stand up. Someone's watching me. The weird feeling, I got at the creepy mansion is back. Lucas takes my hand.

I stop and look to the left and then to the right, but no one stands out in this crowd. Lucas looks around as well. "Sweetness, what is going on?"

"I don't know, but someone's watching me. I know we are in Vegas, but something is weird." We all look around, but there are so many people. How could we decipher who it is?

Lucas frowns and says, "Let's hurry up and get back to the hotel." I never knew these guys could walk as fast as they are walking. Lucas still has my hand, and he is pulling me along. We are waiting for the streetlight to turn red.

Of course, the guys are getting stared at, but the main one is getting stared at is Lucas. No matter where the Hell we go, the women are all attentive.

Oh my God, are you serious? This hoochie just walked up here and rubbed her body against my Lucas. Lucas pushed her off of him, and she almost got run over by a car. She dared to look at him like he did something to her. I look at him and tell him to make sure he has a good shower tonight. Lucas laughs and says, "I'll have a great one if you join me." I am shaking my head, because he knows that is not going to damn well happen.

CHAPTER 27

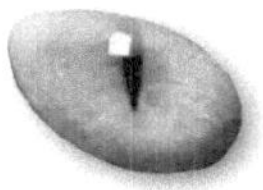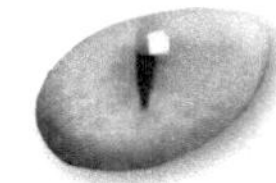

LYSSA'S PAYBACK

Lucas

WE'RE walking out of the elevator, and I'm holding Sweetness's hand. "You still don't remember what you wanted to tell me?"

Sweetness shakes her head. "I think I'm going crazy, because I don't remember what I was going to tell you. I'm sorry. Maybe I'll remember tonight before I go to sleep or tomorrow before the club." As we get closer to the door, she frowns more, because she cannot remember. I know what it is, but I'll wait for her to say it.

"I'm damn ridiculous that I can't remember what I have to tell you, Lucas. I know it's something important."

"You're not ridiculous, and stop saying stuff like that. You are smart; no, you're fucking brilliant, beautiful, and the most caring person I've ever met. I won't accept that. Hell no. I damn sure won't. I want you to know that right now; I'm not going to take it if you or anyone else is negative about you. So you got to cut that out, because it's unacceptable in my presence."

She looks at me and smiles. "You know what? You are so sweet to me, and that's why I feel like something really incredible is happening here with us. And thank you for not pressuring me or anything like that, because I really think we can be something special." Wrapping her arms around my neck, she pulls me down, slowly kissing me.

"You know everything the old lady on the elevator said is so right when it comes down to relationships. Going the distance. And I would love to have that, especially with you; that's why I'm taking my time. We can really get to know each other and see what we can do, like I said earlier. Oh damn, one more thing. I don't think this was what I wanted to tell you before. Can you add Josh, Christopher, and Jay to the VIP list for tomorrow? They'll be here to surprise some people."

"Yes, Sweetness. I sure can put your cousins on the VIP list." I lean over to her and give her a quick kiss, but she holds on, deepening it. Suddenly, we hear coughing and throat clearing in the background, and we pull away, breaking our kiss. She pouts a bit, and I laugh. I give her our special goodbye. For some reason, Sweetness's skin is extra warm.

"Lucas and Lyssa, you two are like a fire that can't be extinguished." Janae and Sasha are standing there, waiting for us to move since we're blocking the door.

"Sweetness, I'll see you tomorrow, probably at the club, since I have meetings. Good night, Sweetness; maybe I'll see you in your dreams." I grin and wink at her.

Licking her lips and smiling, Sweetness moves over for her cousin to go inside. After they close the door, she says, "I was hoping you'd have some kind of surprise in store for me, like you promised me at the falls." A sad expression forms on her face, then she sighs exaggeratedly. "Oh, well, I guess promises are meant to be broken. Good Night."

Placing her hand on my chest, her fingers lightly touch me down to the waist of my pants. I catch my breath; this woman is teasing me and testing my patience like no other. Blowing a kiss to me, Sweetness turns and walks inside the penthouse. She's driving me crazy, and it's official: I'm the fucking ridiculous one. Laughing to myself, I unlock my door and walk inside.

Since their cousins are coming tomorrow and it's our last night here, I'll definitely have to link up in her mind tonight. Sweetness wants to pretend that I let her down, not giving the payback I promised earlier? We'll see. I'm going to have her needing me to the point that she'll be near tears.

When I first read Steve, I saw that Josh and Chris both shift into their animals. I'm not sure about Jay, but he's twenty-one, so he should also be a shifter.

Lyssa

I GO into the penthouse thinking about the performances. That concert was excellent. My cousins are singing one of Caprice's songs, and I join in. We sound good for the most part, because Delia, the bad singer, is with Steve.

"I've got to give the guys their props, except for the scary-ass, murder mystery mansion. We had a fun day and a great night. Who can say I'm not right? Either speak up now or forever hold your peace, dammit."

Ava smiles and zips her lips; Janae, Sasha, and Naya laugh and give the thumbs-up sign.

"Tomorrow night is the last night here, and it'll be fever time. So, you know we've got to look fierce, right? You, too, Sasha—I need you to wear your favorite dress."

She frowns, opening her mouth to speak, but I continue. "Just do it for me, sis, and I promise you will not regret it, and we can take pictures and videos. We'll get to have some girl time, too. It won't be the last time seeing the guys, because they will be Lake Tahoe's newest residents and our neighbors, right?"

Janae voices her thoughts. "I'm anxious to get home to see what happens, especially since they're going to be our new neighbors."

I know they don't think of it as I do, so I just keep it to myself. Janae, Sash, Naya, and even Ava will be looking forward to seeing the guys. Don't get me wrong, I look forward to seeing Lucas too, but it means back to my reality. I'm dealing with my loss, but I think the only reason it is not chasing me down is because I'm here. Lucas may have been distracting me, and when I get back home, it'll be waiting for me.

And I don't think I'll be able to see him, because I'm going to go back into my shell. I don't know what's going to happen now. It's one thing to think about something that you know you probably can't have. It's another thing when what you want becomes something you most definitely can have. Can I get it together at home, so I'm able to sleep at night? I've been able to rest here, and I hope it continues at home.

Do I need to deal with what I'm going through first before getting involved with Lucas? Maybe I should've thought about that before, because I'm entangled with him already. That question is moot, though, because we're involved, so never mind. I'm just scared that I will get home and be like I was before I left—a basket case. I can't even talk to him about it. Then again, the only person I've opened up to is Auntie Amy.

"Yoo-hoo, Lyssa, earth to Lyssa," Janae snaps her fingers in front of my eyes.

"I was deep in thought; what's up, Janae?"

"I was saying that since it's one in the morning, maybe we need to call it a night. I'm damn exhausted."

"I'm going to hop in and take a hot shower before I crash on the wonderful bed. Good night, Fam," Naya yawns as she starts walking up the stairs.

Janae walks over to Ava. "Come on, Sasha, let's help our Sunshine Pixie upstairs." Sasha stretches, then walks to the chaise to help Ava up.

"Good Night, Sash, Janae, and Ava."

"Good Night, Lyssa, sweet dreams," the three of them say—and not in unison at all.

I stop in the kitchen for a bottle of water on my way to my room. My cell rings; looking at the screen, I see it's Lucas. "Hello, Lucas."

"Hey, Sweetness, what are you doing?"

"I'm getting a bottle of water and going to take a shower. What were you doing before you called me?"

"I was thinking about how we didn't have time for me to give you some of that payback I promised you."

"That's not my fault that you all planned so much into the day. Maybe another time." Walking into my room, I open my water.

"I've got something even better, Sweetness. How about now?" The sexiness in his voice resonates through me.

"Now, what?" I know he's not saying what I think he is.

"Are you okay, Sweetness? I said, how about now? Meaning spend some time together so I can repay you for earlier today. You know you want to, and if you didn't, you wouldn't have mentioned it before going inside." His voice is silky smooth, like honey. I'm not going to have sex with him, so what will it hurt?

"Give me a few minutes to take my shower."

"Maybe you should hold off on the shower until you come back. You'll get too relaxed, then fall asleep."

He does have a point. "Okay, come to the door." I get up from the chaise, leave my room quietly, and get the card key from my purse. I open the door, and Lucas is standing there chewing on another sugar stick. Closing the door behind me, softly, we both hang up the phones. Lucas takes my hand and leads me into his penthouse.

This penthouse is precisely the same as ours. Strangely, I don't have any reservations or second thoughts about coming here. I trust Lucas more than any of the few men that I've known for an extended time.

Lucas grabs the remote, turning the music on, and since it's so late, it's easy to find slow and sexy music playing. "Sweetness, do you want a drink?"

I think I could use a drink, but I don't even know what I'd want. "No, I'm good, Lucas. Wait, I'll take a bottle of water."

"Come on, Sweetness, let's go get it." We go into the kitchen, and he gets a bottle of water from the refrigerator. I turn to go back to the living room, but Lucas stops me. "We can go to my room. As you know, there's a sitting area. No, I don't want you uncomfortable. We're going back in the living room, come on."

I take a quick swig of water. Maybe this wasn't a great idea. My body is not cooperating with me. I'm tingling everywhere, and all Lucas did was hold my damn hand. It started when I heard his voice on the phone.

Smack! Lucas just smacked my ass, and oh, damn, how can I feel so turned on by that? I turn around to look at him, and Lucas smiles as he pulls me to him. Quickly inhaling, our bodies so close together, I feel his sizzling heat. Lucas's scent is intoxicating, and it makes me woozy and hungry for him. He stares into my eyes, and a flash of blue fire is in my mind, but it only makes me hotter.

I lick my lips, and Lucas lets out a growl. He swoops in and attacks my lips with his. Parting my lips, I grant him access, and our tongues collide. While we're kissing, he walks, guiding me as I walk back into the wall. Lucas has me pinned against the wall with his body, and it's an inferno. Electricity is surging through me, and my core is throbbing.

His hands move to my breasts. My bra is strapless, and the material is thinner than usual. His palm grazes my erect nipple, and trembling overcomes my body. I need something, and I think he's what my body is craving. My heat has ignited into an all-consuming blaze. Lucas squeezes both of my nipples as I nibble and suck on his lip, and it causes me to get even wetter. It's like a damn waterfall in my panties.

I pull his shirt out of his pants and clutch it on each side, pulling as hard as I can. His shirt rips loudly, and his buttons pop and go flying, hitting the walls and the floor. Lucas breaks our kiss, looks down at his shirt, and shrugs out of it. He pulls his sleeveless undershirt over his head and throws it across the hall.

"Hmm. Sweetness, do you have a tiger hiding somewhere? You ripped my shirt like a tigress would."

"I'm too hot to talk about a damn Tigress, Lucas."

I bring my hands to his naked, tanned, eight-packed waist, which is even warmer than before. Each rippling abdomen muscle is so damn sexy, and I let my fingers roam down to the waistband of his dress pants. Lucas inhales sharply, his eyes never leaving mine. His scent is captivating. I lean into his hot chest and lick his nipple, then I give him a small bite. Lucas groans.

My fingers rub across the top of his waistband, and I let three fingers slide in at the top. Lucas growls much louder. Before I can look at him, he's grabbing me by the waist and picking me up, then putting me over his shoulder. *SMACK!* He smacked my ass again! Dammit, why is the sting make my va-jay-jay feel so good? Uh, he's bringing me into his bedroom!?

"So, Alyssa, my Sweetness, YOU'RE having fun teasing me, right? It's MY turn, and when you say stop, I'll stop, or I'll stop before we reach the point of no return. I know you're not experienced, Sweetness, but woman, you cannot tease me like you just did." Entering the bedroom that's the same as mine, Lucas carefully lays me on his bed.

I should be worried or nervous about him lying on top of me. I know I'm safe, and he'd never hurt me. *Our Mate.* Okay, crazy me, cut it the Hell out. Alyssa, it's not cool to talk to yourself in the third person. Putting my focus back on Lucas, I search his eyes for any menace or anger, but there's none.

Rubbing the top of his waistband, Lucas gives me the sexiest look I've ever gotten. "I also owe you from earlier. Get ready for me, baby. I'm going to make you feel like you've never felt before."

A shudder goes through me, and it's nothing like what I experienced earlier outside today. Lucas takes off his shoes and walks over to the bed. He takes my shoes off, too. The bed dips some as Lucas crawls up to me. My heartbeat is quickening from the anticipation that's building for what he's going to do to me. Lucas is next to me and has his pants on, and I'm in my dress. What a contrast.

"Sweetness, I'm not going to take off your dress unless you're comfortable. You know that we're not hitting the homerun." Lucas's eyes have enchanted me, and I sit up, turning for Lucas to undo the back and getting on my knees. I pull the dress over my head. I have on my strapless bra, panties, and half-slip covering my waist to my mid-thigh.

Lucas gets on his knees and lifts my chin with his two fingers, and he kisses me so gently. I am his prize, The treasure he never thought he'd find. *Lucas is ours, Lyssa! Lucas is about to show us how good he can make us feel.* Can you just shut the Hell up, please?

"Sweetness, I'm not going to touch you until you're one hundred percent here with me. I know you have things going on that you're confused as Hell about. Don't ask me what; I can just tell."

I mentally shut whatever the Hell this is down, so I can focus on my man, dammit. Whatever this is, it wants me with Lucas. Let's go!

Wrapping my arms around Lucas's neck, I say, "I'm here with you; now show me what you're working with."

Lucas, laughing, replies, "I can't show you what I'm working with until you're ready to get it, Sweetness. What you'll get is a little taste here and there, and everything when you tell me yes."

My body had never hummed before in my life until Lucas started touching me. He trails kisses down my neck.

"Sweetness, when you say yes to me. I'm going to show you everything that you ever wondered about."

He moves down from my neck to my chest, and he's using that delectable tongue of his, making swirls on my skin. With every kiss from Lucas's lips or tongue, my body temperature and need increase. Touching Lucas's hair, I run my fingers through it. Lucas stops, taking my hands. "Really?" I breathe unevenly, as I stare at him for that.

"Sweetness, I can't have you touching me right now." Lucas shakes his head while telling me this.

"Why, Lucas?" I want to touch Lucas, too. What did I do wrong that he doesn't want me to?

Taking my hand and bringing it down over the thick, long bulge in his pants, Lucas smirks. "That's why. I'm not a robot, Sweetness. I need and want you more than any other female I've ever been with. You know what happens when I think about you when I'm in this type of situation?"

I shake my head at him, because I don't know.

"I have to get some type of relief, and I can't be like this twenty-four hours a day."

My hand is still on Lucas's um, manhood, and as if it heard me, it jumps, and I do too. I didn't realize he was having such a difficult time. If we keep growing like we are, our time will come soon enough.

"Can you keep your hands to yourself, or do I have to tie them?" He flips me on the bed and straddles my hips, waiting for my response.

Blinking a couple of times, I look at my hands, questioning if I can really keep my hands off Lucas. I will try my best. "Honey, I'll try my best because you know you're irresistible."

"Hold on to those sheets, Sweetness."

Oh boy, how am I going to not touch Lucas? I snatch a handful of the comforter with each hand. I'm on a mission.

Lucas leans down, kissing me so tenderly, and something inside me is going to damn break. An impatient groan escapes my lips, and finally, he deepens our kiss. Thank goodness he's not touching my va-jay-jay. I'm wetter than ever, and it's his fault that I'm so sensitive. Earlier today, he did this to me. Lucas breaks the kiss laughing. Can this man read my thoughts? Lucas's tongue is working on my skin, oh yes! He starts at my neck, and more heat and electricity combust everywhere his tongue goes.

My body is throbbing, especially my va-jay-jay, and I close my thighs tightly together. I'm so wet it's just sliding down between my legs. My lady bits are throbbing and swollen up. *We want Lucas NOW!* My nipples are like stones protruding through my bra. Lucas's hot tongue is making a trail as if it were a lit match, and I'm the forest, playing and teasing my cleavage with that tongue of his. He goes lower. Oh my God, he's licking my nipples through the material. I close my eyes, clutching the comforter for dear life. I want to touch Lucas. Crap!

"Oh, my God, Lucas, don't stop, please, baby." My voice sounds like someone else's. A cool breeze settles on my breasts, and they feel a lot less restrictive. I open my eyes. Surprise! My breasts have been freed from the bra.

"Mmm, Lucas." This man is my dream come true that I never knew. Every fiber in my being is on fire, and I don't understand how to calm this down. He just put his tongue on my nipple, exhaling sharply, and I'm pulling the comforter even tighter.

Lucas licks my nipple like I'm his favorite flavored lollipop, and sensations explode through my body to my va-jay-jay. I can't take my eyes off of him while he works. He looks up at me, and gives me that sexy-ass damn smile.

He licks his lips, then goes back to my breast. He puts his mouth over my nipple and sucks like a baby who needs milk. My va-jay-jay is on fire. A gush of my waterfall has my panties soaked, and most likely the back of my slip, too. I'm trembling like I never have before. Something is happening to me, and it wants me to give in, right now.

"Lucas, honey, I'm ready now."

Lucas stops playing with my breasts and stares at me strangely. "Sweetness, what do you mean?"

Lyssa—What the Hell is going on?

Female—You are taking too long! I want out so I can teach you.

Female—Now, I'm in control. The quicker you give in to your mate, the quicker you will become who you're meant to be. Alyssa, I'm part of you. Just watch, and you'll see.

"I'm ready, and my body is screaming for you to take and make me yours."

"No, Sweetness, I told you we were not until you're ready, and I think you're high on passion." Yes, baby, you know that this isn't me at all. No sex until we get to know each other and have emotions for each other. We are on our way.

Lucas

WHAT in the fuck is wrong with my Sweetness? The goal was to get her wanting to have sex but not actually do it. All of a sudden, she wants to have sex with me? Hell, Nah, something isn't right. I can't even read her thoughts right now. What the Hell is going on here? Suddenly, I can't read her, and it's not as if she knows anything. What happened?

"Lucas, honey, please, I need you to make me yours officially." Sweetness's features are different. Her eyes are more pronounced, and there are more of those gold flecks than five minutes ago. Oh, fuck; is her animal trying to come out? I'm going to put her ass to sleep, then get her dressed, and teleport her to damn bed.

I'm still straddling her, so I lean over her, giving her a kiss, and for a second, her eyes were gold. I give her a kiss and pour everything I've got into it. We're both breathing erratically, and kissing her neck, I get to her ear and say, "Go to sleep, now. All you or your animal will remember is that you were tired, and I brought you home because we weren't going to go any further than we did." Sweetness immediately closes her eyes and is passed out.

Concentrating, I'm able to go into Sweetness's mind again, which means her animal isn't alert. I snap my fingers, and we're both dressed. I pick Sweetness up carefully and teleport to her bedroom. I undress her down to her bra, panties, and slip, then I tuck her in and kiss her on the forehead.

CHAPTER 28

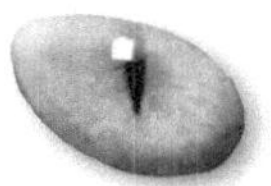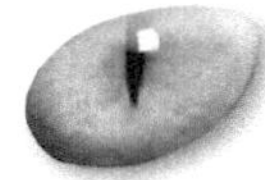

SOMETHING IN COMMON

Lyssa

WAKING up, stretching like a cat does, more bones crack lately, and I don't know why. I look at my phone, and damn, the time shows that it's 4 p.m. Was I that tired from our activities yesterday? I wonder how late it was when my cousins woke up? Are they even awake yet? Pulling off the covers, I get a chill, and I see why. I was so sleepy that I went to bed in my underwear and half-slip.

Getting off the bed, I walk over to the dresser and grab some clean underwear, a pair of shorts, and a top. Making my way into the bathroom, I turn the shower on before using the toilet. Getting in the shower, the warm water sprays on my body, and memories from last night flood my mind. How the Hell did getting turned on make me so fatigued that I crashed in bed like that?

What the Hell was last night about? Do I have a split personality trying to come to the surface? I thought people with Dissociative Identity

Disorder were victims of severe childhood trauma. I didn't have any traumatic issues as a child. If I tell anyone, they're going to think I'm damn crazy. Wait a minute; Ava said the exact thing when she spoke about the biting incident. Something else was inside of her, too! Ava and I have to have a private conversation, probably when we get home.

Lucas told me I could talk to him about anything, but this is crazy as Hell. Hey, Lucas, I have something inside of me that says you are ours. By the way, she can take over my body too. Don't worry, though, she won't hurt you. She wants us to have sex so she can come out and teach me stuff. That would be one of the weirdest conversations I've ever had in my life.

Since this is happening to Ava, too, and we're in the same family, I'm going to talk to one of my uncles; they've got to know what the Hell is happening. Josh, too; he's a male, so he may know something. I'll deal with it when we get home.

I can't wait until Chris sees Sasha at the club tonight. I've got a dress to give Sasha, so she has something muy caliente *(very hot)*. So, Chris will finally see Sasha as a woman, and that they would be wonderful together. I bought the dress for Sasha before we even came here. I saw it when we were together. She loved it, so when I found out that we were coming here and hoping we could get Josh and Christopher here, I went ahead and got the dress for her. I didn't get a dress for myself, because I wasn't planning on meeting anybody.

Sasha's on her way to my room, and I go to the closet to get the dress. I hear a light knock on the door. "Come in," I call out. The doorknob clicks and turns, and Sash opens the door. "Hey Sis, what's up?"

I'm giddy with excitement. "I'm in here, Sash. I've got the perfect dress for you to wear tonight. Come and look at what I've got for you. I brought it here just in case we had a club night." Sash walks in and, "Oh my god, wow, Sis! You got the dress for me; thank you so much. I loved this dress when we saw it." Sasha's jumping, smiling from ear to ear and hugging me.

"Sasha, you know that we're always doing things for each other, and we're family. That's what we do."

Sasha's holding up the dress, with its sequined red halter top, at the floor-length mirror. "I know, but it's just that I wasn't expecting to wear anything special. I'm always at the hospital, you know?"

"Yes, I know, Sash. So now you get a chance to wear the dress here, because it wouldn't be cute if you only wear it to one of those stuffy little Hospital functions."

Hopefully, she'll be getting dressed up more and going out with Chris during her free time from the hospital.

"Did you wake up late today, too?"

"Yup. I woke up about an hour ago, and so did everyone else. You were the last of the sleeping beauties to wake up." She winks and smiles at me. "I'm going to the store with Naya and Janae."

"Oh, boy, the two slowest shoppers in the history of shopping. Make sure you watch the time. You all need to be back in time to get ready. By the way, you're going to wear the Hell out of that dress. See you later, Sis."

"I'll leave their butts if they take too long. And yes, this dress is so hot!" Sighing, she says, "I wish…oh never mind, later, Sis." Sash leaves and closes my door.

I did bring an outfit for the club. It's a sexy-as-Hell, cobalt blue mini dress and pair of shoes Lana got me last year for our birthday. It's brand new. It's the type of material that clings to your body, and it has a v-cut low in the front. It also has thin spaghetti straps, or I could wear it strapless. With this dress, I'll wear my six-inch heels, so I'll be knocking Mr. Lucas the Hell out with it when he sees me in this dress, oh yeah.

I order a light lunch of broccoli and cheddar soup with crackers from the hotel, and it looks and smells scrumptious. I go into the living room and Ava's there by herself, sitting on the chaise with her legs up.

Sitting down in the seat next to her, she inhales and says, "That smells deliciously fantastic. I want some, too."

Placing my food back on the cart and getting my cell out of my pocket, I call her order in. I'll wait for Ava's food to come, and then we can eat together.

Maybe now we can talk about our animal situations. "Ava, I have some weird things happening, and I wanted to discuss it with you. I think we may have something in common."

I have Ava's full attention. "You have a crazy female animal trying to take over your body, too, Lyssa?"

I nod. "Last night, she was talking to me in my mind. Then she took control, but Lucas knew something wasn't right. I'm not sure what else happened, but I was exhausted and went to sleep."

Ava excitedly claps her hands. "This is what I was talking about, but my animal bit the shit out of Griffin. I miss him when we're not together, and you know what? It's a good thing that I'm hurt and can't move around like I usually do. I'd be all over him in a heartbeat."

"I wish I knew what the Hell is going on here. I've been through so much grief, and this animal has never uttered a word. Now that Lucas is here, she needs to teach me."

Ava frowns, confused at what I just said. "Um, excuse me? What does your animal want to teach you?"

Shrugging, "The Hell if I know, and she was too busy trying to get the two of us to, uh, have sex."

"WHAT!!??"

The doorbell rings. "I'll get your food. It's probably room service."

Walking to the front door, I hit the camera button, and up pops Micah. I open the door, and we both smile. "Hello, again, Ms. Alyssa. I guess one of your cousins got hungry when she saw your food?"

"Yup; you are right on the assessment, Micah. Thank you for getting it up here promptly." I give him a tip, which he won't accept, again.

"Ms. Alyssa, everything has been taken care of, and it includes tips. Nothing has changed, and please just relax and enjoy yourself."

Bringing the cart into the living room, he says, "Would you like me to take one of these away?" He points at the serving carts.

"No, I can detach the tray for Ava to use. Thank you for offering, though, Micah."

"Okay, Ms. Alyssa. You ladies enjoy the rest of your day." Micah smiles as he leaves.

I set up Ava's tray, so she's situated to eat and talk some more. "Where were we?"

Ava tilts her head at me. "We were at the fact your animal was trying to jump Lucas's bones, and she failed. How did Lucas know something was off?"

I eat some of my just-right soup, and think about how he figured that out immediately. "I don't know, Ava, but Lucas knew something was not right. I was thrilled that he respected what I told him earlier and didn't go for it. What is so special about Lucas? I want to tell him about what happened, but I'm not sure if I should." I eat some more of my soup, and Ava's enjoying hers, too. Ava's changed, and I never would have thought I could talk to her like this.

"You should tell Lucas. I think there's something special about the brothers, too, but Lucas is even more extraordinary. When my animal took over and bit Griffin, I saw some strange things, and I can't really begin to describe the way I felt. I know one thing: I've never, ever felt anything close to that."

"I saw strange things," I replied, "but it was while we were kissing. It was crazy."

"We have to talk to my Dad and our uncles. Griffin told me that they know what's going on with us."

We continue to eat our soups and think privately to ourselves. I bet Ava can't wait to get home and find out from our family about what is going on with both of us. I also haven't forgotten about Janae and the freaking lion that she's into that licked her damn face.

That soup was delightful, and this movie is interesting. Ava's falling asleep, and it's probably from her medicine. I put our trays back on one cart and lean back on the couch to get comfortable to watch the movie.

I'm with Lucas on a date, walking into a restaurant, and the hostess leads us to our table. Everyone in the restaurant stops their conversations to stare at us. Looking around at everyone, this isn't the regular 'Lucas is sexy' attention from females I've gotten used to. These are filled with anger and hatred. Both Lucas and I are confused.

Lucas—Sweetness, I need you to stay calm. We're in some danger right now, and I can handle it, but you can't, and they'll try to get you, because you're the weak link. I'm going to move fast, so just hold on to me.

Everything on the table is falling on the floor. At the speed of light, Lucas has me on his back. What the Hell?! And Lucas is talking to me in my damn head! Suddenly, the people are metamorphosing. Their skins are sliding off, the shapes of their faces and bodies are twisting, and wings are growing from their backs, revealing beautiful, multicolored, winged giants. What the Hell is this!?

"Get her out of here now, Lucas! They're coming!" The gold woman shouts, and I tighten my grip on Lucas's neck. "Hold on Sweetness." I close my eyes.

"Lyssa, wake up! Lyssa, wake up now, girl!" Freezing cold droplets are hitting my face. "What the Hell!" Jumping up and opening my eyes, I see damn Naya standing over me with freaking ice water.

Naya's cracking up. "Well, I tried to wake you up, calling your name and shaking you. You were in dreamland, so I went up to the next level, and I could have poured all of the water on you, but I didn't."

"You would've been sorry, too, Lil Sis." I snatch the cloth she's using to wipe my face. "Where's everybody?"

"We just got back, and it's a little late, so we're starting to get ready. Sasha and Janae are helping Ava. It's crazy; you and Pixie were both sleeping, but it was hard as Hell to wake the two of you up. It's always hard to get Pixie up, but you are usually a light sleeper. Not today, though; you were sleeping your ass off."

"We had a very active day yesterday, so I'm guessing that's why."

Checking my phone, I see it's much later than I thought. I have crazy dreams, and I have an animal trying to taking over, so she can come out!

I T'S **9 p.m.** and we're about to get ready. I walk into my room, get my blue dress and my lacy blue underwear to match. I have two pairs of the same Jimmy Choo shoes: a blue and black pair with 6-inch heels, and a pair with 4-inch heels. I have the earrings, necklace, and bracelet set that my mom and Dad bought both Lana and me for our 24th birthdays last year.

I turn my music on, so I can get my mind ready for the club. At the moment, I'm not there yet, but I will be by the time we walk out this door. Now that my animal is trying to get our man to help her come out, my mind is in disarray. I wrap my favorite thick, soft, and fluffy lavender towel around myself and pick up my one and only regimen for shampooing, washing my body, and moisturizing my skin. Everyone in my family uses this; we've used this since we were children. It contains a large amount of àwapuhi kuahiwi (Hawaii Ginger), shea butter, and aloe. I love the way it makes my hair and skin feel and look.

I moisturize my skin and put on my underwear and stockings. Naya and Sasha do hair the best, so that's who I'm going to call right now.

"Hey, Naya, are you almost finished getting ready?"

"Almost; how about you?"

"No, I still have to get dressed, but I don't know what to do with my hair. I washed my hair, and it's dry."

"Okay, I'll be over there to do your hair. I just finished Sasha's."

"Just come in when you're ready. Oh, you know I'm not going to put my clothes on until after my hair is right."

Naya laughs, "I know. I'll be there in two minutes."

I'm listening to "*6 inch*" by Beyonce and just waiting for Naya to come. The door opens, and Naya walks in, spinning. "Sis, I'm here to make your hair into a masterpiece that'll wow Mr. Lucas."

"Do whatever you want; I'll be your Muse. Cousin, do your magic."

She laughs. "You know I've got you, Sis, and your hair will be rocking! Oh, you know that's for damn sure." I go over to the vanity and sit. Naya follows; she has her bag of supplies, and she begins to work her magic.

"So, what do you think of the guys moving right down the street?"

Naya's smiling. "I like the idea. That means we're really going to get to know them, because they're going to be right there. We don't even have to wait for them to fly into town or anything like that." Naya's twisting my hair with the curling iron. She had me turn, so I'm not facing the mirrors. "They'll be directly down the street. It's really crazy because you know how I always look at the older guy instead of the guy who's my age. Look who I get: Garrison. I mean, that's so crazy; I could have gotten one of the may younger brothers, but I didn't. I'm happy about it. I like it. The only thing I'm worried about is Ava. After everything we found out, I don't know if she should be talking to anybody right now. I think they need to be friends, but damn; she bit him. Wow, she needs some therapy. What do you think?"

"I've been thinking about that too. When we get home, we'll have to tell Uncle Austin, because this is important. We can't act like this didn't happen or just move on and let her think she can handle this alone, because she can't."

Naya nods. "That's right; we have to, because she has been dealing with this by herself, and it happened when she was twelve years old. Ava just turned twenty-one, so this is nine years later. Now so much makes sense when you think about it. Tia Alicia can probably get Auntie Amy to talk to her. I don't know what Auntie Amy is—a counselor or a psychologist. Someone who deals with childhood sexual abuse?" She's combing my hair and curling with curling iron #2.

"Yes, we have to talk to Tia Alicia, but Uncle Austin has to be first to know, because she's his baby girl. And you know it's going to be terrible, and he's going to want to find him. I honestly believe he would find him and kill him." I think Ava and I should tell Uncle Austin, because we also have to find out about these animals.

Naya nods. "Yep, I absolutely agree with you: that guy's fucking dead, and he doesn't even know it. Voila! Your hair's ready." She spins my chair around, so I can see it. "I love you so much, and my hair's beautiful. Thank you, Sis!"

Bowing down to me, Naya answers, "You're welcome, gorgeous one."

I turn around and give her a fist punch because she has rocked my hair out! It looks like I went to the salon to get my hair done, but I didn't. My hair is full of long, bouncy spiral curls.

Naya's examining her work. "Now, I'm going to go put on my dress or my pants. I've got two outfits, and I'm trying to figure out which one I'm wearing."

"Naya, you don't have that much time. In about thirty minutes, we're all going to leave with the guys, and Lucas is already there. All I have to do is get dressed and put on my shoes and check my face. I'll be right out, and you go hurry up and figure out what outfit you're going to wear."

Naya walks to the door. "I'm going to get myself together now."

CHAPTER 29

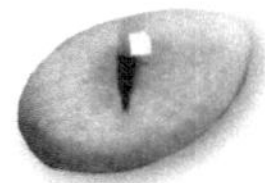

FEVER

Lyssa

LOOKING at my dress, my heart aches. It was the last gift I got from my Lana. I'm going to wear it tonight, because she bought it, and I will treasure it always. Here we go: this is for you, my Lana. I step into the dress, because I can't mess my hair up. It has a zipper in the back, so it's okay to step in because I'm going to need somebody to zip me up.

I put on my stockings, because I can't stand the way my bare feet feel in shoes. I have a little weirdness about me, but it's okay. Going out to the living room, I know somebody has to be ready. I need someone to zip me up. Yes, Ava and Janae are out here.

"Janae, zip me up, please. Help me out." Janae comes over. I turn around for her, and she zips me up. "I'm going to put on my shoes and a little makeup. I'll be right back."

Coming back out, I can pay attention and see what they are wearing now. "I must say we all are looking fabulous. We will have the attention of our dates and then some."

Ava's wearing a silver halter dress with black accessories, and Janae's wearing a black mini dress with red accessories. Sasha and Naya are coming in here, and okay, you know what color Naya likes. We all know she's the pink girl, "a tall strawberry shake," as she calls herself. Naya opted for the black jumpsuit, and she has pink accessories. This girl can't do an outfit without some shade of pink in it.

There's the doorbell, and I know it's not my date, because he's already at the club. So they can go get that, because their dates are at the door. Sasha goes and opens the door, and yes, it's the guys. They come in then stop in their tracks.

All three brothers are in awe, staring at their dates. All three pairs of silver eyes are glued to their women, and slow, sparkling smiles appear on each of their faces. I have my guy, and I can appreciate fine men. I honestly believe that there's not a day that they're not gorgeous. They're wearing expensive jeans: Grayson and Garrison's are black, and Griffin's are dark blue. They're all wearing black lightweight leather jackets. Grayson's wearing a black and grey shirt, Garrison's wearing a grey shirt, and Griffin's wearing a blue and gray shirt. They're all wearing black shoes.

Garrison, says, "I will say this for all of us; you ladies look stunning. Just beautiful." He focuses on Naya while he says this.

Naya smiles. "You and your brothers are looking damn great yourselves. You're looking handsome and sexy. I'm going to have to watch the Hell out of a chick slut hoe if she tries to come up to you while I'm with you."

Then she gives him a beautiful smile, and I'm a female; yeah, she's serious. Naya will punch the Hell out of someone.

Grayson goes up to Janae and says, "Baby, you look gorgeous. I can't wait to take you out tonight, and we're going to have a good time. I hope you're ready to dance till you can't dance more, woman."

Griffin goes over to Ava. "Princesa La Loba, you look beautiful, and I am honored to be out with you tonight. I wish you could dance, because we would kill it on the dance floor." He smiles at her, and she returns his smile.

Sasha, looking bored, says, "All right, you love birds, let's get to the damn club so we can get our dance on."

Garrison opens the front door and holds it open. "Well, ladies, let's go. Our vehicle awaits out front, so let's get going so we can get to Fever. Delia and Steve are waiting downstairs."

I go over to Sasha, so we're the last to leave. "Sasha, let's walk together, because we're dateless for now."

Sasha smirks. "Well, you're dateless until we get there, and Lucas is already there waiting for you. I'm the one who's the dateless woman, so what are you talking about?"

Shaking my head, I reply, "Oh, come on, girl, let's go." We walk out to the elevator and look in the mirror by the elevator, and damn, we look astounding. Just marvelous!

Steve and Delia join us when we get to their floor, so now everyone is all here and ready to go. Delia is looking gorgeous; she's wearing a light blue mini-dress. I like it. We get down to the lobby, and the stretch limousine is right in the front. We enter the limo, and we get to see some of the volcano show at the Mirage, since the traffic is horribly congested. The volcano show is pretty impressive, because they have the drums going, and the shooting fire is on top of the water. It's going with the drumbeat, and it looks pretty cool, especially seeing the volcano erupting from a distance. It looks like lava spouting up. Treasure Island looks like they're about to do something, but we're going to miss it because the traffic is thinning out, and we're getting ready to pull off. Oh, well, maybe next time. We turn onto a street that has a club, but there are a lot of kids here. "Oh man, I'm glad that's not FEVER, because I'm not into the teenage scene," Griffin said, looking at the young people dancing in the street.

Janae's shaking her head. "I know I wouldn't want to go to a Club like that. I'm not into younger crowds at all. I'm twenty-five years old." We all look at her, shaking our heads.

"Oh, well, almost. I don't want to hang out with a bunch of twenty-one-year-olds and younger, because most of them don't know how to act."

Naya's shaking her head. "Well, just remember all twenty-one-year-olds don't act like idiots, and some do know how to act. You're looking at one."

"Okay, we know. Naya, you are a very mature twenty-one-year-old," Sasha says.

"We all agree with you, Sasha."

We drive up to Fever, and, yes, this is a mature crowd. I'm good with this. Wow, is this line for Fever? Damn. "That's one hell of a line, and it better be worth it," I say.

Grayson says, "It's all good, we don't have to wait in that line. Remember; Lucas is VIP. So, we just have to go to the bouncers and give them our names."

We all agree it's a great idea, because who wants to stand outside for god knows how long trying to get into the club? That line is long as Hell.

Grayson leads the way to the bodyguards, and yes, all we had to do was give them our names and show identification, and they let us in. As we walk into Fever and head down the aisle, it opens up into a pretty sophisticated setup. Well, besides the cages with the dancers suspended from the ceiling. Now that I see that, okay…but it's still very nice. I like the red and black décor, and everything is just so red. The chandelier lights hanging from the ceiling are also red. The flashing lights from the dance floor reflect on the walls. The furniture is red and black, and the music is pumping. People are dancing on the stage, and the bar is very nice. They did a great job. Now I've got to figure out where the VIP section is. I think I forgot to ask where it was.

Oh, yes, the music is pumping, and I'm enjoying all of this is. My song, "Damn Girl" by Justin Timberlake, yes, I love that song. I don't care how old it is; that's a good ass song. Since this is my song, I can't help but dance and move to the beat. That beat, you just can't help it. You feel that bass in your bones, and you just have to move. I sense Lucas. I know it sounds crazy, but I can detect him above me.

I'm going to look up to see if he's there. There he is on the second floor, and I think he's just looked at me. Correction; I know he's look-ing at me. Who the Hell am I kidding? I tap Sasha and Janae, who are in front of me, and both turn to see what I want. Pointing to where he is, I show them that Lucas is up there.

We look around for stairs or an elevator. We want to find out how to get up to where Lucas is; we don't know, because it's really crowded in here. On our way to ask the bartender, this intoxicated, sweaty guy blocks me and pulls me so close to him that I smell the strong liquor from his body.

"Yo, baby, I've been waiting for you all my life, girl. Where have you been? I'm here. Give me a chance. I would love to dance with you and feel that sweet body against mine."

I pull away from him, ready to say something, but Lucas is here before I know it. Lucas grabs him by his neck, literally lifting him up with his one hand, and says something to him, but I can't hear it due to the loud music. Lucas drops him down on the floor. The guy jumps up and runs off. My mouth is wide open in shock, because I'm trying to figure out how the Hell Lucas got down here so fast when he was upstairs.

Did he start leaving when he saw me talking to Sasha and Janae? Damn, I don't know; that was crazy, but it was sexy and hot, too, because he just came out of nowhere to defend me. He turns around, comes up to me, puts his arm around my waist, and just kisses me in greeting, I guess.

We haven't talked to each other all day. I'd slept almost all day, and then we were getting ready for tonight and packing, since we're leaving tomorrow.

"Hey, Sweetness, I had to go and do the protective thing. When I got down here, I was walking, and I saw that shit. I said to myself, oh no way in Hell did this dude just put his hands on my woman! The dude is a learning lesson, and he's lucky that I didn't go hard on him, because really I wanted to punch the Hell out of him, like Naya says."

You know, Naya, that's a tough young lady over there. She's knocking brother out. I'm serious. Naya's not playing when she says she's going to get you. She is going to get you one way or another. She is coming after your ass.

Lucas

I'VE been at this damn club for hours waiting for my Sweetness, and when she gets here, this idiot tries to put his hands on my woman! Oh, hell no. He's lucky that's all I did, because I could have thrown him across the fucking floor! I know that would have been a problem. Not really, though I could have handled it and made them all forget, dammit.

So, I didn't do that, and I just let him land on the floor when I dropped his ass. I was looking at the doorway. I knew they were here, and when my Sweetness came in, everything just lit up, because she was here. The room became sunshine for me. That sounds crazy as Hell, but that's what she does for me.

She's in a little shock from seeing me pick up the guy. I'll fix it, though. I turn to her and pull her into my embrace. I lift her chin and kiss her, and she responds immediately to the kiss.

The shock has worn off. Everything is rushing through me with that kiss; damn. Breaking the kiss is what I don't want to do, but we are in a public place.

"Hello, my Sweetness. I had to get that kiss before; I said hello, because I missed you all day, woman. I was ready to come and pick you up just to sit in here with me."

She smiles. "I was thinking about you today, too, but I'm here now."

Looking down, I fully notice her dress. Taking her hand in mine, I hold it above her head and ask her to turn around for me. "Oh, damn, Sweetness, what are you trying to do to me with that sexy ass dress on?" I shake my head then whistle. "That's why the guy came over here like that, woman. Oh no, you're not getting away from me, my sexy beautiful woman. You know that, right? You're going to be with me by my side because you wearing that. You look too damn good, Sweetness!"

Sweetness laughs. "Lucas, we were going down the other way looking for the VIP section, and he blocked me. He was talking crazy, and he was drunk, too."

Grayson and everyone else walk up. "We were looking to see where you went since you left the VIP section. Of course, we saw you over here. We all should've known you'd be over here with Alyssa."

Grayson adds, "Are you ladies ready to check out upstairs? Griffin, there's an elevator over here to the left. Everyone else, we can take the stairs. Let's go."

We opt to walk up the steps. It was a surprise to us that the cousins and their other brother are here I guess they're just going to pop up whenever they feel it's right.

"The music is good, and now that we're upstairs, I'm going to dance with Janae. This should be interesting. I'm going to see if my lady can dance, because she thinks she can. So let's just see if it's the truth, because many people believe they can do stuff but can't. I just hope she can."

Janae rolls her eyes. "Want to bet? I'm super confident in my dance skills; are you?"

Sasha comments, "This is so chic. I love it up here. It's really a different atmosphere up here than downstairs."

Naya's walking around examining everything. "I like it up here, too. They did a terrific job."

Justin Timberlake's song is starting, and I paid the DJ extra for many JT songs. "Sweetness, do you want to dance?"

She pulls my hand and rushes to the dance floor, so I take it as a yes. Moving in beat with the music, she's swaying those damn hips like a siren. I put my hands on her hips and pull her so close to me that we both catch our breath. Sweetness wraps her arms around my neck and says, "I love when our bodies touch. You make me wish for a lot of bad, but oh, the good things we could do."

Oh, shit. Sweetness's eyes have more of those gold speckles. This definitely is a problem. I ease my smoking hot, gorgeous woman to a seat. Maybe not dancing for a few minutes will send her animal back to sleep.

Galveston walks in, and damn, even though he's their younger brother, he's almost identical to the triplets. He goes over to his brother Grayson. "Bro, where are all the people?"

Lucas, tell my younger brother why we have an intimate setting up, please.

Sure, I'll fill him in, Galveston. Can you hear me?

Oh, crap, you can communicate in my mind? Damn!

Yes, I can. You wanted to know why the VIP area isn't full of club people from downstairs? I wanted it to be intimate, just our group. No distractions.

Okay.

"The staff up here can take your orders if you want food. Everything is paid for, so you can make yourself at home and get what you want to get."

Nodding, Janae gives me a smile and a drink. "Lucas, I knew from the first day we met you that you were a go-getter. The first dinner we had when Ava called you a shot caller and a big baller, she was right. What you did with this right here, you're a good guy, Lucas. We can do whatever we want because we have the whole section."

Sasha's looking at some more of the layout. "I like how they got this VIP area. This is nice! Especially the light-up dance floors downstairs and up here, too. Oh yes, we're going to get our dance on. Justin is coming on."

Sweetness jumps up. "Oh, yeah, Baby! Oh, Justin's coming on, 'Bringing Sexy Back.' Time to dance. Come on, come on."

CHAPTER 30

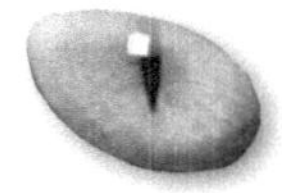

FOOD FOR THOUGHT

Lucas

SWEETNESS thinks she's getting ready to go dance with them on this song. She doesn't know it yet, but that's not happening. This is my song.

Getting up, I take her hand and pull her to me. "Oh, no, Sweetness, this is my song. Right here, and right now, you and I are getting ready to dance." I turn her around; she's facing the dance floor, walking, and I'm right behind her. Actually, I'm pushing her up with my body, and she's laughing.

"Bringing Sexy Back" is on; I get on that dance floor. "Show me what you got, girl. Let's get it."

Sweetness looks at me with this tiny, coy, sly look, and there are a regular amount of golden speckles in her eyes. The next thing I know, Sweetness is dancing for real, and this woman can dance. What she imagined that she would do, in fact, she can do; yeah, baby, let's go.

I start dancing with her, and she opens her eyes in surprise because she didn't know I had the moves.

For a long time, I have been practicing how to dance in case I ever got a chance to dance with some people. Not only am I dancing, I'm doing great, and my mate is rocking it also. Looking around, everybody's on the dance floor. Sasha looks so alone with no one to dance with. Galveston is going downstairs.

Okay, after this song, I will see if I can get to dance with Sweetness and Sasha. Right now, I'm dancing with my woman only, and she's keeping up with me and everything. I'm glad I was wrong, and that she can dance.

"Sweetness, how about you get Sasha so we all can dance together? She seems lonely over there by herself." She can share her with me; it's just a dance, nothing else. She goes over to the table where Sasha's sitting and pulls her up. Sasha's shaking her head no, but my woman isn't trying to hear that, and Sasha's on the dance floor with us. Another fast song comes on, and Sasha starts dancing the boring two-step.

Sasha's too young for this, and she needs some better moves. Wow, Sasha. Oh, my God, now she starts doing the bump. Woah, I know the bump; I've seen it in a lot of souls' memories from a long time ago. It's a fun dance to play around with. Okay, that's good, let's do it. That's what Sasha wants to do, so I start bumping Sasha and Sweetness, too, enjoying this crazy dance. These ladies are going down to the floor doing the dance. We have to get her to do some other dancing.

While we're dancing, Christopher's walking into the building. His thoughts are loud as Hell about Sasha, and he knows all about her. Chris has been waiting for Sasha for a long time. He's a shifter, too, and she's his Reveinah. He's always known about her, but because she's so young, he had to wait. According to their rules, Chris has to wait until Sasha's at least 24 to approach her.

Chris is planning on asking permission to date her, but as soon as she turns 24 on her birthday, he is claiming her. He's also an Alpha, but he wasn't told about being able to bypass the rules. This group is weird, anyway, with all these damn secrets. Well, Chris is no dummy;

he has been stealthily watching Sasha. Sasha thinks he's unaware of her, but he's been aware of her for years. When Sasha thinks, Chris doesn't know she's watching him; he knows she's watching him too. That's too damn funny.

Right now, Chris is walking up behind Sasha. Sasha has a dance partner now. This is going to be funny, and I've got to watch this while I'm dancing. Alyssa doesn't see him either. Chris just comes behind Sasha, grabs her by the waist lightly, and starts dancing with her.

Sasha inhales and recognizes Chris's scent, and she lights up like fireworks on the Fourth of July. Chris turns Sasha around to face him. She jumps into his arms, hugging him, and they look like they're in love, but he just has to wait. Chris needs to find out that he can bypass the rule.

Sasha will be twenty-four in a few months. Yeah, Chris can go ahead and start talking to Sasha, and he can be just like a boyfriend for now. When she turns twenty-four, he can do the marking, and then when she turns twenty-five, he can marry her, I guess, right? It makes sense to me.

We're all dancing, and a song comes on for a group dance, so we all try to follow directions. You move to the right and left in the back, spin around and do a little dip thing, back then forth. That was fun. By the end of the longest song I've ever heard, we mastered the moves. We sit down at the longest table so we can all sit together.

An excited Sasha is focused on Chris. "Oh my God, Chris, how did you know we were here and everything??"

Christopher grins. "Josh and Jay were coming here, and I didn't have anything else to do, so I decided to come too. Most importantly, I hadn't seen my girl Sasha in quite a while, so I had to come and check you out." Chris licks his lips with sparkling fire in his eyes. "Look how grown-up you are now. You're not that little girl anymore."

Chris touches the side of her face, and she leans her face into his hand. Josh adds, "Yeah, I talked to Lyssa the first night y'all got here, and she told me about Ryan. And she said y'all were going to be here today, so I figured we could come and that we'd all leave together tomorrow. Since Jay will be twenty-one very soon, he can get his first taste of Vegas. As big as he is, look at him; no one would think that he's younger."

We all laugh at that because, yeah, as big as Jay is, he'll pass for older with no problem.

Janae clears her throat. "Josh, let me introduce you to Grayson."

Josh says, "What's up, Gray? How are you doing, man? I haven't talked to you in a minute. What's up, Garrison and Griffin?"

Josh knows the brothers already. He's shaking all their hands and yeah, they are very familiar with each other. Janae isn't too happy; she thought she was making the grand introduction.

Fierce heat rushes from my leg straight to my damn shaft. It was hard already. Now Sweetness is rubbing her shoeless foot on my leg and going higher. I have to see if it's her or her animal. I sneak a peek and go into her thoughts, and yes, she's herself. So, she wants to play games? Okay, I've got something for her to see if she's ready for my games. Yeah, she's having a lot of fun over there; damn, she's really reaching for my shaft? Oh, yeah, she really is.

Griffin says, "Josh, I brought that land close to your Uncle Austin's home. Plus, we need to check on Phase 4 of the land we're building on already. I'm meeting the contractor and the architect tomorrow."

Josh quizzically looks at Griffin. "Why move next to my uncle?"

Griffin laughs. "There's only one way to say this, Josh. Your cousin, Ava, bit the Hell out of me yesterday. So, I'll be meeting your Uncle Austin tomorrow."

Josh goes pale and quickly looks at Ava, and she smiles guiltily at him. Garrison nods at Josh and his confused damn expression.

"Well, that leaves everyone besides me, and the rest of my family thought they were going to come. However, since the project isn't finished, there's no need for them to come yet. With our family, we may live on the same land, but we're not living together. We have our privacy, and we live in different homes."

Sweetness says, "So, Grayson, are just the three of you coming to Lake Tahoe, or are more of your brothers coming? You have a sister, too, right? You know what? Yesterday while we were on the plane, I came up with a bit of a game for Garrison and Naya to play to help them get to know each other, and we should do that now for y'all. That sounds cool, right?"

Grayson answers, "Right now, it's just the four of us, and Garrett's coming too. We'll go from there to see how everything goes with the rest of the family. They may stay where they are or they may come here—after everything is ready, that is. I'm in to play the game."

Sweetness is ready to give the game instructions. "This is how it works. Let's say this game is really for the couples who are right here, so you guys can get to know more about each other. You're going to pick the subjects: sports, food, favorite movies, and favorite hobbies. When it's your turn, you're going to give your partner the question on a subject, and they will provide you with their top five answers. Then they ask you the same thing or something else, and you'll have to give your top five answers, as well. And then what you'll see is you've learned something about your partner."

Chris calls out, "Hey, can I play too? I want to play with Sasha." Everybody looks at him in surprise.

Sasha looks shocked. Well, Chris is next to her anyway. "There's always something we can learn about each other. I bet there are things that I don't know about you, and there are things you don't know about me, Sasha." She's kind of blushing right now, but she said, okay. She's not okay in her head though. She's nervous and excited.

"So, we have our couples. Sasha and Chris, okay, that's one; number two is Janae and Grayson; number three is Garrison and Naya, and number four is Griffin and Ava. Those are the four couples playing this game. Who's going to go first? Or do you want to do rock, paper, scissors, shoot? Naya and Garrison did this yesterday, so they can go last. We can go from oldest to youngest or vice versa, which that means Ava and Griffin will be first, then Sasha and Chris, then Janae and Grayson, and last Naya and Garrison."

"Ava and Griffin, select a subject: Food, Sports, Favorite Hobbies, or Favorite Movies."

Griffin sees that Ava isn't ready to go yet; she's looking kind of shy, so he goes first. "Okay, Ava, I'm going to ask you about something that might be pretty easy: your favorite foods, top three, first. No, I don't want to know your favorite foods to eat. I want to know what your favorite foods to cook are."

Oh, you see where he's going? Griffin wants to know if the little Hellion Ava can cook, yeah. It's always okay to know what somebody likes to eat, but it's better to know what they can cook, because you know what they say about cooking. Yeah, cooking is essential…well, for some people.

I can cook spaghetti and meatballs really well. I can make homemade chicken noodle soup, I can make delicious cheeseburgers, and I can make fried chicken really good and make a tasty roasted chicken. Those are the top five things I can make. Griffin looks like he's really involved in thinking about what she said she can make. He may just call on it one day soon.

"Okay, it's your turn now, Ava. What do you want to know about Griffin?"

"Well, I want to know the same thing." Griffin starts laughing, and then Grayson and Garrison start laughing, too. I think I know the answer. Griffin can't cook a damn thing. "Pizza, The best ramen you ever tasted, Buffalo wings, fried chicken, and sausage and peppers."

Sweetness is up to the next couple. "Sasha and Chris, what do you want to know about each other?"

Sasha's looking all shy and nervous, and Chris is just grinning at Sasha. Sasha says, "I guess we can just ask the same things that they just asked. What are the top five things that you can cook?"

Chris claps his hands, and that says *I'm ready for this.* "My number one is meatloaf," he says, and Sasha looks surprised. "My number two is shrimp scampi." Now she's looking more and more surprised. "My number three is that I love making Chinese food: all varieties, from fried rice to lo mein, beef, chicken, shrimp, crab, lobster, and every now and then, pork dishes." He's known her favorite is Chinese food since she was a teen. Sasha really loves that, and she's smiling about that one. Fantastic job, Chris, and you know Sasha will want you to make Chinese food for her. I see what Sweetness's favorite foods are, and I can pretend that I'm making them. No, I'd try to make it but have a backup if I ruined it.

Chris continues giving his full attention to Sasha. "My fourth dish is lasagna. My fifth dish is gumbo."

Sweetness evaluates. "Chris, I have to admit that I am impressed with that list of foods that you can make for Sasha." Sweetness beams at Sasha, and Sasha's cheeks are flushed and reddening more.

Sasha takes a sip from her drink and says, "Chris, you ready for me?"

"I'm always ready. As a matter of fact, I was born prepared just for you," he says.

"Hmmm, whoa, those are the words; you better get him, Sash." Ava has a point. "We need to discuss that asap then."

Chris gives his question. "Here's my question for you. What are your top five favorite foods to eat?"

"Okay, my number one favorite food to eat is going to blow your mind, but it's gumbo." Her number one favorite food has Chris beaming. You know what that means, guys; he's going to make her some damn gumbo, yes.

"Number two are Chinese food and lasagna." *Hot damn; she got two of my favorite meals that I can cook. Oh, I'm all right.*

"Number three is baked macaroni and cheese."

A lot of people love baked macaroni and cheese. That's an excellent favorite meal. Chris should've asked her if she could make the dishes. Chris is grinning from ear to ear, and he knows how to cook every favorite meal Sasha has.

"My fourth favorite meal to eat is fried chicken, and you can't have that all the time."

Chris is about to explode from happiness. "Boom! Sasha, guess who can make some good damn fried chicken? You're looking at him right here. I'm the man. I can make some desserts, too. It's just that I forgot about it."

You see where this is going. One more thing, and Chris probably can cook that too. He's going to love cooking for his girl.

"Now, I'm thinking of my fifth favorite food. I got it…black beans and rice pro bono family, and that Cuban pork that Tia Alicia and Mommy makes. They showed me how to cook it, but I forgot how. I'm always at the hospital, you know?" There's disappointment in Sasha's voice.

Chris leaps up like he just ran the marathon and won. "Hell yeah, Baby, I can make that too. Tia showed me how."

"Janae and Grayson are next; who going to go first? Janae or Grayson, which one of you are going to ask about your top five whatever?"

Janae replies, "I'll go first. I want to know the top five things that you can cook, Grayson. I want to hear how to make it. I'm wondering if you're like your brother."

Grayson cracks up laughing and shakes his head. "Oh, I can cook, sweetheart. Let me think about it. Give me a second. The first dish I can cook is chicken marsala."

Sweetness, scrutinizing the brothers, says, "That answers my question if he can cook better than his little quadruplet brother. I cannot wait until we find out if Griffin was for real about those meals. Both of you laughed at your brother, so I'm suspicious."

Grayson continues, "Okay, the second meal that I've gotten compliments on is one of my favorites: paella."

Janae says, "This guy, okay, I see you. I know where you going. I'm liking what I'm hearing."

Grayson adds, "I like to cook my third dish. I'll say prime rib with herbed garlic mashed potatoes and glazed carrots. Booyah! Oh, yeah, I'm the brother here who can cook prime rib."

Steve sighs. "Yes, you are all making me hungrier. Man, Chris and Ava, your best foods made my stomach realize I need some damn food. We have to order something to eat." Steve points to the controller and the screen. "I think it's cool that this room is soundproof. A button turns the music off and on. There's an enormous damn screen to show what's playing, and the menu choices are there, too."

Grayson continues. "I'm going to go simple with this one—my fourth favorite dish to make and eat. When I get home, I fire up my grill. I put a couple of steaks with pepper on there. I cook them to medium-well, and when I take them off the grill, I spread some garlic herbed butter on them, and I can just add whatever to it, but that main thing is that just-right steak with that garlic herbed butter, which melts soon as it's put on the piping hot steak, and it just melts right in there, and glazes it up, and it's perfect."

Janae, rubbing her stomach, tells Grayson, "You better invite me to your damn place for dinner, Grayson. What is going on? Why didn't I know you would come out like this? You can cook, man."

Steve doesn't even know him like that, and he's getting really emotional about this food. His stomach's growling, and he's licking his lips.

Grayson continues, "Now my fifth dish is a meal that's my own creation. It has shrimp, beef kielbasa, nice chunks of chicken thighs, sauteed onions, red and green bell peppers, and jalapenos. I either have it with rice and some type of roasted vegetable on the side or in a soft roll. I also make my special sauce, and I add just a little bit of cornstarch in it to thicken it up a little, but it's delicious."

Steve complains, "Grayson, man, seriously, you've got my mouth watering for all the stuff you just said. None of that is on the menu here tonight, and I think I'm being punked. I don't like this game anymore, and I don't want to talk about food anymore. No more food talk. Oh, wait, Grayson; when you move in, we've got to come to your house, man. You're going to have to have all of the food you mentioned and have a damn feast for us, so we can taste all the scrumptious food you make. Chris, you're not off the hook, bro; you need to bring your food too."

Steve looks like he just had an epiphany. "How about this? All of the people who said they make good food can come together and have a party with that food at someone's house. Y'all got me hungry, and Chris, I know I had your food before, and it's flavorful and succulent. I love it. Bro, you said you were going to make some more. Now we can set up a date for all of the delectable foods to try."

Sweetness's stomach growls loudly, and she laughs. "First, I ordered something to eat, but nothing here sounds as good as all of the foods

I've been hearing about. Garrison and Naya are next, so if the subject is food, you should ask the top five things you both can cook, pick who's going to go first, and bring it."

Garrison laughs, "We've got this, okay, it's all good now. Do you want to go first, or you want me to go first?"

Naya answers, "I'll go first. Well, I have a culinary arts degree, and I'm a chef. So I'm the gourmet, okay? I just want to put it out there. Working 16-hour days equals I'm not eager to cook when I get home. If I cook some of my favorite foods, number five would be handmade spaghetti, homemade spaghetti sauce with garlic and fresh basil, and homemade meatballs, Italian sausage, turkey, or pork with a great garlic bread made from scratch. Number four would be sauteed shrimp and rice with limoncello vinaigrette grilled lobster. Number three would be grilled steak made with my special herbed garlic butter. Number two is homemade beef, spinach, and cheese ravioli with a basil sauce. Number one is any barbecue food. I'm a grill master!"

Steve claps his hands. "Oh yeah, Chef, you're in! Naya, you need to add your food to the party. Okay, let's go, Garrison."

"Well, I like good food, and I cook. I will go from what I make all the time. I know it's terrific; my number one meal is homemade spaghetti with sausage and meatballs, a four-cheese sauce, and some mozzarella shredded on top of it. Number four is a slow-cooked pot roast with vegetables that I serve with a side of some rice. Number three is black beans and rice with Cuban pork. My number two meals are gumbo and fried chicken, and lasagna and jambalaya are tied for number one."

Steven has more to say. "Well, you know what? I like every one of those meals that you mentioned, Garrison. Oh man, can you imagine? That would be 30 meals we can have at the party! Y'all bring those meals."

The servers bring the food: platters of seasoned curly fries, buffalo wings, nachos with everything, mozzarella sticks, jalapeno poppers, and two trays of sliders. These guys will kill one tray of sliders by themselves.

CHAPTER 31

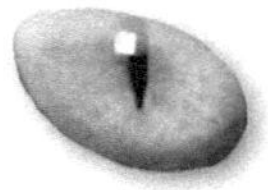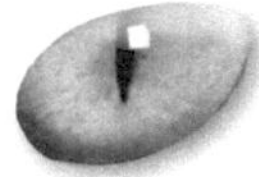

SPORTS & THE GOLDEN ONE

Lucas

SWEETNESS is fixing her plate but still into the game. "Okay, last round for now, then we can get back on this dance floor. We did the cooking questions; let's go for sports now. Ava was first before, so Griffin, it's your turn; ask for five sports she likes."

Griffin's rubbing his chin thoughtfully. "Okay, Ava, tell me your top five sports and which ones you actually play."

Ava's grinning and all perky. "The five sports that I like are football, basketball, swimming, tennis, and bowling. Now the sports that I play: I love swimming. I play tennis, I bowl, and I tried basketball, but I sucked, and it didn't work out."

Griffin's turn. "My five sports are football, basketball, skiing, surfing, and lacrosse. I play all five sports."

Sasha speaks up. "It's my turn, and my top five sports are lacrosse, swimming, basketball, football, and synchronized swimming. Out of those, I'm a synchronized and regular swimmer; I play lacrosse, basketball and you know I can throw a football."

Chris grins at Sasha. "I'd love to see you doing synchronized swimming again. Do you have any recent videos I can watch?"

Sasha gives him a sarcastic look. "You know I was kicked off of the team, Chris. Remember your little prank that caused it?"

Chris laughs. "Damn. Never mind; anyone messes with you, and its Hell to pay. I love diving, running track, basketball, football, swimming, and, as a former navy seal, swimming was a must. I play those sports I mentioned and some others. Sash, I need a private show from you at the pool. I know you can still make some fantastic poses."

Slowly licking her lips, Sasha answers Chris. "Maybe one day soon, if you can stay home long enough. You're always flying somewhere."

Smiling, Chris takes Sasha's hand, and Sasha quickly exhales, breathing heavier. "I'll be here, and I won't be taking any out-of-town trips unless it's essential. I think we need some private time. Come on. Sasha's eyes widen in surprise, and her beautiful smile appears." Standing up, he leads Sasha to the other side of the VIP room.

Sweetness says, "Well, Chris and Sasha have some things to discuss. Next up are Jenae and Grayson; who wants to go first?"

Janae excitedly volunteers, "I love dancing, ballet, tennis, racquetball, bowling, skiing, and snowboarding. I do all of them, awesomely."

Grayson's turn. "My top five sports that I also play are snowboarding, surfing, football, and basketball. I play more, but those are my top five, like you said."

"We have four people who go snowboarding and three people who go skiing. All of you want to play basketball, and most of you are into football."

Naya says something to Garrison, and he nods. "Guys, we know the sports answers already. We did this yesterday, and we have finished eating. Who's ready for some dancing and music? We've talked a hell of a lot."

"Yes, music. It's dancing time!" everyone answers.

I click the button to turn the music on, and, of course, it's JT playing. I pull my Sweetness up out of the chair and step onto to the light-up dance floor.

Lyssa

W E'RE going to dance, and I'm ready to get my man hot and bothered. All we have to do is touch, and it's on. Just playing footsie under the table has me in a pool of fire that's burning more than I was on this dance floor earlier. *"I'm Bringing Sexy Back"* is coming on. Oh yeah, we're all moving to get our dance on. *Smack!* Oh, yeah, I owed Lucas a smack on his sexy ass. Lucas chuckles.

I've got to say my man is fine in his green shirt, that tie with its green and blue designs, those black jeans, and the black leather jacket that's hanging on the chair he was sitting in. Bouncing and swaying to the beat of the music, I move my hands down Lucas's chest. I turn around so my back is to him, and Lucas grabs me so I'm against him. Sparks shoot through my body as we move to the rhythm together. My body responds to his body, which is glued to my back, and I can feel all of his muscles.

Opening my eyes, I smile at seeing Sasha and Chris dancing just as close as Lucas and I are. My sis has her man, finally! Lucas leans down and kisses the side of my neck. I sink back into him, and he nibbles on my ear. The music changes to a slow song, and I turn into Lucas's arms, wrapping my arms around his neck. Lucas's arms tighten around my waist. I breathe in his scent and lick my lips, because I want to kiss him so damn bad.

Female Animal—Lyssa, you need to listen to me. Lucas is our mate, and we have to have sex with him tonight. Our relationship with Lucas is opening gates that have been closed. It's waking up sleeping—I'll say things that people aren't familiar with. You and your cousins are unique, but you, your brother, and five more of your cousins are extraordinary. We've been detected.

Lyssa—Can we discuss this tonight or tomorrow? I've accepted that you're here, but I'm busy right now. I'm putting all my focus into Lucas right now.

Female Animal—Lyssa, this is important! When you're alone, I hope you're ready to talk to me.

Lyssa—Mmm-hmm.

Female Animal—You know you want to, dammit. Just have sex already.

I'm not paying much attention to my other half, or whatever it is. I know time is flying, because we've been dancing for a long while. Ava and Griffin are table dancing; he sat her on one of the empty tables. She moves to the beat while sitting on the table and holding Griffin's hand. Ava's swinging her arms, hands, and both legs, too. That Ava will make sure she has fun, no matter what. You gotta love it.

The introduction of one of my favorite songs starts playing, with its heavy beat and bass line. I could never dance the way I wanted to with a man because it's just that sexy. I can now, though. I'm drawn to this man. Lucas is sex personified, and he is all mine—oops, ours. "Lucas, give me the remote for a minute, please."

"Okay, Sweetness. I have to get it from the table."

I follow him, and he hands it to me. I examine the remote and find what I need. Selecting the darkest dimmer setting, the lights fade out. Yes, no one will be able to see me teasing Lucas. Taking Lucas's hand, I lead him away from the group, so we have our own spot.

Going over to the other side of the decorative room divider, I turn around and place my hand on Lucas's chest, trailing my fingers to his belt and pulling it. I can feel that damn eyebrow arching at me, but I don't utter a word.

I maneuver him against the wall and let the music guide me. Swaying my body in tune with the beat, I take Lucas's hands in mine. I raise our hands over our heads, but I didn't consider that his arms are longer than mine. Laughing to myself, I say, "Keep your hands against the wall. Please."

"Whatever you say, Sweetness. Remember, my turn is coming, woman."

Pressing myself against him, he parts his lips and quickly inhales. I run my hands over his chest and to those monster abs of his. I take my time bending my knees until I'm down by the floor. Slowly getting up, I touch his legs and feel his lengthy, thick member on my way back up. Lucas groans, and I know I'm in trouble.

Raising my knee, I gently rub Lucas's thigh and stop at his cock. Swaying against him, my breasts are enjoying this, and my nipples are tingling and hot, like everything else. Turning around, I slowly bend over and wiggle my ass against him. Suddenly, Lucas grasps my waist, snatches me up, and spins me around, facing him. *Smack, smack, smack*, on my ass, really? "Sweetness, game playing is over. Tonight it's on, mmm-hmm." Lucas's eyes say it all. I think I went too far.

"I have to go to the ladies room." I walk shakily across the dim room.

"Lyssa, wait, I have to go too." Ava's slowly using her crutches and hopping, too.

Waiting for her, the lights brighten some, and I don't have to glance at him. Lucas is watching me, and I'm burning up.

"Lyssa, are you okay? You're looking flushed." Ava's smirking.

Shaking my head, I reply, "Yes, Pixie, I'm fine."

We enter the bathroom, but it's out of order. There's no running water.

"Dammit! I have to pee!" Ava is upset, but so am I. "Come on; we have to use the elevator and go to the regular bathroom that's probably crowded as hell."

I sigh and shrug. "Let's go downstairs before one or both of us have a damn accident." Lucas and Griffin are talking by the table, and Griffin laughs. Lucas's smoldering eyes are on mine; my legs are weak, and I'm almost tripping over my own feet. We walk up to them, and I say, "Ava and I are going to have to use the bathroom downstairs."

Lucas glances towards the bathroom. "We'll go down with you two, Sweetness."

Narrowing my eyes, I say, "Lucas, I do know how to use a bathroom by myself. I can help Ava if she needs me. What can happen? We're in a crowded club."

"Okay, then. I'm sorry about that. I don't mean to sound paranoid or anything."

"I'm good." Getting on my toes, I give Lucas a quick kiss. "Come on, Pixie."

Ava and I go downstairs on the elevator. Walking to the back with Ava hobbling on those crutches isn't safe, and I messed up; I left my cell upstairs in my damn purse, and Ava can't hold anything besides the crutches. "Excuse us," I say to people who are in our way. We're on one of the sides where the couches and other furniture are. It's so congested.

"Why don't they move? People see us but won't move! If I start swinging one of these damn crutches, then they'll say I'm wrong. I can't help it; the music is excellent, and I'm doing the walk dance."

Seeing the restroom sign, we walk towards it, "Ouch! What the Hell?" Ava swung the crutches and hit this young lady! The young lady is crying and grabbing her leg, and, yes, it's red. The restroom line starts in the dance area.

One of the servers come over. "Ladies, we have two guests who will be moved to the front area. This young lady has crutches, so under state law, she's disabled." I help Ava hop along to be the fifth person on the line. While we're waiting in line, two weird guys watch us.

"Umm, Lyssa, what the Hell is going on with these strange guys? Ava nervously glances from them to me. They're looking over here at us intently."

"I'm wondering too, Ava."

I don't know if it's us; I think it may just be me. I'm not sure. Well, one of the men is coming over here with his bald head, purple tattoos, and rings on his face.

"Hello, Golden One." The voice pierces through me.

Oh my God, goosebumps are prickling on my skin. Every single hair I have is tensed. My insides are like an earthquake and a tornado attacking at the same time. I stumble, and some of the ladies catch me. I stay in the line, away from the two guys. That feeling is back, but one hundred times stronger. Why the Hell is he calling me Golden One?

"After you're finished in the ladies' room, would you like to have a dance with me?"

Shaking my head, I answer, "No, thank you, my man is here. I have him to dance with, and he'd definitely have a problem with that."

He leans in, and he sniffs me! I lean back the opposite way. What the

Hell is that? How you come up smelling on people? Has he never heard of personal freaking boundaries? And who smiles at people like that?

Ava swings the crutch and hits him on the side of his leg. "Hey dude, move back! Haven't you heard of personal space?!" That's Ava, yes.

"I'm sorry, but you just smell so good, and I just can't help myself. Are you wearing a particular perfume or something? I've never felt the need to smell anyone like this."

What the Hell is this? I've never had anyone coming to smell me before in my damn life. All the ladies are looking at him crazily, as I am, because this is bizarre. It's almost our turn to go to the bathroom, and the guy is still standing over here. He's really sniffing me, and there's no security guard around here or anything.

Bending to Ava's ear, I tell her the plan. "Ava, if one person comes out, we'll let the person behind me go in. We'll go in together if two people come out, okay?"

Nodding, she replies, "Yep, I got it, Lyssa."

The door opens, and one lady exits; I turn to tell the lady behind me she can go in, and Ava goes into the bathroom. What the fuck?! Shaking my head, I push the door open, and instantly, I can't move. Something ice-cold is ripping through my body! I'm immobilized, and I can't even open my mouth.

Lucas! Help me, please!

Female Animal, with a painful roar—NOW LUCAS!

I can't see anything. Everything is in darkness, and my body is floating. Oh God, I'm either dying or unconscious.

Lucas

I SHOULD'VE gone with her, but she was giving that "are you a damn crazy man" look. I'm not going to invade her privacy. Sweetness will be back shortly. My head feels weird, and I'm cold. Sweetness!

Lucas, help me, please!

LUCAS NOW! Her animal's screaming!

ALYSSA!!!!!

ALYSSA!!! I scream as I speed to the lady's restroom!

About T.L. Reigns

T.L. has dreamed about this story and characters for many years. When her sister, Yolanda encouraged her to go and write, even if it was just with her two fingers on a tablet. It took quite a long while, but the first story is completed. T.L. lives in the Southeast part of the United States. This is the beginning of a series that will take you on a ride that you will not forget. The Ride Starts Now!

To get more information about *The Hidden Beasts* series, *Chronicles of Hidden Beasts* novella series, and find out when Book II will be available, signup for T.L. Reigns Newsletter at www.tlreignswrites.com.

www.ingramcontent.com/pod-product-compliance
Lightning Source LLC
Chambersburg PA
CBHW061306190726
48288CB00002B/372